A W

She was stark naked and almost totally black, like ink or charcoal. Her skin was almost peeling off from the radiation. What little hair hadn't been burned or had fallen out was nothing more than gray wisps.

"You!" she shrieked. "Of all the people who might have survived—you!"

"Y—you know me?"

"I know *everyone* in this miserable circle of Hell. We've been fooling ourselves that we're in some big machine, but we're in Hell, you and me and whoever else survived when the universe fell away. They want you to press that button. Then we'll be reborn again and again, trapped in new hells, each more terrible than the one before it. Well, it stops here!"

I had no doubt she was completely crazy, but how could I get past her? Then there was a sound from behind her, and one of the Black Hairs launched into the burned woman. They were so intent on each other, they had forgotten all about me. I didn't have time to think. It was now or never.

I pushed the red button as hard as I could.

There was a sudden sound of alarms ringing just before everything, including us, winked out of existence . . .

By Jack L. Chalker
Published by Ballantine Books

AND THE DEVIL WILL DRAG YOU UNDER
DANCE BAND ON THE TITANIC
DANCERS IN THE AFTERGLOW
A JUNGLE OF STARS
THE WEB OF THE CHOSEN

THE SAGA OF THE WELL WORLD
Volume 1: *Midnight at the Well of Souls*
Volume 2: *Exiles at the Well of Souls*
Volume 3: *Quest for the Well of Souls*
Volume 4: *The Return of Nathan Brazil*
Volume 5: *Twilight at the Well of Souls: The Legacy of Nathan Brazil*

THE FOUR LORDS OF THE DIAMOND
Book One: *Lilith: A Snake in the Grass*
Book Two: *Cerberus: A Wolf in the Fold*
Book Three: *Charon: A Dragon at the Gate*
Book Four: *Medusa: A Tiger by the Tail*

THE DANCING GODS
Book One: *The River of the Dancing Gods*
Book Two: *Demons of the Dancing Gods*
Book Three: *Vengeance of the Dancing Gods*
Book Four: *Song of the Dancing Gods*

THE RINGS OF THE MASTER
Book One: *Lords of the Middle Dark*
Book Two: *Pirates of the Thunder*
Book Three: *Warriors of the Storm*
Book Four: *Masks of the Martyrs*

THE WATCHERS AT THE WELL
Book One: *Echoes of the Well of Souls*
Book Two: *Shadow of the Well of Souls*
Book Three: *Gods of the Well of Souls*

THE WONDERLAND GAMBIT
Book One: *The Cybernetic Walrus*
Book Two: *The March Hare Network*
Book Three: *The Hot-Wired Dodo*

THE HOT-WIRED DODO

BOOK THREE
OF
THE WONDERLAND GAMBIT

JACK L. CHALKER

BALLANTINE BOOKS • NEW YORK

A Del Rey® Book
Published by Ballantine Books

Copyright © 1997 by Jack L. Chalker

All rights reserved
under International and Pan-American Copyright Conventions.
Published in the United States by Ballantine Books,
a division of Random House, Inc., New York,
and simultaneously in Canada
by Random House of Canada Limited, Toronto.

http://www.randomhouse.com

Library of Congress Catalog Card Number: 96-95200

ISBN: 0-345-38692-2

Cover design by Kayley LeFaiver
Cover art by Paul Youll

Manufactured in the United States of America

First Edition: February 1997

10   9   8   7   6   5   4   3   2   1

To Roger and to John,
neither of whom I can truly accept as gone.
Roger, I think, would have approved of this one;
John is somewhere with Isaac, adamantly refusing with
his old colleague to believe that there is life after
death. I miss you both.

A NOTE FROM THE AUTHOR

This is the third and probably final chapter in *The Wonderland Gambit* saga. It's been a lot of fun to write and explore, although some may be upset with me for, well, borrowing a trick at the end that you all should have expected but that, all things considered, was absolutely essential and inevitable. Don't worry. Next time I have this terrific new original ending featuring a great white whale . . .

During the course of writing *The Wonderland Gambit* saga, I've lost two very close friends who kind of remained in my mind while I completed this book. Roger Zelazny was very close; I helped him move to Baltimore in the early sixties, and he was active in the Baltimore Science Fiction Society and was a cofounder and hidden financier of early Balticons. We'd have dinner often, or just talk on the phone for long periods, and he often called when stalled or unhappy with something and used me as a sounding board. I may not have my own Hugo, but I'll have you know that the little scene in *Lord of Light* in which the peasants discover their first toilet and try to figure out what it's for is mostly me.

We weren't as close after he moved to Santa Fe, but we still kept in touch and got together occasionally at conventions to marvel over how things had gone and occasionally plot new mischief. The last time I saw him, about nine months before he died, he seemed the happiest he'd been since the old Baltimore days. For the past decade, he was just far enough away physically but still so close in spirit that there's an emotional part of me that knows he's still just out in New Mexico someplace.

John Brunner was also a friend, and a good one. We met originally at conventions, and somehow tended to wind up trading stories—sometimes just the two of us, sometimes with a huge entourage—in a hotel pub or local bar for hours on end. Politically, John was far to the left of my militant centrism, but there was something there between us that was *simpático*. I was toastmaster at the World SF Convention where John was guest of honor.

He looked good at Glasgow last August Bank Holiday week. I saw him on Wednesday across the hall, and he saw me, waved, and called my name. I shouted back that we'd rendezvous as usual sometime before the last day of the con. Well, he headed out to dinner and returned with contract offers and a new resurgence in his career, and then he went around and partied all night and we didn't connect. But, what the heck, the con was just beginning.

Timing, John! It's all in the timing! It's one thing to go out at a Worldcon on the upswing of a career that had been down, but on *Monday*, John, not on Thursday morning.

I thought of them when I wrote *The Hot-Wired Dodo*, and there's certainly a good deal of Roger in segments here, and a little bit of Brunner as well, particularly in the moral dilemmas faced by some of the characters and the arguments they make.

I just wanted you to know that they were good people, and that I see them sitting around with Phil Dick and many others now gone and raising glasses to the future, never suspecting they're in a brand-new virtual world.

John wouldn't believe it anyway.

                                                          Jack L. Chalker

I

WAITING FOR THE END OF THE UNIVERSE

When you're waiting around for the end of the world and you know beyond a shadow of a doubt that you've got an immortal soul, you tend to worry less about being good and lean a little more to the bad.

Not that this helped me much, but it did help a little. I mean, I looked like a woman, but I had no reproductive plumbing, no particular sexual urges or desires, and no hair, either, so what the hell. I was more than ready for a new incarnation, but I didn't have any say in when the button would be pressed, and we would have precious little warning when it was. When months went by, though, you did tend to get more than a little bored, particularly when stuck in the middle of nowhere. The most positive thing I'd accomplished since coming to the backup area in central Washington was that I'd managed to mostly break myself of the Brand Box–induced habit of referring to myself in the plural.

I was also "overwhelmed" with depression, but stuck in a body that was constructed in one of Al Stark's little worlds, I really didn't have much capacity for emotion. I was shaped female, but a sexual neuter. I was hairless, and needed a wig

1

just to look presentable. I didn't even have much in the way of taste or smell; it hadn't been necessary in that giant "we're all the same" supermall. I had memories, but it was hard to conjure up physical feelings and emotions when reliving them. So, I used chemicals to feel an approximation of pleasure—and not even all those worked. I was also hampered in doing a lot of the things I would have liked to because we all knew that there wouldn't be much warning when Lee or whoever was now running the institute finally took it through to the next plane.

I certainly understood the setup all too well, having survived two such moves, but I found myself eager to move on from this reality, which had been the worst in several key areas, and impatient that I had to depend on somebody else, somebody I hated. That emotion I seemed to have no problems with.

Thinking through the long term was also more in my line, too, particularly because those thoughts were uncolored by some of the usual human feelings. I had to wonder if in fact we who thought of ourselves as "real" and the rest of the universes as filled with ghosts, or "spooks," created by computer in some vast virtual reality were in fact any more real than the spooks were. Maybe we were even less so—nobody had ever been able to go backward and find out if the rest of the old universe was still there.

Suppose *we* were the electronic creations, going through a series of parallel realities? Suppose the great missing genius, Matthew Brand, almost our god figure in all this, had in fact found the gateway to infinite numbers of parallel universes, each as real as the one in which he'd been born? It wasn't out of the question or more Lewis Carroll–type nonsense; the far-out edges of New Physics postulated parallel universes anyway, and used them to explain a lot of anomalies in "reality." Okay, so suppose that was it. Suppose all the rest were real and *we* were the creatures of fantasy created by Brand. It could be that *we* were the Mad Hatters and March Hares and Mock Turtles, Duchesses and Caterpillars, and those who seemed so "normal" really were just that. Instead of *me* as Alice, I was really the Cheshire Cat, fading in and out of realities, but alien to normality.

It was possible.

That, damn it, was the trouble. *Anything* was possible.

What in hell had any of us learned after all these worlds, all these lives, all these existences? Callousness and cruelty? Well, I guess we brought that with us. Lusts for power and back-and-forth combat? Ditto.

Damn it, after all this time, at least some of us must have learned something! Surely it couldn't have been entirely wasted!

Those aliens and their classic little flying saucer, for example. Who were they? Where had they come from?

"The Boojums showed up in a world where we literally got invaded by another planet," Walt reminisced. "No, not them— at least not right off. Even nastier things. Kind of like *War of the Worlds* slimeballs. The Boojums were from someplace else entirely doing some kind of research work and they got blamed for what the 'Slugs From Beyond' were doing. I remember Matt took a chance on them, I think after seeing them battle one of the slug ships, and tried contacting them. Didn't take, until the slugs knocked one of their saucers out of the sky almost on top of us. Matt saved 'em, and, ever since, they've been like high-tech hunting dogs, loyal to a fault and with no place to go."

"But they shouldn't have translated to the next universe," I pointed out. "Nobody else did, except our people."

Walt nodded. "Surprised hell out of us, too. Everybody except Matt, that is. As you've probably noticed, they haven't got a spoken language, and old paranoid Al wanted to blow 'em away and they knew it. Matt got to them, somehow, through the VR interfaces and the Brand Box. I just can't be positive, but I'm pretty damned sure they had no idea of all this until he and they connected. They made a lot of the improvements, in fact—the Brand Box we know today was developed from the early work between Matt and them using their interface with the saucer. That's how Cynthia, or anybody, really, can fly the thing. You put on the head mount and you *are* the ship. It's that easy. Of course, I get the very distinct idea that the little guys and the ship are connected automatically, like the way you had a head mount inside your head. They let us fool with it, but we always know they're there. They're always connected—to the ship and to each other. The principle of the synergy between alien and ship is the same that went into the final Brand Boxes. The material, however, that makes up the core of the boxes also came from the spare parts supply on the alien ship, which is why we can't build any more of them."

That explained that. "But he had the principle before this, I gather, and the meeting with these beings just allowed him to perfect it?"

Walt nodded again. "If you call this perfected, I guess you can say that. What we didn't figure on was that Matt had some concepts and ideas *these* little aliens didn't know. So, in exchange for the manufacture of the existing Brand Boxes that we interfaced to the life-support pods—mostly in the Command Center but also in some backup areas like this—*they* took a lot of the concepts and math from Matt's computers and repaired and rebuilt their ship. When we punched through to the next level, they all got in the ship, and, although most of us didn't know it at the time, they punched through right with us, using the ship as an alternate command center and its life support as their version of the pods."

"Huh? How come you didn't know it at the time?"

He shrugged. "Well, they shifted under cover. They don't tell us much so we all called 'em Boojums, like the Lewis Carroll stuff Matt was so fond of. They don't seem to mind. I doubt if they have names in our sense, either individually or collectively. Matt shifted them here, and sent me and Tanaka up to help 'em out. Cynthia came along for . . . well, long story of no consequence. Anyway, the slugs found the Mojave Command Center and forced a punch; we couldn't get down there and thought we were done for. Dan tried to make it anyway and got creamed, so he wound up in the reincarnation bin. Cynthia and I stayed here, and were surprised as hell when the Boojums pulled us on board and hooked us up to padded sections around the wall on the center level of the saucer. Hell, what choice did we have but to go along? I don't think the Boojums themselves knew if it would work, but they set it up for the punch, and when Matt punched through so did we. Surprised the hell out of us. Inside the ship, we didn't even do an incarnation. We just rode straight through, believe it or not. Just as we were. Pain in the ass—I was already over forty. Since then we've used the boxes; the Booj, they still punch through their way. Never changed, never got any older, and never got any fewer."

"Huh? I saw several get creamed back in Yakima a few lives back," I reminded him. "I even—well—I hit one with the car."

He nodded. "I know. You can kill 'em, burn 'em up, but come the next punch the same bunch comes out of the same saucer just the same way and in the same numbers. They probably *do* reincarnate—but if they read minds, or have some built-in connection to a kind of master Brand Box in the ship, then they're gonna get all the knowledge and memories back the moment the reincarnation happens. Must be nice. That's what Al's been trying to do, I think. Make it a certainty that his complete memory goes through even if he gets blown away as he did this time. He hasn't made it yet, though. I'm pretty sure of that, although the Brand Boxes can record enough of your old self to really get you oriented. It's never *quite* the same, though—usually a different sex for starters, then a slightly different background that makes it seem like you're a peeping Tom in somebody else's mind. I know what it's like. The memory's there, but it's never, somehow, *real*. You get the knowledge, but not the personality."

I nodded. "I know what you mean even if I can't relate to the experience. I remember at least two past lives, but they don't seem to have been *my* lives. I retain the skills and knowledge, but it's like I'm taking it from a recording, not from experience."

"Yeah, that's about it. I sometimes wonder if we *are* the same."

All this explained a lot, but not nearly enough to even start solving this.

"Walt, I think everybody's been too damned passive, particularly since you lost Brand," I told him. "Nobody's really attempting a concerted, long-term program to solve this mystery. Nobody's really looking for the way out, if there is an 'out.' Instead, you're just fighting each other, going back and forth, trying to gain a little power and advantage that's always local at best."

He shrugged. "What can we do? We don't have the Boojums' automatic restoration. When we die, we wake up ignorant. You know that. And there is no team effort from life to life, universe to universe. Everybody's too busy stabbing everybody else in the back. You can't force that kind of programming change. Matt could do some of it, a lot of it maybe, but when he vanished, so did any hope of getting out of this."

"Maybe not," I sighed. "Maybe it's time we said to hell with what should be, worked with what is, and tried to find the answers come hell or high water. Force it. Anybody who wants in, fine. Anybody who doesn't, we shut out."

"With what? The saucer and these few Brand Boxes? Not enough, and definitely not enough computing power."

"Then with the Command Center, the institute, or whatever we want to call it."

Walt gave a dry, humorless chuckle. "To use that, you'd have to take it away from Al and Lee and that crew, and I mean take it by force."

"Then that's our first objective," I responded, already thinking about how to proceed.

Walt laughed. "And what the hell do you think we've been trying to do these past several incarnations? Do you know how many of us there are on this side, not counting the Boojums? I'll tell you—seven. Seven members of the March Hare Network. Now, with you, and if Wilma comes through the next punch, nine. Rick was certainly with us this time, but we'll be back to square one with him again next go-round, and that's part of the problem. I got you into the center to give you a chance to get us inside with the main computer, but it seemed you only got partway into the system before they caught you."

I shrugged. "Look at what my alter ego was able to accomplish inside that grid, and even beyond it. What betrayed me in the end was that I'd hit a stone wall. I'm no Matthew Brand. I did a hell of a lot considering how far back in my memory I had to reach for those skills and how outside my area some of it was—not to mention the fact that I was working under the noses of people who didn't trust me. I had to play coy with everybody just to stay on the plane at all."

"Well, we've been fighting this out for a very long time," he said. "The thing is, though, I'm really beginning to wonder about the competency of the enemy we've been going after for so long."

"He's done pretty good so far."

"Has he?" Walt responded, chewing thoughtfully on his cigar. "I wonder. What has he learned? What the hell have any of them *done*? They've been in charge now for at least the last nine incarnations, maybe longer, ever since Matt vanished into that box. Al was really in charge of it, longer than that, I think, with his toadies and the ones he seduced who think they're smarter than he is. Matt was just too preoccupied to notice. We really started getting somewhere, too, until Matt was taken out. Since then—*nada*, nothing, zilch. All those power games but no real progress. Using the Brand Boxes as their sadistic toys, for playing with their old enemies like you or trying to indoctrinate others through those fake lives. Progress? Any more info on how to get out of this trap, or information on just what the hell we're caught in? Nothing."

"I'm not sure Al really cares anymore," I told him. "We had

lots of talks, you know, once he had me inside the box. Talks about lives and relationships that I had no memories of at all. Playing God is Al's game. I don't think he wants much else. If you weren't keeping the heat on him, I don't even think he'd punch through to a new incarnation until we were all old and gray. Lee—Lee's a follower. He likes being around power and basking in it, but he's not the kind to make the hard decisions on its use. Rob has a lot cleaner, more innocent sort of soul but is otherwise the same type. Tanaka has real talent, and to some extent so do Cholder and one or two others, particularly when working together. McKee—she has the will, the administrative experience, and the smarts to run the place as an alternative to Al. I'm just not sure she'd be an improvement."

He nodded. "I know what you mean. My own feeling is that the best hope we have is to get the Boojums in there along with somebody competent at interfacing the system with others. That's you, mostly. A few others on our side can help with the basics, but not a one of them is equal to Tanaka in terms of programming in that medium, and nobody else but you can do that mind-to-machine interfacing. See, they didn't care much about your abilities in that direction, but we need it bad. Or don't you agree with the overall goal?"

I shrugged. "Anything's better than doing this over and over, but I'm not sure just what will happen if we manage it. We don't talk to those people, we interact with them."

"Huh? What d'ya mean?"

"Just that. We don't have conversations with them the way you and I have been speaking. Oh, I think they understand what we say, all right, at least inasmuch as it relates to their own perspective, but we have no real exchange of ideas. They're here. They help out. They hang out. But why? If they know so much from their time with Brand, why are they still stuck here with us? What are their long-term objectives? What makes them occasionally risk life and limb to help us out? In other words, there's no disputing that they're our short-term allies in the sense of fighting Al and his group, but are they our long-term friends? Or are they just after this technology, the solution perhaps to their own puzzles over these principles?"

"I don't think they're any kind of long-term threat. I've been with 'em for so many years, it's impossible to count. They've fought with and for me and our people and pulled me out of a lot of jams. More important, I don't think Matt was scared of them, and he got closer than anybody. No, somehow, I just can't bring myself to worry about that."

Driving always had been something I did as much to think and get things out of my system as to actually go anywhere. I don't mean driving to the store or to the big city—just long drives to nowhere and back.

I was down in southeastern Oregon, driving through the desolate remnants of ancient volcanic fury, and I felt depressed but still irritated. Something wasn't right. I kept going around and around, though, and I couldn't get it out of my head that I wasn't being told the whole truth.

Part of it, I guess, was Good Old Walt with the fast, pat answers. The same Good Old Walt that I'd known as a boss lifetimes ago, and as a friend as well, straight through to the core, only . . . where was the Walt that had coldly shot that kid? He was in there, somewhere, but he'd never emerged, not in front of me, anyway.

Al and Lee and the institute were one thing—they represented the devils I knew. Walt, though, and Cynthia, and Father Pete, and the rest—these were the devils I didn't know, not really. They might have been fighting Al, but they sure didn't do anything to help me or Rick until very recently. They were chummy but still, well, distant. I had this eerie, paranoid feeling that there were still lots of meetings to which I wasn't privy, and lots of things they weren't about to let me in on.

Even paranoids have enemies.

Those aliens—somehow I still couldn't trust them, either, or at least believe that they were just regular good old boys with

one hell of a pickup truck. The story about them and Matt rang
a bit true, but it seemed, well, simplistic. The elusive, mysterious Matthew Brand was always so, well, *convenient*.

  "How're we gonna explain this?"

  *"Hmmm. I dunno. How about Matt Brand went out to his
garage and built this supercalifragilistic hypo-blaster . . ."*

He was Einstein when somebody needed an Einstein, God
when somebody needed a god, and he was missing, which
made him too damned convenient.

After all this time, after prowling through the institute and
having dialogues with Al and others there, I still didn't really
know a lot about them or the institute itself. I'd pulled off some
incredible stuff—or, at least my alter ego who thought she was
me had—but it was the tip of the iceberg. Who were those
people in the Brand Boxes? Who or what were those *presences*
just below the institute? And how had Les or Al whipped up a
convenient portal out of the last universe just when Wilma and
I needed one? It was hard to forget Al's sheer power in that
vortex, even though we had considerable power there as well.
He knew and controlled more than he was supposed to in his
role as the power-mad security chief.

Les did, too. A medical doctor who could conjure up a hole
to the spaces between the universes. That kind of power would
otherwise be attributed to Matt Brand, but Les wasn't Brand.
He wasn't even a programmer, yet he'd managed to divert Al
with a wooden club and open up an escape route for Wilma
and me in the middle of a warehouse.

And Walt—Walt was the March Hare, all right, and his
cronies were more of the opposition to Al, but who was the
Caterpillar, and who had left the Dodo? We'd bumped into
him in a kind of mental plane outside the virtual universe;
Walt's group later took credit for it, sort of, but clearly were
making up their story as they went along without any real
knowledge of what had happened except what they pulled
from my memories.

For that matter, many lives ago, we'd watched Walt and Cynthia open one of those portals, too, right over the backup center, and the Boojums had been inside, off-loading supplies.

When I'd asked about that, Walt had sloughed it off as a misinterpretation of what I had seen from a distance, that they were really only off-loading from the complex below the desert floor.

It was difficult to focus with real accuracy on such distant memories, but I was pretty damned sure I'd seen what I had seen.

And then there was Wilma. I missed her terribly; she was the one real friend I had in all this who hadn't changed or lost continuity. She also had that power, that way of dropping into that bizarre shaman's plane and often dropping me in there, too. It had saved our asses more than once—but where and what was it? Was it real or some other construct? Was it, somehow, a Brand Box, or outside of the system altogether? While she knew a lot more about it than I did, I felt sure that even she saw it veiled in the terms of her beliefs, not really knowing how it fit into this entire system.

Now, thanks to Al and the institute, she was a vegetable, kept alive in one of our life-support pods, waiting for the next translation when, we hoped, we'd at least get the rest of her back. My only real hope was that somehow she'd managed to opt out, to somehow mentally drop down to the shaman's world, but I had no way of knowing if she'd managed it or even if it was possible under those conditions. I had dropped in there once or twice under stress, apparently following some subconscious pattern, but I couldn't do it voluntarily. I'd tried. I'd tried all sorts of ways, including hypnotism and meditation, and I'd failed.

One thing was for sure—wherever it was, it wasn't in the linear progression of universes we were creating as we lived and died and moved on. The same shaman's world that I'd first encountered in a half nightmare in my previous universe, I'd gone to again from this universe.

And just where did I fit into all this? Everybody seemed to

want me around, but nobody seemed to want me very badly. I
didn't have the same killer instincts, nor did I have Tanaka's
programming brilliance, or other special skill. I was the one
who hooked up the wiring so it all functioned with minimum
fuss. And nobody, but nobody, either trusted me or cared to
trust me with what they knew. Sure, I understood that no
matter who or what they were and what powers they had, Les,
Al, Walt, and the rest really didn't have a clue how to escape
from Wonderland. But they knew a lot more than I'd been told.

Off in the distance I could see a row of ancient volcanic
cones looking like they'd been formed only a few years ago
instead of thousands of years past. For some reason, that made
me think of assassins and snipers.

Assassins and snipers? Why?

Well, you couldn't create a new plane, a new universe to
move to, until you'd zapped the person who created *this* one.
Basically, you had to figure out which one of our happy group
was God and kill him, her, or it before anybody could get out
alive. Okay, maybe it wasn't that easy, but it was possible.
Then you had to anoint a new god to create the next plane, or
universe, to which we could move, and you did that, dead or
alive, by being the first one into the next level. It was the
reason that Al kept so many of us in the Brand Boxes, so he
could control things to some degree. You wouldn't want to kill
the God Incarnate right away, even if you knew who it was.
Not unless you could also be the first one through the next
time. Or maybe control who that one was enough to fashion
the next plane *through* that God Designate, leaving yourself in
command but not in the crosshairs of either side. Maybe that's
what Al was trying to do by sticking people he couldn't otherwise dominate inside the Brand Boxes.

Whatever the truth was, the one thing the evidence suggested
was that both sides in this had long ago given up trying to get
out and were instead just trying to tailor their own worlds.

It was a pretty fruitless task, I thought. Even if you got what
you wanted, which was unlikely, then what? In the end, it was

still an endless no-win video game that just happened to involve real lives and real people. I wanted *out*, period. Who knew just how long these entire lives really lasted, for one thing? Suppose we were all lying somewhere, hooked into real versions of the life-support modules, all networked together in this bizarre program, but still growing older and totally dependent on the efficiency and maintenance of the LSMs. A batch of thirty to forty dreamers, lying there, dreaming their real lives away, caught in this madness until something went wrong and they died for real.

Rich had opted to live a real life here rather than incarnate. It wouldn't help him escape in the end, but, for now, he was probably the happiest of the group. In a sense, that's what I wanted, too, only I didn't want the illusion.

Networked together . . .

Now, there was a thought. The LSMs weren't really networked together; the Brand Boxes were all independent little universes that could be monitored from outside and entered if one wished. Each Brand Box was its own tailor-made virtual environment.

Like this one . . .

It was a thought that hadn't really occurred to me before for some reason. The schematic, as limited as it was at this stage, was nonetheless clear. X equaled the number of people hooked into this thing—probably no more than thirty-five. Each was attached to the server running a master program, which could also run programs independently on top of this connection—the Brand Boxes, for example. Like spokes on a wheel, with people stuck in the ends. The people so connected were not directly connected to each other, but were connected through the central server.

So I was the Maddox spoke, and off of that three programs were now running as subroutines on the end of my link, of which my current incarnation was one.

It was a simple, obvious concept, but where did it lead? Was the institute, or Command Center, the server? It survived in each transition. It went through to the next plane. But it was still limited by the constraints of the master program—it couldn't move until the conditions for a new plane had been met, making it nothing more than a program itself. A different kind of program, though, which was why things could be accessed there and nowhere else.

It was a shell. Like a pretty interface on clunky old operating systems that shielded the user from having to know, see, or understand what was really doing the work. In the same way, it, and its extension shells like the backup region, were merely devices to hide what was behind it. What the Buddhists called the That Which Is Behind All That.

When Rini had tapped into the system, she'd really just tapped into the shell. She'd not been a real person in any sense, although she became one later. Al, or maybe Tanaka at Al's direction, had created her as an object on the shell rather than an object through which one could access the shell. She'd never been "human" in the sense of anyone else in this world, either we incarnations or the folks who went about their lives in ignorance of the greater forces within the plane. In a sense, the institute was a real, live, three-dimensional representation of the server desktop. We interact *through* the desktop to whoever or whatever it hides. The average person here operated according to the rules of the greater shell, the universe so created and left to run as a mathematical model. But Rini—she wasn't of the universe and she wasn't of what was hidden as we were, the two types of objects the system generally dealt with. She was instead a creation of the desktop.

No wonder she could move through its base structure, mentally and physically, and interact with whatever was connected to and through it. Al had created a monster, and that's what eventually bit him. He was lucky—if Rini, or the knowledgeable part of me she carried with her, had actually understood the concept, she could have controlled the whole damned institute. It was passive, waiting for us to click on a program or routine, but Rini was a part of it that not only was not passive, but

was so integrated that she didn't show up in the command procedures. She had owned the place, lock, stock, and barrel; she
just hadn't known how to use it.

But would I have known? In any event, it was a new class of
being, one that, once created, could be created again. I couldn't
become one, nor could any of the rest of the Elect. We ourselves extended beyond the workstation desktop. Still, inside
the institute's computers, somewhere, on some memory
module or segment, was the data on just how they'd done it. If
that routine could be found, and used judiciously, then whoever the new creation trusted, or had personality elements
from, would be able to alter the entire great plane and become
virtually a god.

Al had stumbled on just what he'd been seeking, only he
hadn't recognized it when he had it. And the programming
team, and even the head programmer, probably Dannie
Tanaka, had been so intent on creating what Al wanted that
they hadn't once thought about all the implications.

Me, I wasn't a genius programmer, I wasn't a key brain in
this, just a mechanic, a systems integrator who took all the
stuff the smart people created and put it together into something that worked. A high-tech and somewhat abstract builder,
who took disparate elements made by others and eventually
came up with something that was greater than the sum of its
parts. Not an architect, since I was using the parts they gave me
rather than designing them myself, but an engineer who could
take off-the-shelf parts and build some neat things with them.

I had the keys to the Command Center, if only I could get in
and gain access long enough to put it all together. Once I had
that access I would be able to strip at least one more layer
away. Rini still hadn't been able to fully perceive the powerful
intelligences she saw as lurking below the station, but she
didn't know what she might be facing. Fear always limits
vision, and she was so awed by the power she felt that she was
afraid to look, afraid that, like Moses and the burning bush, if
she *had* looked it could have blinded or consumed her.

The problem was, how the hell could I get Walt to take the center, and then give me unlimited access to it, without being able to explain to him just what I was doing?

That problem would have to wait, though. In spite of this very universe being the one that gave us the best chance at an opening, it had come too late.

The March Hare's beeper went off before I got to Crater Lake, and when I called they said, "Get back here as quick as you can if you want to incarnate. There was kind of a palace revolution down South, and Lee's been pretty well deposed for indecision and maybe being a little too heavy-handed with the wrong people. Rita Alvarez is now running the show, and she's ordered a packup and rigging for a punch."

"How soon?" I asked, concerned.

"It could be any time, but it'll probably take them eighteen to twenty-four hours. That's just a guess, though."

"I'm on my way."

I can't tell you how fast the drive back was. While Oregon isn't a very large state when you're traveling south to north, it's big enough, and in this world, the interstate highway system wasn't as comprehensive as it had been in the last one I remembered. Still, I got to the backup site after about six hours of steady driving, and turned down the dirt road leading into the Air Force firing range hoping that nobody had jumped the gun. Rita Alvarez had done a lot of nasty stuff to me in this life; it would be just like her to unknowingly polish me off.

Fortunately, everybody was still there, including the backup station. In fact, getting in was almost an anticlimax, since they were mostly sitting around and waiting.

The March Hare Network looked far less impressive in their human forms, and not very threatening. There was Walt, of course, and Cynthia, Father Pete, and an older man I'd seen once before, down at the institute long ago, introduced to me as Dr. "just call me Herb" Koeder, who, it turned out, was a pale-ontologist. Also present was a slightly built brown-skinned woman with corn-rowed hair that I'd never seen before and who was introduced as "Mabel," but that was the only new face.

I looked at Walt. "I thought you said there were seven of you," I reminded him. "Aren't you still missing a couple?"

Walt nodded. "You've never met Doc Koril, at least on this plane. He got himself abducted by Al's boys and taken into the institute. We haven't seen or heard from him since, and I suspect he's one of the folks inside the LSMs there and most likely one of the people our Rini ran into. He's a brilliant man, a research psychiatrist, and I doubt if Al ever thought of him as a threat, let alone on our side, until he made some slip or something. At any rate, he won't be joining us until we can spring him somehow."

"And the seventh?"

"Adrian Martinez. A good-looking Latino with the heart and soul of a certified public accountant. He died in a car crash last winter. Doesn't seem to have been any funny business—he just ran into one of those bad breaks. It's quite possible that this boring piece of shit was his creation. It sort of has that Gary, Indiana, feel to it." He sighed. "So, we're still seven, counting Wilma, who's already in and set up; eight, with you. We'll see who else we can recruit. I've got Brand Box recordings of Adrian and Isaac, as well, if we can spring him sometime, and we'll certainly be looking for others to bring on board. You have any new insights while we wait?"

I decided that it would be better if I didn't discuss things too far. "Not really. Some ideas that are still coming together. What caused the big flare-up that brought me back here and has us all sitting around?"

"Well, we can monitor their general traffic from here, even if we can't do much of anything about it, and we got the word. They've gathered just about everybody left alive on their side who they want to take through, and I expect it's pretty much a done deal. I've got a fair roster, here. There are a few interesting omissions, I notice. No Lee Henreid, no Harker, Santee, Cholder, or Prine, and no Standishes, either, although I think Bernie drowned in some big storm while he was back East."

I looked over the sheet of paper he handed me. Rita Alvarez, Danielle Tanaka, Robyn Henreid—that was interesting!—Dorothy Sloan, also interesting, and Les Cohn, of course. He always seemed to be on the winning side.

"Les is our Talleyrand," Walt noted.

"Who?"

"Talleyrand. Started off as a bureaucrat under King Louis the Sixteenth. Just before the mobs pulled Louis down, he sought out the revolutionaries and signed on with Robespierre. When Robespierre's time was up, there was Talleyrand on the side of those dragging the dictator to the guillotine. He shows up prominently as Napoleon's foreign minister, but is also the fellow who, years later, engineers the return of the old monarchy. You see what I mean? A real knack for always being on the winning side before it's clear who will win. That's Les. If the good doctor ever approaches us and wants to join, we'll know we already have won."

I stared at him. "I didn't know you knew anything about history."

He shrugged. "You pick up a lot of everything when you live as long as I have. Makes you wonder how smart I might have been if I hadn't been killed at some time in the past, doesn't it?" He grinned. "Just kidding. It gets boring as hell, you got to do something. I already did the alcohol business once, I've never been comfortable with drugs because of that experience, so, well, you do other things. You'll see, if you make it as long as I have."

"How long has it been for you, Walt? How many lives, I mean?" Al had made it through nine lives before we finally plugged him.

He shrugged. "Ten, maybe a dozen. I don't even think about it anymore. Too long, so much wasted time . . ." He began to look glassy-eyed, almost as if he regretted those lives rather than being proud of surviving them. He quickly tried to change the subject.

"You pretty clear on what will happen when the alarm comes?" he asked me.

I nodded. "I think so. We head for the LSMs, hook into the systems, and wait."

He nodded. "Understand, though, this won't be like before. The body will not survive, for one thing. For another, you won't be in Brand Box heaven—you'll be aware the whole time until the dissolve. The difference is that the Box is going to keep your memory codex with you when you slide into the rabbit hole. Everything will be like when you did it before, and I can't tell you which or what type of hole you're going to go through, or whether you'll be alone or with some of us, all of us, or even one or more of *them*. Remember, if you don't get to the dissolve, you don't incarnate. Because you'll be going through this way, you'll stay connected to the backup center here, so no matter what happens, we'll be able to locate you or you will be able to locate this place. Because of that connection, you may well be disoriented when you get into phase with the incarnation. You might not have all the background from the incarnate's life at the start, or you might not remember in detail what you do now, but it'll slowly merge. Give it time."

"Do you have *any* idea of what it'll be like? Next time, I mean? Will it be another variant of this, or what?" The only two I could really remember were pretty similar.

"Not a clue," he responded, "only I don't expect the next one to be even *close* to what we've been having. It's almost dead positive that Alice McKee—academic, tough, radical, and an anthropologist, God help us—will set the tone, but not consciously. Not that, at least. Her subconscious will do it. Give a pattern. The computer shell will then provide all the detail flowing logically from that premise. I'm not at all looking forward to this one, if you ask me. I think she's the kind that, deep down, wants redress for past perceived grievances. I remember when Ben Sloan was the object. You wouldn't have believed he had any deep-down problems like that at all, but the world we had to survive in was one that the Black Muslims would have been proud to live in. It was mean. Changed him, too. After that one, he was almost drained, a company man. Strange. Sort of like it all came out of his system at once. I was lucky to survive that; a lot of us didn't. I'm not sure we aren't in for another like that. Brace yourself."

I stared at him, and the others all looked uncomfortable. "You really think it's going to be that bad?"

"Could be. Depends on which way you come out the other end, I think. I really wonder if some of us wouldn't be better reincarnating than going through this way, but no matter how good a recording, it's never the same as the real thing, never without losses. I—"

The air was suddenly filled with loud bells, going on and on at earsplitting volume, amplified by the concrete bunkers and metal cabinetry.

I looked at all of them, and there weren't any who didn't have fear on their faces and in their eyes. None of them wanted this, but it was go through with it or be left behind, to be reborn totally anew. Even Cynthia had been uncharacteristically silent and somewhat sullen, and not at all the confident and bossy bitch that was her trademark personality.

Still, nobody hesitated. If you did, you'd wind up not only being left behind, perhaps, but also totally deaf from all those bells.

There was a name on each LSM. I found mine and quickly stripped and entered, pulling the door shut. I heard it hiss and felt the air pressure change, and I also suddenly found myself if not quite in silence, at least well insulated from the bells.

These LSMs were far more automated than the ones used at the institute, or at least the ones I'd seen. Walt and the others had done an impressive job. The breathing mask fitted over my face fine, and there was a spongy material that expanded and form-fitted around my body, holding me firmly in place. I felt all sorts of pinpricks on various parts of my skin as small needles and IVs entered, probed, then settled into place.

Things become totally unreal, and all sound ceased except the noise of my own breathing and heartbeat.

Here we go! I thought, nervous, scared, but excited, too. If, of course, I lived to reach the dissolve once again . . .

> *'Round and 'round and 'round she goes,*
> *Where she stops, nobody knows . . .*

Sound suddenly washed over me like a great ocean wave; not loud, obnoxious, or unpleasant sounds, just *sound*. It was the sound of a hollow area, like a cave or large room with smooth walls.

The life-support module melted away, and I stood there a moment, naked, looking out at the tableau. It wasn't bright; instead, it was a great dark room the floor of which was made up of hundreds and hundreds of round colored disk-like lights glowing red and green and yellow and blue and white. They would burn steadily for a little bit; then the colors of just one block of them, perhaps six rows by six, would blink once, twice, three times, then change into a different color pattern. A short while later, a second block would do it, then a third, and so on. When all that I could see had undergone this change, the first one would do it again.

A maze, I realized instinctively. *Some kind of mathematical pattern.* But how did you determine what it was if you hadn't seen anyone or anything else run it? There had to be something more to it, something basic and perhaps even obvious.

I had hopes of seeing a Dodo or some similar creature who might give me a clue or some sort of help, but it didn't look like any were going to show.

There was nothing to do but study the changing patterns and see if there was any logical progression. Certainly the temperature was comfortable, the air dry with a faint metallic odor, so there wasn't a problem taking time that way. The only thing was, I appeared to have consumed my last food and water in this life; I either made it across and was born again, or I died in that maze and said good-bye to memory. Of course, having gone out attached to the LSM, I could get some of it back, but even my older selves present by direct memory seemed ghosts of another life, another time, growing a bit dimmer with each incarnation. The Box could feed back facts and knowledge, but not firsthand experience and wisdom; it was more like borrowing somebody else's data than recalling and using your own.

I didn't want that. I hadn't any knowledge of having done that before, but something in my subconscious said that it was better not to remember at all than to remember that way.

Every transition for the living began with a video game, it seemed. Some sort of challenge that you had to solve to move ahead. Last time it had been giant spiders in a human pinball machine; now it was a complicated version of the kids' electronic game Simon. Simple, really. Figure out the pattern and see the repeats. If you can repeat the pattern, the game would give you a longer, more complex pattern, and so on. This was a clear variation.

I watched it for what seemed like hours, and after a while I was getting pretty good at predicting things. Whoever or whatever set this up wasn't some maniacal monster; it would have been easy to make these tests very nasty. It seemed designed more to require you to at least have some sense, and desire to do it, nothing more.

Take this one. Six-by-six grid, thirty-six lights, but only five colors. Every pattern had the colors in the same relationship to others of the same color—in other words, the reds might well be 1A, 2C, no 3, 4B and 4D, and so on. Looked pretty random, but it repeated the same way. Each color was the same in relation to the other five in terms of positioning on the grid. Funny thing was, this left six of them that turned out to be red-green-blue-yellow-white-red each and every time. Finding the pattern was pretty tough, but you were given a fair amount of time

to isolate this one combination. Once you had it, you had a
kind of outline of a walkway, maybe not straight, but always
present. The confirmation was that the next adjoining block
continued the master pattern of the first and always linked to
the six-in-a-line combo. The tricky part was that you'd have to
run it during the period when it was static, after all the blocks
had changed, and that period, by my count of several cycles,
amounted to but one minute before it started to change again. It
wasn't a long distance, but you had to see the whole pattern,
run to it, and get through all in that minute; then you were hus-
tling with little margin for error as the rest changed behind
you. Not hard, but not child's play, either.

I looked around, somewhat surprised that nobody else was
here. For a moment I had the horrible thought that, starting in
the LSM, this wasn't a real punch-through at all, but rather just
another Brand Box experience. How would I really know?

But, of course, that had been the problem from the start. The
hell with it. Having now predicted five patterns in a row and
finding myself growing very thirsty, I decided that the next one
was it.

The pattern as path seemed obvious; I was either right or I
was wrong, but there didn't seem to be any alternative inter-
pretations, so I stepped out and walked, not ran, briskly into
the sea of lights.

It was easy to get disoriented the moment you were inside,
something I'd thought about, so I'd simply reduced the whole
thing to a grid and began repeating the directions. 3F to 2E to
2D to 1C to 2B to 3A. Walk forward, and the next block should
start the same sequence; find 3F again and you were on your
way farther in. I didn't want to rush it; I felt that the two major
traps here were running through—too easy to slip or miss a
step—or becoming so cautious you overthought, second-
guessed, and wound up with the changing pattern catching up
behind you.

*Don't think about the pattern behind. Keep going, keep
going . . . 3F, 2E, 2D, 1C, 2B, 3A . . . 3F, 2 . . .*

Halfway through, I got that uncertainty edge—you know, your mind goes not quite blank, but what you know as well as the back of your hand suddenly seems totally wrong somehow? Was it 1C or 2C? Keep going, keep going.

The thing had its share of surprises; noises and menacing forms waiting in the dark down various wrong turns, almost like everything lethal was prepared for you to make one wrong step—and it probably was.

I was near the end and could actually *see* the great wall of gray static, a giant television tuned to no channel at all, waiting for me, just one more row . . .

All the lights changed around me.

For a moment I stopped, panicked; then I heard all the shadows that seemed to have been lurking just out of sight start roaring, spitting, and scuttling toward my position.

The hell with this! I thought. *What the hell difference is it if it's only one row?*

Now I kicked off, running out past the lights and straight toward the wall. I heard the things behind me, whatever they were, and something brushed against my thigh, but I didn't look back, didn't stop, and I dove right into the void.

II

THE WORLD DARK
ALICE MADE

I began to see why Walt and Al and even Cynthia had made it through so many times after the first one or two. The first time I could remember going through one of those mazes or puzzles, I fortunately had Wilma with me to help out and give me courage. I'm not sure either of us would have gotten through without the other. Still, here I was, past the first danger point and into the queue section; I hadn't panicked, hadn't fallen for any of the tricks, and I'd done it on my own.

I couldn't help wondering if that rabbit hole didn't always change the lights when you got to the last row. I was sure I'd run it in more than enough time; that hadn't been six minutes by any measure. All those creatures in the dark were there to divert you, scare you, make you forget your pattern or where you were, and then that last-minute free-for-all was the final trap. Nothing could really reach you if you just sprinted—but if you froze . . .

It may have been a simple enough game, but the son of a bitch who designed that one had a sadistic streak. Deep down, I hoped it wasn't some earlier version of me.

This second stage had only one trap in it, one I'd fallen into last time and was determined, if possible, not to fall into again. At least here, time didn't really seem to exist, or at least I wasn't conscious of it. I'm not even sure if the existence in the holding area was real in any sense, or just a form our minds created to make sense of a status that had no other interpretation.

It still seemed like it was a factory, and I was on a conveyor belt. Around me were all sorts of exotic shapes and unknowable, futuristic devices designed less to do something than to take as many unnecessary steps as possible to convey you from point A to point B.

It had a pleasant feel, and you could sense other presences, other minds, like you, riding along in a pleasant, timeless fog, with only a mild awareness of place and no concerns at all. That would be the case until the last of us passed from that crappy world we'd been in to here. Then, stacked up but in the order we'd entered, we'd be processed for the new world. In the meantime, it probably gave the master computer, whatever and wherever that was, more than enough time to construct the universe of the first in line, the late Sister Alice Mary McKee, Ph.D.

I earnestly hoped we wouldn't all be nuns.

A world of cultural anthropologists wouldn't be much better, maybe worse. Her work was more about urban folks than South Pacific aborigines, so it wasn't likely to be Polynesian. Too bad. That might have been fun; at least the climate would be great.

It didn't matter. All of us, including her, were stuck with whatever her subconscious mind had come up with, and it was not only possible, it was likely that she wouldn't like it much more than we would. Or, maybe she would, but it might not be what she would have consciously created. This sort of thing tended to be built on emotion, not rationality. Walt, who seemed to go back farther than anybody, had once told me in a worried tone about a society where torture and self-mutilation and even nastier stuff was the norm. That wasn't even Cynthia's sort of place, and it wasn't certain who had "created" it. It sure wasn't the kind of society anybody we knew of would build rationally. Still, it had been built because, while we were rational beings, we were more than that, too.

I did have the same question this time as last. The normal rule was that if you died, you reincarnated without conscious memory of the past life and as the opposite sex; if you came through alive, as I was doing, you remained the same sex and retained your memories of the past. The problem was, in both cases I'd begun male and had been changed in the first case to female, in this case to a female-appearing neuter. The odds were, though, that I'd wind up male this next time, and while that didn't bother me, it sure as hell worried me. I mean, McKee was a hyperfeminist superwoman who had no strong relationships with men but plenty of casual stuff before becoming a nun. Would she want to get rid of men, or get even with them? Somehow I didn't think equality was a concept that would trouble her very much.

The point was, *it didn't matter*. At least, it didn't matter right now. What mattered most was not repeating what had happened last time, when I'd taken a risk and wound up coming in crippled beyond the ability of medicine to fix. I knew you couldn't come in too early—a five-year-old with a graduate engineer's knowledge and vocabulary would have been pretty obvious and not very clever—but I didn't want to repeat that kind of pattern.

As it turned out, I needn't have worried, at least not on that score.

As Walt had warned, I *did* feel a difference from having started in an LSM attached to a Brand Box that had recorded all my memories and personality. The backup center somehow moved into the new reality, as would the main Command Center, but they would have to be sought out over time and activated. The master computer that created these universes had the one advantage of being able to back-engineer the new world—first specifying that, say, the Command Center must exist, then going back to create a probability line that would put it there. Even if it turned out to be a nontechnological society, somehow, somewhere, the artifact would exist.

That, of course, might well present a golden opportunity for the "outs" to move "in," except that whoever was in charge when they punched through had programs that could limit access. Rita would be the controller if she was the one heading the operation, and it would proceed in a hierarchy down from her. By the same token, I was now in the backup-center hierarchy, although probably way down the list.

Before, when the process started, I had been able to view my next life from birth as a sort of movie on fast forward, and pick where I was going to enter and when. I'd then entered as my new self, and my old self had crept in, like an old friend rather than some stranger, over the next few months. In this setup, it appeared somewhat reversed.

What I saw now was a dizzying kaleidoscope, moving fast and in a very disorienting way, keeping me from making any real sense of the new world and my place in it. The scenes were odd, confusing, bizarre, and moving at a great speed that was not easy to slow down. Still, I was getting enough to know that I shouldn't waste much of that life if I expected to do anything at all there, and that whatever happened would be pretty tough anyway. None of us, I knew, in all our wildest dreams, had imagined that Alice McKee would come up with something like *this*.

The hell with this crap, I thought, and just inserted. The only hope I had in this new life would be if I could find some other key players, or just somehow get back out alive.

The strange line of souls marching through the celestial factory vanished, to be replaced by a deep but very ordinary sleep.

Okay, now, how best to explain this place where I awoke to somebody who was never there?

Think about spiders. No, no, I don't mean we all had eight legs and ate flies. Think of insect sex.

The females are pretty well dominant in the insect world; males in general exist for only one function. They tend to be small, often colorless, and rather weak, and it's not unusual for the female to devour her lover. The male has only one job to do, and, once it's done, he is otherwise irrelevant.

They say that the grass is always greener on the other side of the fence, and that's usually true, but we often tend to exaggerate the shade of green. Somebody who starts poor and becomes well educated, rich, famous, and has everything that everybody would love to have is also a member of a subclass that is part of his or her cultural identity. The Utopian Ideal, somebody called it. The conviction that, no matter how much you have, *they* are still keeping something from you and laughing behind your back.

The Alice McKee of both worlds that I knew was from a good home, extremely well educated, never in want, and always assertive and confident. Occasionally, though, like everybody, she'd been turned down. Maybe it was a lover, a friend, a boss, and maybe it was a really nasty encounter at an early age with a male slimeball, but it was always there, coloring her mind-set just below the surface. The enemy was men. Men could do what she couldn't, men got the best positions, men stepped in front of more talented women. She'd always been one of those "banish-the-white-male-culture-from-society" types in academic circles, but she'd never been particularly hostile to me. Still, deep down, it had to have been more than a posture; more than just a set of committed beliefs, it was a firm and somewhat psychotic view consistent with the rest.

That sure explained *this* world.

First of all, it was a modern world not unlike the one in which I felt most at home, a world that went way beyond indoor plumbing to air conditioning, automobiles, jet planes, and all the rest. It was also in the broadest sense a feminist world, not in terms of all the ideological posturing but just in the fact that, of necessity, women ran things. It wasn't because they seized power or there'd been some great social movement; biology and mathematics dictated it.

First of all, women outnumbered men two or three to one. They tended to live into their seventies in the industrial West, and they were physically bigger and stronger.

Men were not just the significant minority, they were physically smaller, four to five feet tall, at most. Having a "short" chromosome, they tended to be weaker as well, and unlikely to pose much of a threat to women no matter what their disposition. They tended to be more sickly and, even in the advanced countries, tended to die relatively young, often in their forties and fifties.

Figuratively, men didn't wear the pants in this society. In most cases, literally as well, but from a more pragmatic cause, for men did have one function in society and it was very important if very basic. Although they were physically quite small, their sexual organs were, well, *huge*. I couldn't help but remember an old silly song from two lifetimes ago:

> *He was dirty and hairy*
> *And full of fleas,*
> *But his terrible tool*
> *Hung down to his knees!*
> *God Bless the Bastard King of Eng-land!*

It wasn't just the "tool," either, but the support structure that, while giving enormous, well, capacity, also made wearing pants impractical. By the time they finished letting out the crotch area for comfort you pretty well had a kind of skirt anyway.

In English they were always called "kilts," to differentiate from a woman's more exotic formalwear, but in practice the guys wore skirts and the women tended to wear pants, period.

Such a physical makeup, and its attendant testosterone levels, did tend to keep a guy always fighting his hormonal urges, which didn't help at all.

Now, you'd think that with this kind of situation men would wind up going around constantly chasing these big women and most of the time getting the crap knocked out of them by their quarry, but that's not the way societies evolve. Still, make no mistake, this was a society that was designed by and for women, although in the image of the familiar as both Alice McKee's background and the computer's world-building methodology dictated.

That same methodology, in which whatever was not specified was simply fitted to the premise, made for some rather comical history, or at least comical to those of us who had known a different society. The Golden Gate of Santa Francesca was only one such example, and hardly the most outrageous. The government, the names, the institutions, and even the religions were all feminized in the generic sense. Men, in fact, were largely excluded from institutional life; there were no male equivalents of nuns, for instance, since it was accepted that men would go insane trying to keep celibate in that kind of cloistered life, and there were no men in government, since men didn't work well in groups or at consensus-building.

My name was Cory Kassemi, the last being my mother's name in the past two incarnations. I wasn't crippled, that was one thing, and I was in relatively good health for my age and sex. Growing up was a somewhat confining experience. After age three or so, most boys were put in a kind of male boarding school called a Primary Center, raised pretty much apart from family and with friends being the classmates at the center, where we lived in a kind of dorm-style setting. Mothers visited often, and quite often took you out for some kind of treat or short trip, so you always had that attachment, but basically you were kept confined to the school, and all the authority figures were older women. We saw men as janitors and gardeners, but even then always under the supervision of women.

We were taught reading, writing, and arithmetic, but not a lot more in the Primary Center. For one thing, it seemed that boys, including me, tended toward a mild dyslexic condition that didn't prevent learning but made it hard and discouraged studying anything beyond the basics.

The center knew this, and was concerned only with imparting a functional literacy. Much of its real lesson objective, what it really taught and was designed to teach, was discipline, discipline, discipline—self-discipline and control, discipline in groups, discipline in interactions with others. The fiction books, television, and movies—dramas and comedies and cartoons— all had reflections of these lessons and all had strong, heroic women and weak, wimpy, helpless, and trouble-prone boys. "Girl" and "woman" were often used interchangeably, but we were *always* "boys." Creative and intellectual pursuits beyond the basics were discouraged, even cut off as soon as identified. Great women and their accomplishments were touted over and over; you sort of knew that there had to be some boys around or there wouldn't have been a next generation of great women, but if you ever asked about it, the reply invariably was, "Well, any boy will do for that."

I think they understood genetics a lot better than that, but we weren't supposed to ever get into those areas of knowledge, and the message was hammered into us constantly.

Boys were nothing. They had ugly, boring, plain bodies, and their one main feature, which really started to develop about age twelve, was ugly and didn't seem to belong. By comparison, women were curved, smooth, and exotic. Boys weren't emotionally stable enough, strong enough, or even smart enough to do the kind of big things women did; they were given a use by society almost because they had to do *something*. Boys were needed for the propagation of the species, nothing more. Women had all the responsibility; they had to gestate and bear the children, nurture them while still working in society, make sure the kids were raised and taken care of, and so on and so on.

At maybe a year after puberty, which started about age eleven to thirteen, each boy was expected to go to work and pay back the Primary Center. This tended to be unskilled labor; the aforementioned janitorial stuff, and cleaning, street sweeping, gardening, and repetitive factory work, although much of that was being automated. There were lots of books, articles, and TV shows on what the idle boy would do when automated out of his traditional jobs.

You were never out in the world alone, or unsupervised for long, but it was still a relief to get out and see what seemed *almost* normalcy, at least on a superficial level. Much to my great surprise, I was no longer in the Northwest or California; I was, in fact, in Texas, in a little town called Larimore near Houston—the latter named, of course, for that great Texas liberator Samantha Houston, who'd whipped Juanita de Santa Ana in a battle back 175 years or so ago.

The job I was given was in town maintenance. I don't want to make that sound more important than it was. Every day, a few of us boys took the bus downtown, and checked in at City Hall with a supervisor, a fat old broad named Miz Snoops, who had gray hair and not all her teeth and who wore a pair of overalls that looked like they dated back to Houston's day. In a way it was another put-down, since any one of us was smarter and more capable than Miz Snoops, but she was in charge and that was that. At least my "raging testosterone" never raged around Miz Snoops.

We'd go out with manual equipment and sweep trash off the sidewalks into these little enclosed dustpans on sticks, and then we'd take poles with darts on the end and pick up trash in the parks and such, and there'd be occasional other small jobs for us to do, like repainting weathered trash cans, checking and sometimes replacing parking signs, that kind of thing. It was minimum wage, and we got to keep ten percent of that, the rest going to "repay" our "education," but at least it got us out, and it wasn't exactly demanding.

I was sixteen, had long brown hair, blue eyes, an increasingly hairy body that was supposedly real sexy, and a soft, high baritone voice that others seemed to find pleasant. I actually looked pretty good in the mirror, at least by old standards. I was in reasonable shape, was a pretty fair cook, and was good enough at mending and fixing that they were talking about letting me try to find a job that paid more and maybe would set me up, with a couple of others, on my own.

The problem was partly scale. It didn't take long to be reminded that I was four foot eight in a six-foot-two society, that I probably didn't weigh ninety pounds, and felt somewhat overwhelmed by everything around me. No matter what, I promised myself, there was no way that I'd ever find humor in short people again, if I ever had.

There were things to recommend the society, particularly if you were female. Just beyond the park you could see schoolchildren, all girls of course, playing field sports and having a good time, then trooping back in probably for algebra and world history—herstory? No, even this world didn't go to *that* extreme. I already knew a ton more than they did, and part of my own sense of self-discipline was hiding that fact both from the women who were my superiors and from my own compatriots, who tended not to be too tolerant of folks different from themselves.

For all the peaceful, unthreatening nature of the town and of society in general, this world was still more dangerous than any I could remember. Women didn't tend to fight nearly as much, or be nearly as violent, but when they *did* fight it was with a ferocity no male could match. The real tragedy was that the society all but consumed the male spirit. Apparently it hadn't always been that way, and there were isolated societies where it was different to some degree, but the gospel assumed that men could not form lasting relationships—most men could and did—and that men didn't care about the children they fathered nor were they competent to assist in raising them when in fact the opposite was true. Oh, there were a lot of the boys who were pretty callous, particularly at my age, but not all. We hadn't actually fathered any children yet, so it was mostly romanticizing and self-aggrandizing rather than real experience that caused the bluster.

And the system insured that we were permanently kept as children rather than as maturing, responsible adults. Still, it produced in most of us a yearning that they wouldn't believe, a yearning for protection and stability. Women lived about the same amount of time regardless of whether they ever married or had kids or whatever; men who were single tended to die by forty, and the older guys were all in long-term relationships.

"Hey, Cory!" Jed, one of my classmates at the Primary for several years, called to me. He'd just been on a detail painting new yellow curbing on some streets.

"Hi, Jed," I called back. "So, you paint the whole town yellow now?"

He grinned. "I'd paint it a lot worse than that if they'd gimme some paint. You doin' anything tonight?"

I shrugged. "Should I be?" It wasn't like we could go out on our own and run wild.

"It's payday, and they're gonna have a bus go down to the mall tonight. Miz Conlon's chaperoning, and she's pretty good at lettin' us go a few places."

"You got any money?" I asked him. "I mean, the few bucks we're gettin' tonight won't buy much."

"I been savin' up. Got enough for a coupla games, I think."

That's one thing we did, we boys. We played a lot of games—exotic card games, role-playing stuff, all sorts of things.

"What? Nothin' to impress the babes?"

He laughed. "Maybe. Depends on how much I got left. If you got a little, you oughta come along. Maybe we can put what you got and I got together and pick up something cool."

Okay, let's face it, even in this new situation there were some things that didn't change. Neither Jed nor I nor, in fact, most of our friends cared a lot about appearance. Sure, there were some guys who were vain, but mostly we were okay if we didn't look mud-soaked and took regular baths. What you *did* care about, though, was that women cared about such things, and they were always on our minds.

Fashion was different from what I was used to in the past. I mean, aside from the kilts, which had a practical reason for existence, the use of more male jewelry than a watch and a ring wasn't too common in either of my past worlds. Here, though, the girls liked that on boys, as well as on themselves, and there was a whole kind of guy-jewelry industry that matched guy colognes and guy shaving lotions. Jewelry and wildly colorful clothing was how we compensated for feeling that we all looked dull and ugly compared to women. Hairstyles were also important, and there was a sense of male fashion way beyond what I was used to in past lives, male or female.

The funny thing was, for all that, the women didn't dress real mannish. In fact, they dressed pretty much the way they always had, which was another part of the problem. I mean, it was hard not to stare and fantasize just watching the world go by. I really was turned on, almost obsessed, with scoring, but between the size differential and the psychological conditioning, I wasn't able to be as forward as I had as a young man in other worlds. Boys didn't go out alone, and they didn't go into bars or other hangouts, and the idea of initiating a new friendship with a girl was as scary in reality as craved in fantasy. I'd been shy in what I considered a conventional world setting; here it was much, much worse.

I tended to wear light, sleeveless shirts and very loose, pleated kilts, and I had earrings, a neck chain, some rings, and fairly short hair because it didn't take any real upkeep. Most boys grew mustaches or beards, but I'd never much liked them in any incarnation and tended to keep myself smooth-shaven. That sort of maintenance was pretty easy, since I had allowed my facial hair to grow in once and I thought I looked awful. Some heads had it, others didn't. Mine definitely wasn't designed for facial hair.

Still, if some girl had come around and said she loved goatees, I'd have grown one without a second thought. None, unfortunately, did, neither saying that nor much else to me. I was a real wallflower, but I wasn't alone.

With the social atmosphere, I admit that there was a lot of jerking off and a lot of boy-boy stuff, just as it was clear looking at folks in town that there was a lot of girl-girl stuff, too, but from my point of view it was mostly a pale shadow of what I wanted and needed and just barely enough to allow me to function without going nuts.

There were some places where you might meet and impress the opposite sex, and these weren't to be ignored. Church was one, of course, even if boys and girls sat in different sections, and there were places like the shopping centers and general work environments, things like that. There were also shows, carnivals, and other areas where there might be some interaction, or at least one side strutting for the other, but it wasn't a constant, day-in-and-day-out type of thing.

I don't know; the women here didn't seem to need it like we did, and weren't in much of a hurry about it, either. It seemed like a lot of marriages were with women far older than we were, while the younger girls might take a fling now and then but were mostly interested in one-night stands. I have to admit that my life mostly consisted of either dreaming about sex, compensating for its absence, or doing things to take my mind off it. I did, however, have enough sense and self-control, probably thanks to the other Corys deep inside my head, that I wasn't going to take any quick way out. In fact, I knew I had a real problem here.

On the one hand, I wanted to get out, get some measure of freedom, and link up if possible with anybody else from the March Hare group, even if, God help us, Cynthia was probably the one of us with the most power in this world. It remained to be seen how Wilma came through, or *if* she came through, considering the gauntlet she'd have to run in her condition. Maybe the link to the box via the LSM had made it possible for her to get through, but even if it did, how sane she might be was a question. Who knew? Maybe that mysterious Mabel, about whom I knew little, was more important now.

Even if Cynthia were running things in her madcap way, it would be preferable to the alternative. Rita Alvarez would be Mistress in Charge of the Command Center now, freed from just about all restraints and highly unlikely to be open to Les tempering the folks in charge since Les would have remained male and thus be in no better shape than me. Knowing Rita, the first thing she'd do after locating and reestablishing control of the Command Center would be to seek out Al, who would be ignorant of his past thanks to Rini and me, but he would be a woman here and thus *still* on the power curve, damn it!

Well, it wasn't like I could do anything. In fact, I might even have caused my own problems. I'd been so skittish about patiently inserting myself that I'd come through relatively young. It was entirely possible that it would be years before all the factors would come together to permit any kind of action. I couldn't count on it, them, or anybody. I couldn't even necessarily count on anybody even setting out to find me, although I suspected that both sides would as usual try to gather in the scattered sheep for purposes of power and control.

The thing was, I was powerless, helpless, in any of that. I was either going to have to commit suicide, wait for a new reincarnation, and wipe out all that I now remembered, or learn to get along in this cockeyed universe. I didn't want to lose my past, or what knowledge and experience I might have gained, but I sure as hell couldn't live in that set of past lives.

So, after a month or so of adjustment, I put the past aside. Not easily, and not eagerly, but out of necessity. It would be useful only when and if my life here intersected with the other groups. Until then, it was pretty damned irrelevant and wasn't going to get me laid or out of these damned barracks.

My new attitude seemed to gain some notice when it became more consistent. I found it a relief not to brood so much, to take things one day at a time and just go with the flow. And there was at least one area in which this situation was a positive rather than a negative.

Somebody once said that a man's adult life was always a series of "have-to's." You have to work at a job you hate because you have to earn the money and you have to play ball with your kid and you have to take out the garbage. Not here. Here, you were a kid forever, a kid with a real super sex drive. You weren't expected to be more than an immature little guy goofing off when possible and having few if any responsibilities to others or to society. There was in fact no real pressure to do anything other than satisfy your own urges and do the minimum to feed, clothe, and shelter yourself, with a society designed to support you if you for any reason couldn't or wouldn't. Adolescence, in that sense, never ended. You were not expected to exercise responsibility, nor allowed to.

After a while, Mom stepped in and decided that I should at least be put on some kind of track that would get me securely married off. She worked for a design firm in Houston—not clothes, things like parks and civic centers—and that brought her into contact with the politicians and companies that were in the tourist and promotion business. She wangled a position in a hotel-industry training course for boys, and that led to a job with a chain-affiliated hotel in Galveston—close enough to Houston so she could keep an eye on me, far enough away so I'd be really on my own for the first time.

It was almost traumatic, leaving the Primary Center after all that time, but we all promised to keep in contact somehow, and I was damned excited. Galveston was a resort city on the Gulf, informal, lots of beaches and swimming, and lots of young people. While the money for this fairly menial starter job wasn't great, it was, with a staff hotel room and staff restaurant privileges, enough.

It was only at this point, after all those virtual "years,"

which were as real to me as if I'd been born and lived them all
through, that I learned that a lot of guys didn't go the route I
had but grew up on their own in society. I found the beach
area littered with them, some fairly normal and working the
usual male jobs, others living as bums, gigolos, prostitutes,
hustlers—you name it. All of them were on the make, all after
the well-off and vulnerable tourists. I hadn't realized how
naïve and sheltered Mom's choices had made me until I was
really out in the world.

Most boys were sort of in-between types, and those I found
myself most comfortable being around. I particularly latched
on to Harry Petrosian, a hustler who was maybe pushing thirty,
looked older, and had been born and raised in the city and had
worked the city and the Madre Islands offshore since he was
small. He wasn't much bigger than me, but he had this thick
bushy beard and hair so long I swear he'd never had a haircut
or shaved. He had these big, thick arms and a barrel-shape
chest and he was a sight. I think he was attracted by my fresh-
faced naïveté, and kind of adopted me. He smoked long, thin
cigars and always wore sunglasses, even indoors and at night. I
never saw him without them, and he tended to take them off
only to clean them.

"Yo' mama sent ya heah to git some street smahts," he commented, flicking the ash off his cigar into the street. There was
a big move against smoking going on, but it didn't bother him.
It was something you could do to annoy that wasn't illegal and
stated your independence and contempt for authority, even
though it might be bad for you. "Furst thing you got to
remembah is not t'fall foah them sweet young thangs y'see all
'round in them topless string bikinis and shit like that theah.
They's on the make, tha:'s all. Want t'suck yo' in, make
anothah virgin, then drop you like a hot kettle of steamed
shrimp. You been heah a couple weeks now—how many times
you been propositioned by them bitches?"

"Seems like all the time," I told him honestly, not even realizing that it might also sound a little egotistical.

"Yep, they can smell a virgin five counties away. How come you ain't took one up on it?"

I sighed. " 'Cause there's always somebody else around who can stop me, that's why! Mama seems to have spread some tips around!"

He roared with laughter. "Well, y'all keep yo' kilt on a bit! Ah'm gonna show you how to pick 'em and keep things safe and still have one good time."

I won't go into the sordid details, but I can tell you that, riding along with Harry in his various tourist vehicles, from pony carts to an electric tram that hit the hot spots along the tourist beachfront and the expensive downtown specialty shops, I got a long narrative tour that didn't get broadcast.

Finally, he introduced me to Trina, who was not my idea of a first sexual partner at all and, fortunately, wasn't intended to be. She wasn't just big, she was huge, nearly six foot six, three hundred pounds, with breasts like watermelons, and the kind of face and voice that said that no matter what you could think of, she'd already been there and done that.

"Harry! He's so *cute*! You didn't tell me that!"

She was to be my escort, along with a couple of other women, only slightly smaller but definitely just as worldly, to some of the tourist spots I was too nervous to go into on my own.

A part of me from the past lives still found things uncomfortable, even more so in a nightclub packed with tourists.

"These folks're mostly computer geeks from Austin and Santa Fe who don't get down to the shore much," Trina told me. I was still getting used to being with somebody two feet taller and two hundred or more pounds heavier than me.

I knew basic dancing from the Primary Center, and Harry had taught me some of the more modern stuff they were doing, and it didn't take a lot of watching before I could get the hang of it.

The one thing about this universe was that there were a lot more women than men, so, no matter how small, insignificant, ignorant, and ugly we might be, in this setting Harry and I were honey and half the room were flies. When Trina and her friends left to do their own kind of socializing, leaving the two of us sitting there at a table gawking at all the noise and music, the flies just started swarming.

Harry was used to this and in his element; I was panicky and nervous and shy but had been put in a position with no escape. His advice wasn't much help in the cacophony around us: *"Pick the one who'll also talk to you."*

It sounds like strange advice, but I learned what he meant and it was good advice. I mean, I was walking all over beachfront Galveston like I was wearing a sign saying "horny virgin," and that, in the end, had been the real reason I'd exercised my self-discipline there. All the VD lectures in the world wouldn't have stopped me from doing it early and often, but my shyness and the fact that I was being regarded as a thing, just another souvenir of "my vacation in Galveston," that turned me off.

The problem wasn't being talked to here, though; rather, it was in understanding amid the loud music and crush of bodies what anybody was saying.

So, when Harry seemed to vanish, and nobody else came back, and I had no other way out, I did the only thing I could.

I danced with whatever girl wanted to dance with me.

I can't really say much else about it. I was more than a little drunk, maybe a little high as well, and while I pretty well remember, in a kind of blurry way, all the rest of the night and the sunrise the next morning, I prefer to skip to that sunrise, which found me kind of in a male fantasy, lying on an air mattress on the deck of a rental condo, listening to the sound of the waves crashing in, sandwiched between two naked girls who were as drunk as I was.

They had smiles on their faces, though. That, at least, fed my ego and sense of self-esteem. Experience had counted, and I was the most experienced virgin anybody in this world ever knew—only, of course, I was also endowed as never before.

All things considered, and in spite of the headache and sourness in my stomach, I began to wonder if maybe I wouldn't start to like this place after all.

They were both still asleep, or passed out, and I had to slowly wiggle out from between them. First, I needed a bathroom, and then to find my clothes. The more I moved, the more I began to feel like a couple of trucks had run over me, but it didn't matter. For the first time since insertion into Alice McKee's revenge, I didn't feel hyper-horny and wasn't any more turned on than I would have been in this circumstance in any of my previous male existences. Instead, I felt, somehow, I'd done what I was designed to do.

I took a quick spray shower, toweled off, and unearthed clothing and sandals. I really needed to sleep for about two days, but I knew I would be up for a while, so I found some coffee and made a pot in the drip coffeemaker. Deep down I was impressed; some of my personal tastes carried from life to life, it seemed, and one was that I liked coffee. Most women here seemed to like flavored decafs and teas with unpronounceable names you had to be a chemist to understand. There was, at least, next to the pound of Bavarian White Chocolate Coffee, whatever *that* was, a pound of regular, solid Colombian. It even had the image of Juanita Valdez on the foil pack. Just its existence meant that my hostesses at least had *some* taste.

I started surveying the contents of the kitchen while the aroma of coffee wafted through the one-story condo. Oddly enough, because it was shared by two women, it didn't have the usual step stools I was used to using to reach high places, but I made do. There was enough food to make a decent all-around breakfast of several types, and, if they didn't stay passed out until I got bored or had to leave, I could fix omelets, crepes, or waffles. I owed them that much, even if I was pretty damned sure I'd given value for value.

And I had, too. In fact, I stayed with them most of the week, leaving only to go to work and check for messages and make sure Mom thought I was being a good boy. Harry was back on the streets, having other things to do himself, but he proved a handy man to run interference, look out for any problems I might not know about before I got home, and provide some local transportation. I actually was saving a good deal of my microscopic spending money, too; I wasn't paying for much of anything at all.

I told you I was going to skip the gory details, no matter how much you might enjoy them, so let's just say I did a lot of dancing, swimming, partying, and sleeping around over the next . . . well, it became kind of a lifestyle. Word got around when you were good; I was good and I knew it. I suspected early on that it was because I'd come from previous lifetimes when the men had been the movers and shakers, and these women hadn't had much experience with guys who were really assertive in bed. I'd also inhabited a woman's body long enough to know where the maximum effort was rewarded in a maximum payoff. In fact, I often wished that I'd had more experience, real sexual experience, as a woman that I could recall clearly—Rini wasn't me, remember—but apparently there was enough left in my subconscious to more than meet the needs.

With my increasing confidence and reputation along the beach, I began to *like* being a boy-toy, particularly when it served all *my* immediate needs. I let myself go, never looked back, and pretty much lived for the moment. You might have said that I forgot where I'd come from and where I'd inevitably go sooner or later, but that wasn't quite true. I just filed it away as something I couldn't control and didn't let it interfere with enjoyment.

The neatest thing was, none of the women I was sleeping with were locals, all were on holidays of fixed duration. None of them were looking for anything beyond a knowledgeable companion with whom to have a good time, someone who knew all the best clubs and local hot places. I certainly picked up that information, along with quite a reputation among the locals as a kind of conceited but still undeniable King of the Beach.

It never occurred to me that the kings in *Alice in Wonderland* tended to be short and not terribly aggressive and dominated by huge queens. The king, like the chess piece, wasn't a real power here when compared to the queen, but he sure as hell had a privileged position. It just took guts to play his advantage for all it was worth.

How long I lived this life I can't really say. Time became blurred, and with the exception of some minor VD scares and a few bouts of illness, it was all kind of fun. I'm not even sure how sober I was during that period. Not that it was just booze, of course; when you knew, deep down, that no matter what, you were going to wake up fresh and start over without paying for what you did in the past life the way the churches all preached, you didn't worry about things like that.

I think it was several years before somebody found me.

It was the winter season, and while the activity in the resort areas never really stopped, it did slow during this period because the weather could change and become pretty cold, even if it was palm-tree territory. You could get a week of hot, almost summery weather when the wind blew from the east or south; then the temperature would drop to just above freezing, particularly at night, for several days when a big system plunged out of Canada. Not exactly blizzard city, and certainly no Chicago or even Seattle, but it cut down on the number of visitors and drove a lot of activity inside.

By this point I was staying with Harry and his huge women and pretty well living off the tourist girls. I wasn't charging— they just liked to buy me things and give me gifts, so I didn't ever need much. By selling or hocking the items and keeping the proceeds, I was pretty comfortable.

There was something of a chill in the air and there were a lot of clouds building just offshore when I headed out one February afternoon to Mary Jo's Barbecue, a Tex-Mex place serving everything from ribs to shrimp. I never had a big appetite, but I did have good taste, and I knew her cooks were the best at what they did.

I wasn't looking for any action that day, but I couldn't help notice that a couple of classic-looking women in casual dress were eyeing me as I went by, and I flashed my smile at them. When they didn't immediately take me up on the invite, I didn't mind. I just kept walking, but, after another block or so, I began to get the strong impression that somebody was following me.

Knowing the territory, it was easy to position myself to see a half block or more in back of me via reflections in glass storefronts, and it didn't take a lot of smarts to know that the pair I'd passed and smiled at were the ones behind me.

The fact that they both seemed a bit grim-faced and professional told me that they weren't likely to be after me for my charm and services. I took them for cops, but they sure weren't local, and I almost immediately pegged them in my mind as probable narcs.

Well, I had a small amount of marijuana on me, but that was easily disposed of along here with just a little sleight of hand. I also had a small concealed pistol in my shoulder bag, but this being Texas that not only wasn't illegal, it was almost taken for granted.

So, if they were narcs they soon had nothing to pin on me, and if they were something more sinister, the worst they'd get would be a small handgun, if I didn't get a chance to use it, and maybe ten greens in dinner money.

I couldn't shake the feeling, when I was within sight of the barbecue shack, that they were somehow *familiar*, although I was quite sure I hadn't seen them before.

Not in this *life*, something whispered to me, and I suddenly picked up the pace a bit.

I needed a closer look at them, but not out here on the almost deserted and darkening street.

"Cor-ree! My so cute enchilada!" Mary Jo Hernandez

called to me as I entered, feeling some relief. She caught my worried look and particularly the relief. "Something is wrong, *sí*?"

"Hi, M.J.! I'm not sure if anything's wrong or not. Two tough girls—maybe cops, maybe not—followed me."

She laughed. "But the girls they *always* follow my little friend, do they not?"

"Not like this. I dunno. Maybe I'm just crazy or somethin', but it don't feel right."

She decided I really was serious. "Well, you sit and eat in here! If they come in, they will deal with me and Conchita and some very big knives. You will be safe here. Then we'll call a cab for you to go home, eh?"

I felt much better on hearing that, and giving her my patented smile, sat down to at least get some decent food.

"What kind do you want today?" Mary Jo called to me.

"Shrimp. Shrimp and a Corona will do. The platter."

She nodded and went in back to start the order. As she did, I saw the pair looking in the window, then at the menu, and, nodding to each other, they both entered and took a table about as far from me as they could. It wasn't a big place; most of the business here was carry-out, so we weren't sitting all that far apart, and not nearly far enough.

Without seeming to stare and maybe tip them off, I started playing the identity game with their features. Both *did* look very familiar, yet neither looked like any women I'd known here, nor any I'd known at least in the past life, the memory of which was already growing dimmer and less detailed as time passed.

Maybe I'm wrong, I told myself, but the fact was that the longer this close proximity lasted the stronger the sense of familiarity, and danger, became. Something was registering in my mind, but not on a level I could yet tap.

Face it, there weren't that many that were a real threat, considering. Neither of these was Dorothy Sloan, for sure, and certainly neither was Rita Alvarez, or Dan Tanaka, and they absolutely bore no resemblance to Cynthia or the newer and little-known Mabel.

Mary Jo brought the platter out herself, and leaned over. "Them?" she whispered.

"Uh-huh," I barely muttered under my breath.

"See what y'mean," she commented, but then went over, spoke to them pleasantly, and took their orders, acting like everything was just fine. I knew, though, that I was being watched over, at least a little bit, by friends, and it sure helped.

I was actually through the tiny bit of salad and starting on the shrimp when it suddenly occurred to me that I'd been going about it the wrong way. I had assumed these women, or at least one of them, would be an incarnate, but what if they were *reincarnates*? It was tough to mentally turn the two women into men, particularly since my view of men had been so prejudiced by this world for such a long time, but I managed.

Nawwww . . . Couldn't be!

The resemblance wasn't exact, but the smaller of the two, at maybe six feet even, very well built, muscular, tough-looking, still bore at least a family-type similarity to . . .

Oh, my god! It's Stark!

Stark made a hell of an imposing female figure, as we'd all feared would be the case. The surprising thing was how feminine his manner was, how different from the usual military demeanor. Still, with the jacket off, she showed muscle every time she flexed an arm, the kind of muscle one got from passionate bodybuilding. It wasn't everybody who could project a somewhat sexy, exotic, tough-girl look while still giving a strong impression that breaking a steel bar over her head might only irritate her.

The other one, the blonde, was even bigger and more statuesque. She had longer hair, expertly applied makeup, nice earrings and bracelets, but it was only an attempt to disguise a mannish face and chunkier construction. There was a kind of

Nordic pioneer look to her, and it took me almost to the end of my meal to peg her.

Lee Henreid. But—I'd left Lee alive, and he'd taken charge of the institute when Al was shot.

Clearly Rita's palace revolution was bloodier than we'd been led to believe.

So both these characters had died last time, and now were back as women. Okay, fair enough. It meant they really weren't quite the folks we'd known before, but they still wouldn't necessarily be candidates for Friends and Lovers of Cory Kassemi, and they were here, stalking me, which said volumes.

They knew who I was. Somehow, they'd found me.

I might dodge them here, but not for long, that was clear. If they could recognize me here, and follow me this closely, then they weren't going to be put off by an escape by taxi and maybe a few days hiding out in Corpus Christa or Austin.

They might well not want to tangle with Mary Jo and Conchita, either, although both these old "friends" looked like they could take maybe a dozen strong women with their bare hands if they wanted to.

The fact that they were eating sandwiches instead indicated that they didn't want to make a big fuss here and draw attention to themselves. They clearly hadn't been a hundred percent sure it was me at first look, but they knew now, if not from Brand Box memory then from briefings.

The two unanswered questions were whether they were aware that I knew who they were and that they were after me, and, of course, whether that fact mattered at all to any of us.

III

CATERPILLAR
EMPOWERMENT

Mary Jo came out with my check, and I paid it. "Called you a cab," she whispered. "It's sitting out front now. Juanita's a cousin and she was right down the street."

"Thanks, I owe you," I whispered back, and got up and walked confidently toward the door, almost past them.

They got up and started to follow, but I could hear Mary Jo's booming accented voice stopping them cold. *"Hey! You two! You got to pay before you run out on me!"*

Lee fumbled quickly for a bill and I knew the two were going to just leave it, but I was out the door by then, saw the taxi sitting there, and got in without any problems. I'd used Juanita before. She could be quite handy, if she happened to be anywhere close.

She floored it the moment I was inside, sending me reeling into the seat. "Ow! Take it easy!"

"We don't know if they got a car handy or what," Juanita called back. "Till then, we lose 'em a little, huh? Don't worry—put the call out on the radio. Ain't no cab gonna pick dem up for at least five, ten minutes!"

Well, that was a help.

"Where you want to go when I'm sure you're clear?" she asked me.

That was a good point. Where could I go that they couldn't find me? And what kind of life did I want to lead? It had been one thing, so long ago, to cut out for the hinterlands with Riki, but who did I have here? And, unlike Riki or me in that world, I didn't have any good way to go it alone, particularly without much in the way of assets.

There was only one possibility, as bleak and as hopeless as that might be, that would at least afford me some protection.

"Juanita, baby, I got to get to Austin. It's my only hope to really shake those goons."

"Hey! I like to help you, *muchacho*, but Austin's a little out of my meter district and I got choir practice at eight!" She thought a moment. "Maybe I could let you have enough for bus fare, that's about it."

"It'll have to do. You can stop by Trina's and they'll be able to pay you back out of my lockbox there. I know they can all open it. I can count."

She laughed. "You are something else, my little one! *Sí!* I have maybe fifty greens here. That should be enough for a one-way ticket to Austin, I would think, if there's a bus leaving any time soon. Maybe a couple of meals as well!"

I thought a moment. "Not the bus station, then."

"Sorry, I don't have enough for air!"

"No, no. I just was thinking that I'd have to go via Houston and probably Dallas, too, and change coaches at some point, so if you could take me to the west-side station where the locals stop, that would keep me from being in the main bus station, where they're sure to look."

"Not bad. Cheaper, too, if slower. All right, then! Hold on!"

I don't know if Al and Lee—or whatever their names were here—were really trying to follow me at this point, but I felt a lot better when I got to the small corner minimall on the west side where they sold coffee, Cokes, and local bus tickets to all the small towns from here to Houston.

The run to Houston was hourly. I bought a ticket on the first bus that came along, figuring I'd play each stage by ear, and by whatever was left in this modest bank.

I did start feeling a little paranoid, though. Damn it, it always seemed like I was either running from them or trying to live a life they then moved to ruin! It wasn't fair! Al could be a sadistic son of a bitch and have fun, Cynthia always seemed to enjoy herself, and the others got to play around with all sorts of things, but me—I was just a damned target. If they wanted me, why the hell didn't they at least make me feel like the kingpin in the grand plot to rule all the universes? That at least would feed my ego and make my suffering a little more meaningful.

As usual, I got some attention and some pickup lines on the bus, but I wasn't in the mood. For the first time since I could remember, I wasn't in the mood. Everybody seemed to take on a slightly sinister cast all of a sudden, and there seemed a dark cloud over my head that I might not be able to keep from descending on top of me.

Obviously, if they figured out what I had done, they would either race ahead to Houston—the local took four hours to make the basically little more than an hour drive, stopping everywhere in East Texas—or they'd call ahead for others to be there and stake out every arriving bus.

I began to hate Alice McKee for stacking the deck so solidly against men in general and me in particular. I wasn't any angel or role model, but, damn it, even Rini had been given more outs than I had here. There were far fewer males, so we stuck out. There was no disguising anything, since we were simply not big enough, strong enough, or important enough. Hiding out, going underground, these just weren't valid options, and when everybody who could help tended to think of you as some kind of child it was even worse. I was on the run, and there was very little I could do about it except scream for Mama, who might not even care. I didn't dare give her a call; not now, not from Houston. They'd surely have that angle figured out. Maybe from some rest stop along the way, some pay phone, but not now.

The fact that it was Al, personally, made it all the more intolerable. I'd been partly responsible for this, I knew; damn it, Al should be in my place in this kind of world and see how it felt for once!

I was still pouting and feeling sorry for myself, though. If I'd really been on a crusade for truth, justice, and the American way, I sure as hell wouldn't be running home to Mama.

The more I thought about it, the more I realized that even Mama wasn't going to be a lot of protection. I looked out the window at the cars speeding past in both directions and considered the ultimate solution: getting so lost even I couldn't find myself.

That had been my first impulse in times past, hadn't it? I'd done it with Riki in what I thought of as my "original" world even though I now knew it wasn't, and Rini, thinking she was me, had done much the same thing getting out of the institute—and for what? Riki and I had wound up as drugged-out bums out on the barrier islands not too far south of Galveston, and ultimately getting sucked into what proved to be the shaman's world. We'd run for nothing.

Rini had run right into the hands of a pimp, which was even worse. That could be my fate here, too, of course; the reversal of sexual roles here didn't change everything. There was always a market, there were always lonely people, and the weaker boys could always be forced into it, kept there by drugs and lack of options.

Still, it was tempting. Get off, start hitching, see if I couldn't get picked up by some really good-looking babe who'd fall for my charms and take me away from all this.

And what had I argued about with Walt? That we should take these bastards on, make somebody and something *move*, not just continue in this endless petty skirmish for control. Big talk, but what the hell could we do about it? Walt was surely no bigger or stronger or more powerful than me, nor were the others. Father Pete couldn't even be a priest here, and the biggest intellect who could make things happen in that group was who—Cynthia? Gimme a break! Cynthia versus Al, Lee, and Rita!

Still, I needed to make a series of decisions and I needed to make them quickly. What, exactly, did I want to try to do? Run? That would be consistent with my current personality, but some part of me kind of drew the line there. I'd spent most of my time up to now goofing off, seeking pleasure, and never looking beyond tomorrow. It was time I grew up a little. If I ran, lost myself in a hedonistic life, and died young, I would only wind up in their hands anyway without any memory of what was going on.

Not this time. Been there, done that.

Run directly to Mom? Well, as an expedient, that might be necessary. Mom here wasn't the nice little old lady of my youth; she was still a very strong and influential person, still in her fifties, an executive with some clout, and she did offer the largest measure of cover. The problem was, she wasn't going to be very easy to convince that I wasn't just trying to come back and live off her. I mean, what could I tell her? She wasn't even one of us, so latent memory wasn't even a factor.

"Gee, Mom, I know this is hard to believe, but you are a construct created by a giant computer someplace, see. And just about everybody you know is, too. Except for maybe two or three dozen folks who keep getting reincarnated, and they're after me 'cause I'm one of them. I know you remember me being born and that every moment of my life can be traced, but, see, that's all just part of a program . . ."

Sooner or later—probably sooner—I'd be put in this nice place in the country with bars on the windows and doors while folks in white coats attempted to convince me, by any means necessary, that my hallucinations were really brought on by my sense of powerlessness.

So Mom *could* protect me and give me cover, but not without me giving her a whale of a convincing story, one she might doubt but still go along with. I hadn't really thought of that.

And even if I did come up with a good idea, one she'd accept, then what? I'd have a target on myself, because that's one place they were sure to have staked out already. I'd be nailed eventually and that would be that.

The fact that that pair of goons was out and about meant that the Command Center was definitely up and active in this world. And if it was up, so was the backup, I guessed. Where the hell was it? Or was it up? Only three of us from the March Hare Network were women: one I didn't know, one who was a vegetable the last I saw her, and one who was more than a little insane and working with a lot of little men from outer space.

Wait a minute! Maybe I'm going at this the wrong way! I told myself. What, in fact, did the areas I had been in so far have in common? Anything? Western Washington State, the Bay Area in California, now East Texas.

No, that was wrong. Not East Texas—Austin. At least that's where I was eventually headed, right?

In all three worlds, all three areas were centers for computer companies and high-tech industries.

The Command Center had been in Yakima the first time, but at Stanford the second. Why couldn't it be in the middle of Texas this time? Austin, perhaps, or College Station, where the big university was?

It was a thought. If the Command Center was now in Texas, then maybe the backup was relatively close as well. Unlike the CC, the backup had been in the same place both times, though, and that might as well have been a million miles away.

That had to be it. The Command Center moved, but the backup didn't, perhaps so it could always be located. That of course brought up a question: Why hadn't the CC folks taken a crack at controlling it, too? But there were forces behind all of this that might have blinded them, or it might just be too damned well protected, somehow. Certainly the saucer was there.

If that was the case, then I was half a continent, fifteen hundred miles or more, from any allies, and I was as of now heading toward my enemies' headquarters. That seemed a bit stupid.

But forty Georgia Washingtons weren't going to get me a distance like that, and I sure had no way to get there otherwise.

Maybe running away from here was the best plan, but not running toward them. Maybe I should run away from here and aim toward someplace else.

As the local finally pulled into Houston and headed for downtown and the main bus station, I seriously considered making for central Washington. I could hock my watch and rings for a few bucks, maybe, or luck it out if I got the right set of hitches. Hitchhiking from here to beyond Yakima, though, would be a long and dangerous haul. I was up to that part, I felt sure, and it was only the fact that it was already pitch dark outside that stopped me.

It was February. It wouldn't be so bad in June or July, but I'd now been in the Gulf area so long I was forgetting that I was proposing not only heading north, but heading through the high mountains. I had no heavy winter clothes, and I was proposing hitchhiking through all that snow and ice and wind and subzero cold?

Even Al didn't seem quite as threatening as that.

Pulling into the Houston station, I was still unsure of what I was going to do, but I was on the lookout for suspicious folks who seemed like cops or other agents. It wouldn't have to be a big government group out to get me; Al could just have asked the local cops to pick me up saying I was wanted for something.

There were a couple of faces like that, but they were kind of cruising the platforms and there were a lot of buses with people moving in and out, back and forth. This was one time, too,

when being small helped; I just got in the middle of a bunch of
the biggest preoccupied women I could manage and did my
best to keep pace. In no time at all, I was through the loading
area and the terminal doors, and I slipped easily to one side and
down a dark alley toward the street on the far side of the bus
depot.

Houston . . . Who did I know in Houston? I kept close to the
storefronts and moved rapidly away from the bus station and
into the general hustle and bustle of the city downtown. I
fought off the feeling of paranoia that was the natural out-
growth of being a tiny man in a world of huge women and tried
to keep focused. I didn't stand out, anyway; while it was true
that most of the people you saw were women, there were men
of varying ages and economic situations about, and the big
trick was to just look as confident here as I was in Galveston.

Although the Primary Center wasn't that many miles down
the pike from here, I wasn't really familiar with or comfortable
in Houston, a place more of the mind in my growing-up years
than in reality, where one was taken to the zoo or to a movie as
part of a big trip but which wasn't really familiar. It was
always hard to remember sometimes that the destinations of
tourists and pleasure seekers were actually real places with real
citizens and not just abstract Disneylands.

Still, something resonated about Houston. Somebody had
come from here, somebody I'd known well.

Jed Crocker! Sure! My old buddy for several years at the
Primary had come back here to live and work when I'd left for
Galveston. But where to find a Jed Crocker in a city of maybe a
million? Maybe he'd moved. Maybe he'd gotten married and
wasn't a Crocker anymore. Well, it didn't hurt to look him up
and see.

I found a phone booth inside a small diner and wrestled with
the phone book, which seemed to weigh three tons. Reading
was slow and hard, too; I really had to concentrate, and I had
the distinct impression that I badly needed reading glasses.
Still, I managed it.

There were two and a half pages of Crockers, and it was unlikely he'd have a listing himself. His mother's name was Edna, I recalled, and there was an Edna Crocker listed. Hell, it was worth a quarter.

"Hello?" The strongly accented voice was that of an older woman, but not the Spanish/Mexican accent I expected. This sounded almost British. "Crocker residence."

I suddenly became a little shy and uncertain, but it was too late to back out now. "Uh—hi! My name is Cory, and I went to school with a Jed Crocker at the Larimore Academy. I'm trying to get in touch with him. Is this his mother's residence?"

There was a slight pause, as if the person on the other end was thinking it over; then she said, "Yes, madam has a son named Jedediah. I'm afraid he doesn't live here, though." My heart sank. It was too much to ask, but it was a big hope. "He has a flat—an apartment—of his own with some other friends. I can give you the number if you would like."

I was soaring again. "Yes, very much, thank you!" I had nothing to write it down with, but I wasn't going to forget *this* number.

"Five-five-five, nine-five-one-oh," she told me. "Please do not call here again. I'm afraid Master Jedediah and the mistress are not currently on speaking terms."

There was a click, but all I was doing was concentrating on that number.

I fished out another quarter and dialed the number. It rang for quite a while, and I got worried that nobody was home, but finally an unfamiliar guy's voice answered. "Yeah?"

"I'm looking for Jed Crocker and I got this number," I told him. "He's an old friend of mine. Is he there?"

"Naw. Not right now. He'll be down at the store till midnight. You oughta check there."

"I'm from out of town and it's been a while. What store is it and where is it located?"

When he told me, I had at least part of the answer for Jed's estrangement.

I couldn't find my way around Houston on a bet, so there was nothing to do but to spring for a cab. The cabbie shrugged and we went maybe a mile and a half northwest, through a kind of small business area that had seen better days, and pulled up in front of the store. It wasn't the kind of neighborhood I'd have found on my own.

It wasn't hard to figure out what was sold in a store called the Hard as a Rock Place. The real clue wasn't the rather plain window that just said BOOKS—MAGAZINES—PICTURES but the graffiti scrawled all over it and around it, mostly too high for folks like me to reach.

In this society, women swung both ways most of the time and usually had a real relationship with another woman while using us boys mainly as studs, but it wasn't too popular for men to have much interest in other men once they left the confines of Primary Centers. It was hard to establish a real relationship with a woman, though, or to think about any sort of exclusivity, so this sort of thing wasn't at all unusual, if officially frowned upon.

I hardly recognized Jed behind the counter, with the long earrings, heavy makeup, chains, leather, and lavender beard and hair. For a moment he wasn't sure it was me he was seeing, but then his mouth opened and he gaped at me. "Cory? That really *you*?"

"I should say that line to you," I responded. "Man, I knew you liked it where we were, but I didn't expect *this*."

He gave kind of an embarrassed laugh. "Well, the look is kinda for the commercial part, y'know. I don't think I'd dye the hair otherwise. The rest, though—well, this is the real counterculture, Cory, my boy! We live as much as possible in a world of men only. See the scale here? It's echoed in the apartments and other stuff as well. It fits us. We have our own restaurants, our own nightclubs, our own social groups, and we interact with the world of women only when we have to."

"Doesn't sound like you'd make a lot of money that way," I noted.

He shrugged. "Money isn't everything. A lot of us hold regular jobs, it's true, but we're better organized than you think, almost self-contained in some ways. And we even got a couple of fair-sized ranches where no woman's been in ages. You don't know the freedom you feel in them." He paused. "But I don't think you're that far to my side. Never did. What made you go to what must be a lot of trouble to find me?"

I sighed. "I didn't know where you were or what you were doing, but I need help. I'm in trouble, and I'm on the run. I need to hide out until I can sort things out. Maybe get hold of my mother to run interference and fund a better getaway."

"Shit! What'd you do? Rob a bank?"

"No, nothin' like that." *Think fast. This has to be a convincing cover story!* "Fact is, Mom works for Lone Star, and she's high up in management. They do a lot of computer stuff for the government. Well, somebody's trying to put the snatch on me, and I'm certain they want to get information from my mom in exchange for me. Sounds real cloak-and-dagger, don't it?"

"You're tellin' me!" But he was swallowing it, hook, line, and sinker. It wasn't that hard to do.

"So what do you need right now?" he asked me, sounding very willing to help.

"I need to get out of Houston and essentially drop off the end of the Earth for a little bit. That at least will get the heat off me."

He nodded, thinking. "Waxadoches Ranch sounds like the best bet, and I don't think you'll feel all that uncomfortable there. Ain't no women gettin' in there without a fight. It's private and flat enough you could see somebody lookin' in from miles away. Course, you'll need me to even get you in there, so stick around. Let's see . . . It's Thursday now. I got to work tomorrow, then I'm off until Monday at six P.M. We oughta be able to get you down there and settled by then. In the meantime, relax. Take a look around the store. There's lots of real interesting stuff here."

He wasn't kidding about that. The leather kilts, the silk and dark red leather codpieces, the whips . . .

I spent the night and the whole of the next day with Jed and his companions in their small, seedy apartment in a run-down section of town, and felt at least temporarily safe. The two other guys who shared the place seemed fairly nice if a bit odd, but it wasn't too different from the years I'd spent in the Larimore Academy. As long as they didn't ask me to join in their lifestyle, I was satisfied to cook them some decent meals to pay for my taking up space.

I didn't watch much TV back in Galveston, and even less did I watch the news, but it happened to be on one day while I was cooking lunch and I kind of glanced at it now and then. I suddenly froze and became raptly attentive, though, when one story came on.

"A High Mass will be celebrated this Sunday at the Cathedral of Saint Joan the Divine in honor of the recent elevation of San Antonio's Bishop Alvarez to Archbishop of East Texas. The new archbishop, a Houston native, shown here at her consecration in Rome . . ."

I didn't need glasses for this. The picture shown was absolutely that of a rather good-looking, statuesque Rita Alvarez in full white robes and high, white bishop's hat being escorted down a big cathedral aisle by two others, at least one of whom was one of the Standishes—no, *both* the black-garbed priestesses with Rita were the Standishes. Looked like one had died in the old life, the other hadn't, and now they were *both* women, happily serving God. They'd always been fundamentalists, and this church wasn't all that friendly to fundamentalist beliefs, but if you were a holy woman inside the Church power structure, there was probably a lot of compensation.

Well, okay then. The fact that Rita and the Standishes were Texans, and that their district ran from the coast to Austin and then to San Antonio, meant several things, much more important than just seeing Al and Lee. First, the gang was all here as adults. Ages would vary, of course, depending on when the insertion was chosen, but the bottom line was that we were all in the world. So many in this region, particularly those who were at the institute when it punched through, had to mean that the Command Center was here as well. Not necessarily in Houston, but certainly between here and San Antonio, and probably somewhere between Austin and San Antonio, since that was where Rita was based. She certainly wouldn't dare be this publicly and this prominently visible unless she was damned secure, too.

On Saturday morning, I got in the sidecar of Jed's motorcycle and we headed off out of the city south and west toward the ranch. It was kind of harrowing to ride that openly, but I didn't drive and this was what was available. Little Jed, with the leather jacket and helmet, seemed dwarfed atop the big roaring Harlette, or as they were often referred to, Harlots.

Being so exposed, I felt like everybody was looking at us, and they probably were. But most people wouldn't remember many details of what they'd seen ten minutes later.

It was a good ride, almost three hours, to the ranch, barely "next door" in Texas terms, but I couldn't help notice when we turned off the highway and onto the approach road that there were lots of posted warnings, a set of mighty mean-looking gates, and an elevated guardhouse that would look more appropriate for a prison entrance. The guys in the tower were seated and seemed fairly relaxed, but they had fixed machine guns mounted in the concrete wall in front of them.

I stared in amazement. "Expecting an attack from Mexico?"

Jed laughed. "Nope. But the Church, that's something else again, and sometimes just our ever-lovin' friends and neighbors. There's folks who'll attack anybody they think is different or who don't play by their rules. We got lots of places where there's heavy weapons here."

Once I'd been introduced, inspected, and okayed, which included a pat-down search of my person, we were allowed past and continued on for a ways. Jed was right: there were two other fixed towers on the way in, although no gates.

The ranch itself was less spectacular, but still impressive. In fact, it looked like a dude ranch, rustic hotel, and working cattle farm all rolled into one. There were three main buildings—a big ranch house that was clearly administration, two long barracks-like structures that had big air conditioners on them, several barns and outbuildings, silos, and a corral with horses. It was pretty damned impressive.

"From when we passed the gate, you were in an area where no women are allowed," Jed told me proudly. "Men built all this and men run it. It's nearly self-sufficient. We raise plenty of beef, some pork, and have a separate sheep range for wool and mutton. Our fields grow corn, wheat, veggies, you name it, and way down the road there is a massive chicken house that provides eggs and poultry. We trade with other ranches for cotton and building materials that we don't have locally. Electricity's from our own generator, and there's been a few oil wells paying off so that helps fund the whole thing. We move a lot of stuff up to Houston—would you believe we hire on independent women truckers to come to a loading area and pick up the stuff? They drive it up and drop it in the wholesale farmer's markets, and bring back what we need."

"So some women do come in to pick up stuff?"

"Nope. See them tracks over there? Little electrical railroad can take stuff from here to the loading docks, and there's spurs to the areas. We bring it in here by wagon and cart the old way."

I looked around, amazed. "But who *owns* this? I mean, it's such a huge operation!"

"A foundation owns it. Lots of inheritances here, and bequests, all building on a will years ago that one of the pioneer families that had only boys set up so they'd always have a place. Then there was a reformatory over half a mile that way that closed and we bought and annexed it, and it's just kinda been growin' since. This is one of the few places in the country, maybe in the world, where the guys run things."

Well, of course, it was something of a surprise, and I couldn't deny their pride or their industry, but it was founded as much or more on male insecurity as on male aspirations or even sexual orientation.

Alice McKee's subconscious had created the conditions for all that. The women were in charge, and the men were physically and numerically crippled so that they could in fact only perform one role. You couldn't be a scientific genius—hell, reading and writing and arithmetic were hard thanks to that dyslexia nicely put in the Y gene. Boys could do art, but the critics never took male art seriously. I was surprised that when we'd had a crack at computers at Primary, I didn't even excel in that area. The type of programming and the way of operation was so visual and object-oriented that it was beyond anything I'd known, and it sprang from an entirely different origin. The end product was the same as the computers I'd known, of course, but it had evolved from the female spatial and problem-solving thought-stream rather than the linear mathematical male model and was obtuse to the old guard like me.

Face facts—there was only one thing the male body and mind were designed to do in this life, and that was easily and quickly done and did not require further participation in society.

So, for all its impressive scale, Waxadoches Ranch still had a kind of sad, almost pathetic aura around it, particularly when you saw how many of the small, weak guys it took to do what one Texas cowboy of my earlier world wouldn't have thought twice about doing. They had created an almost cartoon society rejecting the "outside," meaning women.

I always had the impression in the past that there was some genetic or biochemical component to homosexuality. I still did, but most of the homosexuality here wasn't as outrageous as indicated by the store back in Houston or the way Jed and some of the others dressed; it was more rebellion, rebellion in the only way they knew how, and rebellion in a kind of silly, immature way. Only when you knew other worlds and other societies did you realize how pathetic this attempt was. But it was all they had.

They were delighted to get a new cook, and hired me on the spot. Nobody asked much about me or where I'd come from or why I was there, although the ranch boss, a man named Fedders, who looked as old and worn as the stables, had gotten the word that I was hiding out from some sort of kidnap plot.

"Well, nobody's gonna come here and do a snatch," he assured me. "Too many folks around too much of the time. You're never really alone here, which is the other good thing. If anything gets dangerous, whether it's uninvited guests or rattlesnakes, you just give a holler and you'll be surprised how fast everybody shows up to help."

For what it was worth, I believed him.

In the very meager stack of reading materials in the main house was a book called *If Men Ruled the World*. It was a fairly simplistic book, large type, very simplified language for easy reading, but basically it theorized that if men ran things instead of women there would be world peace, mutual trust, brotherhood, safety, and goodwill. They could hardly conceive of how naïve they were.

The problem, of course, was that finding a hideout had never been a serious problem for me, although sometimes getting out of that hideout had been difficult. This time, though, I was determined not to do that, not to fall into that trap. I wanted to be a player; that's what that LSM hookup at the backup station had been all about. Using that backup, assuming I made it through as I did, whoever reactivated the center should be able to find me without problems. Maybe it was Cynthia, and she wasn't too great about those kinds of technical things, but there would be the Boojums with their fancy little flying saucer to help out, and they and Cynthia had looked right cozy the last time I'd seen them together.

Well, that wasn't much of a hope. I found that the communications shack had phone books for half of creation, and I began looking through the various yellow pages starting with San Antonio and Austin, trying to find something that would sound like the institute or the Zyzzx Software Factory or anything that would indicate "Command Center." The problem wasn't that there was a lack of candidates; on the contrary, there were more possibilities than I could count.

The real problem was how the hell could I go incognito in a society like this?

The answer struck me about my fifth day there, when I was watching some of the boys just horsing around in the corral area. That's just what they looked like—boys playing. I still had a pretty good head of hair. If I shaved especially clean, and if I combed and styled the hair right, then dressed in girls' clothing, I just might be able to pass for, oh, a prepubescent eleven- or twelve-year-old girl. With a little care about how I spoke, and if I didn't talk much, I might also get away with that part. Hell, I knew what it was like to be a girl; now was the time to put those memories into a kind of method acting. The one outstanding problem, the oversized member, could be handled with baggy-cut pants and some restraint, physical if need be, against the thigh. I was sure I could pull it off, at least for a few days. Long enough, I hoped, to reconnoiter the likely suspects.

The other problem would be transportation. Twelve was a bit young to be using motorized transport alone and these were fair-sized cities, particularly San Antonio. A *lot* of area to cover. There was no way around it, though. Once I got in, I'd have to use either public transit or a bicycle. Anything else would be more than obvious and would certainly attract attention.

There were some guys on the ranch who could help, too. I'd

never thought of cross-dressing as part of a power trip, but it could be in this nutty world. They even had stilts to gain quite a bit of height, and the clothing could be padded out, but I knew it would take far too much practice for me to get convincing with some of that. On the other hand, the hairdressers and seamsters and makeup specialists could create a pretty convincing proto-teen out of somebody like me. They even dyed my hair a kind of strawberry blond, and brushed on stuff that made my eyebrows match, dramatically changing my looks, particularly with the kind of pixie cut they gave me. One thing for sure I'd proven last lifetime was that I had the kind of face that could be either sex. This really proved it.

The neat thing was, they took it as something of a challenge, a creative endeavor; nobody once asked me why the hell I was doing it or what it was all for. Everybody had their own secrets and motives, and nobody much cared so long as it wasn't a threat to the group. There was even a kind of lozenge you could suck on that lasted for hours but didn't taste all that great. It coated not only the throat but the larynx and other air passages and actually shifted the voice a half octave. It didn't work forever—about ten minutes after it was completely gone, or if you drank hot liquids, the effect wore off—but it would be handy. Getting used to the taste, though, which was kind of a cross between Listerine and day-old grass clippings, was a problem. Apparently any attempt to flavor it also caused it to lose its effect.

Almost as bad was this bath they called the "sheep dip," which smelled and looked a lot like its namesake. It was kind of acidic and greasy, and you didn't bathe in it, you had it applied to you, almost *all* of you, and it stung like a bad all-over sunburn. After it hardened to a dark, glistening substance, it was dissolved in a very soapy and very hot bath. When it was over, you'd lost almost all your body hair. Most of your body was kind of a pinkish red, too, but that went away after a few days. What didn't was the effect. That stuff pretty well killed hair at the roots. My hairy body had been reduced to just the pubic area and what was on the top of my head. When it was all over, and I put on the specially tailored clothes and cowgirl hat, I looked very much like a young girl. To be frank, it wasn't at all comfortable, but it *looked* right.

I knew that playing this role wouldn't be a problem, but if I got caught, or couldn't find what I was looking for, then things would start to get tough. Still, I had a number to call to get a ride back to the ranch if need be from anywhere in the big-cities corridor. The only thing I really lacked was money. Fortunately, Jed had managed to get in contact with Harry in Galveston, and Harry had gotten Trina to transfer the funds I had there to Jed's store. I could then draw it at the ranch. Not nearly as much as I'd like, but it was a few hundred bucks.

"Enough to get a kid knocked over or worse," one of the guys at the ranch warned me. "Make sure nobody sees more than a tiny bit of that money."

He didn't know the half of it. The fact was, for all the problems, there was a hell of a lot less crime and violence in this country than in any incarnation I could recall. There was still petty crime and bigotry and intolerance, things that knew no gender barrier, but it really was pretty safe to walk most streets at night.

These people, even the guys, had no idea what kind of defenses you had to have back in my old worlds just to go shopping downtown. Still, I wasn't about to argue with the sentiment "Lead them not into temptation."

In fact, everything was going so perfectly that it wasn't until I was studying street maps of Austin and looking at the university area, office buildings and industrial parks along the area where the computer companies were, that somebody asked me the question that should have been the first one asked.

"Don't want to get nosy, and I'm not, but what happens if you find this place you're looking for?" one of the guys asked me. "These sure ain't your friends or you wouldn't be goin' to so much trouble."

He was right. What if I *did* find the Command Center?

Would it matter? What could I do? Walk in and say, "Okay, everybody up against the wall. I'm taking over now"?

All I could do was press on for now and keep improvising. Hell, the odds were I'd wind up dead and buried anyway. Still, I responded, "Well, there's friends as well as enemies in this. Once I know where the bad girls are, I figure I can search for the cavalry next."

It was pure bravado, but, damn it, I was bound and determined that this time, the time when it made the most sense to lay low and let everybody else fight, *this* time I was gonna be front and center, right in the middle of things.

I got a ride to Austin with a long-haul trucker named Gail. She seemed real protective, bought the story about me being poor and needing to get home from a work-study program in Houston for the spring-break holidays. The spring-break cover story was handy but limiting to me; I had only a little over a week to be able to get around without somebody asking me why I wasn't in school.

With the aid of the lozenge and by relaxing my mind-set, Gail and the fellow truckers we met at truck stops along the way bought me as a young girl. The guys had done a hell of a good job, and I was able to bring up my previous Brand Box persona enough to keep things convincing. I knew how to move right and, if need be, how to talk right.

In fact, everybody was so taken by me that I had to fend off women trying to buy me things or do me favors. It was a whole different world, a world denied men in this society. I'm not sure what they'd have done if they discovered what I was, but no matter how uncomfortable things were for me, I was bound and determined to keep up the act to the end.

I actually slipped away from Gail at the terminal in Austin; she was talking about taking me directly home, and I didn't want any of that sort of thing. I suspect she'd probably put me down as a runaway of some kind and be worried, but she wouldn't press it. It was a big city and you couldn't solve the world's problems.

The first object was to find a base of operations where I wouldn't be subject to a lot of questions. That probably meant roughing it, although Austin in April was certainly warm enough. I wanted real concealment; the last thing I needed was cops and Juvenile Services and all sorts of questions. This masquerade wouldn't last long under the kind of exam they gave, and my prints would be on file at least at the state level, so they'd know who I was and that would go out on the police wires. It didn't take a lot of imagination from that point to figure who'd show up to claim me.

I found an old pipe—a big one—down in a hollow in a city park that wasn't bad. It would give shelter, wasn't going to fill up with drainage, and a little work with some grass provided just enough comfort for sleeping, with my oversized purse as a pillow. It would do, and did, for my first night there.

The next day, after a fast-food breakfast nearby and some fix-up work in the mirror of the women's bathroom, I set out with a bus map of the city and a lot of change and decided to check out the more public areas. You never knew; I could get lucky.

Naturally, though, that was the last thing that happened, and it became a pretty boring routine. What exactly was I looking for, anyway? I mean, in both cases the Command Center had occupied a two-story administrative building and, in one case, a second warehouse-like building where all the real work was done, with a third for storage and cafeteria. In the last incarnation, it was just one large, two-story building that wound up having a couple of levels buried deep underground. The common elements were few beyond that, and not much help.

In both cases, Al had worked for the government, but in one he'd been plainclothes and in the other a navy security officer.

After three days of riding all over the city and meeting lots of dead ends, I had to face it. Unless I saw and recognized somebody, it was hopeless. I might as well call for a pick-up now.

That night, dead tired, discouraged to the point of depression, sitting on the grass near the old pipe worriedly watching some lightning and hearing the sound of distant thunder, I began to wonder what the hell I thought I could do.

The fact was, I just wanted to do something, *anything* other than going back to being a beach bum or a bull cook for a herd of gay caballeros, and, most of all, I didn't want to wind up crawling back to Mom.

It was very dark in the park, except for the occasional distant flashes of lightning through the trees, and the insect noise and thunder made it both dramatic and more than a little bit scary. I wondered just how solid that pipe was in a downpour, and whether or not it was metal.

Not in any kind of real sense, but in a kind of vision in my mind to which I was but a third party, a visitor looking on, I suddenly saw and heard—someone.

"*Who* are *you?*" the caterpillar asked.

"Cory, same as always," I responded automatically, the way you respond "Fine, thank you" to "How are you doing?" even if you're about to jump off the Golden Gate Bridge.

"*Wrong!*" responded the caterpillar. "*Holy, shit, Maddox! Haven't you learned* anything *yet?*"

"Huh? What . . . ?"

"*You always were the most clueless idiot of the bunch, but I'd hoped by now you'd at least have a little more grasp of things. You've had all that experience now, all that knowledge, and you have the benefit of Rini's own power trip as well. And you've learned* nothing?"

"Huh? What do you mean? Who *are* you?"

The caterpillar sighed in frustration. Finally it asked, "*You see that approaching thunderstorm out there?*"

"Yeah, sure. So?"

"*Make it stop.*"

"Huh? I don't get you at all."

"*That is becoming increasingly obvious. Still, for the first time in a long time you have an advantage here. You are still linked to the master computer through the backup systems.*"

That's the key, you know. That's how they draw the power for the saucer, that's how they become the March Hare or the Mock Turtle, that's how they open up rabbit holes and get out as well as in. When Rini connected to the March Hare Network when imprisoned in the house with the pimp, she connected to the main computer through that same backup. She'd already been processed by Al through the central nexus, so she was conducive to the hookup. You didn't need that processing. You exist in, through, and beyond this shell. Before, though, you weren't connected. You didn't come into a new incarnation still attached to the master computer. This time you did. You have the power. Use it. Or do you think all this is somehow real?"

"I—I don't know how. Even if I followed what you were saying, I don't know how!" I felt close to tears.

"Rini had no education at all and she could do it. You know why? She didn't think about it so much, she just did it! Think of objects! Everything, everyone, objects, collections of objects, sets, classes, subclasses. You're not God, not even here. You can't manipulate them all. But you sure as hell can pick one."

What the hell was I being told? That I had more power than I realized? Or had I just gained that power when I incarnated through the backup center? Even so, the implication was that I'd had it all the time I was here. Had it then, have it now.

The first time I'd connected to the greater net, the caterpillar had done it, and given me a choice. The second time, I connected by mere proximity to the massive power being drawn in by the experiments in Yakima. Connected so completely that I could switch bodies, travel along lines of force and wires of copper . . .

And then Rini, set up as a separate object within her own world by Al and Dannie at the institute and reprogrammed as an alternate "me." She, too, had drawn from the institute, from the main computer, while a prisoner there. Enough to actually influence things, escape, get away. And, later, in Vern's place, at that basement computer console, she had been able to tap

into the backup center and receive just what she needed—
empowerment, a direct link.

The caterpillar was saying that I didn't need that. That I
could do it without having some program merge in my head.

Program? Wait . . . Damn it, it was so obvious! I mean, we
knew that this universe came out of an interaction of Alice
McKee's subconscious and the master program. The whole
thing, one vast shell, and we were all objects on it. No, *everything* was an object or collection of objects on it!

A little knowledge was a dangerous thing, and the power
was as limited as that knowledge, but it was *something*, by
god! I wasn't powerless! None of us were, if we understood
even the most elementary part of what we were really doing.

That was one reason why they tried so hard to either conceal
it all from us or get us all under control. Otherwise, we few
were potentially the most dangerous people in the universe—
any universe, at least any one we were in.

I tried to clear my mind and manage wireframe mode the
way Rini had, but I couldn't quite get it. She'd had a device, of
course—but the damned device was really just an add-on piece
of code, an object, as well. She had needed the code patch, but
did I?

*Concentrate . . . concentrate . . . the hell with the thunder
and lightning, it's just there to distract, a running subroutine . . .*

The night and the park came alive in ghostly off-white outline. It was fascinating to see, to watch. I put out my hand and
looked, and saw that it was like some white-on-black pencil
sketch, but slickly animated. I kept looking, and saw that the
hand and wrist were far more complex underneath, with structures almost too complex to follow . . . with number and letter
codes and occasional little rectangular labels with long Latin
names on them.

How far down could I go? Would there be labels or part
numbers or reference numbers for each cell, each component
of a cell, each *atom*? If you blew it up enough to see, would a

cell have little labels saying MITOCHONDRIA and GENETIC HELIX? Or would it be even more detailed?

The storm suddenly broke all around me and I got very, very wet in a hurry even in the shelter of the tree. I was extremely pissed off at this interruption to my wonder. I looked up at the storm and saw its wild fury as a sequence of numbers, ones and zeros changing faster, faster, ever faster, but not quite a blur.

I didn't make it stop; I ordered it to keep away from me, and it moved damned fast off to the north.

Being soaked was miserable and uncomfortable, but I could see where the storm had created the patch set and I simply deleted that patch.

I was suddenly completely dry, as if never rained on.

This thing had real possibilities!

"One last thing!" I heard the caterpillar call, his voice seemingly growing fainter as if falling fast. *"When you do it, they can monitor it! I'd get the hell out of there and stop playing games if I were you!"*

IV

A MESSAGE FROM
THE OTHER SIDE

In the recordings of Rini's experiences with this sort of thing that I'd gotten from the Brand Box in my past life, I knew something of what it was like and what it could do, but, frankly, the real thing was something else again. I did have a sort of godlike feeling, knowing I could influence various things, that I was suddenly at least a minor programmer in the universe's largest AutoCAD simulation.

This had been what the caterpillar had been grooming me for since the start, the assumption of some sort of power and control. And, like Dorothy in *The Wizard of Oz*, while I might have had the power all along, I needed to go through a lot before I believed it.

The last warning from my ally, whoever or whatever it might be, was the flip side of this new power. It *was* limited. You didn't just tune in to something this complex and change it to suit you. And the others certainly knew how to handle it, at least most of them. Al wasn't as much of a threat, I was certain, since he would have lost the firsthand knowledge, the feel experience would give him, and the others would have as much or perhaps slightly more control than me thanks to living a few more lives. I wasn't sure if I was ready for Rita yet, for example. Still, the two most powerful would be men in this woman-dominated world—Les, wherever he was, and Walt.

And Cynthia Matalon as well, I suddenly realized. Flaky, uneducated, she shouldn't be underrated because of her nuttiness.

Well, if I had to take care in exercising this new power not to reveal myself, there was an advantage. Now that I knew how to sensitize myself to this kind of energy, this programming mode, wouldn't others also be obvious to *me*? Perhaps there was a different, more absolute way to the Command Center.

I let my mind go nearly blank, casting out in all directions and letting sensations come in, sensations beyond those that mere mortals could perceive.

There *was* something. Somebody. Several somebodies, in fact. Over there, maybe a mile and a quarter from the park, over by the Capitol building. They were moving, probably in a car, but I sensed them, or, rather, sensed their difference from all the other people in the city.

I cast my net a bit wider, not wanting to draw attention to myself in the same way, and sensed a sudden, more powerful concentration of the same sort of beings out beyond the city, but not very far. There were too many beings and too much of a sense of throbbing power for it to be just a few of us going here and there. It had to be the Command Center in whatever guise it existed in this universe.

I was too tired in spite of my excitement to do much tonight toward reaching that goal, but now that I knew how to zero in on it, I might well be able to go right up to it. What I'd do then I didn't know. I sure didn't want to fall into Rita's hands at this stage, but I really wanted to know who and where and what they were.

I brought the cast back in, looking for any local threat. The ones in the car were several blocks past by this point and heading away from me, but I suddenly felt a contrary cast and a sensation of puzzlement. What I could do, they could do.

Still, the power and skill of whoever it was wasn't anywhere near being up to mine, and I was just beginning to experiment with it. Even one-on-one, I felt pretty sure I could take these folks in a contest of wills.

I wasn't so sure about the others, and I wasn't at all certain, either, that just because something wasn't real it couldn't hurt or possibly even kill. People had delusions all the time—the old bit about believing you were Napoleon or Alexander or that somebody close was possessed by the devil was very real to them—and I had felt enough pain, even in *this* life, to know that there were levels beyond which you couldn't go no matter if it was "real" or not.

I waited there, just "listening," but none of the presences I could perceive grew any closer or more familiar, and, finally, I decided to get some sleep and see what the bright light of day would bring.

It turned out that control, the ability to either turn this power off or to make it unconscious in use, was the key to survival. If I were in Chicago and none of the other "incarnates" was within three states, it would make no difference, but here, in Austin, where a number, perhaps the majority, were congregated, it was something I had to master and fast.

I was getting dirty and it was tough to keep myself presentable, particularly masquerading as a kid. This was really the day; I either found what I was looking for or I packed it in.

I took a bus as far as I could in the direction of the strongest presence, and felt the almost magnetic attraction grow stronger and stronger as I went south and west. Eventually, I ran out of at least the knowledge of how to continue on by local bus, so I got off and started walking. It filled most of the morning and half of the afternoon, but I was too close now not to follow the draw even if it took till past midnight. The walk through the suburbs and local small business districts did give me an odd sense of this world, or at least the North American take on it, whose details hadn't really struck me. Perhaps it was getting closer to that energy source, but it seemed as if more and more of the old me, both old versions of me, surfaced, and for the first time I saw this world through an outsider's eyes rather than as an inhabitant.

As Cory Kassemi, I'd focused mostly on my own role and my own interrelationships. Most of my experience, though, had been in a resort city and in a downtown urban setting. Things that I'd pretty much not noticed or had taken for granted seemed to leap out at me now, maybe because of the energy, maybe because I had little else to think about.

There was little in the way of single-family housing, even out here, for one thing. Oh, there were large homes with lawns and gardens, but they seemed more like group homes, with two or three women living there together, sometimes with one male, sometimes without. There was also a certain casualness I doubted would have worked in my past worlds without causing a lot of trouble. It was kind of startling to see bare-breasted women even though I'd seen a bunch of them in Galveston. Again, it was the setting—mowing the lawn or getting a tan on a lounge chair. Not everybody had the body for it, of course, and not everybody who didn't have the body for it refrained from exposure anyway, but it was the casualness of it all, the lack of concern. Men were around for the one function for which they were needed, but they weren't any threat.

There were kids around, more than I thought there would be, and they, too, showed a remarkable lack of concern for their safety and well-being. There were all sorts of nationalistic and cultural differences that divided the world up, and lots of tensions, but on a local level this world simply had less violence.

In the affluent areas, the kids tended to be almost exclusively female. Male children were either kept inside, sent away to cloistered boarding schools like I'd been, or given over to some common greater family care. Only in the poorer neighborhoods did you see boys, who tended to be dirty, bruised, picked on, and often just plain miserable, with nothing

but giant diapers or ankle-length pullovers to wear. Their relative status and value was clear from the contrast with their
sisters.

I recalled what Walt had called this. A revenge world, he'd
said. Not justice, but reversal. Deep down, Alice McKee
hadn't wanted the equality and social justice she had preached
and probably had convinced herself she wanted; deep down,
Alice McKee had wanted to get even with men and make them
suffer under an exaggerated sense of social oppression she
firmly believed was aimed at women in the worlds she'd lived
in. Sort of like slaves decrying and hating slavery, until they
revolted and became the leaders and, instead of abolishing
slavery, enslaved those who'd once been their masters. So
much for principle. It was proof of a cynical view of the human
mind, but in none of the worlds did it look as if humanity had
produced a majority of saints.

Shortly after five in the afternoon, I found the Command
Center. I can tell you the exact time because of the huge church
whose bells pealed the passing of the hour just before I found
what I'd been searching for.

It wasn't in the church or on church property, although that
wouldn't have surprised me much. Just beyond the church,
which had the usual Tex-Mex, Spanish Colonial look about it
and seemed as large as a cathedral, there was a small service
road that a sign on the corner said led to the APPLIED PHYSICS
LAB. Exactly whose lab it didn't say. I guess you were supposed to know.

At any rate, I turned down the path, and felt very strong
presences just to my right as I passed the church. The home
of Rita and the Standishes and maybe others? I wondered.
Probably. Its proximity was just too convenient.

The road ran into a fairly dense grove of trees perhaps two
hundred yards beyond the back of the church and its rectory, a
grove I felt sure had been planted to shield any view of what
was beyond from the street. Until now I'd played the casual

walker, but as soon as I reached the woods without anybody grabbing me, I got off the side of the road and headed into the shelter of the trees.

It didn't matter. The trees were maybe a city block thick, and then I hit the fences. In some cases, the outermost fence actually threaded its way between the last stand of trees. Looking back toward where the road was, I could see a gatehouse and a whole set of controls for access. Looking up at the fence, which was maybe fifteen feet high, I could see nasty barbed wire on top and a lot of other even more gruesome devices to impale anybody nutty enough to try getting over it. At my height, it was absurd to even think of it.

Beyond the first barrier was a second fence, looking much like the first but having an array of incredibly fancy gadgets on top, the purpose of which I couldn't guess except that it wouldn't be nice for anybody climbing it to find out. You could hear a steady sixty-cycle hum coming from it as well, and I suspected it wasn't just to power whatever they had on top.

Beyond that was a grassy area with wheel ruts, as if made by Jeeps on countless patrols, and beyond that was a solid green fence with an angled top that prevented any view inside. Beyond the green fence was the source of the power I was feeling, but that was all I could see, feel, or understand.

There were two sudden thoughts rising in me, each at war with the other. On the one hand, if I had the power to divert a storm or dry myself instantly, I almost certainly had the power to walk right through that line of fences and alarms and live. On the other hand, since others like me could sense the use of such power and since those others were pretty well concentrated here, to do so would be to invite a lot of company real fast.

I had a very strong feeling that all this wasn't to keep me out, but to invite me in and effect another social transformation—male spider to tiny little fly.

Okay, then, Cory, why the hell are you here in the lion's den in the first place?

Good question, one I'd asked myself more than once by this point. Just knowing where the enemy was did provide some advantage, albeit a small one, but the question of *"now what?"* loomed ever larger as I sat there in the gathering twilight. Certainly I wasn't going anywhere until after dark, maybe until well after dark.

I took out my last candy bar and nibbled on it idly, wishing I had brought a canteen as well.

Having gone into the den, though, I at least decided that I'd get as much of a look at their setup as I could. I eased myself through the trees, checking as carefully as I could to insure that they hadn't also put some kind of booby traps here, and got to a point where I was still concealed but had a fairly direct view of the gatehouse and road going in.

At least the sign on the gatehouse—not the one warning of dire consequences for unauthorized entry—told me what I was supposedly outside of. TEXAS STATE UNIVERSITY APPLIED PHYSICS LABORATORY, it read, and, in smaller lettering, OPERATED FOR THE PUBLIC GOOD BY TANAKA INDUSTRIES.

Yeah, uh-huh. Nothing like not bothering to be subtle. When you paint a target so big and so obvious that all your real enemies can see it and then you scream, "Kick me!" said enemies have a right to be suspicious. On the other hand, said target might well be overconfident. Rini, who hadn't even been one of us, had stumbled into and managed to outfox and even destroy quite a number of these selfsame bastards. If they had enough power, if they could draw up and switch on like they had before, then I knew well that none could sense another presence, not in that level of energy field. The same thing that would give them vast power both collectively and as individuals would also mask an enemy. It had more than once before, and I learned real well.

At least, I hoped I knew what I was doing.

There wasn't a lot of traffic going in and out, but the occasional car indicated that this was a twenty-four-hour operation, all right. The gates were nicely angled so that nobody could see straight in, and it was next to impossible to get an idea of just what was beyond the green fence and its gate. You could probably see it fine from the air, but it would look much like any of a hundred other private or public research facilities, either government or corporate, in the surrounding area and would be unlikely to reveal anything. Somehow I suspected that the air defense was pretty good, since they'd had to figure in the outlandish possibility of a flying-saucer attack.

I doubted that the Boojums would be dumb enough to go that route anyway, although they had been convinced once to try a ground assault.

Most of the cars didn't give me a sense of having fellow-incarnates inside, although one sleek one with two tough-looking women inside it, one smoking a big cigar, sure did. The night was too dark and the car was moving too fast for me to get a really good look at anything, but there were several incarnates, even Danielle Tanaka, who could give off that kind of strong energy signature.

I began to wonder if the concept of an energy signature might not be literally true. I hadn't really been able to determine a sufficient variation in anything except amplitude that would let me differentiate one from the other, but might there be some way to do it, reliably, even from a distance, without going to wireframe and risking detection? I wished I knew. I wished that the damned caterpillar had given me more information than he did. If it was so important to him that I grow and learn to use this power, then why the hell didn't he hand me an operator's manual?

I sighed and settled down for what I hoped would be an uneventful night. After a while, just out of sheer boredom and awash with the proximity I felt to the Command Center, I dozed off.

And promptly fell several feet onto hot sand.

*   *   *

It had been quite a while since I'd been here, but it hadn't changed very much. The shaman's world still had the varicolored beach; the black, warm, eerily still water; and the huge, gnarled forest that went up thousands of feet toward the cavernous fairyland ceiling.

I still didn't understand what the place was, or why it had such stability, but here it was, and I was almost getting comfortable with it, alien though it was to anything in my "human" experience.

In the past, I had arrived in the form of some sort of gargoyle, or flying monstrosity, but not this time. Just as Rini had been able to somehow access this place and arrive in her own form, this time I was there as my Cory Kassemi self, only naked and exposed.

Maybe I was small and not terribly strong, but at least I knew my way around here a little. I walked back off the beach, whose sand was not only sticky but also hot, and into the vast tangle of roots and deadwood from the trees that were so huge that even their remnants created habitats and pathways large enough to travel through. I knew that there had been a shaman's pit of some sort over to my left a few hundred yards or so, and I made for it as deliberately as I could. If someone, *anyone*, else was here and could speak with me, it would be a breakthrough. If Wilma had recovered and was somehow here, that would be even better. Except for my first experience, Wilma had always been here, or had come, when I'd fallen through. She could do it any time she wanted to, if, of course, she still remembered how.

I found the pit after a short hike, but there was no one there and the fire was cold. It looked, in fact, as if no one had been there in quite a long time, perhaps since the last visit that registered in my memory. That worried me; Wilma wasn't the only one who'd been able to make it here, and my last visit had been a lifetime ago. Was this place somehow dying, or losing its ability to draw those who could find it? That was a very disturbing thought. This strange place had initially frightened the living hell out of me, but, over time, it had instead turned into a bedrock of sanity, a safe area where only those I could trust might be found.

Why was I here now? Had I been brought here, or had I unwittingly triggered a subroutine in the master program that controlled my own existence that tripped me into here? I had wound up here most often when I had felt particularly lost, alone, abandoned, and with nowhere else to turn; while that summed up my predicament, I hadn't had the sense of outright *desperation* that had triggered my other visits here.

This was a world of magic, elemental creatures, and minor gods. Perhaps they, too, were nothing more than computer-generated creations, but, if so, they were outside the continuous, endless progression of realities.

I sat at the fire pit for quite a long time, just staring at it and wondering why I was here, for how long, and just what I was supposed to do.

There was a rustling, a wind in the giant trees, that was eerie and startling; this place had the most static air I'd ever experienced.

I looked up, but could see barely a ripple in the trees or feel any real movement of air on my body. Still, the sound of rustling high above came in waves, like a breeze in the faraway topside regions of the ceiling-sky.

"Light the fire . . ."

I frowned. It was an eerie sound, more like a great creature's exhale than real speech, yet it sounded as if the breeze itself were speaking to me.

"Light the fire . . ."

I looked around. Suppose it was some sort of message, some kind of sentient attempt to reach me by one of those mysterious "Powers" that seemed to always be hovering around? Not the caterpillar, certainly. Not here. But something else, something powerful, nonetheless.

"Light the fire . . ."

I frowned again. "With what?" I asked, aloud, more puzzled than upset. I had no matches, no lighter, and even if I'd had a lens there was no sun to give me the energy to focus it. Still, there had to be *some* way to do it. I seemed to remember that the shamans hadn't exactly arrived in business suits.

Rub two sticks together? Hell, I'd tried that many times. It was possible, I knew, but without a bow to help generate the necessary friction, you could get the sticks hot, but not hot enough.

But what about the rock?

"Light the fire . . ."

I looked up to the heavens, irritated. "I'm trying! I'm trying!" I told whoever or whatever it was. "You want instant gratification, next time teleport a Boy Scout!"

I searched frantically for something to work with and finally saw several well-worn stones on a small bed of straw near the fire pit. I could recognize flint when I saw it, and the straw was incredibly dry. I had no idea what was the proper way to do this, so I just started experimenting, putting the larger well-worn rock down into the straw and using the rounded second one to draw along the first in a fairly rapid series of motions. I got sparks, in some cases big sparks, but nothing seemed to catch.

In all my lives I remembered seeing news stories about huge fires caused by carelessness, accidents, or a freak of nature that would burn down half a country. But when I was presented with the basic tools to start a blaze in dry grass, it didn't seem to work.

Momentarily giving up, I finally examined the pit itself. There was a kind of liquid there, viscous and smelly, with a kind of scum or oil slick on top of it. Some sort of fuel for the bigger fire? Maybe, but what good did it do me? I wasn't going to try and spark flint into it. I'd be more scared it would flare up and engulf me in the flame as well.

But if I could either hold my nose and scoop a little out onto the straw, or maybe dip some straw into it and put it back in the pile, then . . .

It was worth a try.

It wasn't a very professional job, but I managed to get a thick clump of straw together, dip it in, swirl it around, then put it back on the pile. I figured I must be on the right track; the old ghostly voice hadn't kept nagging me. Maybe I hurt its feelings.

My wrist took a beating and I still wasn't getting anywhere after repeated attempts to ignite it. Finally, I sighed, sat back, and decided that maybe putting the big stone right on the wet straw wasn't smart. How about angling it over so the sparks would leap out?

I took a deep breath, planted the stone, and tried it. First try, nothing. Second try, nothing. I decided that third time was either the charm or I'd drop back ten yards and punt. One more time . . .

The oily straw exploded into flame, and I fell backward, off balance and momentarily blinded by the unexpected brilliance. Still, it was burning almost as fast as flash paper. I rolled back over, tried to grab the little bit that wasn't still in flame, and tossed it into the fire pit.

For a moment I thought nothing had happened or that the flame had been suffocated before it could ignite the rest of the oily liquid. Then, suddenly, I was pushed back again by a wave of heat and the flames shot up in a huge vertical column.

I scuttled away, sliding rearward on my ass, not wanting to take the time to get up. The column looked much too regular and symmetrical to be natural.

It rose up and up, but never quite reached the height of the trees or the ceiling, and seemed to terminate abruptly like the top of a Doric column.

Closer to my level, at least seven or eight feet up from the pit, what almost looked like a fearsome, ghostly face formed in the column, which had become a uniform yellow-orange. I couldn't really make out much, but there were definitely eyes there, and a mouth, and perhaps some semblance of nostrils, although what such a creature might breathe is beyond me.

"G . . . down . . . rub . . . ter and cover you . . . wi . . . san . . . "
it said, the words broken by crackles of static. *"Need . . . cond . . .
Hurry! The con . . . last long!"*

For a moment I couldn't figure out what the hell it wanted.
There wasn't enough information, and my face mirrored my
confusion. "Need cond"? Cond what? *Think!* "G'down"? Get
down? Go down? Go down, next word had to be "to," but to
where? "Ter"? Ter what? Or what ter? *Water!* Go down to the
water and cover you—

All of a sudden, I put two and two together. The last time I
had a vision of this place, a bunch of the shamen all covered
with colored sand had been sitting around this *thing* that had
formed from the smoke in a far less active pit. I got up and
hurried back down the path to the water. I jumped in over my
head, getting myself nice and wet, and surged back to the
beach and rolled around in the sand until I was literally covered with fine golden grains that stuck to my skin like glue.

The sand must be some kind of electrical conductor. The
damned thing was a communication device!

I tripped several times on the way back, but the column was
still there when I finally returned. The burning column was
maybe half the height it had been and was very slowly
shrinking. It wasn't kidding. This connection wasn't going to
last long at this rate.

I came up as close as I could, feeling the heat, and sat down.

"Think!" the voice commanded, far more clearly, sounding
almost human now. *"Concentrate!"*

"Who are you?" I shouted.

"It would be meaningless to you if I told you. What you *can*
understand, I believe, is that I am not inside the matrix that you
are trapped in. You *do* know what I mean by that?"

"More or less. You're not stuck in this never-ending series
of lives and programs. I'm talking with somebody from the
real world."

"Who can tell what the real world is?" it responded, not
very reassuringly. "At least I'm not in your fix. I know what

you're going through. We've been working on this for some time but we've been able to reach very few people who can figure out we're not gods, demons, or dementia. Listen carefully, because time's very short and I don't know how many times we can do this before we burn out the connection."

"I'm listening!" The top of the column was getting lower and lower, almost to the level of the ghostly face, which began moving down the column to compensate.

"We believe we have developed a solution to get you all out of there, but it is complex. We are going to transmit the programming sequence if time permits. It must be administered to the Core Computer, not the backups, via a Brand Box connection. There's not enough time to explain any more at this time. If you trust us, if you want a chance at getting out, then you must reach into what is left of the flame and do it *now*! Without hesitation!"

"But I'll burn!"

"Do you think that this body is any more real than the others you've had? *Now or never!*"

The hell with it. So what if I burned up here? Somehow I knew I was still also asleep, or comatose, back in the world. I leaned forward and plunged both hands into the column.

The sensation wasn't what I expected at all, less a burn than a tremendous electric shock, and then my whole mind, my whole consciousness kind of disintegrated, and I felt a mass of incomprehensible stuff just flooding into unused areas of my head. I was frozen, unable to move, unable to act, unable to think, just experiencing.

And then it stopped, and the column was gone completely. The last thing I got, and the only thing I could rationally comprehend, was *"Transmission terminated by loss of connection."*

I felt very dizzy and not a little nauseated. I fell back onto the sand, so stunned I didn't even look to see if my arms were still there.

Before I passed out, there was enough rationality left inside my mind to wonder, *Loss of connection? Did I get the whole thing or not?* And what had I gotten? I felt weird, light-headed, dizzy, and confused, but I had no access at all to whatever they'd sent, and no knowledge of how to interpret it anyway.

Sensation suddenly roared back into me, and with it an incredible wave of pain so bad that I screamed and passed out completely.

The tolling of the church bells woke me up well into daylight, and the area had a busier sound. I could hear lawn mowers and the sound of highway traffic just beyond the trees. I hadn't done a precise count of the number of chimes, being still groggy from the experience and the nearly comatose sleep that followed, but it seemed to last pretty long. Nine, maybe ten counts.

Finally I managed a look at my watch, but since it said 10:42, it was no help at all. Something had knocked it off.

The first thing I had to think about once my head cleared enough was whether or not what I'd experienced was real even in the sense in which I now understood reality. Had I actually translated into that strange shaman region or did I just wish that I had and allowed my dreams and exhaustion to fulfill the desire? And, if it was real, what, exactly, had happened? Did I, somehow, actually make communication with people outside of our endless existence? Was there now code in my head to rescue us, and, if so, did it all get transferred before the connection was lost? And, finally, assuming it was all true up to this point, what assurance did I have that the ghostly face in the fire and the transferred code were what he'd said they were?

The proof that I'd had at least *some* transcendental experience was clear when I absently looked at my hands. I'd been white and fair-skinned before; the hands I saw were a deep golden brown. I looked down at my chest and at my legs and saw the same thing. I was pretty sure I hadn't changed form; something had turned my complexion very dark. I rummaged in the purse for the small compact and looked at my face in the mirror. Yeah, it was still the same old me, but the coloration had continued to darken me beyond the usual levels of a good tan. This wasn't any suntan; it was a real change. My hair hadn't gone the same way, though—it was white, giving me a very strange, almost unearthly look.

The code, or whatever had been transferred to me from the fire column, had done this, perhaps in connection with the sand. I suspected I was permanently changed, but that it was some side effect. All it would do would be to make me less recognizable to those who knew me, while making me stand out in any crowd even to total strangers. It was not helpful. No matter what else happened, one very quick purchase was going to be some black hair dye. Even my *eyebrows* were white! Good thing I had bathed in the sheep dip to get rid of my body hair, though. I could just imagine the effect of all that stark white hair on somebody who was now very dark and still looked twelve years old.

Enough of that, I told myself. No easy way to wash up or get breakfast around here, or so it seemed. There was a mini-mart that I'd passed on the way, about three blocks down the road, but those places never had rest rooms, not even in this female-dominated society.

Of course, I could just walk up to the installation and introduce myself, but while that would have gotten me cleaned up and most likely fed, I wasn't too thrilled about the dinner possibilities.

Okay, so what now? I had code I couldn't use unless I could get inside the Command Center, I had some power that I couldn't use without alerting all my worst enemies, and I had no allies in this world that I knew of or at least that I knew where to find.

Damn it, Cynthia! Where the hell are you when I really need you?

Hell, what did I know about anybody's condition here at the

moment? I'd been in touch with nobody, and I'd been tracked down and was on the run from my enemies.

What I really needed was just somebody else to talk to who wouldn't immediately call the psycho ward. The face in the fire had also warned that the backup facility wouldn't do; I'd need a Brand Box from the Command Center, since it was the only one with a direct connection to the master computer. That meant here, not central Washington, if in fact that was where the damned backup center still was. If the big one was here, they might well be anywhere.

This level of virtual reality was becoming the pits.

There was no way I was going to sit there hungry and thirsty all day long; besides, I needed some time to think. Walking out the way I came in, though, wasn't practical. There were too many people around now. Best to see how far this stand of trees really went and what was beyond. If I intersected with a less traveled street a few blocks down, it wouldn't bother me a bit.

I could *feel* them around me, beyond the fence, in back of me, in and around the church. There was no way to shut the sensations out, and I could only pray that just having this sensation wasn't necessarily drawing them to me. Of course, if I could sense them, the odds were pretty good that the reverse was true, but unlike them, I wouldn't necessarily expect others of my kind to be around.

Texas is mostly flat and it's mostly prairie, even if it's often overdeveloped in spots. That means most "forests" are planted and most high cover is deliberate, so the trees gave out pretty quickly after I reached the limits of the APL grounds. Unfortunately, that also was the limit of development in this direction; I was looking out at a more typical flat landscape with only mild contours. In the distance, the road by the church, whose twin steeples I could still see behind me, melded with the interstate going south and west from here. At that point there was an interchange with the usual services: a gas station, minimart, and restaurant. I wasn't too sure I wanted to eat in that restaurant, considering that it might well be used by locals on a break, but that kind of minimart was designed for travelers and it would have a rest room and snacks that would be sufficient. I doubted if it would have Clairol, but you never knew.

I was pretty rank and I knew it. I needed more than just a quick wash by this point; I needed a bath with heavily scented bath soaps, I needed industrial-strength shampoo, and I needed to cremate these clothes with full military honors and find new ones. None of that was really in the cards at the moment, but what the hell could I do?

There wasn't much business at this time of the morning, which suited me fine, considering my changed look and gamy appearance. I made right for the women's room and took a good look at myself in the mirror. Gross. I washed up as best I could, then went to a stall, shut and locked it, and relieved myself.

I tried at least to brush off as much of the grime as I could and was thankful that my hair was short and I had a hat, as limp as the hat was by this point. There was nothing I could do about the sides or eyebrows, but it didn't look too ridiculous.

Back in the minimart, I picked up a couple of doughnuts and a big bottle of grapefruit juice and took a look for hair dye. No such luck.

I popped one of the voice-changing lozenges into my mouth after eating and drinking, figuring I was going to have to do some acting for a while, and went back outside. It made no sense to call from here; that just would keep me nailed close to the Command Center and increase the likelihood that I'd be picked up. Until I could figure out what I wanted to do next, and maybe experiment with this newfound power somewhere away from Rita and company, I figured I'd taken enough risks for now.

I walked over the overpass that took traffic to and from the road heading back toward the city and looked down at the traffic. Hell, hitching was illegal, but it was worth taking a chance. It was close enough to the city line that I figured the state police wouldn't bother coming this far, and the city police would be staked out farther down the road to catch speeders.

I walked down the entrance ramp and stayed carefully on the shoulder, but I walked just enough ahead that I could be seen by people coming from under the overpass in time for them to decide whether or not to stop. I wasn't sure what the initial reaction would be to somebody my size and build hitch-hiking there, but I could lie like the best of them, and I was only trying to get back downtown.

I stood there for about twenty minutes in the increasing heat—even early April can be pretty damned hot in central Texas—and several cars slowed down, but no takers. Finally, a low, dark-blue sedan slowed and pulled over. I ran to the window, hoping that nothing had screwed up the voice change. The woman inside didn't have a dangerous feel to her, and looked pretty ordinary. Thirties, maybe, short black hair, Hispanic-looking, and with a nice smile.

"Where you goin', sweet thing?" she asked in a heavy South Texas accent.

"Just downtown. I was ridin' my bike and got a flat. They said up there they'd hold it for me, but I gotta get back and ask my mom to help when she gets off work."

"Com'on. Get in. I'm goin' past theah."

I opened the door and slid in, hoping that the woman didn't have much of a sense of smell. I no sooner closed it than we were off.

"You look like you been on the road a good long time," she noted. "You sure you don't want me to run you all the way home?"

"No, thanks. Couldn't get in anyways. I don't like to bring stuff like house keys and all when I'm ridin' out of the neighborhood. I'll get a ride home from Mom at work."

"Wheah's she work?"

"National Bank Building, just across from the west side of the Capitol. Just let me off at the Capitol and I'll make it the rest of the way."

As the danger point receded from view, I felt some relief. The fact that the nice woman had bought the story and asked no questions of any importance also helped. I began to feel really relieved.

What had taken me the better part of a day to get to by bus and on foot took twenty minutes to retrace by car. Austin, for all its government, industry, and educational institutions, really wasn't a big city by anybody's measure, and certainly not by Texas standards.

As we neared the Capitol, I found myself almost involuntarily going into that curious wireframe mode while staring ahead. When I realized I'd done it and saw how strange everything looked, I glanced over at the woman and realized just how easy it would be to reprogram her to do anything I wanted her to do, even drive me to the ranch. I resisted it, though, since the power it would require would surely register back at the Command Center. Maybe if I had been in New York, Chicago, or L.A. I would have risked it, but not this close to them.

I risked only one slight use of the power as she pulled up on the west side of the Capitol building and I got out and thanked her. I told her to completely forget that she'd done this or ever seen me, and she seemed to freeze for a moment, look confused, then lose interest in me and drive on, as if wondering why the hell she'd stopped in the first place.

I kind of liked this sort of power, if only I could use it in a less restrictive environment. I particularly liked it in this world, where I was part of the minority of humanity that had no power at all. I think that was the worst part of being a male in this society. It was sort of like blacks in the Old South must have felt, living in a nation that had the freedoms, the affluence, and the rights most folks only dreamed of, and because of color in that case, and gender in this one, there was simply no way you could ever share in or have any part of that.

There were a couple of presences in the area, so I decided to get on the move. Even that little use of the power might have attracted somebody, and it would be stupid to stick around.

Damn it! What good was all this power if it betrayed you? This was almost more unfair than not having the power at all. This was kind of like getting all of Superman's powers only to discover that everybody else got God's.

I walked down into the business district. It was getting late, but some of the stores stayed open after five and I found my hair dye and got something decent to eat—a hamburger with lettuce and tomato, anyway. That was one advantage of being so small and so light: I didn't have much appetite, and I didn't run to fat.

All through downtown I felt several of the presences, at first in different areas; then, later, I got the distinct feeling that there was some kind of pattern to it. All of a sudden, I had the really strong sensation that they knew I was here and were coming for me.

All thoughts of calling the ranch and then waiting around the bus station or some other public place until they could pick me up just vanished. I walked on, trying to suppress panic, and got on the first public bus that stopped. I had no idea where it was going, but the odds were it wasn't going anywhere near the APL.

It wasn't. It headed out, slowly, as I made my way toward the back and tried not to be crushed by the standing-room-only crowd. Somebody in back took pity on me and gave up her seat; I smiled as gratefully as possible and sat down. It was one of the seats that put my back to the window, so I was able to look either forward or back, more or less, and I wanted to look back.

If you ever want to really make somebody trying to tail you miserable, take a city bus at rush hour. No matter what you do, you can't be inconspicuous following a city bus that stops almost every block or two. Auto traffic just doesn't work that way, and you become much more obvious when the bus leaves the city center and there's some space between cars. There was no question, though, in spite of inflicting such grief on the presences, I was spotted and they knew I was on the bus.

So now what?

We came up to what seemed to be a major transfer point. I got off with a whole crowd of women and made my way back toward several apartment buildings and across a children's playground. You couldn't drive a Chevy through here, which put my pursuers on foot, and I was pretty sure that there were no more than two of them.

I had no idea where I was going and I didn't care. I just wanted to shake them, one way or the other.

One of them had gotten out where I'd left the bus and was in back of me, coming at a brisk but not running pace. The other seemed to be still in the car, and circling around, and I figured they were going to try and squeeze me between them when I inevitably had to emerge from the playground. Both were incarnates, neither seemed so overwhelmingly powerful that they were likely to be really dangerous compared to me in a confrontation. On the other hand, they probably had more practice and more confidence in using their power than I did, and there *were* two of them.

Well, hell, maybe it was all over, but if they knew who I was and what I was, then why shouldn't I at least *try* them on that level?

I quickly left the playground and concentrated on an alley between two apartment buildings, trying to imagine a sleek, fast racing bike with headlight and horn. One seemed to draw itself in outline in front of me, set against the brick wall, and then slowly filled, became three-dimensional, and finally clattered against the walk. I picked it up, jumped on it, and started off. It was a perfect fit, just exactly what I would have wished for.

Win or lose, this was kind of fun. But winning would be better.

I certainly threw them off. The one in back stopped, totally confused by the slight burst of energy and then the sudden more surprising burst of speed I'd shown.

The one in the car suddenly wasn't too sure, either, since they apparently didn't have easy contingency plans. That's what they got for taking me for granted, I thought with some satisfaction.

And Texas, even the towns, is a good place for bikes. Flat, like I said. I didn't want to expose myself at the street level any longer than I had to; that would neutralize the car to an extent, and, possibly, prevent them from a visual sighting that they might not have had.

I could sense that one of them, though, was calling for help, and that was a problem. I could materialize a bike, and be very good on it, and even open up some distance between us, but I was totally lost in this neighborhood and darkness was coming on fast. They knew the city well, and there wasn't any way I could see to dematerialize their two-way radio.

Now would be a good time for the saucer to show up and beam me aboard, I thought frantically. That had saved my ass once, in a past life, but I wasn't counting on it here.

There were several cars converging now, some not having the same kind of danger feel as others but clearly being coordinated with one end in mind. I was getting desperate. I turned back into a massive, two-story development and suddenly found myself in a nearly endless, pitch-dark lane. When I switched to wireframe mode, riding the bike became more like some bizarre computer game in which you had to steer a center course, watch out for obstacles in the path, and still make it to the end of this strange outline landscape. It was not only tense and somewhat disorienting, the fact was I was also growing more and more exhausted. Boys' bodies weren't designed for the amount of exercise I'd been getting today, and I'd had several days of irregular and improper food and drink as well.

I got out of the courtyard but it didn't seem to matter. Bright, ghostly figures moved through the wireframe landscape inside the walks and gardens that were in the center of the four big apartment blocks. At that moment, I suddenly realized that my only choices were to either give in to them or figure out some escape that they hadn't prepared for before they caught up to me.

I began to wonder if I could call up a rabbit hole. I didn't know how to do it, but I hadn't known how to materialize a bike, either. Hell, if I could escape alive into a rabbit hole and through to the void, I was more than content to let them play out this world and start again with full knowledge. I aimed for a spot I felt I could make on the bike before anybody got to me and I tried to fix on that spot and concentrate, concentrate, concentrate.

It began to form! I actually could *see* a circular motion beginning dead ahead, developing into a more substantial cavity with every passing moment. I pedaled as hard as I could right for it.

Something or someone hit me in the head. I had the sudden feeling of an enormous shock and the eerie, almost disembodied sensation of flying through the air.

I don't remember landing.

V

THE HOLY ROLLING

My first disappointment was to regain consciousness and discover I wasn't in a tunnel past the void or in the waiting area, but very much alive. I didn't even have a headache, and when I felt my head where I was certain I'd been struck by someone with something hard—nightstick, truncheon, or blackjack—there wasn't a trace of soreness or matted blood.

Either I'd been brought down by some kind of VR weapon or that same ability had been used to completely heal me as soon as they'd determined that I wasn't dead.

Still, I was hurt on the psychological level by the contempt my very status now showed. They hadn't even bothered to restrain me. I was on a very fancy covered bed—silk sheets, ornate posts, and even a canopy that showed a kind of sunburst pattern. The room itself wasn't large but it was ornate and opulent. What looked like gold I suspected probably was, and what looked like marble certainly was.

I got out of the bed and looked back, half expecting to see the remnants of bloodstains there, but there was only the faint outline of my body, looking pitifully small in the wide expanse of the bedding.

I did, however, still have an odor about me, so, having no other alternatives at the moment and suspecting that even my newfound powers weren't going to get me out of that door, I walked over to a smaller door that was open, apparently by default, and clearly led to the bathroom.

There was soap and shampoo there, as I would have expected, along with a hair dryer and the other usual amenities. There were even oversized towels, washcloths, and a bath mat.

I looked at myself in the mirror. The black dye-job looked pretty phony, I thought, but the dark golden-bronze complexion wasn't bad on me at all.

I was still very achy from all the exercise I'd done, and none too steady, so I opted for the bath over the shower, at least until I washed my hair. Just getting into hot, lightly scented water, soaping up, and reclining there was heaven after what I'd been through.

The question, of course, was just what had I been through? All those sensations of incarnates in the park—I had to be in the hands of the Command Center, but this wasn't exactly what I pictured as being behind those fences. In fact, while I could sense a few incarnates around this place somewhere, none were even close. They had that little fear of me!

I had to worry a little just on that score. I mean, I wasn't much of a threat, but I had given them something of a run, hadn't I? Lying there in the bath, totally relaxed, I let my mind go and tried to put everything here into wireframe mode and see what I was dealing with.

There was a sudden blast of colors and sounds and total disorientation. There was nothing that I could hold on to, nothing my mind could make sense of. It was like falling into a deep swimming pool with sharks all around and no knowledge of swimming. And it hurt! I withdrew in seconds, and found myself gripping the side of the big tub and gasping for breath.

What the hell was *that*?

I decided not to try any more experiments, not while mostly immersed in a bathtub, anyway.

When I went to shower and wash my hair, I got another surprise. The water seemed to run jet black, ugly, like black ink
rolling off my body into the tub. I was so unnerved from the
first experience that I froze for a moment, then I realized what
was happening and relaxed.

The hair dye, as ugly as it was, hadn't seemed to have
bonded to my hair. It was washing out with soap and water, all
the way down to the roots.

When it was running clear again, I stepped out of the tub
and immediately went to the mirror, pulled over the stool,
stood up over the sink, and brushed away the fog from the
mirror. My guess was right—I was to have bronze skin and sil-
very white hair from now on, it seemed.

The more I looked at myself while drying myself and my
hair, the more I began to think that there were other changes,
perhaps not quite so obvious. I had to do a mental comparison
with my old life to work them out. Not that it wasn't my face
there, but . . .

I was much thinner, a lot thinner than you could expect from
just the past few days. I didn't have an ounce of fat on me, and,
from the apparent weight of the rather ordinary hair dryer, not
much muscle, either. I didn't look emaciated—far from that—
but I sure looked soft enough that a three-year-old toddler
could whip me in a fair fight.

The question was, were the modifications part of the file
transfer, or had I been gone over by experts after my capture?
If you could make a blow to the head that hard and that dam-
aging go away, then what else could you do while your subject
was unconscious?

I went back out to the bedroom, sat in a chair in front of the
dresser, and tried to access the wireframe mode again.
Instantly I got the same painful, disorienting sensations as I
had in the bath, and I stopped instantly. Whatever it was, it had
shut *that* door just as it was getting to be fun.

I considered it a moment and realized that it was exactly
what I would have done if our places had been reversed. No

worries about me charming the help, particularly the ones with guns, as I had the driver of that car, and also no problem with me conjuring up any rabbit holes.

So, when they'd healed me and treated my wounds, they'd "appended" my code, as it were, using a basic principle first reported in detail in my memory by a fellow named Pavlov. Make what's a threat untouchable by making it too painful and too unpleasant to try. It wouldn't take too many attempts to teach me *that* lesson, particularly if each attempt seemed to be more intense.

My plumbing also seemed to be a bit more stimulated than usual. I was somewhat turned on, far more than in the past. I had the strangest feeling that in most circumstances I wouldn't just enjoy sex, I'd need it. That time wasn't quite here, but I wasn't sure just what it would take to push me over that edge into addiction. Not much. But not Rita Alvarez. For some reason thinking of her really helped me keep control.

Well, the clothing, or more accurately lack of it, in the room made it clear that this wasn't an accident or hyperactive hormones. What I found was a selection of very sexy satin codpieces and not much else. There was, however, an assortment of jewelry, cosmetics, and perfumes and body colognes. Well, what the hell—if it would get me out of here . . .

I don't know if the use of the makeup, and making myself into a girl-toy fantasy, was really a voluntary act or not, but it seemed like it, and I certainly understood how these minds worked by now. Still, if this was programmed behavior, I probably wouldn't know anyway. That was the insidiousness of it when used skillfully and subtly.

I'd been in something like this kind of a Brand Box world before, long ago, and I began to wonder if I was in one again. The last time young women were the sex slaves; now it was the boys' turn. It would certainly explain a lot about this room, these feelings, and my looks. Dan Tanaka had made pretty young women the objects of his desire in his private Box;

would Danielle Tanaka do any different with the opposite sex here in this world?

So I was back again in a Brand Box. When Al had trapped me in one during the last life, it had been a wall-to-wall dump, where sterile identical people all lived in this massive coopera- tive mall-like enclosure. The only reason I hadn't eventually succumbed to it and become mentally one with the others was Al's use of the temporary VR interface to come in and talk to me, taunt me, argue with me, even bargain with me. This time, I was in Tanaka's hands, and all she wanted was my body.

Well, whoever cooked this one up was kind of rutted, anyway. Maybe I was a "boy," but scanty clothing, make- up, smooth skin, and even heels were all trademarks of this mind-set.

Only now I was all prettied up with no place to go.

A speaker buzzed near the door, startling me. I hadn't even realized it was there.

"Come down to the bottom floor and see me in my office!" a woman's voice commanded. It was strong, firm, and yet familiar. Archbishop Rita was about to have some fun with me, a light amusement using a helmet for a few minutes before going off to the real world once more.

There was no question of not obeying. Even if I had been inclined not to, there was just no question of escape. A sub- routine or a plain, outright command, it was nonetheless absolute. They were taking no chances.

I opened the door and walked into a hall, then straight down as if I knew where I was. There were other rooms along the wall to the right, and on the left a railing of gold-plated brass that looked down on a very large and hollow-sounding expanse below. A grand staircase of marble with golden banisters descended, and I came down, the heels clicking on the marble and echoing throughout the structure.

At the bottom, I could see a main entryway but that wasn't for me. I turned right and walked down to the end of a corridor filled with religious pictures, some remarkable sex reversals of classic scenes, and entered an outer office through a plain wooden door, which I closed behind me. I walked past the empty reception area as if I were in some kind of trance, unable not to follow instructions. I found myself before an inner door that had a cross on it and a nameplate I did not even glance at. Instead, I knocked hard on the door three times, hurting my knuckles a bit.

"Enter!" came the almost familiar voice, and I did so without hesitation.

The archbishop's inner office was quite large, with an ornate, decorative fireplace on the outer wall; expensive art and iconry all around; lots of gold and silver; and a plush carpet that was tough to walk on in the shoes they'd given me. In the center, behind a well-organized desk that looked to be solid redwood with a religious mosaic made of tiny bits of colored woods and beads embedded in its top, was Rita Alvarez as she existed in this world.

She smiled when she saw me, got up, and came around the desk. I dropped to my knee, kissed her ring, and bowed my head.

"Stand up," she told me. "We haven't seen each other in this life and I would like to get something of a look at you."

"Yes, Reverend Mother," I responded automatically and did as instructed.

She really did give me the once-over, and that gave me far fewer worries than the fact that I was clearly in a huge church. This was really Rita as I'd seen her on TV; maybe this *wasn't* a Brand Box.

Rita stood in front of me and I instantly felt even smaller, weaker, and more insignificant than I had before. She was instantly recognizable, perfectly proportioned, but something like six foot six. If she hadn't been wearing the clerical garb, I think I'd have been staring dead into her navel.

She'd definitely been here longer than I. Although she still

looked very good, there were lines in her face and neck and
sure signs of exceptionally generous aging. Close up, she
seemed likely to have had plastic surgery, maybe more than
once, and to be covering up gray hair. It was a comforting
thought.

After a while, she gave me a patronizing pat on the head,
went back around the desk, and sat in her big judge's chair,
leaning back and looking very relaxed. "I assume," she said
after a bit longer, "that you are trying to figure out what happened and what this situation is. You probably think you're in
a Brand Box at the Command Center. Let me disabuse you of
that right away. This is the Mission de Santa Paula, the real
world, so much as those like you and me can have a real world,
and Austin's a few minutes back up the interstate. You've been
here two and a half days. As you can see, we did do some work
on you, and certainly improved things a great deal from what
was brought in. You weren't very attractive, I might say, and
you *stank*. Now you smell better and are almost pretty, if that's
a word. We don't need to trap you in a Brand Box for this sort
of adjustment, you see."

I said nothing. I wanted to, but for some reason I couldn't.

She knew what I was going through. "The technique's not
much more than what we've all discovered with manipulation
of local objects, in wireframe mode, by direct mental command. Dear old Al and his doctor buddy kept the rest of us
pretty much under control by keeping that sort of power to
themselves, but thanks to your little clone and your own rather
remarkable escape last time, we learned more than a little of
how to do it. Al would have stopped us from doing anything or
probably remembering anything, but you very nicely stopped
Al for us. Lee had the mastery, but not the skill or Al's down-
right brilliance. Instead of covering up, he investigated how
and why it all happened, and so we all pretty much learned the
secrets. They have made life here *much* easier. Come—you
may speak to me here."

Suddenly I could in fact speak, although in the language of what I was beginning to think of in VR terms as my "scenario."

"What will you do with me, Reverend Mother, if this is reality as I knew it?" I asked her.

"Oh, it is. I promise you that, and I see your point. Somebody like you isn't exactly proper for this place. Don't worry, we have plans for you on that score. The program is Dannie Tanaka's, as you might have guessed, with some modifications. With the direct access to the shell by mind alone, she's able to take years of refined code developed in her research and simply append or overwrite the old code. We just needed *you*.

"We've done it with a number of people. Makes one feel much more secure and everything runs much more smoothly and more efficiently as well. Al was doing it for some time, you know. Making us play out scenarios in the Boxes, ordering up different variations. We always thought it was part of the research aimed at getting us out someday, but what it really did was give him precious code for changes he could graft on to us. There's some evidence that he was the one who made me into a cleric, possibly poor Alice as well. If so, it is a kind of technique I can appreciate, since I cannot conceive of and would not want to have any other life. If that feeling is a program, it is as solid and permanent as I can think of. That is Dannie's current research, though. If this kind of change can become permanent, become part of your core personality that transcends even incarnation, there's no limit. We think we know the code, but we can't be sure—at least until we punch again, and we are not going to do *that* for a while. Not when it is so *wonderful* here." She paused and a playful smile came over her. "You do think this is wonderful, don't you?"

"No, Reverend Mother, I do not."

She sat back and grinned. "Well, it doesn't matter because you are stuck. The programming clearly worked: you have all your memories but you are much more pleasant both to look at

and to have about. We had word that a young girl was seen
here the day before we ran you down in Austin. That was you
in disguise?"

"Yes, Reverend Mother."

She frowned, sat up, and stared at me. "Why did you come
here? Surely you knew the risks! Whatever did you hope to
gain?"

"Reverend Mother, I hoped that I could tap the power of the
center as I had before and take command of my own life."
Damn it, I couldn't *not* respond to her questions, and I couldn't
even think of a lie!

"Very brave. Very stupid, but very brave. Well, we've taken
much of that out of you. Have you had any contact with the
backup people—Slidecker, Matalon, or the others—since
incarnating here?"

"No, Reverend Mother. If I had, I would have gone to
them."

"Indeed. So you're here partly out of desperation. I suspect
that dizzy dingbat's in command and on some sort of power
trip wherever they are. Were there any more women who came
through with your backup personnel last time? Other than dear
Cynthia?"

I hated myself for being unable to stop from spilling my
guts. "Yes, Reverend Mother. One that I did not know. All I
know is that she was named Mabel. She looked at least part
African-American."

I could see that the news was somewhat unsettling to Rita,
and I got a bit of a lift from that reaction. I could swear that
Rita didn't have any more idea who Mabel was than I did.

She thought for a moment, idly chewing on the end of a
pencil, then said, "Well, we'll take a look through the
recording we took; I'm sure over time we'll get your entire life
story. All I want to know at the moment is whether or not you
actually got through security and inside earlier in the week."

"No, Reverend Mother. I didn't even try."

"So, you picked up the secret of the wireframe as we did, from what happened last incarnation. And all of this coming here was for nothing?"

The first part wasn't a question so I didn't feel compelled to answer it. "Not for nothing, Reverend Mother. I believe I was contacted by one from outside our existence and hold code from him." With a lot more prompting, I told in detail the whole story of the shaman's world and the column of fire. Rita listened intently, and I had the idea I was being recorded, as she took no notes.

Finally, when I was done, she asked, "Do you think that this was a real experience? That the code exists in your head now?"

"I do, Reverend Mother."

"Well, we'll have Dannie take a look at it and see what might be there. I can tell you that, using a cursory scan, I can't detect anything. Well, we'll see. Wouldn't be the first of this kind of delusional episode in the records, either."

"I am not delusional, Reverend Mother. It happened. The code is there. If you will permit me to try a transfer of it inside the compound, it may actually help break this cycle and allow us to find true reality once more. I am sure of it. If it is a delusion, then what harm?"

"What harm? *What harm?*" She was suddenly near fury, and it scared me. "You little idiot, you never were one of the brighter ones in all this anyway! If what you say is true then I *guarantee* you I won't let you near that compound, let alone a Brand Box! Don't you understand that we already have what most can never achieve? Immortality, power, an infinite variety of lifetimes without permanent cost? Why in the *world* would we want to go back to whatever it was that stuck us here?"

It was a viewpoint I wasn't surprised to see in some, even Al, but I was a bit taken aback to see it in Rita. Still, she wasn't even the same Rita as last time, let alone earlier than that. Power, fame, and position had given her a real taste of the kind of life she'd only dreamed about, and now that she was on top after all this time, she wasn't about to play the heroine.

It was kind of sad. Understandable, but sad.

She got her self-control back fairly quickly.

"Cory, Cory, Cory," she sighed, sounding tired and patient, as if dealing with a mentally deficient student. "Have you ever considered the idea that none of us are any more real than the spooks? I have."

"Huh?"

"What if this is some gigantic, demented computer game? You've seen the transitions before the void. What if we're just the ones representing the players of the game against whatever background the computer creates? Those of us without players go along a preordained path; those with players can do extraordinary things sometimes, or change whole directions, as you did last time. I don't want to know if I'm no more real than the spooks. I'd just as soon never find out."

We were all uncertain about what was happening to us, particularly now that we knew more of the truth, but I couldn't believe that. I just couldn't.

Rita, however, was more concerned with not thinking about such dark concepts anymore. Her sadistic streak rescued her from melancholy this time.

"Now, I'm going to tell you just what Dannie and the techs did to augment you," she continued. "You can't *not* be the way they programmed you, but I want you to appreciate your situation. I couldn't kill you—I always kind of liked you, even if you were such a little computer nerd. I wasn't going to put you in a Brand Box because you got out before, and I'm not sure what you might be able to do once in there. Now, with what you've told me, I'm going to double that resolve. You're kind of cute, even exotic with that skin tone and hair coloring, and you've got a nice little ass and big brown eyes. Be a shame to waste that. You can also recognize Slidecker's people and even be a magnet that might bring some of them to us. Besides, I owe you a slight debt for the favor of removing Al as controller. Still, we can't have you wandering around. That's why I ordered your reprogramming."

She paused a moment, then continued. "You've certainly discovered that you're rather limited to what boys are *supposed* to be like here. You've got endurance but not strength. The system is natural to you. You *like* being a girl-toy. You must act within the system and as the system demands. You won't lie to a woman, cheat on her, or steal from her. You won't be able to tap into the wireframe anymore because we've added a little conditioning routine developed by Al that we discovered in the archives. You've already experienced it so you may as well forget trying to access it. If you make a promise, you must keep it. You're going to find men more repulsive than sympathetic, and want and need to be around women, making them happy. And, of course, you'll be handy to us, answering questions and maybe solving small problems if something should come up. You know how we're going to do this?"

"No, Reverend Mother," I responded, *but you're enjoying this so much, you're just dying to tell me.*

"Why, you're going to be married! Right here! And by the archbishop, no less! Private ceremony, too, but still just as binding. We're going to hold auditions, you see, over the next few days to see who likes you the best, and maybe you will take a liking to one or more of them. You should have a lot of fun. I am told you had a lot of practice at this sort of casual sexual sin over the past few years in Galveston, so you should be right at home. In the end, if neither you nor any of the women hits it off, well, of course, we will arrange something. Everyone is clear on that, which means it is in your best interest to be serious, settle down, and make a good, true choice. You'll be around if required, but otherwise it's going to pretty much put you out of the war. Want me to call your mother when all's ready?"

I had never once thought that Rita Alvarez was kidding, and she certainly wasn't. They moved me to one of the small

houses on the church grounds, within sight of the woods and
the road into the Command Center, but it was a million miles
away as far as I was concerned. I couldn't even feel the power
there, just vague presences that got irritating and disturbing
when I tried to consciously sense them. They weren't about to
have me digitize into the wireframe or electrical system. And,
over the next few days, even that faded to nothing, and I had no
more sensation of anything extranormal at all. That power had
been completely removed from me. I could get it back in only
two ways: by incarnation or by death and rebirth. Neither of
those seemed imminent.

I was in the most bizarre situation anyone could be in. I
knew how it was done, how it was *being* done to me, because
I'd done it myself. If I could control the mind and memories of
that driver and actually materialize a bicycle out of thin air,
then having it done to me wasn't any big surprise. Rita had
even demonstrated it. As she'd recited each of the characteris-
tics she wanted in me, they were there. Not like some mind
control or hypnotic commands—they were really there, as if
they'd always been there, even though my memory and my
intellect said otherwise. It was a demonstration of sheer power,
of just how much I was totally under the thumb of—well, Rita
first, but any of the others as well, if they knew how to do it.

I was also finding it harder to really think of my past lives as
actual existences I'd experienced. I'd recall lots of details of
something in my head, only to find on closer examination that
it was nonsense. I couldn't follow programming; I barely
understood what that meant, except it was the ultimate power
here. Part of my mind laid out a past incredible to little Cory
here in this life, another part said it was real and the way things
should be. They were playing openly with my mind, my emotions, and my knowledge and laughing about it to my face. I
was, quite literally, their toy, and finally I just cracked. I didn't
know what was real and what wasn't, and I never felt so
powerless, terrified, and confused in my whole life. I felt
insignificant, hardly human at all, and when I saw those big,

beautiful female bodies, the way they walked, talked, and took command, I knew that I could never attain their level. I envied them, yes, but I also loved them and wanted them.

Rita was right. I desperately wanted the security and sense of accomplishment that marriage would bring. I wanted to get married. I knew it wasn't that simple, but the white hair and bronze skin had given me an exotic look that had already gotten me noticed.

Rita set up the auditions, which were a series of dates, sometimes with one woman, sometimes with more, as it was quite common for women to live in small groups of anywhere from two to five. These were among the most bizarre experiences in any of my memories, at least on a personal level.

First, they scared me to death and excited me at the same time. I was bored, scared, and feeling totally defeated; this was at least a chance to rejoin the world, however limited it might be. Second, it was sometimes odd, because the dates would often be with at least one incarnate whom I'd known before in a past existence, and often none too favorably. A couple of them should have had scores to settle with me.

And, finally, some were just what they purported to be—dates. Evenings out to see a show or go to a good restaurant or shopping, and these dates didn't end in some kind of sexual encounter. Hell, I wanted them all to at least end that way, but not all of the women did.

In addition to people I didn't know who were clearly of this reality, I saw and went out with Jamie Cholder, whom I'd once shot dead in a past life; Sally Prine; Betty Harker, who'd lost a hyphenated name in this shift; Bernadette Standish; Dorothy Sloan—Dorothy Briggs here—whose husband I'd digitized into oblivion in the last world; Robin Garnett, who didn't look as much like a horse in this incarnation as in the last; and, last but not least, the inevitable and uncomfortable Danielle Tanaka, beautiful and glamorous as ever.

Standish was a big disappointment. With almost as incredible a face and form as Tanaka, if of a different ethnic background, she was nonetheless still the same dedicated fundamentalist fanatic she'd always been, and so probably the most frustrating and least fun date I could possibly imagine. After seeing her on TV in black garb next to Rita, I thought she was in the priesthood herself. It was a likely career choice, after all. She was, so she told me, not able to overcome her inner demons, which manifested themselves as vanity and lust, and until she felt she could control them utterly she would remain a "lay person," and, in fact, was Rita's secretary.

I was glad Tanaka arrived with two other women, Harker and Cholder, neither of whom had any real grudges against me that I knew of, because, alone, Dannie scared me to death. I used to think Dan was somewhat amusing, but I was getting a whole new respect for that mind now—cold as ice, brilliant in this bizarre business, with the morals and often the attitudes of a Josef Mengele.

It was odd, but the fact was, even though all of these familiar folks brought things back to me, they did nothing to bring my old confidence, my old self back. In fact, I have to admit that after the initial shock I nearly forgot who they'd been and who I'd been and became cute, sexy little Cory. I needed company that much. I suspect each one of them had been primed or prompted, knowingly or unknowingly, to "adjust" me that way. It didn't prevent me from knowing who they were or had been, but, somehow, once we were over the initial awkwardness, it didn't matter.

The one exception, of course, was Danielle Tanaka. There was no way in hell that I could marry *her*.

What was somewhat surprising was who wasn't there. Where were Lee and Al? I knew they were here, and much their usual selves, yet neither was in the group paraded past me, nor had I seen any trace of them since the initial encounter in Galveston. By the time I realized their absence, it was too late to work in questions to learn where they might be. Even more interesting was the absence in any form of Les Cohn. The good doctor was at least as long-memoried as Rita, maybe more so, and thus extremely powerful. For all his faults and evils, Les had been the only person I'd ever known to have the guts to not only thwart Al's fun at the height of his power but also hit the security man with a shovel and get away with it. Even as a male, and hence no medical doctor here, he should have had a harem of women carrying him around in a sedan chair and feeding him peeled grapes. For all I knew, that was going on right now. Les was always the most dangerous of the old crew because nobody was really certain just what he wanted or what he got out of it.

The woman I most wanted to see a second time was Sally Prine. I remembered Sally as a guy in the last life, as unreal as that seemed to me now, and as a good guy as well, even if he was working for the wrong side. I didn't know how he'd wound up dead, but maybe he'd just seen too much and had his fill of it or perhaps had seen too much to be allowed to keep going.

Sally wasn't the best protection against the others, since she was clearly at the same stage in this life that I'd been when I'd first discovered the truth back in Seattle. Still, in the back of her subconscious mind, I suspect she reacted to something she recognized in me from the old days. At least, we started keeping a lot of company together, and without much in the way of moral restraints.

Okay, this wasn't exactly like the kind of thing I'd have done in my previous lives for romance, nor was it a conventional kind of relationship as the old me would have thought of it, but it was a normal sort of relationship for here, and, thanks to Galveston, I knew how to pour on the charm.

Like just about all normal folks in this world, though, Sally didn't live alone. Since being found by the church working as an inventory control specialist in some automated factory in the Midwest, she'd been given a transfer to a division here, then slowly drawn into this group around Rita. Dorothy Briggs had gotten into some trouble with some of the locals in the area, and Sally took her in, welcoming the more experienced hand. Whether this was arranged by Rita or others wasn't known, but soon Dorothy and Sally were sharing a place not far from here, a two-bedroom condo in a nice area that had provided a welcome distancing from Rita Alvarez.

While she had a kind of classical beauty, Dorothy had always seemed to me to be reserved and somewhat distant, with the kind of personality you expected to find in a school principal or English teacher.

Although Sally and I did have fun, it was Dorothy who pushed for the three of us to join together, something that surprised me. After all, she was an incarnate, like me, and she had to at least suspect that I had something to do with her husband's disappearance. They'd been together in the two lives I'd known them, and that sort of suggested a kind of permanence, like Rick/Riki and me.

I did think of Riki, often. She had to have been reborn here, probably ignorant of this whole thing except for occasional dreams and odd memories. More than anything I would have loved to have seen her, to marry *her* in this world. We always made the best team. But with me stuck here, and her whereabouts unknown, it wasn't something that was practical. In this life, we'd have to be apart.

It appeared, though, that there wasn't the same degree of lingering love between Dorothy and Ben Sloan. I didn't get any details, but the impression was there, and Sally later admitted to me, "I think he was kind of rough on her, at least the last time. She almost seems more scared he's gonna show up than that he's gone."

For Dorothy, it apparently was my looks rather than who I was. The bronze complexion gave me a kind of racially ambivalent cast; I hadn't had it long enough to know for sure, and I hadn't been aware of anybody treating me as more than odd-looking for the brief period I stayed in downtown Austin before the chase, but I did see how I could sort of pass for almost any racial type, even a Polynesian or American Indian.

At any rate, my odd looks seemed to attract Dorothy and seemed irrelevant to Sally, so that was fine with me. Dorothy, on the other hand, still felt uncomfortable where they were living and wanted to move to a stand-alone home nearby, one with a private pool, wooded grounds, and privacy. The kind of place women in this society moved to only when they had a high income and were thinking of family.

I was pretty sure that the women incarnates, at least, were sterile, but it wouldn't stop either of them from finding a third or even a fourth who was a spook—what the Command Center crew called "people created by and in and of a particular plane" and unable to live outside of it—who could have spook kids by me.

I wasn't all that sure about that part, but keeping up a place that size would give me something to do and provide a degree of comfort as well.

Still, during this whole process, I continued to be interrogated now and then by Rita and Tanaka, and I began to get some information that seemed at odds with the way I saw the world these days.

For one thing, Rita had run into my mother at some function and was surprised to discover that she looked sort of Near Eastern Semitic—Lebanese, actually—and not anything like I was now. Rita should have known, and I thought the security staff would have it all laid out, that I hadn't looked like this until very recently. I mean, wouldn't the information that Al and Lee had used, and indeed their own reports, have described a different person?

The fact that everybody seemed to assume even now that I'd been born like this meant that either they had bad information, had used their powers to change reality without somehow changing me, or they simply didn't know.

But they *had* to know. They'd sent Al and Lee to get me! That had started this whole thing!

As we finalized arrangements for what I figured was going to be a lifetime, I asked Dorothy about the two former security bosses. She seemed quite surprised.

"Haven't seen them. I'd actually been looking forward to

seeing at least Al as a woman, with no previous knowledge of his past lives, but neither Al nor Lee has been tracked down yet. Why?"

"But I saw them! And they saw me! Chased me! That's why I ran from Galveston!"

She seemed very thoughtful all of a sudden. "Who else have you told this to?"

"Nobody. They never asked, so I don't think it ever came up."

"Well, don't. Swear to me—this is between us, okay? Promise now!"

I was off balance and a bit confused, but I nodded. "Okay. I promise."

I had to keep my promises. That was one of Rita's conditions.

Still, what the hell had all this been about? I mean, if Al and Lee were tracking down incarnates for the Command Center, then what was the big mystery?

It finally hit me, and I felt suddenly even more stupid and inadequate than before.

Al and Lee weren't working for the Command Center. They had tracked me down either for their own purposes or at somebody else's orders. Both had been reincarnations, so, without the CC Brand Box backup recordings, they had no real memories of the past and were operating on personality and habits they didn't know they had. They wouldn't have the slightest idea that people like the incarnates, the Command Center, or Brand Boxes even existed, nor would they believe it if they were told. Al and Lee, then, weren't working for themselves, and it wouldn't have served anybody else, even a potential power like Les, to have this kind of collection operation when there was no access to the main computer.

Somebody had been damned clever, that much was clear. Diabolical, and with an evil sense of humor. Cynthia, perhaps. It would be just like her. Just like her to find and recruit Al and Lee for her side. But because I had no way of being let in on the joke, instead of retrieving me, she'd only succeeded in panicking me into the hands of the enemy.

Yeah, it had to be Cynthia. It was the kind of dumb, impulsive thing she might very well pull.

And so I'd blown it completely here right from the start. I'd become beach bum, then run from the folks who would have taken me to the very people who could have protected me from Rita.

It was the last straw to any self-confidence, ego, or hope I had left.

The wedding took place on a Saturday in June. It hadn't been necessary for me to marry more than one of them, but they'd decided that they were comfortable doing it together. I had no idea what the generally white, working-class Prine and the African-American but highly educated, upper-middle-class Briggs had to bind one to another, but there it was. Both wore white, since even Dorothy had never been married in this world before, and I wore a custom-fitted boy's black formal, which included a fairly tight floor-length kilt and patent-leather boots. The ceremony was presided over by a beaming Archbishop Alvarez with a group of guests that was a rogue's gallery of incarnates. All the Elect who were at APL now or worked in the region were there, as well as two boys, neither of whom seemed familiar at the start. One of the boys had a fully gray beard and not much hair on top; the other had mushrooming black hair and a really drawn, pockmarked face.

The one who looked like an old geezer even though he clearly wasn't turned out to be a very small and emaciated Larry Santee; he looked embarrassed and didn't say much. The identity of the other one, with the drawn, pockmarked face and cartoon hair, still eluded me, but it was a striking look and the eyes seemed so very old.

We got to the heart of the ceremony, and I had accepted that this was certainly the best for me, that I'd already blown any chance to be an active participant in this cycle, when we got to the oaths. I kept forgetting about how Rita's treatment affected me on things like oaths. Up to now, I'd sort of gone through the ceremony with a mental fantasy that these two women were really Riki and Wilma, when the archbishop looked down at me and said, "Do you, Cory Andrew Kassemi, take these women as your wives, and do you by so doing swear to all these witnesses and Almighty God that you forsake all others forever, and will love, honor, and obey your wives absolutely and with full devotion and measure so long as you shall live?"

Sally and Dorothy weren't under any programmed commands, or at least I didn't think they were, but the moment I automatically responded, "I do," I felt a sudden and complete change come over me that I'd never experienced before. Any desire or thought of Riki or Wilma or anybody else completely fled, burned from my brain by a total, absolute, and worshipful love for these two women. I would do anything they asked of me, unquestioningly and without hesitation. I loved them, *worshiped* them; they were the only reason for my existence, the total center of my life and my being.

"Do you all swear that, having this union sanctified before God and these witnesses in Her holy Church, that you will at all times remain faithful and obedient to the Church and Her teachings, and accept the Mother of the World as the authority for your lives?"

"We do," we all responded, and I could somehow sense that this was as binding on the two of them as on me. I found it comforting, for this Church had no divorce and thus we would remain a family unit. With my newfound love and total commitment, I felt actually glad that this had worked out as it had, that I had found such love and union, and I knew that the Holy Mother who was God of All had somehow steered me to this.

I did not lose any knowledge; what I lost were my old allegiances, alliances, and orientations. My sense of unfairness about the world and its system was gone, too. I wasn't on the CC side or the backup side anymore; neither was I concerned with right or wrong. I was on the side of whatever my

wives committed to and believed in, and I totally accepted
their judgments.

At the reception after, we went down and were introduced
to the guests we didn't know, including the mysterious little
man with the exploding haircut.

"I am Allan Koril-Martinez," he said in a pleasant, unusually low voice. "I am the caretaker of the grounds here. My
wives, of course, work inside the laboratory, as yours do."

Even through my rapture and newfound sense of direction
and identity, I couldn't help but mentally skip a beat and take a
very deep breath.

This fellow, who basically mopped up the cathedral and
trimmed the bushes, almost certainly had once been Alice
Mary McKee, Ph.D., intellectual, scholar, and the founder of
this world. It wasn't very often you got to shake hands with
your local god, even if he was totally ignorant of the fact.

It went to show that revenge meant nothing in this system,
because the odds were you were going to come out on the
wrong end of your own perceived justice. I only hoped that he
felt as happy as I did at that moment, because once we went on,
I put him almost completely out of my mind.

After staying awhile, we snuck out the back, got out of the
formal dress and pulled on more comfortable clothing—just an
old kilt and T-shirt for me, shorts, shirts, and sandals for the
women. We went out the back door and into a waiting van.
Sally drove first, and Dorothy and I made use of the space in
the back and its pre-prepared mattress flooring. A while later,
driver and lover switched. I was going to like this, I thought on
that ride from Austin to Brownsville. We were heading along
the Mexican Gulf Coast to Cancún, and we didn't care how
long it took us to drive there.

By the time we reached the coast, I could hardly remember
who I was, nor did I care. I could hardly even remember my
name, which was, now and till death, Cory Prine-Briggs.

VI

THE MAD HATTER AND
THE MARCH HARE

After a couple of weeks of whirlwind fun for all of us, we headed back for Austin once again. My personality and feelings remained radically changed, and totally focused on my two wives. It was probably the cleverest thing Rita could have done, since it in no way affected my knowledge from the past or my long-term memories. I knew who I'd been, I could dredge up old memories, old experiences, and retrace most everything, but the operative word there is "could." I had no desire to do so, no interest in doing so, and absolutely no sense that any of it mattered. I didn't even think on or want the old system anymore; I liked this one just fine.

Whatever powers had been worked on me, they'd also been worked to a far lesser extent on Dorothy and Sally. Dorothy was in a third incarnation here and thus was no slouch at power herself, but Rita apparently went back much farther. With Al out of the way, she'd apparently been about the equal of the indecisive Lee and far more dedicated to control and command than he'd been.

Still, the lusty love I felt for my brides was in some ways reciprocated, and eagerly so, and I got the strong impression that two women had been drawn much closer by all this. All reserves were down when it was just the three of us, and we tended to use pet names reserved only for use by the family. For a lot of reasons, they both called me Doll; pretty good name for a girl-toy anyway. Dorothy was always Dorothy to everyone, but to us alone she was Dee, while Sally was just Sal.

Most of the summer and early fall was taken up with moving and resettling in the new place, which needed a lot of work. This was mostly my job; they, of course, went off to work every day at APL and the Command Center.

No male was permitted inside the gates of the APL, not even spouses. It was as sacrosanct as a women's locker room, and while I was always curious about it, not even my wives described much that went on inside it. Of course, I had an idea what the place looked like, certainly down on the lowest floors, but I admit I wanted to see how different it might be.

Sal was working as a programmer under Tanaka, that I knew, while Dee was in an administrative post with the official title of "scenarist." I got the impression that this involved developing, or overseeing a team that developed new alternative worlds for both Brand Box testing and for possible futures that would then be planted in various of the Elect via the Brand Boxes. Sometimes they took, even without the subjects knowing it, and when it was their turn to become god, the scenario often played out. It just never played out quite the way it was supposed to.

It was none of my business and I didn't press it much, but it was natural to be curious about and interested in what the wives were doing. Me, I ran the house, did the shopping using an electric-powered cart, kind of a giant powered tricycle with a hopper basket on the back for packages. I also picked up things in town for both Sal and Dee when they were too busy or too overloaded, riding the bus in and using one of those pull carts to carry stuff. I was a great judge of clothes and female adornments, it seemed, and if I bought them clothes they tended to look great and to fit perfectly.

What was interesting was that I never felt the least bit tempted to stray or cheat. I respected, liked, and felt most comfortable around women now, but none had the same kind of attraction for me that my wives did. I'm not sure how this manifested itself, but most women seemed to get the same impression, and after a while I found that they tended to feel comfortable around me. Almost all boys were out for only one thing. I wasn't. I also looked exotic and I knew it; heads always turned at the darkly complected boy with the silver hair and baby face. At least nobody who met me during this period ever forgot who I was or missed me a second time. I accented my hair by letting it grow long, doing a lot of styling and pampering, and using male cosmetics and jewelry to make it seem even more exotic, not necessarily to attract anybody but to complement what I felt were the two most gorgeous women in the world.

My whole mind-set remained at all times totally focused on Sal and Dee. Almost everything I did was couched in terms of whether or not they'd like it, not because I had to but because I wanted to.

Occasionally Dee and Sal would work different shifts. I had the idea that some big project was coming up but I didn't know what it was, and if they didn't want to tell me, it wasn't any of my concern, except to make sure that pressures of the job didn't translate to pressure at home.

One time when Dee was working the day shift and Sal nights, Dee arrived back home looking somewhat thoughtful and a little concerned.

"Doll, I been meaning to bring this up for a long time, but for some reason it kept slipping out of my mind," she began over a light supper.

I looked up at her, surprised. "Huh?"

"You remember you said that in this life you weren't always dark with that white hair? Was that true?"

"Sure, honey. I mean, I got turned into this."

"How? I want to know the whole story."

Well, of course, I launched into a detailed account of my hiding out, the side trip to the shaman's world, the face in the fire, the downloaded code, and how I'd awakened this way, possibly from the effects of whatever had been downloaded into my brain.

"You ever have a sense of what's there?" she asked me.

I shook my head. "No sense at all, love. I mean, no dreams, no funny images, none of that. No long strings of numbers or crazy formulas, either. It's like nothing's there."

"But it is?"

I shrugged. "The reverend mother thinks so. She has forbidden me or anyone to act on it, so that is that, I would guess."

Dee looked at me with those big brown eyes. "She didn't forbid me," she responded softly, and I was locked in her gaze. This wasn't like the fear of the power I'd had before being married. I mean, this was Dee. I'd *die* for Dee.

The thing is, I don't remember what happened for a while after that, and I think I know why. If Dee was going to set aside some of Rita's programming so that I wouldn't resist, she had to do some fancy work around the codes, and I couldn't consciously know anything about it or I might betray it. In fact, I barely remembered the beginning of the conversation. It was as if I looked into those eyes, and then there was a weird jump, and we were sitting slightly differently and things moved a bit on the table, all in an instant. I didn't even think further on it, but I did see on Dee's face that she wasn't entirely happy. She hadn't been able to get to the stuff, either.

"Doll, I want you to swear to me that you'll never tell *anybody*, not even Sal, that we *ever* talked about this, okay?"

"Of course I swear!" Hell, I'd sworn to obey, and I'd do that for either of them.

She paused a little more. "Doll—do you know where Ben Sloan is? I mean now? What happened to him?"

The question took me off guard, yet I'd been expecting it since the first time I'd met Dee in this life. "Yes, honey. I do."

"What happened?"

Again, there was no way I was going to hold back and I had total trust in her, so I told her about how Ben had been digitized and sent into the Brand Box Al had prepared for me. As far as I knew, he was still there.

She seemed astonished. "Digitized? *All* of him? Without a body in an LSM?"

"Didn't need it. I didn't know it was possible myself, but I saw it happen. I know where he went, too, 'cause I'd just come from there. It was kind of like his whole body went to wireframe, then broke up into these tiny dots and was just, well, sucked into the Brand Box." I paused. "Do you miss him? I mean, it wasn't something we did deliberately. It just kind of happened."

"Oh, calm down! I'm not blaming you! He wan't the world's easiest man to live with, let me tell you, but I was kind of used to him. I would like to see him in this kind of setup, too, still a man. But how would you get him out of there in one piece?"

"Going in didn't seem impossible, if you were firmly anchored here both in your own physical body and in your mental connection. That's not to say I could do it, but it probably can be done if you have the kind of power that was around that night and somebody had both the will and self-control to use it. But it wouldn't be Ben who came out. It would be a clone of a chubby little sterile female, like I was last time, white and bald. I'm pretty sure if you get completely digitized you don't go through incarnation or reincarnation. I don't know why I think that, but I do."

She seemed lost in thought. "I wonder . . . I wonder how much of a change you could make with this digitizing stuff . . ."

I had no answer to that. Only two people that we knew of had gone that route, and they were Matthew Brand and Ben Sloan. They hadn't come back. Wilma and I had done it the other way, but had emerged initially in the forms in which we'd been stuck in the boxes.

"I don't know what really *is* possible with all that power," I told Dee honestly. "I don't think I want to know. I'm happy with you and Sal right here."

She smiled sweetly. "I know you are, but, as always, events have a way of taking over. It was always Al's dream to bring the Command Center up to full power and lock it there, flowing into us, slowly growing until it underlined the whole world. Enough power and the entire master computer data bank to draw on, that was the dream. Anybody who could draw on it, and that would include the likes of us, would be able to literally be a god, and whoever had seniority in lives would be the ruler of the gods. Then you could make any world you wanted. You'd be immortal, sitting on Olympus, worshiped by the masses. Rita has something of that same dream. She thinks of it in Church terms and calls it the "second coming incarnate." It would be different than Al's dream, but the same idea. But to do it, you have to bring up the power to full and leave it there, stabilized, while everything connects and everyone is brought online. That's what they are going to try to do, in slow stages, soon. Bring up the power."

"You're scaring me again," I told her honestly. "Why does she need to be a goddess? I mean, this world and her place in it isn't so bad as it is, is it?"

She laughed softly. "Don't worry, little one. I don't go back far enough, but ten times Al tried it and ten times he couldn't make it work. Others surely have tried as well. The real question isn't whether she will realize her dream, but whether or not she will destroy some of us while trying and possibly force us *all* into reincarnation." She lapsed into silence, and I didn't know what to say to her.

Finally she gave a chuckle. "Ben in the body of a bald white girl! Might be almost as much fun as seeing him the other way . . ."

I didn't like the idea of a power-up any more than I liked the motives for it. Something bad always happened when they powered up, something bad for me, for everybody. What would all that power do to Rita's cutting me off from it? Would I know when there was a power-up or would it make me dizzy or sick or even kill me?

I guess I got too worried, because both Dee and Sal grew concerned about my moping. Finally, they took me aside and told me not to be concerned, that they knew what was going on and that they wouldn't let this get out of hand. I wasn't to worry anymore.

It didn't keep me from worrying, even if I was supposed to obey, but it did calm me down a little. I mean, it wasn't as if somebody like me could do anything about it.

It was clear something else was up, though. We started having dinner guests on a more regular basis, almost all folks who worked at the Command Center. Casually, carefully, they wound up pumping me for details of what it felt like to be an active mind in wireframe mode, the energy stream, the details of how to control it. They also wanted information on my Brand Box—that is, the one Al had created for me. It was pretty clear that they were going to try to get Ben out, although I wasn't at all sure they could do it. I mean, even if they knew the method, could they even find him, after all these years, in a society where there was no individuality at all and everybody looked, spoke, and acted the same?

There were also dangers in the operation itself. Could they contain that box and its programs if they did a blind extraction? How could they tell who was who and what was what? Didn't they risk turning others into just more of those folks? I definitely didn't want to be one of them anymore. I hadn't liked living that way before and I sure didn't now. I liked being a boy in this world married to two wonderful women. I didn't want it to change.

Of course, like everything else in this woman-run world, I didn't have much say in that.

I did, however, try to find out what the hell was going on by pressing Sal, a reincarnate with very little of the sense that

longer continuous consciousness brings. Not that I could use
any power, but she really couldn't just order me to forget it,
either. She was just not Machiavellian; she thought fairly
straightforwardly and never looked too deeply at people or
events. While this wasn't always a virtue, it did help her stay
alive and out of Brand Box hell, and it gave me at least one
source from which to learn what was going on.

"They're gonna try'n bring up this power grid in the basement," Sal confirmed. "They say that it's been tried and tried
and never worked, but that they're gonna take whatever time is
needed to learn how to control it. I'm not real sure what the
results will be, but I've been running some routines for Dannie
and they don't make any sense at all."

"What do you mean?"

She shrugged. "Well, it's hard to explain if you never been
there."

"I've been there. Not in this life, but I know what's what."

She looked at me funny. "Yeah, I keep forgettin'. Sorry, it's
just kinda weird thinkin' of a boy doin' my kind of work."

"Well, men and women were different in that life. That's
okay. I know what a Brand Box is. I just want to know what
they're doing. I never could figure out this power-up business
when they tried it before."

She sighed. "Well, I don't understand it, either, really, but I
get the idea that it's kinda like, well, like bein' in a Brand Box,
only you don't need the box and you're connected direct to the
control program of the main computer, the godlike thing that
built all this, I guess. I don't know much more. My access is
limited and I'm working around the edges of this. I mean, it
took me two years to get used to that whole system of programming and to learn the language, and I'm just fair at
working with the Brand Box stuff. Nothin' like this scale. I
took a look at some of the math and circuitry and it looked like
a giant bowl of spaghetti exploded in a math lab. And I'm
pretty good at this!"

I smiled. "I know how you feel. Don't feel too bad, honey. I was really good at it once myself, and the more I got sucked into it, the less I found out I actually knew. I'm glad I'm out of that. I just am tryin' to figure out what becomes of us, of me and you and Dee."

She shook her head. "I'm not sure. There's a bunch of folks who aren't too happy about all this, but they just got to go along, that's all. Some, like Dannie, don't even seem to care who's God, so long as they can make this work. She's a weird one. Absolutely a genius, way beyond the rest of us, but with that body, those looks—and all she does for kicks is vanish into her own Brand Box for a little bit. Never really goes out or has anybody she cares about—boys, girls, horses, you name it. She lives, eats, sleeps, and breathes this stuff. What a waste. If I had her looks . . ."

"You're plenty gorgeous enough for me," I told her sincerely. "I assume the Reverend Mother Alvarez will be at the center of this connection?"

"I guess. She's in the middle now, but they haven't gone that far with me. I only get what I overhear and what Dee tells me. They say that whoever gets connected like this will really be a god, at least as far as we're concerned. Absolute power, and absolute rule, forever. It's kinda scary to think that any one person who was born like me can get that kind of power, but I guess it's better to be a holy woman, huh?"

That was not a pleasant thought. As much as I loved what I was doing and the way I was, my opinions of Rita Alvarez hadn't changed one bit. That was odd, too. She could have easily made me have nothing but worshipful respect for her, but she hadn't. Not that I didn't follow the Church, but I understood that being ordained didn't remove the risk of your going to Hell, and I sure knew Rita.

At least now I knew what they'd been working at all that time. Godhead. Al had lost his bid, and maybe Rita would, too, but I could see the attraction, the reach for absolute power. No wonder Rita didn't want me anywhere near a Brand Box with what might or might not be in my head. She'd have killed me just to wipe it away—if she could be sure that it would be erased that way. In the meantime, it was safer to have me thoroughly domesticated and under total control than to let me roam free, even in a new life.

Well, since my only worry was that it might end, I felt little more than natural curiosity. I didn't like the idea of Rita fooling with this, but I did have a sort of gut feeling that, if Al and that crew with all their experience hadn't been able to manage and tame that kind of energy, Rita, who was no computer whiz at all, wasn't going to have any more success, especially with a much less experienced crew. Still, you never know what might come out of it, and for the most part, power-ups hadn't been followed by wonderful things in the past.

I belonged to a suburban Boys' Club. There were many such clubs all over, and I guess just about every guy belonged to one. It was the one place where no girls were allowed, everything was at an appropriate scale, and the boys there were all pretty much in the same kind of lifestyle. It wasn't a big deal. Play some poker or pool, sit around and brag or complain, that kind of thing. I used to go down for a while every Wednesday afternoon, even though I didn't find other boys' company all that big a deal. None of us were really friends, or competitors, and I think we found each other pretty dull overall, but it was sort of expected, and there were occasionally some good practical ideas and tips shared.

It wasn't long after I'd had the discussion about the power-up with Sal that I went down to the club and noticed a new boy there. That really wasn't so odd; what was odd was that nobody else seemed to notice him.

He was about four foot six, and had a pot belly, gray hair with a bald spot in the center, and this oversized droopy gray mustache that made him look like an elderly Yosemite Sam. And while boys generally didn't smoke, he was in the smoking lounge with a couple of others puffing on a big, fat stogie. I would have recognized him anywhere, and he was just the person I didn't want to see at this point in my life. The fact that he'd show his face so close to the Command Center, and Rita, right out in the open, meant something, too.

There was no avoiding the confrontation, so I figured I might as well get it over with.

"Hello, kid," he grumbled, even retaining some of that New York gruffness in his voice and tone. "Have a seat," he invited, gesturing to a chair. "And don't look so much like a deer caught in the headlights. I'm not going to bite you. I just want to talk."

"I don't want any part of this, Walt," I told him right off. "I'm happy where I'm at. I'm not in the war this time."

He chuckled. "Sure you are! We *all* are. It's just that, thanks to Rita and some foolishness on everybody's part, we're on opposite sides for the moment. You keep underestimating me, old buddy. Everybody does. It's one of my most valuable survival traits."

I didn't know what to say. "What do you want, Walt?"

He shrugged. "I want to win, of course. I want to be able to take whatever's been put into your head, stick it in a Command Center Brand Box, and find out what happens. Rita wants to be a goddess of the virtual universe and doesn't give a damn about much else, you or me included. And you should get this part straight: either I win or nobody wins. Rita's goal isn't a realistic option. If she ever actually achieved the level of power and had the interface exactly right, it *still* wouldn't work, because she hasn't developed the kind of control over the power that's needed. Al almost had it, but Al's problem was that he wasn't really an engineer at heart. He didn't have that kind of mind-set. I do, and the only one who could have been my equal was Al. That's why they never attacked the backup center even though they knew where it was after that first time. That's why I had the guts to attack *him*. Standoff both times, although I did get really close that one time while you were drawing Al's undivided attention. Now? Well, we'll see."

"You're talking pretty big for a little guy in a world like this," I pointed out.

He shrugged. "I been in worse than this. So have you, you just don't remember. This is actually pretty handy, overall. Nobody expects the boy to have any power here, or have complex knowledge and skills. This built-in dyslexia was a bit of a pain, but I overcame it. Willpower—other kinds of power, too—all work together. I'm the only one around that's been going for the endgame since Matthew Brand digitized himself into oblivion."

I shook my head and sighed. "Look, Walt, all that was a different me than I am now. I don't even try and follow this. Whatever happens, it's out of my hands."

"I know what's been done to you and that you really believe it, son," Walt responded. "Too bad we can't just do it ourselves. But this caterpillar talks only to you, and we don't know who or what it is except that it's helped you. And even though Wilma could get to that shaman's world, whatever it is, and even speak with whatever was there, this Pillar of Fire contact never reached out to her. Only to you. You got to face it, boy. Somebody else, maybe several somebodies for all we know, has put you in play. I just wanted you to know that we know about as much as you and your side, and that we're here. You won't tell Rita about this. You won't tell anybody. You'll find that our conversation, this meeting, totally slips your mind whenever you want to talk about it to others." He got up to go.

"That's it?" I said, amazed. "No pep talk, no attempt at spiriting me away?"

He laughed. "Why would we want to do that? Hell, son, we want you right where you are." With that he walked out of the room and out the door, again with nobody apparently noticing that he had even been there. I don't know why, but I followed him for just a little bit, past the desk and outside, where I saw him get into a big four-wheel-drive vehicle and shut the door. There were three women inside, and all were damned good-looking. My eyes weren't the greatest of late, but I knew who they were. Wilma was the dark one with the headband; the brown-skinned one was the mysterious Mabel; and the driver, in an outrageously revealing outfit and smoking a cigarette at the end of a very long holder, was Cynthia Matalon.

Walt looked back from inside at me and grinned. Not one of the three women gave me so much as a glance.

Now I was worried, and I think that was the point of the encounter. Walt was demonstrating to me that he had his finger, as usual, on just about everything, that he had the motive, method, and opportunity, and that I was dead meat.

I was just about to call it an afternoon and go home, not being in the mood to do much else, when I noticed a slick black sedan pull out and move in behind Walt's car, maybe half a block behind. I couldn't make out who was in it, but it very well could have been Harker or somebody else working security. Clearly Walt was being watched. Whether or not he knew it was a different story. Whether or not he cared was even more of a question.

The light changed and the two vehicles moved out. Out from a side street pulled a white car that looked other- wise identical to the security car following Walt. I only got a brief glimpse of the pair inside that one, but I could swear that one of them was Lee, in which case the other one was probably Al.

This was getting *crazy*, and fast.

Was Walt pulling a fast one on Rita's people, or was there still a component I was missing here?

I needed help bad. Fortunately, I wasn't alone in this and the others I could go to for help were soon coming home for dinner.

I headed home, trying to figure out what I could do to keep out of this and finding nothing at all. As long as that crap was in my head, they'd be after me—Walt and his crew to stick me in a Brand Box, Rita and her crew to keep me out of one. Why the hell did it have to be me, anyway? Why did I have to be the one who went to that damned shaman's land?

Dee was already home by the time I got there, and I was very happy to see her. The trouble was, other than the usual reasons, I couldn't think of why I was so glad to see her, so I started dinner. She helped, and by the time Sal got in, we were all ready to eat.

I kept thinking that there was something, something important, that I had to talk over with one or both of them, but for the life of me I couldn't remember what, and, after a while, I promptly forgot it.

Dee had to go back to the APL that evening, but Sal and I cleaned up and then had a little fun until bedtime. By that time I didn't have any idea of what was bugging me, and managed to go to sleep almost immediately.

The funny thing was, my dreams remembered for me.

There was a great woods, and a path through it, and just inside the forest there was this enormous oak, its lowest branch looking like the arm of some fantastic creature out to snare the unwary. At the oak, the path split into two forks going off at right angles to one another. But it was not the branch that drew my attention so much as who, or rather what, was on it.

The Cheshire Cat grinned when it saw me. It looked good-natured enough, even a bit silly, but it had very long claws and a great many teeth, which commanded some respect.

"Cheshire Puss," I called to it, rather timidly, worried that it might not like the name, but when it grinned a bit wider I felt bolder. "Can you tell me, please, which way I ought to walk from here?"

"That depends a very great deal on where you want to get to," it responded, in a voice that sounded a lot like Groucho Marx's.

"But I don't want to get anywhere. I'm being pushed into going, but I don't really care to go anyplace I'm being pushed."

"Then it really doesn't matter which path you take," the Cat

replied. "Or, of course, if you truly don't wish to go anywhere, you could simply remain where you are."

"I can't remain where I am," I told it. "I've been trying to do just that and all I do is move."

"Then you might as well move anywhere. It'll get you somewhere, after all."

"Can you tell me, then, where these paths lead?"

The Cat thought a moment. "The one on the left goes to the March Hare. He's mad, you know."

"Yes, I believe I've had the pleasure. And the other?"

"To the Hatter. He's mad, too."

I was taken aback. "Must I only travel toward mad people?"

"We're all mad, you see. I'm mad, you're mad, we're all of us quite insane. Who wouldn't be, after all this time doing this crap?"

"Why do you think I'm mad?" I demanded to know, a bit angry at the accusation.

"Why, of course you're mad. If you weren't mad, you wouldn't be here," the Cheshire Cat pointed out. "Well," he said, sighing, "I must be going. I mean to say I cannot stay, I must be going." He began to sing it as a song, and as he did he began to vanish, starting with the tail and going all the way up to the head, until there was nothing left of him but his smile. Suddenly, the whole head became visible again, and he sang, "I'll stay a week or two! I'll stay the summer through! But, I must be going . . ." And, with that, he faded from sight.

I was having a tough time finding much to argue with in the cat's logic, though. Like the Cat, I had to be going, and if the path to the left went to the March Hare—well, I already knew who that was. Even the Mad Hatter was better than Walt.

I remember taking the right path this time, and heading through the dense woods, eventually emerging at a Tudor house made of gingerbread with a straw roof that looked like it had been designed by a madman, and with a giant top hat for a chimney.

The Mad Hatter emerged, wearing the tall hat—the tag stating size and price visible—the green almost leprechaunish suit, boots, and a rather aristocratic air for a mere tradesman.

He was, of course, carrying a pot of tea and quite a tall stack of cups and saucers in the other hand, struggling not to trip or drop them as he made his way toward a picnic table in his front yard.

He suddenly spotted me and stumbled, and the cups went up in the air, as did the big pot of tea. As they all came down, the pot miraculously appeared to fill each cup, which then landed, one at a time, in saucer, in the Hatter's hand. He flicked each in turn onto the table without spilling a drop. It was such an amazing performance I felt the urge to clap as the last one was expertly placed. He seemed so pleased at this that he turned, took a bow, and got conked on the head by the teapot.

I rushed to help him up, and got him unsteadily to a chair. He held his oversized head in his hands for a few moments, then looked up at me and said, "Well, I hope you're satisfied."

"Huh? Me? What did I do?"

"Caused all that, of course, do you deny it? First you show up here, unannounced, uninvited, and as a result you startle me, and then you distract me when I am recovering from the startle. Oh, my! I need a spot of tea." He leaped up and rushed back into the house. "Back with some in a jiffy!"

I walked over and looked at the half-dozen still-hot cups of tea he'd placed on the table. I picked up one to drink, realized I had no sugar, and reached over to the sugar bowl to get some.

The top of the sugar bowl popped off and the head of a very small creature poked out, then rose to its full height of perhaps six inches. It was a curious creature—fur and tail and feet like a rodent's, but dressed in a nineteenth-century waistcoat complete with tiny pocket watch—and yet the face, the face was very familiar . . .

It was my face. And then it opened its mouth, and in a tiny, slightly inebriated parody of my own voice, it recited:

    "Twinkle, twinkle, little bat.
    How I wonder what you're at?
    Up above the world you fly
    Like a tea tray in the sky."

"Poor devil. Been like that for some time," the Hatter commented just behind me. He was back now and drinking from an enormous teacup.

"What happened to him?" I asked, uneasy at the sight of myself this way.

"Decided he was too little and too defenseless to do much of anything, and wound up getting his mind zapped by everybody as a result. To him, it's always six o'clock and the world's a dizzy place he wants no part of, so he hunkers in the sugar bowl and stays on a permanent sugar high. Sleeps a lot. Utterly useless."

I was getting the point. "But—if he's the Dormouse, then who am I?"

"Beats me. You just showed up here uninvited and unannounced, remember?"

I cleared my throat, a bit embarrassed. "Um, yes. But, you see, I had to come somewhere, and here was where somewhere turned out to be."

"But you also could go anywhere else and still be somewhere," the Hatter pointed out. "You should consider the lessons you should have learned from this experience. Everyone's a walrus, you know, or a carpenter—or an oyster. You look ruddy well like an oyster to me right now. First one that ever wanted to be eaten."

"I don't want to be eaten!"

"Could have fooled me. Tell you what I'm gonna do," he went on, going from a mild, kind of cartoonish Cockney accent to that of a carnival barker. "I'm gonna make you an offah! I'm gonna give you not three, not two, but at least one big chance! For a limited time only, when you feel that powah surge through body, mind, and soul, you'll be free. Just that

once, you'll be free. You can run, you can pick a side, you can do anything ya want t'do! But—that's it. You're also free to crawl back into yer shell and pull down the lid and do nothin', *nothin' but hope no hungry walrus or carpenter comes along with a good shucking knife . . ."*

I woke up in a cold sweat. It was daylight, and Sal was already up and had apparently gone. There was no sign at all of Dee. It was an eerie, empty house, and I remembered just what I wanted to talk over with them.

Trouble was, I knew I'd forget again if I ever tried to actually talk it over.

The Mad Hatter had put it right on the line. I was absolutely alone on this one, and that was just exactly where I didn't want to be.

I didn't know if the dream had been anything more than a dream or not. The *Alice in Wonderland* imagery was growing pretty old by this point, but did I remember it in that kind of detail? When had I read *Alice*? As a kid, sure, but which childhood? I might have read it in the last life, being cooped up like I was; I sure didn't remember reading it earlier, although *Alice* was a theme even then. Damn Matthew Brand! Why the hell all these nonsense symbols?

Dee was dead tired when she got home, and I discovered what she'd been doing on her own, in addition to what they were preparing down there. I wasn't sure I liked it—not that I could do or say much about it.

Dee—with the aid of Sal, who could tell Dee what questions to ask and where to look—had been trying to determine if, and if so how, you could remove a totally digitized person from a Brand Box. I was pretty sure she wasn't going fishing for Matt Brand.

"Does Ben really mean that much to you?" I asked her, a bit hurt.

She smiled and squeezed my hand. "Don't worry—I'm not

looking for replacements. It's kind of hard to explain. For a long time, we were the only two African-Americans on the whole project. Most black folk don't like or trust computers. Too long being on the receiving end of Big Brother's tender mercies, you might say. We stuck together. I'm not sure we were ever in love, and, Lord knows, he wasn't very good in bed, but he was a friend and partner. I can't let him rot if there's a way to bring him out, and I'm pretty sure he'd do the same for me."

"But if it's like it was with me, he won't come out recognizable. And I remember Wilma, after her time in that horrible place, coming out a vegetable. If he comes out, there may be nothing mentally left. No memories, nothing. Just a clone of what I was just before incarnating here."

"Lots of things can mess up memories," she told me. "Blows to the head, diseases, you name it. Brand Box recordings can restore a measure of things, and when we translate again, it'll be there."

"If we translate again," I pointed out. "I didn't think that was the object of the exercise."

She smiled. "Only Dannie and Rita seem to believe it's possible, as far as we know now. We'll see." She sighed. "When we try the first power-up experiments, there may be sufficient energy for us to attempt our own retrieval program. Maybe. I have to try. They worked on this problem a lot, it seems, several lifetimes ago, when Brand vanished into that Box of his. There was a ton of stuff, a lot more advanced than we could ever work out and a lot more complicated than we could even follow, but clearly aimed at only one thing. The difference was, they never really used it. They couldn't locate Brand specifically, if it's possible to locate him, and they didn't want to feed it through the entire energy grid. None of us really understands that, you see, and we have no idea what it will do."

I stared at her. "Then you've found Ben using the VR helmet interface?"

She seemed startled that I could use these terms so easily, but the more she discussed this, the more my knowledge came back.

"It was quite a job rebuilding it," she said with a trace of irony in her voice. "Seems somebody really fried the circuitry. Yes, I've been in there, and no, as of now, I can't tell one of those people from the other. You know, though, it's extremely peaceful in there and the society works rather well. Not a single thing that pollutes all our existences really creeps in there. There's no racism, no sexism, no envy, no jealousy—it's quite amazing. I never had that sense of total *belonging* before. It's quite seductive."

"Just don't think of going there to live," I responded, a little bit alarmed. "I don't want to lose you in there."

She smiled. "But you're in there, too, of course. All of them are based on a version, or vision, of you. Perhaps that's why it's so comfortable. Poor Ben. It must have driven him insane."

I wasn't all too thrilled with extracting an insane Ben Sloan in one of my images, but I wasn't too thrilled about any of this. "Does Madam Tanaka know of your intention to do this?"

"I think she's been so wrapped up in this project, she probably hasn't even noticed. Why?"

"I was just wondering if running your program while the power was completely up, while they were running their experiments, might not cause some unexpected results, that's all. I don't feel good about this at all."

"Don't you worry any about this, Doll. We know what we're doing, and it's a lot less ambitious than what they are doing."

I was still worried, because I wasn't sure that anybody in this mess really knew what they were doing. Al had been startled to see the little alien creatures; nobody figured that you could broadcast a spook through phone lines right into the main computer center; nobody figured you could change minds and bodies until they did it.

Nobody knew anything, really.

Three days later, they began the power-up. Neither Sal nor Dee told me, but I knew by their general nervousness and by the fact that they were working double shifts and staying down at the Command Center. Dee at least knew what it was like; for Sal, this was going to either wake up her residual memory or be a whole new, unique, and not necessarily positive experience.

There was nothing I could do or say to make them not go. They were confident and determined, and I loved them at least for that. I even admired, to an extent, Dee's sense of loyalty to Ben. Still, I knew that crunch time was coming. Not right away—they wouldn't be bringing up power levels and holding them tonight, or for several more nights, but it certainly was starting.

So, was the Mad Hatter real? The March Hare had been, and he was most certainly mad. If the Hatter was real, I would have one chance during this period to make a decision. One chance only, without being hindered by Rita's spells or my specific current personality.

I knew what they wanted me to do. I also knew that what I wanted to do was crawl into a shell, but I was too obvious, the oyster on top of the pile. If I got into that shell and buried my head, I was sure enough gonna get shucked by all sides.

What the hell *did* I want, anyway? I didn't want Rita to win, certainly, and I really didn't want Walt to win, either. I didn't want to lose my wives and my security, but how could I keep that without somebody winning?

That evening, for the first time since waking up in the Mission and going down to face Rita, I felt the power again. I was actually lying down in a sofa chair, listening to some music and more asleep than awake when it hit. It made me dizzy, nauseated, and caused a fair amount of pain, but as it went on the discomfort seemed to lessen, almost as if I were getting used to it. Then it was gone, and things were back the way they had been.

Shaken, I'd gone into the bar and looked for something

strong. I found some Wild Turkey, 100-proof bourbon, poured some in a glass, and drank it down. It tasted good, but it burned. I poured some more, this time adding a couple of cubes of ice, swirled it around, and drank it down.

It didn't take long for it to hit me. It felt kind of like the first power-up; I was dizzy, certainly, and a bit sour in the stomach, but there was no pain and no nausea. In fact, I felt really kind of good, silly even, and very turned on. I slipped out of my clothes and went around turning the lights out. I don't know why I did it; I'm not at all sure if I was thinking at all. Soon the only light was the little one over the bar, and I went over and poured another drink. I took it with me, turning out that last light, leaving myself in total darkness. It was no big deal; I knew the layout of the house better than I knew the back of my hand.

The music was still playing, and I did a little dance, humming along with the music as I went out the patio door and onto the deck in back of the house, stark naked. It was dark and hot, and the air felt very still and heavy, like a blanket of velvet caressing me.

The power-up sensation hit again, but this time it only partly penetrated. I looked off to the south and east of the house and saw the greenish glow on the horizon. Then, suddenly, I looked down at myself and I could see that I, too, was outlined by a very dim aura of the same greenish energy. I wondered idly if anybody could see me glowing in the dark like this, but I didn't wonder long.

"Twinkle, twinkle, little bat! How I wonder what you're at!" I recited to the darkness, giggling. God! I couldn't believe how turned on I felt! If either of the girls came home now, they might not survive me! I wanted them, both of them, and I wanted them bad. I stared at the greenish glow and got drunk-enly pissed off at it. They were over *there*, I thought. Over in that glow instead of back here with their husband who needed them so badly.

Along with love and hate, and all the primal emotions, lust was one of the most powerful. Wasn't that why vampires were always so sexy? If I were a vampire, I'd fly to that green glow and I'd find 'em and do 'em all!

The glow winked out again, and I almost collapsed in the darkness. I was feeling no pain now, but I couldn't find the rest of my drink. I fumbled around, searching for it, oblivious to anything else. I finally gave up and sat down on a chaise lounge, looking around at the darkness. The lights burned in some other houses not too far away, and I could hear the distant sound of traffic.

Gawd! Was I horny! I wanted Dee and Sal and I wanted them here and now, and my growing frustration made me feel like some kind of weak-kneed nothing, and instead of reinforcing my own sense of low esteem, that made me mad.

The glow returned. I stood up and faced it and, with the aid of the booze, let it consume my attention and interest, my desires and my fury. And, in the darkness between the Command Center and where I stood, images seemed to form, images taking their form from inside my own mind.

The Dodo had fallen into a small gully, really only a few feet deep and not much over his stupid-looking head. With a little bit of effort, he could have jumped and grabbed the side and pulled himself out, but this appeared to be the farthest thing from his rather tiny little mind.

"I say, old chap!" he called to me. "Could you toss me down a shovel?"

"A shovel?" I laughed, calling to him, as ghostly as he was, a pale drawing in glowing green. "What on earth do you need a shovel for?"

"I've fallen in, can't you see? So the only logical thing for me to do is to have you or someone toss me a shovel so I can dig my way out."

"You can't dig your way out! You're going in the wrong direction!"

The Dodo drew itself up to full height and looked haughtily back at me. "Sir, I may be a Dodo, but I am more than willing to accept that the Earth is round. Is that not true?"

"Yes, but—"

"Well, sir, it should be obvious, then, that if I dig down, then, sooner or later, I shall emerge in China, and everyone knows that it's quite a bit easier to go down than to labor to go upward. Otherwise why do so many go so easily to Hell and so few, with great difficulty, to Heaven? Now, sir, the shovel? There's lots of digging to do, you know. If we do not dig together, we shall get nowhere at all!"

The vision faded even as I laughed and called to the poor, dumb bird.

Suddenly I had the terrific sense that I'd just discovered something important, something maybe even vital, profound. But it was probably just the booze, I told myself. It was just the booze . . .

VII

PUNT AND
FREE KICK

They ran the power on and off all that night, and I had some weird dreams and even out-of-body type experiences. I was as drunk as a skunk, but the energy was exciting odd parts of my mind that I usually kept under tight control—even some that I didn't know were there.

I also had strange sexual fantasies that I never was sure afterward were only in my imagination: very weird, kinky stuff with anonymous women who kept showing up at the front door begging to have sex with me. The fantasies were punctuated by bizarre visions, animations like that of the Dodo and snippets of scenes from lives I could not remember. I certainly passed out into the deepest stupor I had ever experienced, and coming out of it, like a swimmer rising from the bottom of a pool, desperate for a gulp of air, I had one last vision different from the rest, and therefore seeming much more real.

Dan Tanaka, looking a bit older, paunchier, and grayer than I'd ever seen him, was sitting at a computer bank along with most of the rest of us, all recognizable in spite of obvious physical differences.

"Damn it, Dan, we *have* to use this! If Matt remains trapped

in there, fully digitized, for any length of time, he may wind up
being untraceable! We'll lose him!" Les Cohn was arguing.

"The doc's right. We got to get him out of there!" Walt sec-
onded, his mere presence at such a gathering showing that
whatever rupture had come, it had come after Matthew Brand
had been fully absorbed by his own creation.

Several others nodded and agreed. Sally Prine, Jamie
Cholder, the other programmers who'd worked on the retrieval
system without break since Brand vanished were particularly
adamant.

Tanaka sighed and tapped something into his console, then
looked back at them. "I'll short out the box and destroy it
before I'd allow you inside with what you've got."

"Why? Why are you doing this?" Rick demanded to know.

"Because I've run full analysis of the subroutines you've
come up with. Over forty billion combinations of practical
approach routes and patch points come up, and in not a single
one do we get him back as we need him, if we can retrieve him
at all. In about a third of the scenarios projected, grave harm is
done not just to the Brand Box he's in but also to the Command Center core systems. It would be meltdown—out of control. A practically zero chance of success coupled with a
one-in-three chance of crashing the core program—that's
death for us. All of us. And everybody else in the whole damn
world. I can't allow that. Not even for Matt, and he was my
friend. Perhaps the only real friend I've had in years."

I woke up wide-eyed, terrified, drenched in sweat, and with
a hangover pounding in my head. Worse, I was on the chaise
lounge on the deck and still stark naked. We did have a measure of privacy on the deck, but it wasn't absolute. How long
had I been here?

Enduring pain like I hadn't felt in living memory, I managed somehow to ease off the chaise, only to find standing
impossible. I crawled on all fours over to the door and hauled
myself inside.

I'd been a *baaad* boy.

I tried standing again, but the room kept spinning and my vision doubled and jumped alarmingly. I shut my eyes and it helped a little, but it still felt as if I were walking on a moving ship in a storm.

Taking my bearings by opening one eye for a brief moment and hugging the wall, furniture, and appliances, I managed to make it back toward the bathroom. I got there and had started looking through the medicine cabinet when the sins of the previous night came rushing back and I threw it all up in the toilet.

That actually made me feel better, although it left a godawful smell and an even worse taste in my mouth. My head still throbbed, though, and I looked again through the cabinet and found the leftovers of an old prescription painkiller. It was Sal's, for when she'd wrenched her back. I took one, and even though it was huge, I got it down with water. I then struggled back down the hall to the bedroom, where I collapsed on the big bed and lay there on my back staring at the ceiling.

After about ten or fifteen minutes, the pain began to recede. I decided maybe I could get up, and made the attempt. Whatever that stuff was, it sure was strong. No wonder it had done the job for Sal.

I managed to actually walk back to the bathroom and ran the deodorizer fan. I felt better enough to risk a shower. It was only then that I discovered how bruised I was, and wondered where and how I got the bruises. They seemed to be all over my body, and not the sort of thing you'd get from sitting on a chaise lounge baying at the moon. Well, the dark complexion definitely helped hide them, but I could feel them even through the effects of the narcotic when I touched them. By the time I'd finished the shower, dried myself off, and slipped into something brief but legal, I no longer felt the bruises at all. In fact, I no longer felt much of anything. That was the penalty of taking a drug in a dosage meant for somebody two and a half times your size and weight.

At least it wasn't uncomfortable. I actually felt ravenously hungry, although I usually had very little appetite. When I'd finished eating and finally thought to glance at a clock, I discovered to my complete shock that it was almost four in the afternoon. I switched on the radio and checked to see if any messages had come in.

I kind of figured that Dee and Sal would have called if they were going to be delayed, and they had. Everybody was sleeping in until the initial set of experiments was over. They did start to get worried when I didn't answer all day, but I gave a call over to the lab and left a message that I was okay. Something, though—that last, crystal-clear vision of all of us around Dan at the console—kept haunting me, and I asked that either one, particularly Dee, call me when she could.

When Dee did call, about seven, I omitted a lot of details about my night but described the vision in detail.

"It's in your mind, Doll," Dee insisted. "You just don't want Ben brought back, and you're feeling guilty about it. Your dreams are yelling at you. Was I in the dream? I don't remember ever having a flashback like that."

I tried to think. "I don't remember. I don't think I saw you or Ben. But Sal was there. I'm convinced that there's enough truth to these flashbacks to at least be extra careful. Damn it, run the figures past Tanaka. See what she says."

"Are you kiddin'? Even if I wanted to get close to the Dragon Lady, that's the last place I want to be. She's gone crazier than anybody. She's acting almost like a mad scientist from a bad movie. She's so convinced she's licked the problem she barely even thinks about others except as minor details. No, we're all staying as far away from her as possible. You, too. I love it that you're worried, and I appreciate your concern, but we do know what we're doing here. Lord knows, we've done it often enough!"

She begged off at that point, having been called to a meeting. I felt depressed as hell, and not from the drink or the drug. I'd done my best. I was absolutely convinced that the memory was a reality, and the routine they were going to use to find and retrieve Ben was based on the same one Tanaka mentioned in the flashback.

I was less worried that Mad Dannie would succeed. Something deep down told me that it wouldn't work any more than the past attempts had. Something I'd worked out last night but just couldn't remember, damn it! Could it have been a real idea, or was it just some aftereffect of the binge that convinced me I had discovered something I hadn't?

Something about Dodo on the road to Hell . . .

Forget about it. I was still a nonplayer in this. I was going to try and avoid any more drinking or drugs if I could help it. I couldn't understand what had gotten into me the previous night. I'd never done anything like that. It had been stupid. I could have gotten arrested if anybody had noticed me out there, or, worse, killed myself if I'd taken a header off that deck.

". . . Chance of thunderstorms this evening, possibly severe in places," the radio was warning. "There's a fifty percent chance you'll get dumped on if you're anywhere in the region, and a five-county area is under a tornado watch until four A.M. . . ."

Great. Rita and Dannie would be running their experiments, Dee would be working a dangerous side game that could corrupt everything, and I'd be here, most likely twiddling my thumbs in the dark with no power if one of those suckers hit.

They'd actually run two more power tests during the late afternoon and early evening. Apparently Tanaka wasn't going to go to the next stage until she was dead sure that everything was working precisely as predicted. I'd felt the surges, and again they'd had the odd effect of turning me on. *That's* why I'd taken to the bottle the previous night, I recalled. Trying to dampen down that almost impossible series of animal urges. I could relieve some of the intense physical tension but it wasn't enough.

It wasn't fair, either. If a boy had two wives and only one real function in life, he oughta be able to perform that function with at least one of them!

I was frankly concerned about what would happen to me when the power did get turned up to full. Should I lock myself in a closet or find something to knock me out? Would that help?

The first big thunderstorm hit about eleven that evening, catching me unawares in spite of all the warnings and sending me suddenly around the whole house making sure things were shut down. It made an enormous racket, and, sure enough, the electricity went out within the first few minutes. The pounding of the rain on the roof was very loud, suggesting not only the severity of the storm but also the idea that there might be hail in it. Hail could get nasty in Texas or anywhere else on the plains, and if this storm got any more severe it might well spawn tornadoes. It practically sounded like one anyway, bellowing so much fury and shaking the house that it felt like a freight train was rolling through the living room.

I thought I heard glass breaking, and while frightened by the storm I knew I had to go check on things. I took a flashlight and headed toward the back of the house. One of the patio doors had shattered and there was glass all over, but no sign of what might have caused it. It didn't really look like storm damage, but with all that roaring it was hard to imagine what else it could be.

I turned around to get something to patch it with and the flashlight illuminated a large, standing figure. I gave a muffled cry and switched off the light, but the lightning was more than enough to see by. I was positioned wrong to make a run for it in any direction except through the broken door and out into the storm.

I knew who it was right away. Lee Henreid was unmistakable, female or male, and in this world, where Lee went, Al was surely close by.

It had been a long run, but they had finally caught me.

"Move back into the living room!" Lee commanded over the storm's continuing noise. "Don't run. We have things well covered. Just relax and you won't get hurt!"

I didn't believe that a bit. Not with these two. Still, I had no choice but to obey.

The storm blew through after twenty minutes, although we were still left in the dark without air conditioning.

While Lee held me in the kitchen more with sheer intimidation than with any specific weapons or threats, Al went through the house. I could hear her doing a full-blown search, though I couldn't imagine what they were looking for.

It was a good thing I was faithful, though, or I might well have tried to seduce Lee. As a man, he had been a rather plastic muscle man—good-looking, blond, and with chiseled body, but kind of hollow inside. Nothing had proven that more than his inability to hold on to administration and protect his own ass from Rita in the period after Al had been shot.

In spite of the Mr. Universe form, Lee made a much better woman. I think that would be the case no matter what world we were in, but this one had oversized everything. She had to be over seven feet tall, and perfectly proportioned for that size, which meant that everything about her was huge. I'd gotten a good look at the two of them back in Galveston, but now, under these circumstances, I could be as impressed as I was scared. She was gorgeous.

I wish I could say that Al looked like a man in drag, but, unfortunately, Al made a pretty good woman as well, although not as absolutely stunning as Lee. Al was smaller—six foot two maybe—and had a leaner build, but the face, even with softened skin and nicely understated makeup, still had that same charm and toughness. It would have been criminal for the naturally blond Lee to not have long, thick hair, but Al's short military-style cut looked just right on her. Al also smoked, something that Lee clearly disapproved of but could do nothing about. As always, there was only one boss.

Al came in, lit a cigarette and then two candles she'd found somewhere in the living room. It gave a ghostly air to the proceedings. She then went around and opened the patio door, letting in some cooler post-storm air. She came back over and stood there, towering over me.

"We've met before," she commented softly.

That is an understatement! I thought, trying to keep calm. As always, nothing I could do would change a thing. Still, I had a hunch about these two considering their status in this world. "Yes. In Galveston," I responded.

She seemed pleased at that. "So you do remember us! My name is Almira Starkweather and this fine strapping girl is Lee Ann Henreid, and we're not used to being led around by cute little boys in satin coddies. Why'd you run from us back then? What made you nervous?"

"You looked, acted, and smelled like cops," I responded.

A hand struck forcefully across my face, and I felt tremendous pain, the blow knocking me off the chair and onto the floor amid the broken glass. I shook my head for a moment, feeling both anger and helplessness, then got back to my feet. Al shoved me back into the chair.

"Little boys need to show some respect," she growled. "Now, what was it you just tried to say?"

I rubbed my jaw and tried to figure what bug she had up her ass. No sense in not trying the obvious first. "I said that you looked, acted, and smelled like cops, *ma'am.*"

She smiled and nodded a bit. "You learn fast. What do you think now? Still think we're cops?"

"I—I don't know, ma'am. I have no idea now who you might be, except that my instinct to run seems to have been in my best interest."

Al smiled. "You're right on that, too. Clever little boy, aren't you? We've known where you were, all about you, for some time now, you know. But we had instructions to let you go for a while, until things started to happen. Well, now things have started to happen."

I wasn't quite sure what all this was about, and certainly not how it concerned me. What were they doing here, and under whose instructions were they operating? One thing grew clear as the night went on: nobody had told either of these two who or what they'd been before, and they didn't know me from Adam when it came to past lives.

I was kind of worried about when the Command Center would start doing more of its power tests. They hadn't done one since Al and Lee had invaded, probably because of the storms. Sooner or later, though, they'd start up again, and I couldn't help but remember the effect it would have on me. With these two here, I just didn't know what I would do. I couldn't exactly overpower either one of them, considering my relative size and strength. Al kept checking the phones, but they appeared to be out as well. Whatever had caused the power failure had probably toppled a couple of phone poles, taking both electricity and communications. They were supposed to bury most power cables in this area, but, somehow, hadn't gotten around to it.

I don't know whether power remained off at the APL or not—I thought I heard the Mission bells chime the hour, and they were on an electrical timer—but clearly somebody over there decided things were back to normal enough to start the tests again. I felt a slight sensation, but wasn't sure if they were actually doing full tests again or not. Certainly it wasn't like the night before.

We moved into the living-room area, which had a reasonable breeze even though it felt more humid than was comfortable. Al had gone out to their car and apparently used a car phone to call whoever she was reporting to. I was low on snacks but had some beer and wine. Al took the beer and pretzels and seemed reasonably content with it; Lee passed on the alcohol but chugged down most of a quart of skim milk.

The phone rang, causing us all to jump. I looked over at them quizzically, and Al nodded to me. "Answer it, but no funny stuff, no messages. Just handle it routinely and get rid of them."

I went over nervously, picked up the receiver, and said, "Hello?"

"This is the phone company," a woman's businesslike voice responded. "Just checking to see if service is restored. Thank you." *Click!*

Seeing me look disgusted and hang up, Al asked, "Who was it?" I told her, and she grinned.

Damn it! Who were they working for and why was I now a prisoner in my own home?

And then they started powering up the Command Center again. Ten percent, like last night, was enough to get me started, and I tried to keep a grip on myself. Still, I found myself staring at the two women, just staring, and noting that I wasn't the only one who had felt the tests resume.

As the power continued to go up, I began to lose self-control to the animal lust and desire, but I managed to keep it contained, while my gaze never wavered from the two women. I watched them start to glow, like I had the night before. Suddenly I realized that they weren't the only ones glowing, but my aura was much stronger than theirs.

The tremendous animal urges simply flowed into the focus I was giving them and there was a sudden flash that must have lit up the whole room to any observer. The energy that was coming from the cast-off portion of the power-up flowed into me and then into my captors. I could see their expressions clearly, even feel their emotions: first confusion, then amazement, then feeble resistance to the titanic arousal we were all feeling. At that point, both of them wanted me as much as I wanted them, and all rational thought fled.

It lasted a very long time. I think the phone rang more than once, but it didn't matter. We should have all dropped from exhaustion long before, but something kept renewing us, kept us precisely at our peak in energy and desire, over and over again.

Only later would we be able to reconstruct what had happened. It was the added program that Dee had used to try and fish Ben out of his digitized state. Somehow it reached into the core of every one of the Elect and energized and renewed them, moment to moment, molecule to molecule. Eventually someone—possibly Rita, or Harker, or even Dee—managed to get enough control to make it to a console and shut the power down. At that precise moment, which might well have been hours, even days later, I simply collapsed. When I awoke again, a very different, very warm sun was streaming through the windows, and I opened my eyes upon a scene of some destruction.

The room was a mess. It looked like a herd of rampaging wild animals had come through. The violence implied by the wreckage was kind of scary, particularly since I remembered nothing about it. In fact, I felt kind of distanced, almost as if I were looking at the scene from outside and not quite comprehending or even recognizing it.

I had no idea where I was. I had no idea *who* I was. I got unsteadily to my feet and had enough presence of mind to realize that, somehow, I must have lost my memory. Some big storm or shock or something must have ripped through the room, taking my past with it.

I was naked, but if I knew that it was irrelevant to me. I had no memories, no cultural comparisons, no real sense of right and wrong. I appeared to have bracelets and anklets and something hanging from my ears, but I had no idea why they were there or what function they served. Until I knew, I decided to leave them where they were. They might be important, and at the very least, they didn't seem to do any harm.

I headed toward what turned out to be the kitchen and found a girl there, as naked as I, sitting on the floor behind the counter. Her face and black hair were smeared with some red stuff, and she had poured some more of it from a big jar and was painting with it idly on the floor and on her body. She vaguely matched one of those faces and forms in what little memory I had, but she wasn't going to be much help in filling in the details.

"Hi!" she piped up, like a little girl meeting a friend. "This is fun. Want some?" She scooped up some of it from the jar and held it out to me. I got down on my knees and she stuck it in my mouth. It was sweet and sticky, and we wound up alternately eating it and playing with it like two little kids without a care in the world.

Eventually we got bored and started looking around the place. Although she was a lot bigger than I was, there was no sense of aggressiveness between us. We both heard noises out back and went through the open patio door and onto the deck to see what was making them. It turned out to be another girl, even bigger than the other, with yellow hair, naked and dirty, swinging back and forth as hard as she could on the big rocker. She stopped suddenly when she saw us, but without any fear or even curiosity. "Hi! I'm rockin' on the swing!" she told us needlessly. Clearly she didn't have any more idea of what was going on than we did.

"What's your name?" I asked her, probably sounding just as childlike and stupid.

She frowned and then looked puzzled. "Name?" she repeated, as if the very concept was foreign to her. Almost in self-defense she responded, "What's *your* names?"

That, of course, was the problem. "We dunno, neither," the black-haired girl replied. "I can't—'member—*nothin'*."

"Me, neither," the yellow-haired girl responded, then frowned and looked thoughtful. "Maybe . . . I 'member both of you. We—we made *love*." She came over, picked me up, and hugged me, then put me back down and hugged Black Hair. "I—I love you." It wasn't said with any sort of passion, rather as a statement of fact.

Black Hair turned and looked down at me as well and

smiled. "I love you, too." She paused. "Want to make love now?"

The fact was, I doubted if I was ever out of that mood, but of the three of us I seemed to have most self-control. That in itself was odd, for some reason, but I felt somehow in charge, even though I knew I shouldn't be, as small and weak as I was compared to them.

There was a reason for this. Deep down I knew there was. I just couldn't remember it.

Instead of playing more, I looked around the area in the bright sunlight. Except that it wasn't exactly bright sunlight. There was a yard, and some trees, and a couple of other houses could be seen, but then—nothing. The horizon was a uniform blue with little sparklies in it, not like stars, more like pinholes. And way, way off in the distance the sun was sort of coming up—only it wasn't. It seemed, well, *stuck* there.

My instincts took over. "Let's find something to eat inside," I suggested to them. "Then we can go see what all this looks like."

They shrugged, apparently willing to go along with any suggestion anybody had. In fact, I had the distinct feeling that if I suggested we all get up on the railing and jump down headfirst on the ground, they'd think that was a neat idea, too.

Still, they weren't completely beyond hope. "Is this *our* house?" Black Hair asked as we went back inside. "Ow! Got somethin' stuck in my foot!"

She limped over to a chair, plopped down, and examined the foot, which had a glass shard stuck in it. I looked at it, then pulled it out. It bled, but it didn't seem like it was going to be a real problem.

"Watch where you walk!" I cautioned. "There's lots of stuff like that around here, looks like!"

Okay, so if this was our house, why couldn't I remember it? And if it wasn't our house, whose was it and where were they?

We explored the kitchen and came up with a meal that

should have been disgusting, but since we didn't know any better and it all seemed edible, we ate it anyway.

Afterward, we searched the house. We found a couple of pictures of me with two women, all of us kind of dressed up, but they weren't the same women as my companions.

There were no other clues, though. Some maps, books, and paintings on the walls that made no sense to any of us, but nothing really useful. Finally, we decided it wasn't worth looking much further and went back outside. It felt kind of stuffy and hot inside anyway, and smelly, too. Little wonder, as we gave no thought to personal hygiene or even bowel and bladder control.

"Wanna go see if we can find more of us?" Black Hair asked me.

I nodded. "Somebody's got to be around who knows *something*. I'm gettin' thirsty, too. We got to find water, maybe help, too. C'mon."

There was a car out front, but we found nothing useful in it. The car phone looked promising—but when we picked it up, nothing happened. It was dead.

Black Hair frowned, though, and looked over the whole thing. "I almost 'member how to work this. See—this thing is 'Go,' this one's 'Stop,' and you point it with this round thing here." It sounded reasonable, but nothing we tried would get it to actually come to life, so after a while we abandoned it.

I was getting more and more afraid that something really awful had happened, that it wasn't just us but maybe everything that was screwed up. I mean, it was bright enough, but the light seemed weird, wrong, somehow. And the sun wasn't supposed to stay still like that.

We started walking down the driveway and made it to the main street. It was very quiet, and there didn't seem to be anybody around. No sounds of any kind, really, except us.

I think maybe that got to all three of us more than anything else. The complete, utter silence. We could make noise, and echoes would bounce back to us from the surrounding houses, but other than that it was deathly quiet.

The two women were becoming more serious, getting more focused. None of us had regained any more memory, but we were becoming less childlike by the moment.

"This is creepy," Yellow Hair muttered, and we nodded, there being nothing we could add to that observation.

"Which way do we go from here?" Black Hair asked.

I shrugged. "I don't think it matters, since one way's as good as the next." *Where had I heard that logic before? Think!* I shrugged and picked one at random. "This way."

We began walking toward what looked to be a main inter-section—maybe some stores would be there—water and maybe people, although if they were around they sure were keeping very quiet.

We weren't walking toward the frozen sun, but at an angle to it. I didn't really want to walk to it; it felt warm and maybe a little dangerous.

Black Hair stopped suddenly, pointed, and hissed, "There's somebody in that car over there!"

I looked, and saw a small form in the passenger seat of a van. Although having as good a case of the creeps as the two girls, I wasn't about to be put off by the sight of another person and I walked straight up to the van. Neither the van nor its occupant made any attempt to move as we approached.

I jumped up on the running board under the door, and pulled it open, then cried out and jumped backward onto the grass as the person inside the car pitched over and fell out.

The two women both gasped, but after I got back on my feet, we approached the body as one and looked down at it.

It had been a boy, like me. A bit older, with a medium com-plexion and neatly trimmed jet black hair and goatee. It didn't take but a glance at those staring eyes to know he was dead.

"I 'member him from someplace," Black Hair commented, staring, more curious than frightened now. "I *knew* this guy!"

"Me, too!" Yellow Hair agreed.

I stared at the face very carefully, and got an impression that maybe I'd seen him before, but I didn't have the same shock of familiarity as the two women. It was pretty clear, though, that whatever had zapped this area and our memories had done an even nastier job on him.

There wasn't an apparent mark on him, either. It was like he just . . . died.

"That looks like another one down at the end of the block!" Yellow Hair called to us. "He ain't movin', either!"

I looked up and saw what she was talking about. It was one of those small roadside stands, and it definitely seemed to have somebody inside. We couldn't do much more for this poor devil, so we headed on down the block.

I couldn't make out the colorful hand-drawn sign over the window, but Black Hair stared at it and read, "sno cones one dollar."

Behind the counter was a nice-looking girl of maybe fifteen or sixteen looking out at us and smiling. It was unnerving, that smile, because she wasn't moving at all.

"Miss? Hello?" I called up to her. "Are you dead or alive?"

Getting no response, I walked up to the front of the stand and reached out my hand to touch it.

The stand dissolved—very slowly, as if made of syrup—from the point of contact in all directions, dissolving into tiny dots that swirled and sparkled and then evaporated before hitting the ground.

I jumped back, and we watched the process with wide-eyed wonder. Even the girl dissolved. Soon there was nothing at all left of her or of the stand around her. Nothing, that is, but a simple wooden stake in the ground to which a small index card was attached with a single staple. There was some writing on the card, and Black Hair approached it and squinted, trying to read the simple block printing.

"Sno cone stand, quantity one, with attendant (F)," she read. She straightened up and crept backward toward the rest of us as if the stake and index card were some deadly poison. She looked stricken, terrified, almost panicked, as she gazed down at me and asked, almost plaintively, "What does it mean?"

I sighed. "I wish I knew."

Yellow Hair looked around at the rest of the street. "Will the rest of this dissolve if we touch it?"

There was only one way to find out.

The answer, from a representative sample, was "maybe." Some of the houses and cars dissolved, while others remained as solid as a rock. It made no sense at all.

A few more blocks over, we reached the edge of the Earth.

All semblance of reality as we'd been accepting it ended in a sudden, slightly irregular boundary. The street continued, but it no longer had the solidity or detail of "reality." It became, in a sense, a cartoon, a detailed perspective drawing, white on blue, going off into the distance.

It was a machine drawing, pretty clearly, and it not only had streets and buildings and cars, each item had a label, too. Not index cards, but just little rectangles that said things like WHISTLE STOP MINIMART, GENERIC TEMPLATE NUMBER 14, and CHEVRON STATION, 6 PUMP, GAS AND GO MODEL 12A ONLY.

"I'm scared to death," Black Hair told us, swallowing hard. "But I just *got* to know."

She went right up to the edge, took a deep breath, then kneeled down and put her hand on the blue area where the street was sketched out and labeled. "It's *solid*!" she exclaimed, amazed. "I can feel it. It feels smooth, even a little cold, but it's there."

I just gaped at it. "What the hell is this?" I asked aloud, of nobody in particular.

I didn't much remember the world we'd lived in, but I knew this sure wasn't a part of it.

Stepping out onto that blue world showed that Black Hair had more guts than Yellow Hair and me put together, but once she was out there and started walking around, it became irresistible to follow her.

She was right about it being cooler, and that sort of helped. We were still walking cautiously and carefully, but going up to the drawing of the minimart, I reached out and touched a storefront that was as solid as the footing I was using but felt just the same—smooth, featureless, and cool.

"How far does this go?" I wondered out loud.

"Looks like it goes all the way as far as you can see," Yellow Hair responded. "All the way to the dark edges."

I looked back at the edge of reality and decided that I just felt more comfortable there for the moment. I walked back, carefully, and felt some relief with the heat, humidity, and real pavement under my feet.

The other two looked around for some time but finally joined me, all of us sitting down on the grass staring out at the impossible view.

"Now what do we do?" Black Hair asked, echoing my own sense of complete befuddlement.

"I'm thirsty. We still didn't find any water," Yellow Hair noted.

I sighed. "Well, I guess we're still looking for water. Beyond that, we have three choices. We stay in this ghost town, we wander around out there until we starve, or we go the other way."

"Walk into the sun?" Yellow Hair gasped.

"I doubt if we'll do that. I just don't know what's there, but something tells me that if we're getting all our heat and light from one direction, and there's nothing else here to give us a direction, then we might as well find out what the heck that really is." I paused. "But water is first."

None of the houses that remained had working water or any other utilities. As some rational procedures established themselves in our minds and we got a bit more pragmatic memory back, we began to remember what some things were for. At least there were some bottled soft drinks and juice in a couple of the refrigerators, even though, without power, they were quickly warming up.

It wasn't much, but it was enough. We had to find some way to get out of this or else figure out a way to survive here. Going toward the bright source of light and heat might not even be possible, but it was something that had to be tried. Taking a couple of cans of warm juice with us, we started off toward that side of the neighborhood, using the edge as a guide.

Now and then, on our right, we saw the occasional shapes of immobile people and animals. We found a couple of others like us, women this time, both as dead as that guy in the van and with not a mark on either. The rest of the people we found dissolved at the touch, leaving little note cards in their place.

Reaching the point where "reality" ended, still facing toward what looked like the sun, all three of us felt a little fear. Still, we knew that the blue would support us, and that if it grew too hot or too bright, we could always turn around.

Black Hair stepped off first, then me, and Yellow Hair followed. It was hard for me to keep up with them because of their longer stride, but they always waited for me to catch up.

The blue flooring area soon ran out of drawings and labels and became a featureless plane with long, barlike rays of light moving from us toward that bright central point. It wasn't something we could look straight at, but we could feel it.

It was impossible to measure time, but after a while I was just too tired to walk any farther without a rest, so we sat on the now warm, smooth blue floor and took a breather.

"How long you figure we got to go yet?" Yellow Hair asked us.

"Who can say? Doesn't look much closer, does it?" I replied. "Still, we're getting there. Funny thing is, it doesn't seem to be getting much hotter now, at least. I—"

Black Hair suddenly grabbed my arm and I stopped talking and looked up at her quizzically.

"I hear something," she said. "Or somebody."

We all sat very still, and, sure enough, we could hear something or somebody not far away. "Sounds like . . . *digging*," I commented. I got painfully to my feet and started off slowly in the direction of the sound, the two women following.

It didn't take long, walking at a precise right angle to the sun, to find the source of the noise.

There was a hole in the floor. It was a great crack like the kind you'd see in a broken mirror, a jagged, ugly scar. Somebody, or something, was down in the cavity, and they were working hard. I dropped to hands and knees and crept cautiously to the edge and looked down.

Perhaps fifteen or twenty feet down, a curious creature in funny clothes with a giant bird's beak and two big eyes was swinging a pick ax, chipping away.

"Hello!" I called, my voice echoing along the walls of the crack.

The creature looked startled, and began frantically looking around, then shrugged.

"Up here!" I called.

It stopped again, then finally looked up and spotted us.

"My goodness! *You* again!" it called in a funny accent. "Come back to join me? I'm certain China can't be much farther. I've dug an awfully long way already!"

It was a very odd statement, but it implied that we'd spoken before. "Do you know me?" I called down to it.

"Well, we've never been properly introduced, but we have spoken, yes," the creature admitted. "What? You don't remember?"

"I don't remember anything. None of us do. Something happened up here and it wiped out a lot of the world, killed some folks, and left us without any memories at all."

"Oh, come, now! You must have *some* memories. Otherwise how would you know to speak to me or the words to say? If you had no memories, the way you three look, I might be Dodo barbecue by now! Goodness!"

"Do you know who we are? Where this is?" I asked it.

"As I say, we've never been properly introduced, so how would I know precisely who you are? The other two I don't really know, but they're quite lovely, both of them. Come down! With four of us I am certain we shall come out in China in no time at all!"

"You can't dig all the way to China by doing that!" I told it.

"Indeed? And how do you know that, Mr. Genius, if you don't remember anything?"

He had a point. How did I know that he was wrong? I wasn't too clear on where China was, but I just *knew* you could never get there by digging down through the center of the Earth.

"You should get out of there and come with us!" I told it. "Perhaps we can find a—shorter—way?"

The creature pulled himself up and looked quite proud and determined. "Certainly not! You think just because I'm the last Dodo bird in the universe that you can misdirect me from my purpose! Well, sir, you are quite wrong! I may be the only Dodo now, but, one day, the skies will once more be full of us, the noblest of all bird-dom!"

I pulled back from the crack and looked at the other two. "I don't know what sort of creature this Dodo is, but I'm sure he's not somebody who can help us. Still, if *that* thing is alive out here, perhaps other, smarter creatures are as well!"

There was no way to argue with me on this, and the only way to find out was to resume our journey. The sounds of digging were soon lost behind us.

As we went back on course toward the hot brightness, we slowly began to get used to it. It wasn't any one moment or any one thing that did it, but the closer we got to the source of all this, the more strength and comfort we had, and the less either the heat or light bothered us.

Still, we met no one else on our journey after the Dodo, and it took a long time before we finally approached the source of it all.

VIII

THE DODO'S LESSON

It was bright enough that we all looked like dark silhouettes against the radiation pouring out almost in front of us. There was nothing but blue plane to the left and right of us, but there were cracks, lots of cracks. Here was the center of whatever happened. Here we approached the point where the world had cracked.

Looming in front of us was a massive building, with two tall towers and great doors framed by a vast arch. It looked dark and cold, and we decided not to enter it, walking to one side, where, almost out of nowhere, there seemed to form a narrow street like the ones we'd left back in "reality."

"Another dead boy over there, poor dear," Yellow Hair noted, pointing.

He had apparently been trimming the bushes by the giant building when it happened, just sort of frying him in his tracks, though he didn't look burned. Still, we all were getting the feeling that this was something called "radiation," a word that had popped into our minds without any context for explanation, as we'd gotten very close to this point. A burst of fire that didn't burn you outside but went through you and killed you anyway—that was what we knew it to be.

"Old guy," I noted. "Gray beard, white hair. At least he'd been around a while, I guess." Still, like the first body we saw in the van, there was too much of a sense of familiarity about this one to linger. I didn't know who he'd been, but I was certain that, at one time in the past, I had known.

The road went through a patch of forest and finally reached a guardhouse with a bunch of gates and fences. Black Hair went up to the little building, where a tough-looking uniformed guard stood, frozen stiff like the rest. She was as big as Yellow Hair but not as good-looking.

"The sign says that boys are not allowed beyond this point," Black Hair noted. "Want to stay out?"

"Not unless somebody or something stops me," I replied.

"Fair enough." Black Hair reached out and touched the guardhouse and it and the assemblage of crossing barriers began to dissolve. In a short time, all that was left was a bunch of sticks in the ground with little note cards saying what they'd been.

The second gate also dissolved, although, interestingly, the fence did not, but the third and final one proved stubborn and quite solid. It appeared to be controlled not from the guardhouse but from inside, where some kind of observation tower could barely be seen. Kind of clever.

"We can't let *this* stop us!" I cried. "Not after coming all this way! Besides, there's no place else to go."

The women found some tools, including sledgehammers, but while their banging made a lot of noise, it didn't get anything open. Finally Black Hair vanished into the gardener's shed behind the big building and came out with some rope and an ugly-looking tool that had a lot of sharp spikes.

She tied one end of the rope to the spiked tool, swung the end around her head, and threw it toward the top. After three tries, she still hadn't hooked it, but the idea was obvious and quite clever.

"Let me do it," Yellow Hair suggested. "I am stronger and taller." Still, it took her two tries to hook it and pull enough to insure that it was solid.

This was one case where being small and light helped, although I wasn't too thrilled about pulling myself. Still, I said, "I'm the lightest. Let me go first, and then if I make it, you two follow. If either of you is too heavy, nobody will get over."

They both nodded, and I took several deep breaths, spat on my hands, grabbed the rope, and pulled myself slowly up to the top of the fence by walking up the wall while holding on for dear life.

The top of the wall was pretty damned high; I hadn't thought it would be so high or so scary to look back down.

"It's too high for me to jump down without hurting myself!" I called to them. "Let me use the rope to get down on this side and I'll see if I can open the gate. It's probably not that tough if you're on this side of the wall."

They didn't like it, but at this point there wasn't much they could do but go along.

In fact, while I hadn't thought of the fact that the tower would need power that didn't exist anymore, there was a manual system to operate the gate. It involved turning a big wheel that moved other gears and levers and opened the gates inward. I shouted my discovery to the women, then tried very hard to move the wheel, without success. It needed more muscle power than I had, damn it.

Why couldn't this part of the shattered world dissolve?

I shouted my problem to them, and Black Hair yelled, "Take the rope and claw to the tower. Throw it off the tower to our side. If one of us can get over, we can open it!"

Good plan. *Boys weren't much for thinking and planning, they were strictly for making love and babies.* Now where had that come from? Still, it represented how I was feeling at that point.

The tower was a hybrid, the first I'd encountered. Part of it dissolved—maybe had already dissolved—but the part facing away from the radiation source was still solid. I hoped I could get up there and toss the rope over without collapsing what remained of the structure.

It wasn't easy, but there was a straight-up ladder on the outside that was clearly a backup to the stairs inside that no longer went all the way to the top. I managed to climb up there with the rope, my whole body screaming at the abuse it was taking. From there, I could see the girls and actually managed to toss the rope down to them. Pretty soon, I had it securely latched again, and Black Hair got up it, although it was a near thing. She was over the other side, jumping down athletically to the ground, and had managed to start turning the big wheel even before I started making my way down.

The gates squealed and screeched, and it took every ounce of strength Black Hair had, but the gates swung open just enough for Yellow Hair to squeeze through.

Both Black Hair and I needed a break and we took it. Yellow Hair, who'd had no problems so far, used the time to do a little exploring, then came back and reported to us.

"There's a bunch of buildings just up ahead. Not all of 'em look all together, but a couple do. It looks like some kind of, like, explosion. The part that was facin' the blast, that's gone. The rest—no damage at all. Still creepy. Bunch of cars were there, all dissolved when I touched 'em."

After a bit of rest, I actually felt worse, but my desire to see what was here and maybe learn something about what had happened overrode even the aches and pains and tiredness.

It was a ghostly scene. Here, close to the "blast," things had evaporated or dissolved when directly exposed and it gave the whole place a sense of melting and decay. More unnerving was the occasional sight of what looked like *parts* of people, often just legs in shoes and socks. Most of the people had clearly been either wholly or partly vaporized; virtually all the rest had been frozen in some kind of weird death tableau, ready to crumble when touched. And yet, for all that, it hardly explained the sticks and cards and labels, or why a few people we'd seen had died but remained otherwise as solid as we were.

The tremendous glow that appeared to be a sunrise from afar turned out to be a bright dome of energy over the whole compound. The center and source of this great frozen blast was clearly just ahead, past the parking area near the end of the road, in a low-slung two-story structure with modern lines and a flat roof.

The other buildings appeared to have been offices, labs, or storerooms, but this one was different. Black Hair walked up to it and squinted at the sign. "Applied physics laboratory, TSU," she read, the words clearly difficult for her and of little apparent sense. "Admittance by level badge only. Secure area. Authorized personnel only. All others keep out." She turned to me. "What do you suppose it means?"

"Well, 'keep out' is pretty clear," I answered. "I think some people were fooling around with stuff they didn't know how to control and it blew up on them. I can't think of any other reason for it. Blew up and killed them and most other folks, too."

Black Hair nodded, but looked somewhat troubled. "Why not us, though? Why didn't it do the same thing to us?"

"Why didn't it melt *this* building?" Yellow Hair asked us, feeling as strange and uncomfortable as I did. "I mean, isn't this where it went *bang*?"

"Maybe it did," Black Hair mused, then reached out and touched the door. It was solid, as were the walls.

Yellow Hair walked completely around the very long building, finally coming back from the other direction. "All four walls are there and they are solid," she reported. "But it is warm to the touch."

I began to have a feeling that it wasn't the environment that had changed but rather we who'd changed as we'd come closer and closer to this point. We should have been blinded, burned up, fried. There was no way we should have been able to stand here and survive, we all felt that.

"Maybe we can't die," Black Hair mused. "You remember my cut?" She lifted her foot and showed us. It was dirty, but there wasn't a trace of a cut even though it had been a fair gash. "I didn't feel anything there since we started toward this place."

Yellow Hair looked around with an almost awestruck expression. "Maybe whatever killed them made us like gods or something."

"Maybe we should go inside if we can and see if we can find out anything else," I suggested, trying to shake this sense of being totally alone, the sole survivors of a disaster. Gods may enjoy good food and drink but they sure didn't need it, and they sure didn't feel the kind of muscle aches and bone tiredness I felt.

Black Hair tried the door, and it opened with a groaning sound. With the aid of a hand from Yellow Hair, I made it to my feet and followed Black Hair in. Yellow Hair brought up the rear.

Inside the environment was somewhat different, as if the very air was some kind of solid thing, a greenish-yellow with sparks that seemed nonetheless rather frozen, static. We sort of cut through it, and it felt like walking through cobwebs, tingling and tickling the body.

There were no lights inside, but at least this static energy seemed to radiate sufficient light for our needs, even where there were no windows.

We looked around the first floor before going farther, and found several solid bodies, all women. We were at the point of expecting them now.

The second floor was mostly offices and big workrooms. Much of the first floor had been that way, too, although the whole middle seemed to be filled with all sorts of complicated machinery.

"You notice somethin' funny 'bout the last couple of bodies?" Black Hair asked us.

"Huh?"

"Look at 'em again. It's kinda like they're not made up of one person but two, and those two weren't anyways alike. It's kinda weird, but take a look."

I saw what she meant. It wasn't twisted features, it was more like they had been in the process of melting, but instead of melting into nothing, they were melting into somebody else. Somebody whose body was shorter, chunkier, and maybe bald.

And all with a kind of dark brown skin tone, darker and different than mine.

"Listen!" The word was whispered in a frightened, tense hiss by Black Hair.

We froze and listened. It was a kind of steady whining noise, somewhere in the distance. It didn't sound like anything I could relate to, as little as that was.

"It's comin' from down there," Yellow Hair noted, pointing at a stairway.

"What is it?" I wondered aloud.

Black Hair shook her head. "I dunno, but we didn't come here to run." She looked around, found a metal bar, and held it up like a club. She started silently for the stairs, and, after a moment, we followed.

The noise grew louder as we descended, and when we reached a landing, there was a sensation that we were somehow in a different type of environment, one that seemed only slightly related to the one above.

It was bright and warm down at the bottom, almost stifling hot, and the very walls seemed to blaze. It never seemed to have occurred to any of us that we might be killing ourselves by walking into this radiation; it just wasn't a thought that came to mind. The future was the next hallway, not the next month or week or even the next hour.

We passed down a corridor with a lot of colored lights, all

blazing, and at the end we followed the ones that led left because that's where the noise was coming from.

"You feel something?" Black Hair whispered.

We did. The air, the static, frozen air, was neither static nor frozen here. We were entering an area where the air was moving and there was a definite if slight breeze.

We emerged into a large chamber—completely underground and cut off from the surface except by that corridor and stairs—where things weren't static at all. The same radiation that had seemed so static elsewhere wasn't static here; instead, it throbbed around the room, giving off some heat but shielding us, I think, from the tremendous kaleidoscope of horribly intense lights springing from a point in the floor ahead of us. The lights were swirling around, apparently causing the agitation we saw in the air around us, and they gave off an eerie, colorful show that we could only bear to look at for seconds at a time. All around us was a ghastly tableau.

There were seven women in the room, at least as far as we could tell. There might have been more, but we couldn't see anything past that central area.

They were all identical, and they were all frozen in midmotion, not keeled over like the others we'd seen. They were real enough. One close to me had her mouth open as if she were shouting and was pointing toward the breach in the floor, an expression of sheer terror on her face. Another was frozen in the act of frantically pushing some controls on a massive console, not quite able to reach one last big, round, red button. The hand, clenched in a fist, was maybe a quarter inch from it.

The others were similarly frozen in midmotion, and it was clear from their expressions that they all knew they were in trouble and had been in the process of trying to stop it when it caught them. One sat reclined on a chair and had this helmet-like contraption on that covered her eyes and ears. I wondered what the heck she'd been doing. The thing was attached to a wall console by a thick cable. Her expression was the most curious of the whole bunch—total and complete surprise.

They were all *small*, too, for girls. They were only a few
inches taller than me, bulkier, with dark brown skin. They
were all bald and they all looked exactly alike.

"How come they don't look like us?" Yellow Hair asked,
puzzled.

"It changed 'em," Black Hair guessed. " 'Member the ones
upstairs? Kinda half and half? This is what they was changin'
into, I bet."

I nodded, but it cleared nothing up. "I know what an explosion
is, even though I can't think of ever seeing one," I told them.
"Still, if whatever it was exploded right over there, caught these
girls, and then mostly caught the ones above us, why didn't it
change them all the way? Or us, too, and everybody else?"

" 'Cause it couldn't, I bet," Black Hair, responded, thinking.
"Something stopped it. Froze it in midexplosion. It just sorta
shut everything down, 'cept us. Us and that nutty Dodo we saw
diggin' out there."

Black Hair went around to the other side and examined this
wall of rectangular gizmos. She looked down at them and said,
"There's *people* of some kind inside these things! Look!"

We hurried over and Yellow Hair lifted me up so I could
see. There was a kind of dark glass wall over each, and, sure
enough, inside several were people. They all looked like they
were asleep, or at least had been asleep when all this happened,
and they, too, had been touched by whatever had changed
these folks. They were all naked and had all sorts of wires and
probes sticking into them. They also were wearing those helmets, only not everything looked connected and certainly not
everything fit them.

"See something funny 'bout them?" Black Hair commented.

"Huh? What?"

"No nipples. Weird. Even boys got nipples. Not them."

She was right.

Yellow Hair put me down and I went back over to look at
the girl at the console. That big red button was something
she'd been clearly trying to press. It also seemed to have had a

thick cover over it that had to be unlatched in order to actually strike the button. That meant it was important but dangerous, I guessed. Not something you wanted to push by accident.

I couldn't help but wonder what would happen if it got pushed, or if in fact it was much too late now to have any effect. Black Hair seemed to read my thoughts and said, rather firmly, "Don't touch it! We dunno what it does! It might start it up again with us here!"

That was certainly true. When she was satisfied that I was moving away from the console and wasn't going to push anything, Black Hair turned and almost bumped into the frozen girl who had been pointing and screaming. I don't know why, or what made her do it, but Black Hair reached out and touched the smaller figure.

There was a sudden motion, like the figure was going to dissolve, and I think we fully expected it, but it didn't happen. Instead, even though Black Hair pulled her hand away quickly, a reaction begun at the point of contact spread over the frozen body, a bizarre and increasingly rapid assemblage of black and then multicolored dots that seemed to consume the whole image. Only that image wasn't being consumed, it was being changed, even *growing* as it attracted more mass from the whistling color bands shooting out of the hole in the floor.

In only thirty or forty seconds, it became an absolute, detailed, duplicate of Black Hair, even to the dirt and crud that covered her body. And it became *alive*, and gasped just as Black Hair gasped and pointed just as Black Hair pointed. They both said at once, in the same voice, "Did you see *that*?"

"Wow! Neat!" Yellow Hair commented.

I stared at the two absolutely identical girls, who now had caught sight of each other. "Uh-oh," they both said at once, looking each other in the eye.

I looked up at the new creation and asked, "Do you remember anything about what went on here?"

She looked puzzled. "Course I don't. I came in here with you!"

"No you didn't," the other one said. "*I* did. You were one of those until I touched you!"

"No! It's the other way around!" the first one insisted, each one so much like the other it was already confusing to tell which one was which.

"It don't matter!" I yelled. "One of you touched one of these things and it became another *you*!"

They both seemed to accept that as at least a starting point. "But which one of us is which?" they both asked.

"Don't matter, I told you! Unless . . . unless the new one's faking it. I doubt it, though. Whatever changed them into the identical girls still works in here. It changed one of you into Black Hair. Don't touch—" I began to warn, but it was already too late.

Absolutely intrigued, Yellow Hair had touched one of the frozen figures, and the same process happened again, only this time, the frozen figure became an animated duplicate of Yellow Hair. Now there were two of each of the girls! Two sets of absolutely identical twins!

"This ain't fair! There's four of you and still one of me!" I complained. "Maybe I should—"

"*No!*" both Black Hairs shouted at once, and I stopped dead still. "Until we figure more of this and get food and water, no more touching folks!"

I bent to that logic, but hoped Yellow Hair—both of her—wouldn't think it was neat to have a tribe of her around. They were big and strong enough that there was no way we could stop her.

"The thing is," Black Hairs both said, "if touching these folks changes 'em into us, then whatever did all the rest is still active in here. That's why the lights and the moving air. In here, we got to be real careful."

That was an understatement. "Then let's move out of here for now and see if we can find that food," I suggested. "We got all the time in the world to come back."

Both Black Hairs nodded. "Agreed," they said.

"I hope we can find some cold drinks, too," I muttered. "There is nothing I want more than a real cold drink."

The same energy stream that had transformed the frozen clones into duplicates of the girls came out in a smaller but equally deliberate manner from the hole and arched over toward me. I got nervous and backed up, but it hit the floor in front of where I'd been. Or, rather, it stopped maybe eight inches above the floor, and began to flow into a shape that, in a matter of seconds, solidified into a waxed-paper soda cup with ice cubes and orange liquid in it.

I reached down, picked it up, and took a sip. It was orange soda and it was really cold.

"Hey! Could *we* do that, I wonder?" the Yellow Hairs asked. They crouched down, looked at the floor, and said, "I wish I had a big, cold drink."

Two identical drinks just like mine were formed in front of them.

The Black Hairs followed suit. We needed drinks more than anything else, and, frankly, while we also could have used some food, that was tougher to wish for. We didn't have a lot of memory of just what we were supposed to eat.

"Wow! This is fun!" the Yellow Hairs commented, drinking their sodas.

"Maybe it is, but I think we oughta get out of here!" I shouted to them. "Look at yourselves! I don't think it's doing any of us good to be in here for too long!"

Their skins had become dark, like they'd been tanned by the sun, and I was beginning to notice that they seemed to be changing slightly, their figures and features becoming more exaggerated. If that was happening to them, then I couldn't guess what was happening to me, but I couldn't hide the fact that I was becoming turned on again.

We headed for the corridor, all five of us now, and were soon back at the bottom of the stairs. It was weird to go back into that stifling, static environment again, but a relief to get out of that bizarre room.

"Wait a minute!" Black Hairs both called to me. "My eyes aren't adjusting right. I can't see my hand in front of my face!"

"Me, neither," both Yellow Hairs agreed.

I looked around and could see just fine.

"Link hands and follow me," I told them. "You keep hold of my hand, and the others keep hold of the one in front. I'll lead us out."

It was a little tough with the stairs, but we managed, and I finally got us all outside. Things seemed normal to me, if a bit bright. "Any better?" I asked them.

"No," they all responded just about in unison. "I can't see a thing!"

I had to face a fact that they hadn't yet allowed themselves to consider. That, for some reason, the radiation hadn't affected me, at least in this way, but it had them.

I had four blind goddesses on my hands.

We didn't try to find food after that; besides, we were too tired, too scared, and too confused. The grass was soft, there was no weather, and nothing seemed terribly threatening, so I suggested that we all try to get some sleep and see if that might help their eyes. I was totally, completely exhausted.

None of us, of course, had any concept that we might be in a severe radiation field, or that there was any other remaining danger. It simply didn't occur to us. It was likely that if we had retained our memories, we probably would have had more sense than to come here in the first place.

Then again, maybe not, since the food was going to run out fast back in that little patch of remaining reality, and death here attempting an escape would be far preferable to death by slow starvation over there.

As achy and exhausted as I was, and without a lot of memories or recriminations to dwell on or worries about a technology I was rediscovering and misunderstanding, I went out like a light.

* * *

They were all there, all lined up at the tea party, all looking starved and thirsty and forlorn, since the Mad Hatter and March Hare had wasted the tea and the Dormouse had eaten all the biscuits and crumpets.

I knew their faces; I knew all their faces, save perhaps one or two, whether they were male or female, big or little, weak or strong. Even Black Hair and Yellow Hair were there, although not copies of them. Of the short, plump woman with no nipples who was cloned in the big room there was no sign.

When I approached them, they all turned to me with pleading eyes and empty teacups and moaned, groaned, and pleaded with me for help. For some reason they believed that only I could help them.

But I wasn't myself. Or was I? I looked down and saw two enormous bird's legs below me, and feathers all around, and my vision was indeed blocked in part by what I'd taken to be a very large nose but proved to be a hard, bulbous beak. I was wearing a waistcoat and tie, and my four-fingered hands held a pocket watch attached to my coat by a gold chain. The watch said that it was one minute to twelve.

I was the Dodo.

But I couldn't be the Dodo! I'd seen the Dodo digging and had spoken with him on more than one occasion. I'd even argued with him, or dismissed him as not worth arguing with. Digging through the Earth to get out of a hole instead of taking a hand and being pulled out—it was absurd. Yet, now, I was having a hard time remembering why the logic was absurd. I was beginning to think like a Dodo!

A small child, eyes big as saucers and twice as sad, came up to me, showed me an empty plate, and asked, in a plaintive, heartrending voice, "Please, sir? May I have some more?"

I looked down and hardened my heart at the sight. "Forget it, kid! You're in the wrong book!" I snapped, then took out my pipe and began to fill it with tobacco. When it was ready, I lit it *with a burning piece of straw I pulled from one of the torches outlining the meadow and puffed hard. The smoke billowed out, far disproportionate to the amount of burning weed, and it swirled around and began to take form.*

"So you've gotten to that point, have you?" the Cheshire Cat asked, although in the smoke, only the eyes, nose, and mouth were visible.

"What point?"

"Must everything have a point?" it retorted. "Why, I'm quite round. Very few points on me, except at the claws and whiskers, I suppose."

"But you said—"

"No, I said that you *have gotten to that point. There's a difference."*

"Indeed? What?"

"Well, someone else could have gotten to a totally different point, for one thing."

"This is nonsense! I can't remember much of anything right now, but I know that this is not real. It can't be."

"Indeed? It's not as believable as drawings of a city, dissolving cars and people, and a bunch of identical girls who turn into whoever touches them? Oh, my, yes! Now that's *a realistic, believable scenario! This, on the other hand—a lot of folks sitting outside waiting for something to eat and drink and hoping you'll be a provider. Oh,* that's *unbelievable, fantastic. Yes, quite so. And you don't believe you are mad!"*

I felt very uncertain at this conversation and didn't like its direction. "Am I mad?" I asked it.

"Well, ordinarily I'd say yes, that we're all mad, but since you're a Dodo it might just be stupidity. You know they just stood around and let themselves be killed? Didn't even try to get away? 'Dumb as a Dodo' has more truth than madness in it! No, Dodos might be too stupid or too dense to be mad. But these people—the rest of the group—they're quite clearly mad, because they're putting their lives and futures in the hands of a stupid Dodo bird!"

"I'm not a Dodo! This whatever it is just made me seem like one! Perhaps I'm dreaming!"

"Ah!" responded the Cat. "But what if you're not? You have no idea how difficult it is to communicate on any rational basis with somebody with a birdbrain."

I hesitated a moment. "Is that what you are doing? Communicating?"

"Well, I'm hardly tap-dancing with you! Of course I'm communicating! Whether or not you can hear me and understand me with all this fog in your Dodo brain is a different question."

"It looks quite clear today to me," I noted.

"Now, see, there you go again!" the Cat said disgustedly. "You've been given as much information as can be gotten through. You are one of the few hopes left that anything can be done. At this very moment, you are the only hope. If you blow it this time, there's no tomorrow. Your friends played with things they didn't understand and they crashed the whole damned program. You don't know what that means because you're a Dodo."

"Stop saying that!"

"Okay, because you're a giant stupid ugly bird. Better? If you weren't, you'd listen. When everything went down, it took your memories with it. Shock blew it mostly out, but now vestigial remnants have returned. You're starting to remember, but you don't have the data to put names to faces, places to events. Right now, you are running on momentum and inertia, almost a little piece of independent action in a world where it's all gone. That's because of the backup link, which you also don't remember, but it won't remain forever. You can use it if you act quickly, but you are drawing very close to the point where the backup itself will lose what little power is left there."

"Call me a Dodo, then, but I do not understand you," I told him.

"And you'll understand less and less if you don't use what you've got and act! Do I have to spell it out for you? Okay—

Push the damned red button. *Is that clear enough? Otherwise, get your shovel and start digging."*

And then all of the people and all of the creatures around the tables in the meadow turned to me and called, in torment and with a heartrending plea, "Help us, Obi-Wan! You're our only hope!"

I drifted off into a deeper sleep where the dreams no longer were of the sort I could remember, and I slept solidly for an unknown period, since time no longer existed.

When I awoke, I half expected to find myself transformed into a giant bird, but I was just a very, very achy boy with a bad headache.

The women were still out cold, and that suited me just fine. I still didn't remember much about the time before the world exploded, but I remembered the dream very well indeed. Most of it seemed nonsensical, as dreams often do, but out of dreams sometimes came sense. Had I been acting like a Dodo? A dumb bird that walked up to its killers and tried to be friends? It wasn't flattering, but it might have made some sense.

And if I was the Dodo, then the one we saw digging out there was me, too. Thing was, we all saw it, so how could it be me?

The main point, though, was that my dream, which maybe was me, too, said to push the red button inside or else we'd start losing it again and finally kill ourselves and everybody else. How I could kill those others, all but a handful of whom were already dead, I didn't know, but somehow I felt that it was true. Maybe, like the frozen women down there, those folks who seemed dead lumps weren't really dead at all, but merely waiting for somebody to do something so they could come back to life.

Not touching them, not changing them. But what?

Pushing the damned red button was what.

I knew that if the women woke up they'd try and talk me out

of it, and I had enough conditioning from the world as it had been that I'd probably let them dominate me. Was that the Dodo and its killers? Maybe. I wouldn't hurt any of them and I didn't think they'd hurt me, but if not acting would kill us all, then what difference did it make?

I took a leak and then walked slowly but steadily back toward the building we'd explored, going in as silently as the creaking door would allow, and entered the silent, grim halls.

As I walked back along the route from "yesterday," whenever that really was, I got a sensation that maybe I wasn't alone, that there was somebody, something, living here.

No, that wasn't right. *Nothing* was living in this world anymore. At best, like me, other would be surviving. That was what made this a fairly easy choice for me. The alternative was this nightmare existence.

I went down the stairs, still filled with self-doubt. Was I about to do something incredibly dumb based on a stupid dream? Did I really know anything? Was I really getting any real communication from somebody, or was it just my compulsion to push that red button? I mean, I had to face it. I really had been tempted to press it the day before, and didn't only because Black Hair didn't really want it.

The closer I got to that bizarre room, though, the more nervous and uncertain I felt. What if this was all there really was? What if we could have a long time just eating and sleeping and screwing? I could have the most fun of all if we turned these frozen folks into Black Hairs and Yellow Hairs and none of them into me.

What if that button blew up the universe or something?

No, that was stupid. Somebody already had blown up the universe. The button couldn't possibly do that. That thought, at least, was a logical comfort to me.

And then, there I was, in the breezy room with all the flashing lights, all the noise, and the power—and that damned red button.

It didn't seem quite as breezy as it had the day before, and it didn't seem quite as bright. There was a real sense, even though it was slight, that things were starting to run down. Made me wonder what the place had been like just after the blowup. Must have been a real mess.

I got a tightness in my stomach as I looked over at that woman, her mouth open, her expression both frightened and determined, and that hand poised just above that button. So close . . .

I think I was most worried that nothing would happen, that it would either be an anticlimax, too late to have any effect, or simply not work anymore. Or, maybe it would just ring a bell or activate warning sirens. That wouldn't get us anywhere.

I approached the console with its ever-frozen occupant and looked at the button. I wasn't even sure I could keep from touching her if I was to press the damned thing. The chair she sat in was on rollers—maybe I could gently roll her away to one side.

It moved at least a couple of inches before it jammed on something, but a couple of inches was enough.

I stood there for a moment and just stared at that big red button, not really thinking, not quite sure if I should really push it at all . . .

Something took hold of me and violently flung me away from the console. I was so surprised that I was on my back on the floor before I realized what was happening. Above me loomed this huge shape, and a strange woman's face that glared at me in lunatic triumph. I'd never seen her before that I could remember, but she had the same sort of familiarity we felt when we'd first found the other dead ones. I was pretty sure she was at the big gathering in my dream.

She was stark naked and almost totally black, like ink or charcoal. Her skin was peeling off in little bits from whatever radiation was coming from that hole, and what hair hadn't been burned or fallen out hung there in gray wisps.

But she was still plenty big and strong enough to stop me.

"You!" she shrieked, voice cracking. "Of all the people who might have survived—*you!*"

I figured it was better to just lie there. "Y—you know me?"

"I know *everyone* left in this miserable pesthole circle of Hell. That's where we are, you know! We're in Hell! We've been fooling ourselves that we're in some big *machine*, but what kind of sick mind could have dreamed up the kind of depravities and violence and hatred that these worlds contain? Now it's out of the bag. *We're in Hell!* You, me, and maybe the handful of others left when the rest of the universe fell away from lack of interest!"

"I—I don't understand . . ."

"They *want* you to press that button. And you know what'll happen? We'll be reborn, again and again, trapped in a whole new sequence of hells each more terrible than the last. They want you to think that maybe the next one will fix things, but they know better. We're all in Hell because, at heart, we are evil! And the evil in our hearts is what keeps creating horror after horror! Well, it stops here! The true death! *Oblivion!* Here we stop it and cheat the forces of Hell! We worked hard to do it and by damn we did it! And I'm not going to let anyone, particularly not *you*, cheat me out of my cherished goal!"

There was no question she was crazy, but she was one of those crazies that had a whole logical line to their madness. No giant vanishing cats and big stupid birds here. She *wanted* this destruction, which made it all the more important that, somehow, I survive long enough to figure out some way to push that damned red button. But how could I ever get past this madwoman?

"Look!" I cried to her, trying to get her to calm down. "I don't know who you are. I don't even know who I am, let alone what this place is or what's going on here! I'm not trying anything! Why didn't you show yourself when we were down here before?"

She hesitated a moment, as if unsure whether or not to

believe me. In the end, it appeared that she decided it made no difference. "I wasn't here when you first came down, although I've been coming here at least once a day since it happened just to make sure things were untouched. When I discovered two of my pretties were missing, I had to wait and see who it was who had taken them!"

"Nobody took them! My companions brushed against them and they turned into doubles of my companions!"

"They—what? *Stay on the floor, you worm!* They—you have companions? And they have—doubles?"

"Yes, he does!" came a firm voice behind us. The burned woman looked up, startled, and saw the two Black Hairs standing there. "Interesting," one of them muttered, mostly to herself. "Can't see worth a damn out there, but I see fine in here. Who the hell are you?"

"*You!* You came to take it away from me!" Burned Woman shrieked at Black Hair. "I will not permit this to happen! *I will kill you!*" she screamed, and launched herself at Black Hair.

The other Black Hair launched into Burned Woman, and they both crashed to the floor. Burned Woman was crazy, though, and, being crazy, had the strength of ten, physically throwing off her attacker. Seeing this, the first Black Hair looked at the frozen figures still around and her face suddenly brightened. Even as Burned Woman was getting up for the attack, Black Hair went over and touched another of the frozen figures. Burned Woman's jaw dropped as she saw the shimmering transformation take place and the new figure come alive. Now it was three against one.

As two of the three Black Hairs came after Burned Woman, the crazy one looked around in panic, and spotted the figure sitting in the chair I'd moved away from the button. She went over and put her hand on the one in the chair. Instantly the change and reanimation began to take place.

I counted seven or eight frozen figures, not including the ones sealed in the boxes. I climbed to my feet but hugged a point against one of the consoles to keep out of the way as a remarkable contest ensued, with Black Hairs rushing to transform the remaining figures before the two Burned Women became three.

I suddenly realized that they were so intent on each other, nobody was paying any attention to me at all. When the action shifted to the other part of the room, and I glanced around the console to see a fair number of Black Hairs launching themselves toward at least three Burned Women, I lunged for the wall console. One, maybe all, the Burned Women saw me move and turned to rush at me, to stop me by any means, but they were too charged up, operating too much on emotion and mad hatred to think straight. I was at the button cover before they could reach me. I, too, didn't have any time to think. It was now or never.

I pushed the red button all the way in just as hard as I could.

There was a sound of alarms ringing all over, and then, quite suddenly, as all the women stood there frozen at the clamor, the colored display seemed to suddenly flare anew, and everything winked out of existence, including us.

IX

MIND OVER MATTER

Death was nothingness, but it was also timeless. Existence vanished, as if a flame on a candle had been suddenly snuffed out.

There was no sense of being dead; the moment I pressed the button, the entire universe had ceased to exist, including me. The next thing I was aware of was a kind of flicker, as if a television was on but receiving no signal. Suddenly there was at least the attempt to broadcast one. This flash produced no cognitive recognition; it was a sensation I was aware of only in the past tense, after having experienced it.

Zip! Buzz! *"We almost got her! Hang on!"*

Buzz! Zip! *"Damn it! Reel her in! Reel her in! Trap! Trap! We don't want to have to go through this shit again!"*

Zip! Buzz! Zip! Zip! Buzz . . . *"Shit! Stand by! Reinsert! Digitizers on! Autoseek on! Go! Go! We'll lose 'em forever! Stand by! We'll get 'em next time, people! Okay, by the numbers, everybody! Backup energized and running. Very good. Equalize. Autonexus locked. On my count . . . Five—four—three—two— one . . . Reset!"*

The first thing I was aware of was awareness. If that sounds strange, try being dead first and then returning to life, for that was surely what had happened to me. Happened not just to me, but to everybody . . .

I opened my eyes and sat up.

Something was very wrong here, according to the rules as I understood them. I had . . . memories. I knew who I'd been, if not who I was supposed to be. I remembered Cory Maddox, the networking whiz kid; I remembered the other Maddox, confined to a wheelchair and out of the action. And I remembered Rini through her stored memories, and the nameless, faceless clone in the Brand Box hive, brought out and back to life. I remembered Cory, the little boy in a world of giant women. I even remembered breaking into the compound with Al and Lee after they'd blown reality sky high, even if they hadn't remembered who *they* were. Funny . . . Even as amnesiacs, we'd made a pretty good team, the three of us. Probably because we *were* amnesiacs.

What had happened? I'd received a lot of excess power from the Command Center trials, we'd had some kind of blind orgy, and that, somehow, had protected us from whatever had destroyed the universe.

What *had* gone on there?

In hindsight, I could deduce what had likely happened. Dee had been so hell-bent on getting Ben out of the fully digitized domain of the Brand Box that she'd run that old program they'd come up with to rescue Matt Brand, even though it wasn't at all clear that Matt Brand had wanted to be rescued. And the program, stopped the first time by Dan Tanaka, had proven just as dangerous as the chief programmer had feared. It had ripped apart our reality, crashed the whole damned program that ran the universe, and left many of us dead, many more in a frozen deathlike state, and just a few alive. Al, Lee, me, and Rita . . .

And, in spite of Rita's efforts, I'd pressed the button. Some kind of super reset button, I guess, considering that it was what the technician sitting there had been so close to pressing herself. My guess was that she'd been caught by surprise, hesitated, then scrambled to get that plastic cover off, but the disaster had caught her just before she could do it.

Well, I'd done it, in spite of Rita, with Al's help.

But where *was* Al? And Rita? And Lee?

And if I'd died, why had I awakened as a woman, not just as a woman, but naked, without jewelry, without anything at all, here, in this pastoral setting?

I didn't reflect on it at the time, but the nakedness itself instilled no modesty in me at all. It seemed so natural to be completely au naturel that I never had a second thought about it.

It was pleasantly warm, and there was a slight breeze that whispered through tall trees and felt quite nice as it caressed my exposed skin.

Nearby, a small waterfall carried what must have been snowmelt from the white-capped mountains nearby down into a river that bubbled and flowed off into the forest.

There were certainly insects, and some birds, and maybe small animals about, although I couldn't see any. No people, though, and no sounds of civilization.

Oddly, though, I also felt no fear. Curiosity, yes, and puzzlement, but no fear at all, even though I had no idea what might live in the area or who. It just didn't occur to me to fear anything or anyone in this place.

There was a duality in my mind that I recognized but didn't reflect upon. I had all those memories, and could ponder all of those events and use that knowledge and experience, but they had no relation to the "me" of the here and now except in the abstract.

As for the physical part of the new me, I had no perspective, so I might well have been six feet or four, but I was almost perfectly proportioned, lean, olive-skinned with long strawberry blond hair tumbling over my shoulders and down my back almost to my behind. I couldn't tell what my face was like, but for someone in this sort of environment with nothing to protect any part of the body I was remarkably free of blemishes, scars, or stretch marks. I felt in absolutely perfect condition, as good as I could *ever* remember feeling, and when I moved, in spite of the unfamiliar form and very long hair, it was with an effortless sense of total freedom and confidence.

The water didn't provide much of a reflection, being in frothy motion, but it was cool and refreshing. I wouldn't have hesitated to get in it, and swim across it.

After getting a drink, I decided that some exploration was in order. This was either a Brand Box or a new incarnation. The Brand Box seemed more likely; otherwise how could I enter like this, without passing through the void, without playing one of those stupid games, and still come out the opposite sex?

I also seemed to have, well, no physical flaws. The body was young and absolutely perfect. Even more interesting, I had sufficient continuity with my past lives to feel a bit odd-looking this way. Rini's memories were there but they were as if I'd seen a movie of her experiences rather than lived them, which, of course, I hadn't. My own experiences had been basically male, with the last one being male in a rather inferior social position. Still, I couldn't exactly knock the change. It was just too *comfortable*; a perfect fit.

It wasn't hard to find food in the forest and glades, with no particular work required. There were trees with fruit on them, wild vegetables springing up everywhere I looked, short trees with nuts and bushes with berries by the ton. I had no craving for meat of any kind; strictly vegetarian here. No hunting or cooking was required, either, to get more than enough to give all the vitamins, minerals, and nutrients a healthy body needed.

There were lots of pretty flowers around, too, and these often had oily secretions on their petals and leaves that turned out to have a variety of sweet scents that could be daubed on like perfume.

There were plenty of insects around, mostly doing what insects do, and it suddenly struck me that, while I had a lot of exposed area, so far I'd not been bitten once by anything.

That, too, was very unnatural, although I wasn't complaining about it.

More and more, though, I was getting the impression that this was the inside of a Brand Box, not an incarnation or reincarnation at all. It was too perfect, too convenient, to be anything else. But whose Brand Box? Certainly not one prepared for me, nor any that I'd seen before. No buildings, no structures of any kind, no artifacts, nothing.

And no other people, at least not so far.

It was only now that I remembered coming to, and the bits and pieces of conversation heard in the distance. Not God, surely, but a man's crisp voice giving orders and working at something, working at, perhaps, saving me. The memories I had must have come from the backups, which apparently had survived well enough to allow for transfer. Into what, though? A construct body in a Brand Box? Was this some kind of holding area where I could live until they would figure out how to get me out without crashing the computer again?

I kind of hoped it was something like that. It was starting to get kind of lonely, and I just didn't feel like communing with the birds and the chipmunks too long. I wouldn't make a very good forest fairy or wood nymph. I needed people.

I decided to find out if I could get to a height where I could see out over the forest, and tried some climbing. I was as sure-footed as a mountain goat and moved so naturally and so confidently that I barely realized just what I'd done until I was well up the slope and poised, balanced, on a small outcrop. The forest continued up with me, though, and I couldn't tell just how high I might have to go to get a clear view, so the thought came to me to climb one of the high trees.

Again, although I was quite human, I scampered up a tall tree as if I were a monkey or a squirrel and was soon high up in the complex branches. I was awed by my strength and balance, but, again, not once did I feel any fear, even leaping from tree to tree, hopping across to some very small limbs that some part of my mind assured me were big enough, until I eventually could make the top of one venerable old tree and looked out at my world.

The garden extended as far as I could see. There were larger open glades and areas where different sorts of plants grew, but from the mountains all the way to almost the horizon, it was a lush, verdant subtropical paradise. Only at the horizon did there seem to be a larger body of water, perhaps a coastline of an ocean or a huge lake.

It didn't matter. I needed to explore, to move around, to see who, if anyone, was here and what the rest of the place was like. An island or a whole world, it was certainly much larger and more formidable than the Brand Boxes I'd experienced in the past. If this was a Brand Box, and I was certain it had to be, it was the largest and most elaborate I'd seen and much more complex than I'd been told was possible.

Getting down was almost as effortless as getting up, and the odd thing was, I didn't feel winded. I'd not gotten a scratch or as much as a hangnail from all that work. It was almost as if, within the very primitive confines of this world, whatever I needed was provided and whatever I wanted to do within those limits was effortless.

It was certainly true that whenever I felt hungry there were substantial vegetables, ripe and ready to eat, all around, and if I felt thirsty, well, there were juice fruits and clear bubbling streams. The animals were mostly small, at least the ones I saw, and had no fear of me nor any need to fear. I had not the slightest desire to harm any of them.

At sundown, I felt my entire system slow to a tired crawl. I found a soft bed of moss, lay down on it, and was soon fast asleep. I slept the sleep of the dead, because I had no dreams I could remember and I found myself rising just after dawn. I'd had no fear of just going to sleep, no particular concern for the dark, and, when I awoke, I felt alert and anxious to start a new day.

There was a clamminess on my skin; a great mist had settled on the forest overnight, and it still cloaked the trees in the early morning, a gray, wet mass of fog that seemed to have risen to a height of many feet and soaked about everything, including me.

A nearby stream provided a morning swim that made me feel cleansed and tingling, and by the time I'd emerged from the water, wrung out my long hair, and picked breakfast, the mist was dissipating, vanishing first into the heights of the forest and eventually into the air, warmed by the rays of a bright new sun.

This was a Brand Box all right, no matter how large the scale. Nothing was this peaceful, and this paradise-like, in any kind of reality.

It was also, like most paradises, pretty dull. It was particularly bad without other people, but even with others there was only so much you could do in a place like this. There was no need to cultivate, no need to divert streams or rivers, no need to create weapons against nonexistent threats. That left little else to do except to keep exploring, maybe toward that coastline way off in the distance, in hopes of finding *something*.

Over a period of several days, I thought I was getting closer to the horizon glimpsed from the heights, but I was also moving more slowly and with less resolve. There was no way I could count the days, which, one being exactly like the one before, all ran together anyway. The forest was so uniform and unvarying that it was tough to measure my progress, and after a while I was just sort of going for the sake of going when I felt like it, and not going when I didn't.

I finally saw my face, not in a still pool of water, but in an outcrop of what seemed to be obsidian polished by the elements. My face had a kind of classical beauty to it and really fit in with the rest of me. The result was very pleasing indeed, although it was startling how very young I looked. Fourteen? Fifteen? There was a totally unspoiled, almost childlike look to my face and form in spite of its obvious development.

I wasn't surprised at being beautiful. Everything else was so perfect here, why not me?

More unsettling was that it was a stranger's face. There was no hint of Cory Maddox in it, male or female, nor anyone else I knew. It was such an innocent face as well; Eve before the Fall. The thought being the same as the deed, there was certainly no such childlike innocence inside my mind and soul, but something there longed for the state of being that was reflected back at me whenever I stared into a smooth surface or still water. No worry, no fear, no insecurity: all things accepted at face value and with childlike joy.

Was this, in fact, Eden or some virtual-reality concept of it? If so, where was Adam, and, more important, where was God?

All of these worlds were programs; programs, in fact, created by a great and complex machine playing God's role. Even the simplest of these worlds had far too much detail to be the product of a human mind—or minds. What kind of a machine could contain, manipulate, even access that kind of database? How enormous would it have to be, and how fast? Unknowable, inconceivable, mind-blowing—it was as good a definition of the human concept of God as I could think of.

More to the point, no matter how much memory or vestige of personality remained, no matter what our talents or predispositions, in every new world we had been as much a part of the program as the "spooks" created just for that existence. First and foremost we had to act according to the program; not a script, but certainly clearly defined paths and choices.

The whole idea of those mini–Brand Boxes in the control center, after all, had been to condition behavior, to try and set us on new, prescribed courses. Removed from that environment, such conditioning hadn't seemed to carry over in the long run, but it certainly had in the short term, steering to some degree the rest of the existence in that plane. I knew that all too well. I'd tried to fight my own "ultra-mall" existence and pretty well lost. If it hadn't been for Al showing up to taunt me every once in a while, that world would have engulfed me in spite of myself. Even with Al, I had grown into that program until it almost felt wrong to be out of it.

This existence, now, was different. It was wider, certainly, and so far lonelier, but that vision of myself, and the way I felt, without pressure, without fear or pain, was very, very seductive. Would Adam or God or Satan show up sooner or later? I didn't know. I only knew that every hour, every day in this place those questions seemed to recede more and more, and the memories of the past, of the many pasts now, also seemed to fade. It wasn't that they were gone, although one day they might be from lack of use, but rather that I no longer paid much attention to them.

There did remain a sense of playful curiosity. None of the animals that I'd encountered either feared or troubled me, and I regarded them much the same way. One morning I found a band of monkeys at a small water hole. They didn't fear me nor I them, and I was soon in among them, larger than they and, in spite of my flowing blond hair, certainly less hairy as well, but they seemed willing to share their meal of plantains, bananas, and fleshy fruits gleaned from the high trees and even to go through my hair, grooming it clean of whatever might have gotten in there. They were fun to play with, and I remained for some time—days, at least—before the bull monkeys started making overtures that were unmistakable. I declined, having no particular interest. I knew, though, that if I was not going to join them, I would have to leave them; it would be wrong to do otherwise, and I moved on.

I had many such experiences, each one seeming new and fresh and fun to me. I ran with the deer in the early-morning mists, and fed birds from my hand. I experienced everything and there was always something new. When I heard unusual sounds or saw something unfamiliar far off, I went toward it, never afraid of what might be there but rather in anticipation of finding something new.

I barely felt a sense of self at all after a while. I existed and interacted with the peaceful environment; that was enough. I could spend days in beds of fragrant, exotic flowers, watching insects that never bit go about very structured activities that were as incomprehensible as they were fascinating. I think it was less the program than just the total lack of threat, something I'd experienced before. Deep down, I just wasn't that much of a person of action, no matter which sex or role I was placed in. I was somebody who was dragged into action kicking and screaming, and quite content to let others do the heavy lifting. It wasn't cowardice, it wasn't anything like being self-important, it was just that I wasn't cut out for such responsibility.

One day, without conscious thought or plan, I made for the seashore. I think it was the pounding of the surf and the screech of the birds that attracted my curiosity, and when I reached the beach I wasn't disappointed. This was no calm inland sea such as the one in the shaman's world; this was a vast salt ocean, attacking the shore with huge, magnificent waves that rose up to several times my height and then curled, frothy white at the tops, before collapsing and crashing onto the white sand beach.

There was a lot of driftwood and organic debris washed up on the shore, almost forming a barrier to the beach, but once I got beyond it, which wasn't easy, I was out onto the hot sands and wondering how courageous I should be in the face of those waves.

The remnants of the waves rolled up the shore, finally reaching where I stood. The water was warm and seemed to surround and even grasp my ankles lightly, and I felt myself sinking a bit in the wet sand. Then it receded again to go out and meet the next wave, and I was able to pull myself free of the porridge-like sand and await the next one.

As I experimented, I grew a bit more adventurous, although something inside me knew that I could go into the water only so far before I risked being carried out to sea by the undertow. I finally decided on what should be a safe margin and actually sat down in the sand, letting the next wave crash in and almost engulf me, knocking me back just a little. The feel of the warm frothing water was a nice break from the hot sun.

I noticed after a while that I wasn't alone on the beach. The waves were not only bringing in occasional driftwood, they were also bringing little organisms and tiny, glittery shelled creatures that either would be washed up too far and eventually die or would remain in the wet sand, waiting for the next wave to take them back out. On these, I saw, a veritable army preyed, scuttling forward after each wave receded and feeding on the tiny sea animals, then scurrying back to the safety of the dry sand as the next wave crashed in. They were small themselves, although larger than the shelled creatures, and were the color of the sand itself. From a distance, you could only see them when they moved, and I managed to make my way back to see what they were.

Some kind of crab, it appeared, or maybe tiny lobsters. They were an intent bunch, but they certainly were no threat to me, even if they had a big claw they used to grasp and crack open the little shells. I watched them for quite some time, fascinated by their predictability. All day they seemed to do nothing but wait, then come forward at just the right time, seize and open one of the tiny creatures, eat it, and retreat until the next wave came in. It was like clockwork, a choreographed dance of the crabs. It was funny to watch, but it didn't seem like much of a life.

Still, I had the oddest feeling that it was supposed to mean something. Exactly what I wasn't at all sure of, but the feeling just wouldn't go away.

For the first time in so long I could not tell when, I began to think about the past and present. Maybe my subconscious had been thinking about all these strange experiences I'd had and rolling them around and around trying to put something together.

> *"The sun was shining on the sea,*
> *Shining with all his might;*
> *He did his very best to make*

> *The billows smooth and bright—*
> *And this was odd, because it was*
> *The middle of the night."*

The words came as a whisper, almost a taunting whisper, partly from the sound of wind and wave and partly from some hidden corner of my mind.

> *"The Walrus and the Carpenter*
> *Were walking close at hand;*
> *They wept like anything to see*
> *Such quantities of sand;*
> *'If this were only cleared away,'*
> *They said, 'it would be grand!' "*

It was so familiar, yet as foreign to me as Mongolian. It made no sense at all, yet I felt that it was telling me some things that were important, even profound.

> *" 'If seven maids with seven mops*
> *Swept it for half a year,*
> *Do you suppose,' The Walrus said,*
> *'That they could get it clear?'*
> *'I doubt it,' said the Carpenter,*
> *And shed a bitter tear."*

Where was this coming from? What had triggered it from the dark recesses of my mind, and why here and now?

> *" 'Oysters, come and walk with us!'*
> *The Walrus did beseech.*
> *'A pleasant walk, a pleasant talk,*
> *Along the briny beach;*
> *We cannot do with more than four,*
> *To give a hand to each.' "*

I could almost see their faces, almost remember the names. All I did know was that in one instant on the beach I'd gone from not thinking about anything to trying to think about too much. It was certainly easy to do here, in this setting; the monotony of the crashing waves and the march of the crabs provided few distractions, and I had nowhere to go and nothing else to do.

> "But four young Oysters hurried up,
>   All eager for the treat:
> Their coats were brushed, their faces washed,
>   Their shoes were clean and neat—
> And this was odd, because, you know,
>   They hadn't any feet."

But there were no oysters in the corners of my mind, but rather people; human faces, familiar faces . . .

> "Four other Oysters followed them,
>   And yet another four;
> And thick and fast they came at last,
>   And more, and more, and more—
> All hopping through the frothy waves,
>   And scrambling to the shore."

There were quite a number of people. Young ones, old ones, men, women, brown, white, yellow . . . *Volunteers all.* Volunteers for what? Who were they? When was this? And were any of those people me, or was I the point of view?

> "The Walrus and the Carpenter
>   Walked on a mile or so;
> And then they rested on a rock
>   Conveniently low;
> And all the little Oysters stood
>   And waited in a row."

The scene dissolved into the dance of the crabs on the beach before me, winking in and out, the people all prepped and lined up, the little sand crabs running forward and then dashing back, the people all stepping forward . . . *Step back! Step back! If you don't step back the waves will overwhelm you and carry you off!*

> " 'It seems a shame,' the Walrus said,
>   'To play them such a trick.
> After we've brought them out so far,
>   And made them trot so quick!'
> The Carpenter said nothing but
>   'The butter's spread too thick!' "

Yes, they'd followed the Walrus, all right, filled with promises of adventure and riches and perhaps immortality, and at least a chance at wonder. They'd been beguiled, all right, but by experts who'd spread it on way too thick. They were too smart for that. They knew what they were getting into. After all, weren't they all *experts*?

The thoughts seemed so clear when they came, yet the sum made no sense at all. Who were "*they*," anyway? Whose faces *were* those? I suddenly felt more confused and alone than ever, and the two sides of me—the one who was trying to figure out these profound questions and the other who not only didn't want to figure out the questions but didn't even understand what the questions were—collided in confusion.

I shorted out, more or less, and spent the day pretty much where I was, ignoring the dance of the crabs and just staring out at the monotony of the waves.

Near the end of that day, though, as the sun grew huge and orange and made ready to touch the waters, even that perfect symmetry was broken.

Something was out there.

Out in the water, perhaps a quarter mile or more offshore, there appeared to be some kind of boat, or floating island, with a periscope-like stick just ahead of it. As I squinted to try and make it out, I became aware that it was no longer going parallel to the shore but had turned and was coming in toward the beach, growing larger with each passing minute.

The big structure I'd taken for a boat now seemed more like an upside-down bowl, much larger than I was, and what I'd thought of as a pipe or periscope seemed an undulating thing that was clearly attached in some way to the great dome behind it. It was a great, long neck at the top of which was a huge reptilian head. This was some great, prehistoric creation the like of which I'd never seen before.

And, in another moment, the other side of me whispered, *"Yes, you have. But not this big, and not in this world."*

It was a turtle of some kind! A monstrous turtle whose neck and head alone were the size of my entire body.

For the first time since waking up here I felt a twinge, if not of real fear, at least of anxiety. I got up from the sand and walked backward toward the driftwood piles and jungle in back of me. I was reasonably certain that nothing that big and hulking could move fast enough, particularly on land, to catch me, but I really didn't want it to even make the attempt. I found a spot behind a huge driftwood log and settled in, quiet and motionless, to see what the great turtle would do once it reached the shore, and hoping that it would before the sun vanished completely and the whole area was plunged into darkness. I didn't want to still be there, listening to some great beast I could no longer see! I made very certain I could make it back into the jungle area, so I'd be protected and also have a quick exit.

With a final lunge, the creature almost plopped onto the sandy beach, making an explosive noise that scattered the sand crabs. And then it did something totally unexpected. It pushed off with its powerful front flippers and stood up on two legs! Two legs that weren't at all flippers, but actually had knees and enormous hooves, like some giant hippopotamus. Its tail was huge and wet, but was more a donkey's tail than a stubby turtle's tail. Even the face no longer looked so totally reptilian. It was sea green and leathery all right, but it more resembled the face of a cow than that of any cold-blooded creature.

It looked around, lumbered forward to a dry area about halfway between the high-tide mark and the start of the driftwood, and then it used its flippers to dig a hole in front of it. I was convinced that it had seen me, but its gaze went on past and it grabbed a large driftwood log and tossed it into the hole, then another, and another. I began to wonder if it was making a nest.

Then the right flipper reached toward the underside of the great shell and actually pulled open a heretofore invisible pouch there, reaching in to remove something that it managed to grasp in the curled end of the flipper. It was so fascinating I quite forgot my position, and the sun's last light vanished.

There was a spark, then several more, and suddenly there was a big flame that illuminated the creature. It reached down and with whatever had caused the flame it set fire to the nearest log. It sat back, staring morosely into the fire, and that cowlike face grew infinitely, almost pityingly, sad and I could actually see tears welling up in those big brown eyes.

It sighed, an unhappy, hopeless sigh, and then it muttered something I couldn't catch right off through the still pervasive sound of the ocean waves. It repeated it several times, finally in a loud enough voice to make sense to my ears.

"Soup!" it moaned. "Beautiful soup!"

I was too curious and the creature too strange for me to fear it. In a way, I almost pitied it, but only because of its melancholy manner. The fact that it spoke, though, and in a tongue I could understand, made it even less threatening, somehow. I moved a bit in my hiding place to try to get a better view of what the creature might be doing, then froze as the head snapped toward me, its two strange catlike eyes seeming to peer right at me.

"Alice? Is that you, girl?" it called, sounding more curious than knowing. "Come, come! Stand up! I shan't eat you. I'm not well equipped for that sort of thing."

I could have run off, I suppose, but the sense of menace I'd felt before had not returned with this creature. I stood, a bit shyly, but did not approach it or say a word at first. In fact, I'd said nothing at all since I'd arrived in this world, and I wasn't even certain that I had a voice! And something about oysters rattling around in the back of my head kept me from fully trusting even the friendliest of monsters.

"Oh, my! I like your taste in clothing this time around," the creature commented. "And, my! How you've grown up!"

"Sir, is that who I am? Alice?" My voice was there, all right, but it sounded strangely high-pitched and breathy.

"Of course! Of course! Who else could you be? Hmmmm . . . On second thought, perhaps not. More like the Red Queen, in some respects, only a lot better looking. The hair certainly befits a Red Queen. Perhaps a Red Princess? Don't remember *her*, but, then again, my memory isn't all that wonderful anyway."

I did not follow this. "Why would you think I am a red queen or princess?"

"Why, it's obvious as the—er, well—as any prominences on your body. You run and you run and you run as hard as you can and you always stay in the same place. The Red Queen has understanding but to little purpose. She understands that she must run as hard as she can just to stay where she is. Alice, on the other hand, runs and runs and has no under-standing of where or why, but at least she moves. I see ele-ments of both, in equal measure, in you, so I shall call you Alice the Red."

I didn't particularly like the name, but it was as good as any. "And what shall I call *you*?" I asked the creature.

"Me? Goodness! Why, I'm a mock turtle, of course! Can you have forgotten so much without dying first?"

"But mock turtle is called that because it isn't really a turtle!" I objected.

The creature brightened. "Indeed? You remember that, then? But, of course, it's wrongheaded. One gets mock turtle soup from mock turtles. Where else?" He sighed mournfully. "Soup! Be-u-tiful soup!"

I didn't want him sinking into self-pity again, so I asked, "Do you know how I came to be here? And what is intended for me?"

The Mock Turtle froze, then looked confused. "Why would you want to know that? Do you want to leave?"

"Well, it *is* very peaceful here, and quite wonderful, but it is also quite lonely, and existence seems without a point."

"Point? *Point?* We are born, grow up all too quickly, become old and infirm all too soon, then we die and are food for worms. The universe either expands forever, in which case it grows cold and dies forever, or it contracts and tries again but in the process wipes out all that has come before, thus making everything and everybody—every action, emotion, song, poem, great discovery and damned good wine—irrelevant, for it all might as well not have ever existed."

"But I do not suffer here!"

"*Precisely!* So why leave? Why trade pointless peace for pointless suffering? At least here no one will make you into soup!"

"I should hope not!" I responded, a little unsettled by the thought. "Must it all be suffering beyond here?"

"All. For this is Hell, nor are we out of it. Eden before the Fall was mere ignorance. Apes in a gigantic garden without two profound thoughts in their heads. Suffering and dying was the price of becoming human."

"But I am not ignorant here!" I protested.

"Indeed? And what do you know?"

I thought a moment. "I know mathematics, and some history, and geography, and biology, certainly."

"Useless!" snorted the Mock Turtle. "You don't explore in any systematic way, you don't plan, nor have you any objectives. You grab your food off handy trees and you run through the jungle and up and down hills and beaches. You may count all the sand on this beach, but what will it achieve? Does it matter one whit if you know that you have two arms and two legs and two eyes? Why bother to count the fruits and nuts? They are all around you! History? Here, one day is just like the last or the next, so what good is it? Geography? There are mountains, jungles, grasslands, deserts, beaches, and bodies of water. End of geography lesson. Biology? You eat when you are hungry, you sleep when you are tired. Big deal.

"You do not *need* any of your knowledge here, which is why you have been losing it. You are reverting to the ape from which your ancestors came, and even that is more than you need here. Soon all that will be left will be the physical shell. When you no longer even think on *that*, you will lose that, too, and begin physically reverting to the form you require."

As he spoke, I could feel my whole body tingle, and the hair that had trailed down my back now blended and became one with my body. My arms grew unnaturally long, my feet took on handlike attributes. I felt myself bending over, balancing on my knuckles, but still looking forward at the creature. I panicked and tried to scream "Stop it!" but all that came out were guttural grunts.

I was becoming, if not a orangutan, certainly a creature more closely related to that ape than to *Homo erectus*, possibly the common ancestor we and the orangutans shared long, long ago.

I tried to grasp at thoughts, any thoughts, but everything began slipping away. All the knowledge, all the language skills vanished, leaving only emotion, instinct, and a kind of simple pictographic thinking that was entirely devoted to the situation at hand. In moments, the only thing that remained was the sense of panic, which I instinctively dealt with by bounding back across the driftwood and into the jungle, effortlessly climbing the tallest tree. Once high up in the leaves, I wrapped arms and legs around a branch and, feeling safe and comfortable and having no remaining memory of why I was up there, I went to sleep.

How long I lived as an ape I can't say. In some ways it was the same existence as before, only freed from thinking beyond the moment, comfortable with my ability to leap between trees and secure in the feeling that the jungle was my element. I ate a lot and I slept a lot and had no thoughts more complex than whether I wanted the big round fruit or the little red fruit.

It was as boring as it sounds, but without real cognitive thought, it didn't bother me at all. In fact, I'd quite forgotten just about everything except for one traumatic event, and that was why I stayed away from the beach. Still, even that fear was hard to hold on to, and eventually I wound up randomly coming out close to the ocean shore again. Emerging in the middle of a bright, sunny day with no odd sounds or scents to alert me to any dangers, I came abruptly face-to-face with the Mock Turtle once more.

I froze, filled with panic and fear, then tried to run, but it was no use. Something had hold of me, paralyzing me at first, then drawing me to the big creature whether I wanted to go or not.

The Mock Turtle looked down at me with its almost comical half-cow, half-pig face and seemed to smile, then it reached down, pushed an area on the underside of its shell, and a door popped open. Had any real part of me remained, I would have recognized the helmet it removed from the compartment, realizing that it was a version of the direct neural interface that I'd helped develop for the Command Center, but all I could do now was tremble as the creature placed the helmet over my ape's head and then gave it power.

The orangutan brain I now had wasn't capable of fully

absorbing all the complexities of a human life, let alone the kind of memory and skills I'd built up over several life-times, but enough came through so that I could remember things right up to the time when this impossible creature had turned me into an ape with a comment and a gesture. It also allowed me to understand, within some limits, what he was saying.

"Ah! I was wondering when you'd show up!" the Mock Turtle commented as it replaced the helmet in the compartment and closed it. "I'm sure you're wondering what *that* was all about, and who and what I am."

I tried to speak, but only ape sounds emerged.

"Don't bother with that," he cautioned. "You don't have the vocal equipment. However, as to who and what I am, I am a computer program, a subroutine masquerading as a creature. So are you, which is how, with a bit of rewriting and some access to the operating system, I was able to change you. The one difference between us, however, is that I have no independent life beyond this vast electronic illu-sion machine. I exist because another created me to be here and told me what I was supposed to do. You, on the other hand, are mentally here but physically *there*. The problem, you see, is that you haven't been very good at doing any-thing about your situation. You have occasional flashes of ingenuity and outright guts, but they are few and far between and just as often motivated by fear rather than a sincere attempt to solve the problem. You have such pitifully modest wants, you are almost as boring as this place. Fulfill those meager needs, and you don't want to rock the boat. In that sense, are you any different than the ape I made you become? Simple wants, simple needs, easily satisfied. You exist, but want little and get just that much, and nobody cares and nothing moves. You don't create or destroy. You don't act, you react. For all that, you've gotten nowhere. You might as well be an orangutan."

I would have liked to have protested, to have argued my

own case, but I realized with some shame that even if I were capable of doing so it would be a sham to just prop up my own ego. What the creature said was true.

"I am going to assume," continued the creature, "that you can recall enough about computers to at least understand a few analogies. Then we'll go on from there. We are in a holding area, a kind of limited backup region. The fools in the last incarnation caused the equivalent of a network crash. The system and its requirements are a bit too comprehensive to allow for a mirrored backup, so what was backed up and stored were the memories, personalities, and experiences of the true humans connected to the network. It has taken quite some time and considerable work to bring as much as this little world back online. A great deal of cobbling together, pirating of material and resources, and outright kludging was necessary. The bottom line is, we have it running and it is stable—for now. It may continue to be so for a very long time. It took quite a while to crash it the last time. However, we have no way of knowing for sure how long it will last or whether the self-repair mechanisms that were adequate before will continue to be so here. And, if there is another crash, there is no longer a backup. We had to splice all that in. If the system goes down again, you will die, utterly, completely, and forever."

That was something I could understand, and well, and it scared me.

"So, we come to the point of the exercise," the Mock Turtle continued. "There are those who are working to get everyone out of this trap before it is too late, but this sort of neural inter-connect is unlike anything seen up to this time. Human minds could not create or maintain it. It was not even designed by a computer. It was designed by a vast assemblage of computers that were in turn designed by an even more vast assemblage of computers, proceeding back to, at some point, a human designer. In other words, the people who sent me haven't the vaguest idea how to get you out without killing you. If they did, they would have done so by now. They cannot do it, at least not alone. They need to be met halfway, from inside the machines, where we are now. Until now, it was guesswork in the extreme to send any sort of messages here, and all that were sent tended to be twisted and turned into metaphors. That is because you and the others actually control what's happening here. You just don't do it on a conscious level. Those who sent me are convinced that the metaphors have given you sufficient information to get to that halfway point. The problem is, only you, not they, can see and hear the metaphors. You must interpret them as if they were some obscure Biblical text and discover what they are trying to tell you. You must actively pursue and reach the point where we can maintain direct communication, not just intermittent images. You are bright and levelheaded and this is one reason you have had so many encounters, but you must find the courage and the will."

I didn't like that. I wasn't sure I wanted it. I certainly didn't want the responsibility for it all. The Mock Turtle, however, knew my thoughts and feelings.

"You are at the moment of decision," it told me. "You must seize and hold the lead. You must be the one up front, for nobody else better qualified has survived the system crash unscathed. Others were far more qualified and some were smarter than you, but they are now back to the baseline and all their pasts are but dreams and visions and nightmares. If you refuse this last chance, all may pay the price. But, if you do, we will wait, hope, and pray that nothing else happens until another one can be brought back up to the levels where they can do the job. In your case, I give you two choices. Choice number one is back there. If you turn and go back toward the jungle, all that you now remember, even this encounter, will fade. Then you will meet a band of true orangutans led by a dominant male and you will be incorporated into the band. Since nothing truly dies here, that is the way you will remain until the final system crash or until all others are out and there is a shutdown. Until then, every day will be like the other. You will never have to make a decision or think a complex thought. But no one, *no one*, will ever come for you."

It was not something I found appetizing. It sounded in its own way very much like brain death. Still, I could not help but understand his point. If I could not lead in this circumstance, I was only an impediment.

"The other choice is to go through *there*," the Mock Turtle said, pointing toward the ocean, which now opened to reveal a great spiral, a tunnel into the depths of the metaphorical machine. There was certainly no question in my mind that I would enter it. It was a relief just to know that the system was back up. No sketchy half-realities and posts with signs on them. A real world lay beyond that point, a world that may be virtual, but that still would be as real and solid as any ever known to me.

"I see your decision," the creature noted, "but I give you fair warning. Your sole reason for existence now is to interpret the subroutines and the experiences, both past and future, and come up with a plan. If you die in the attempt, well, you will still be one with them. If you do not shirk your duty, you may succeed. But if, after a while, you find your old habits coming back, if you voluntarily run to the security of the shadows, then you will find yourself becoming just what you are now. You will never *quite* be alone; I shall have my mark on you!"

It was a sobering, scary thought, but I had no choice. I was forced into this position by circumstances and the system, and if that absolved me of some overall responsibility, I felt I could hack the rest. I didn't know, didn't even really believe, that I could solve it, but I sure as hell was gonna try . . .

"I should tell you," he called after me as, bounding on all fours, I raced for the open tunnel that parted the seas, out of Eden toward a new Purgatory. "We've not had all the time and resources to rebuild the system, so some things have been rather jury-rigged. It should, overall, make things easier, we think."

I hardly heard him; my sole purpose was to get *out* of this Eden into that familiar tunnel and on to some other existence. I made it and hit the hard floor, splashing a bit of water that had made its way in through the open tunnel mouth. Behind me, receding into nothingness, came the pitying wail of the Mock Turtle, crying "Soup! Be-u-tiful soup! How we are all in such a soup!"

X

EQUAFEMININE
INTUITION

The Mock Turtle hadn't been kidding about things being more rudimentary than I remembered. The smooth, seemingly artificial rocky coating inside of the transition tunnel was the same, and as before it led, eventually, to a huge open area where vast electronic gadgetry like some giant circuit board stretched out and all around me. But it *looked* different, *felt* different, even *smelled* different. Still in the body of the orangutan, I wasn't at all clear whether this was truly a difference or just the result of the altered senses of the animal body.

Beyond this point had always been one of those petty games with deadly holograms and silly puzzles, and, for a moment, I stopped and looked around at the vast electronic region. The orangutan wasn't built for speed, but it was certainly built for climbing. It was enormously tempting to change the pattern this time, to slide off the walkway and try to climb using the stuff that was on the vertical circuit boards and see what was up, or down, there. Up, most likely would be the most promising. The vastness above and the bottomless pit below didn't really bother me; climbing was so automatic that the idea of ever falling was simply unthinkable. What was intimidating was that the endless expanse above, going up to the vanishing point, provided no goal to work toward. How much of a climb would it be? Hours? Days? Weeks? All without food or water, most likely.

And what if there were no way out? This wasn't reality; I wasn't sure at this point if I could truly recognize reality if I saw it. In a virtual world, you really *could* keep climbing into forever . . .

No, the smartest thing would be to keep going as usual and see if I could still somehow vary the pattern. It would be interesting to bypass that staging area for once, to emerge without having to grow up in that other world, an alien, an invader.

I also couldn't help but wonder whose world the next one would be. Usually it was created from the mind of the first one through or the first to die, but in this case there had been a reset. It was quite possible that whatever world I entered would be something out of my own subconscious, my own dreams and fantasies.

Wasn't that what Al and the others had been trying for? To create their own worlds, their own ideal existences? And hadn't they all failed miserably on that score?

What was rolling around in *my* head, anyway? Gender confusion, that was for sure. Deep down, I really wasn't sure which sex the original, the *real* me, was. I'd been comfortable in both male and female roles, and found them both a bit lacking as well. Still, being a neuter hadn't been much fun. I'd sure have liked to have been smarter, tougher, or, at least gutsier. What kind of dreams had I had? Not much in *this* existence—after all, apes didn't exactly have high imagination levels. In the past, it had been mostly a blank, with my dreams unremarkable and thus unremembered. A few had been wild fantasy types, but nothing I could put my finger on.

Hell, the program would probably build the world at random taking pieces from all of us. There was only one way to find out.

The puzzle was almost tailor-made for me, a halfhearted

gesture. Kind of a big jungle gym, very dark, with a lot of nasty, snarling, snapping things in the total darkness below. The thing was, this ape wasn't about to misstep on such a simple and natural device.

The gateway at the end of the rabbit hole was easily in view. The test wasn't so simple that you could just climb to it, but it was within a few meters of the end of the bars and an easy, effortless leap for a big ape like me. I didn't even hesitate.

This time there was no holding area, no staging, no setup to a new life. It was as if the orangutan body hit the white static of the reentry window, was immediately reshaped, and emerged, running, on the other side.

And I was running, or, more accurately, trotting. I was erect and feeling human again, my arms at my sides, but I was still going forward on all fours! It was a momentarily eerie sensation that took me completely by surprise. I came to a stop, first looking around and trying to get some bearings, then examining myself.

The immediate area seemed fairly normal. In fact, it was an extremely well maintained dirt road through a bountiful, green region of leafy trees, rolling meadows, and gentle hills. It was warm but not particularly hot, and the sun was angled upward but still to the east, or so something told me. Midmorning in— where?

And what the hell was *I*?

Of all the lives I'd lived to this point, save that of the ape— and that was a special case—I'd been human. Male, female, or other, but nonetheless human. I still *felt* human, but I definitely wasn't. My long strawberry blond hair was back in billowing amounts, and my skin was darkly tanned but not weathered. Ordinary-looking arms and hands, if perhaps with fingers longer than symmetry would suggest, and very large but firm breasts. The arms were muscular; I felt like I could lift somebody my own size.

All of which, of course, went down into a horse's body. A *centaur*! I'd always liked centaurs; to be sure, I'd also liked other mythological creatures as well, but there was something alluring, powerful, even sexy about a centaur. The waist was a marvel of engineering, almost snakelike in its ability to move and twist. I could lean far forward, and if I was careful of my balance I could almost touch the ground with my head. I could also turn almost all the way around, enough so that I could easily reach the hindquarters with the very long arms and fingers. I could certainly mount, cinch, open, and shut the saddlebags I had in the middle of my back. I also had a really long tail that was moved by an enormously powerful tailbone. If it weren't for the weight of the hair, the tail could have been dangerous.

There was some sense of civilization, or minimalist modesty, anyway. The breasts were supported by a kind of halter top and I also wore a light open tunic of brightly colored cloth. Nothing really concealed the very human vagina at the base of the torso, although thick soft fur made it nearly invisible. I was surprised that it was there; it hadn't ever been in any concept of a centaur I'd ever known.

Also impossible to conceal was the very large appendage that hung between the two rear legs. I could even bend down, look back between my forelegs, and see it.

This was a human female form mated to a stallion's body.

Unisex centaurs. I could hardly wait to see how they mated.

Other accoutrements were noted and cataloged. A very nice jeweled pendant around my neck showed real craft, not some primitive workings. Two simple gold bracelets, one for each wrist, showed taste. The horse's hooves, too, were notable, not only for being obviously well maintained but also for being shod. I pressed a leg into a soft bit of dirt, then leaned down and looked at the print. Reading backward, I could swear it bore the words "Rebock Sport" but couldn't be positive.

Jogging horseshoes?

Maybe that explained the wristwatch. A stem-wound affair, but still a nice, tasteful piece of functional jewelry that showed the time to be roughly 9:45.

So what did this tell me? I had hooves, which would explain the lack of paved roads, but there were also deep, clear ruts that indicated some kinds of wheeled traffic for which paving would be best. Nice handcraft, but nothing high tech. That wouldn't be so handy if I had to find the Command Center. It would be here, someplace, but it would be an artifact, hidden, impenetrable until somebody who knew what it was came to it. And where would it be? Texas? Washington State? Why not Mombasa or Berlin, Buenos Aires or Yokohama?

Well, nothing would be gained by standing there, that was for sure. I wasn't exactly in Times Square, and I needed to find some measure of civilization if only to learn more about this world.

There hadn't been any preliminaries to this existence; no birth and childhood and no firm memories. Perhaps they would come, but not now, not yet. The Mock Turtle had said that things would be a little different, a little basic, and he was right.

I stopped, reached around, and rooted through the saddlebags. Combs, some makeup, some bottled pills and remedies I wasn't at all sure about, a deck of cards, and a wallet. I pulled out the wallet, opened it, and discovered first a large card with a face staring back at me. My face, I supposed. I hoped so. It was a damned pretty one, even in its kind of sepia-toned old-fashioned look. Next to it was typed, obviously on a poorly maintained typewriter, some vitals.

If found, return to Jayce Magnus Cord
Rural Route 4, General Delivery,
Sharpsburg, Marysland.

Jayce—pronounced Jay-See, I knew—Magnus Cord . . . No more Cory Maddox? That, or a variation of it, and my middle name had been a part of all previous existences. I'd assumed that just as Al Stark had always been Al or Alberta, I'd always be named something close to Cory Maddox. This was bad. It would make it next to impossible to find any of the others, none of whom would remember anything about the past. Even discounting being a centaur, I didn't look or sound anything like I had before. It meant I was totally on my own here.

On the other hand, the program did tend to get us entangled in spite of ourselves. This protected me as well as inconvenienced me. Al might not remember, but Al would still be Al no matter what the face or form, that I was pretty sure of.

"Marysland . . ." Close enough. Sharpsburg. That rang a bell somewhere, but I couldn't remember why. Something in history happened there, only it probably hadn't happened here. In any event, other than that one famous thing, it was a small town by any stretch of the imagination. In fact, just thinking about the town brought it to my mind's eye, and it really was small and rustic, although just off the National Pike and near transportation.

Hmmmm . . . So knowledge of this world was going to come in pieces, but it was going to come. That, at least, was something.

The card gave a birthdate for me, but it was meaningless since I didn't know what year it was now, or from what historical marker the years were calculated. A twin-sexed centaur Jesus just wasn't something I was ready for yet, although the moment I thought of it, just such an image popped into my mind. I still wondered how they would crucify a centaur, and at the same time I didn't really want to know.

My occupation was listed as "messenger," and my employer as the Beneficial Insurance and Trust Corporation of Richmond, Virginia. Exactly what I carried for the company was unstated; I had by this time noted that among the pretty green trees on my left was an unmistakable line of telephone poles. This world had phones or at least telegraphs.

The road went up through a notch in the hills and opened to a panoramic view of the countryside. Below me was, I knew, the National Pike, a large, wide road, a kind of freeway for the horsey set, well paved and maintained with two very wide and separated lanes. It was also quite busy, with centaurs pulling wagons—small wagons with one centaur; larger ones with teams of them—going back and forth in great numbers. I trotted down toward the pike as if I knew where I was going, trying to let myself go on automatic until my memories filled in.

It was already amazing to me how easily and comfortably I seemed to handle this new, very large body. I liked it. It had both beauty and power. When I got in among the rest of the folks, though, I discovered that, as in all the other worlds I could remember, not everybody met those two positive attributes. A lot of folks were just plain ordinary; there were old folks, young folks, people who were definitely fat and people who were ugly under any circumstance. Most of the horse parts were colored brown or black, but there were all sorts of others here and there, and a lot of them clearly had dyed the hair on their bodies to rather distinctive shades. Racial features tended to be about what I'd expect in this area of America in any of the worlds, although the only really light-complected people were the rare ones whose equine parts were white and golden yellow.

A lot of them were ratty-looking, too, and few had the kind of coiffured hair and billowy tail I did.

I couldn't help but wonder if I'd created all this somehow. It struck a cord with me, definitely, but I couldn't remember imagining or dreaming anything remotely like this.

My new self did seem to know where it was going, joining the stream of traffic at the junction, keeping left and allowing the wagons and carts to pass on the right, and galloping along at a pretty good clip. No demons or faeries or other mythological creatures made any appearances but there was certainly animal life. I spotted some deer off in the distance at one point and there were dogs, cats, and chickens around. Birds and insects abounded but hardly in a supernatural way. This was simply a bizarre alternate evolution of the dominant species, although, of course, you could argue that the two-legged ground-hugging ape with the big brain was about as likely. It *did* seem that every creature, at least every mammal, was dual-sexed; there were no males and females in the warm-blooded animal kingdom.

The major problem with a dominant race this large—even though I actually stood maybe five-six or -seven and was proportionate, and the others ranged from a head shorter than me to a head taller—was that there was a need for a great deal more food and drink than a normal human would need, and because we walked or trotted or galloped most places, we got enough exercise moving our large bodies that we definitely needed greater quantities to eat. The solution was huge blocks of what I could only call oat or straw cakes. They had kind of the feel and consistency of, say, Krispie Treats, but instead of rice, they were made up of what tasted like shredded wheat. They appeared to be cheap to make and plentiful as well. I felt like a pig considering the number of them I would eat at road-side vendors, but supporting the extra weight made it essential. Meals, which were highly spiced and included meat and meat products as well, were also large, but it was the ingestion of huge quantities of what were called orn cakes, or "ornies," several times a day that made it easy to last between meals. In a pinch, the omnivorous race could eat plain old grass or leaves or piles of oats, but these were about as appetizing as dirt.

When I got to the train station, I found quite a milling throng of all shapes, sizes, and ages. It was also an education in a bit of the biology here, what with mothers having breasts hanging out and babies in a part of the anatomy I hadn't noticed in my self-exam before, a kind of marsupial pouch in what I thought of as the stomach region. Sure enough, I had one, too, but if one didn't have a nursing child, the opening of the pouch was so tight that it seemed more like a flap of very tough, leathery skin. And the child needed the pouch, too, as it turned out, since it seemed that babies here were born with faces, necks, and tiny arms, but with no equine legs. Sort of like big, fat worms. As they grew, the forelegs came in first, and they looked out on the world with the tiny forelegs hanging out of the pouch; ultimately the rear legs came in and the children were on their own. Just the thought of hooves inside a pouch pressing against my chest gave me shivers. Still, the computers were continuing with their fine detail; I couldn't help thinking that the evolutionary tree here must be something to behold.

There wasn't much unusual about the station itself except that it seemed designed to keep the throng outside. The tracks looked pretty much like normal railroad tracks, so I wasn't at all sure what I would see, but after I had bought a ticket—to Georgetown, Marysland, my inner voice instructed—and waited, munching ornies with the rest, we heard the train coming and soon had it in sight. It was a big, black smoker, a steam train, not some antique on a nostalgic ride at an amusement park, but a real, working engine.

The cars had no seats—as I was learning, nobody sat in this world—but a trainman hit some kind of control and row after row of doors popped open just like on European trains. We went in and entered a roomy, padded stall. There was space for two to stand in each compartment, plus a large open area beyond that, which proved to be a corridor about wide enough for one person to pass. You definitely weren't supposed to move on this kind of run; as it turned out, the corridor was used by the conductor to collect tickets, and then by vendors with carts selling everything from more ornies to large centaur-sized subs and meat pies and the like, as well as heavy, sugary soft drinks, beers, ales, and honeyed mead.

My mental state through all this was one of wonder and curiosity, as if I were suddenly dropping in on an alien but familiar planet as an observer. I didn't feel that I *belonged* here, not in the way I'd felt I'd belonged to the prior lives I'd lived. My memory was spotty, and while I was becoming more comfortable with the nonhuman form, I never felt born and raised to this. Still, it being the first nonhuman world I'd

entered, at least that I could remember, there was this nagging
question in the back of my mind that wouldn't go away.

Everything you think you know is wrong . . .

What if the ape-human form was merely a string that consisted of the worlds I could remember? What if it wasn't my
true or native form? I wasn't sure that *this* form was native to
me; it seemed too strange and the world a little too backward.
Still, the mere fact that I was now living in this world and in
this form undermined my fundamental assumptions about my
origins and the true form and nature of the others as well. This
was a virtual world, real or not in an objective sense, as were
all the others. If I could be an orangutan, a man, a woman, a
consciousness that could ride electrical circuitry, and now a
centaur—where did that leave my concept of "reality"?

Suppose we were more of those little aliens in the saucer?
Or were there ever any aliens at all? How could anyone know
the truth, even about themselves? And, worse, would we
know the truth when we saw it?

Somebody knew. Somebody sent the Mock Turtle, somebody who sounded an awful lot like a programmer in a control
room, got through to me on the demonic highway. Somebody
was the caterpillar right at the start of all this. The March Hare
Network members were just others like myself, but who was
the Mad Hatter or the Cheshire Cat? And who or what was the
Walrus that seemed to follow me?

This world seemed ill suited for such answers. Not only was
I just winging my way around, but the more I saw of it, the
more I was convinced that the technological level here was far
too primitive for the kind of computers and government and
university research that centered around the Command Center
and made it an integrated part of the other worlds. This was
certainly a developing world, and a potentially interesting one,
but it was unfolding at a much, much slower pace. This wasn't
the nineteenth century, it just felt like it. The cities had electricity, of a sort, but not everyone had it in their homes. It was

mainly for business and commerce, and the big steam generators that created it did so without real controls. Rural villages
and farms had no power at all, and even in the city you had to
have money or be a fancy commercial place to have it;
common folks used oil or kerosene.

It seemed that steam technology was well developed,
but that storage of electricity from steam generators was extremely poor.

Also poor was much of the population. The masses seemed
on the whole illiterate and ignorant, but working twelve-hour
days six days a week kept them from having much time to
reflect on that condition. The mere fact that I was both educated by this world's standards and attractive gave me two
limbs up on the crowd. True, my "education" seemed to have
resulted mostly in my being able to read, write, and do simple
sums, but it was sufficient in this world to get me into at least
the second level of society.

I was, in fact, being sent to the city by my clan—a sort of
large family unit that was the norm here—to make my fortune,
with references from the bank and some limited experience in
travel. I carried a letter of introduction from our Eldest, Ebana
Magnus, to Senior Delegate Charl Linton Brown, who was a
kind of distant relative or something, with hopes of getting me
into the civil service, since Georgetown was just across the
river from Alexandria, the district capital.

As the large marble and red brick city across the river came
into view, the native part of me gasped in some awe at a city so
large. The rest of me, the older me, was surprised at just how
modest it seemed. Except for some enormous pyramidal structures in the distance, it was quite low, with nothing higher than
four stories and two being the norm. Of course, stairs weren't
very practical for this equine form, and wooden or grooved
concrete ramps were used in most buildings, so this wasn't a
big surprise. The pyramids were something of a mystery, but
until I got the chance to get closer, there'd be no way to tell

just what they were for. Not religious structures, anyway; single-story churches and cathedrals abounded, many with modest steeples.

Finding the delegate's house wasn't all that hard. Georgetown was the genteel part of the capitol district, with a lot of old houses, lots of expensive dwellings, fancy-looking restaurants, and law offices. It was quiet and smelled quite fresh, compared to the Pike and the train, which, frankly, had smelled of sweat and dried dung.

The streets were mostly cobblestone and quite well lit; almost the whole area save the back alleys was lit by primitive but serviceable electric lights, as were most of the buildings.

Brown turned out to be a middle-aged character in pretty good condition but clearly with hair dyed and deliberately kept short to minimize the thinness. My voice was fairly high-pitched, even to my ears, but Brown's was a medium tone, more in the male than female octave range, although this was fairly common for the race as it aged. So, too, was being over-dressed on the human part to minimize other signs of aging and, particularly, confirmation of menopause, although one look at the face, even as good a one as money could buy, told me all I needed to know.

"So, Cousin Ebana's youngest comes to the big city," the delegate commented, looking over the letter of introduction and chuckling. "Bank messenger! I remember that bank. Still got only one teller window?"

"Yes, cousin. Just the one. But there are a number of branches—"

"Never mind!" Brown snapped, cutting me off. "You can get settled in one of the spare rooms on the second floor. There's a ramp at the back. I seldom eat here, but there is a pantry, kitchen, and small dining room for meals, and there is running water, even *hot* water, inside. The privy is in the basement. Make sure you use it! I want no nasty smells around this house!"

I was taken aback at the idea that I would do such a thing,

but I was very clear that, in the delegate's mind, I was one real country rube.

I was also a sexy and attractive country rube, though, and we were very distant cousins, so there was a certain lecherous radiation from my host and benefactor that I hadn't really counted on. Fortunately, at least at the start, it stayed there.

I spent about a week getting oriented in the area, occasionally meeting with Brown's associates, mostly political types and lobbyists. I played the role of cute little thing from the country as well as I could, while trying to use some common sense. If someone or something was manipulating me to a degree, then I was here, in this place at this specific time, for a reason. Since the technology and culture were obviously not at the heart of things, and since the system crash had scrambled our names and faces, giving me the only long-term memory of the bunch, then it was clearly something that only I could make use of.

Had the Command Center melted down or did it still move with us? It wasn't in too great a shape the last I remembered it, but I was convinced that it had to be here somewhere. What would these people—who had yet to perfect the battery or know the wonders of vacuum tubes, let alone the miracles of silicon in the same role—think if they actually found the center? It also had to be empty, deserted, at least insofar as the folks who usually ran it would be concerned. Some people might have survived in life-support modules and Brand Boxes, but they'd still be trapped. Could their bodies be maintained for that period, or were they now only consciousnesses inside the boxes?

Now that was a thought. If I could find the Command Center and get in, and if the power was self-contained, then there might well be allies in there, and maybe even means of communication. Certainly there was a connection to some pretty damned powerful computers. If I had control, things would be effectively reversed. *I'd* be in control of it in the way Al and Dan and that crew had been in all my past memories. Not just a backup mechanism like Walt and Cynthia had, either. The whole thing. The control panel for reality. The Dashboard of the Gods . . .

There had been other times, other worlds, other lives. There had been worlds more primitive than this by far, and worlds filled with magic and mysticism, superstition and a limited cosmology, and the Command Center had always been there. Inside the Keep of the evil vizier, beneath the sands of time, buried, hidden, sometimes unknown deep within ancient caverns, it nonetheless had always been there. And always in someone else's control.

I really didn't want to dwell much on that system crash; too much was potentially lost, not just ancient enemies but friends and lovers, and a great part of me as well. All wiped out, erased. All that was left was my own memory of them. It was depressing as hell.

I finally got work as the secretary to a medium-level bureaucrat in the department of the interior. It wasn't like the department I had known, the one that ran the national parks and protected endangered species. This department was more like the ones in Europe and the Far East, the department that included much of national law enforcement and internal security. If these people had been a mean and nasty lot, this would have been more of a KGB or a Gestapo, but this just wasn't that kind of world. True, there had been wars here, but not in modern times, not on any big scale, and people in general weren't all that rebellious. Still, the seeds of discontent, even full-blown class warfare, were certainly present, and the department's job was to insure they didn't get out of hand. I had the impression that the department actually ran half the underground revolutionary movements and secret societies in the country—all the better to insure that they never got together and really rocked the status quo.

Most of this I learned just by playing the dumb sexy little thing that was a junior secretary to Proconsul Marcial, somebody with only slightly more brains than they thought I had but no looks to compensate. The place leaked information like a sieve, though, when people were relaxed and didn't feel exposed. True, thanks to my family and age and clean background check, I had a high security clearance, but I never had the need to know anything. Marcial, the child of a very wealthy mining clan in central Pennsylvania, was here because of that wealth and those family connections, but nobody with real authority had any intention of giving the proconsul something important to do. Instead, the office was mostly involved in taking polls and surveys of the underclasses to see what they really thought. Since our superiors already knew what they thought, our work was basically to research some campaign or action they'd taken to confirm that it had an effect. Mostly, though, it wouldn't have mattered if anybody in my office ever came to work.

Marcial, of course, believed that he was a vital cog in maintaining the security of the state against all enemies, foreign and domestic.

Mostly I compiled meaningless reports and statistics from the field offices, typed them up, mimeographed them, and sent them on in triplicate to offices further up the line. I never was sure if they made it past the incinerator chutes on each of those higher floors, but it made no difference, either.

What did make a difference was that I got to see a lot of data, I got to overhear a lot of interesting conversations, and I got access to the libraries of state and similar repositories to follow up leads. And when information led to dead ends and roadblocks, I wasn't above sleeping with whoever had what I needed to keep going.

Thus I learned how we made love. These bodies were very limber, and the rear legs had a kind of joint pivot that allowed them to lie flat. In the "female" position I would be stretched on the floor or pads, about nine feet long not counting the legs. The "male" position, of course, was to mount over somebody who was lying flat. I know it sounds weird, but even though there were some who always preferred "male" and some who always preferred "female" positions, there was something kind of wild and even democratic about being able to do it both ways in one session. I did note that the higher up somebody was the more "male" they were during sex. No chance of being burdened with complicating kids, or maybe it was because the kind of ruthless aggression their jobs demanded was more of a "male" personality trait. Although I enjoyed both ways, I admit I tended to like the "female" more, which was perfect for what I was out to achieve in this casting-couch, social climbing routine anyway. More reward, less work.

At any rate, thanks to this activity and to my research both inside the department and in the libraries—those great pyramids were major national libraries and museums, it turned out—I got an education on this world but not a lot of leads on the Command Center. If it did exist here, I was convinced that nobody had found it yet.

What I hadn't figured on was that they might have found it and not known it.

It was when I was on a break from work and just idly touring the National Museum of Nativist Archaeology that I spotted what might have been, if not an indicator, then a forest of billboards.

I hadn't really been in this museum before except for a quick look, and I don't even know why I took the time to do it at all that day, except that I was intent on eventually going through the whole set of national treasures.

It was a reconstruction, more of a simulation, of a building in maybe one-quarter scale. A temple of some sort, of an ancient Native American empire that had once apparently controlled a good chunk of the Southeast. It was a step pyramid, with a steep ramp going up about twenty feet on the model, which meant that on the original it would be about eighty feet without a rest platform. Anybody who could climb that with hooves and no shoes had both my respect and my admiration.

At the start of the ramp were two statues characteristic of this empire, whose name was far too long and complex to remember and made up by archaeologists so only they could say it. The statues were a pair of stylized North American gryphons looking menacing. They had nasty eaglelike faces, a lionlike body, and mean-looking clawed legs. The middle pair weren't legs at all but instead turned up and went back as great stylized wings. Those big beaks had sharp teeth in them, too.

It wasn't these that fascinated me, but the fact that other creatures, apparently from this empire's heyday, flanked the impossibly steep ramp all the way up to the small but flat gold-tipped top.

There were all sorts of archaeo-babble names for each of them, explaining what they were and their place in early Southeast society, but I knew it was probably all bullshit. They were as stylized and as weird looking as the gryphons, but what they were was clear to anybody who knew the story.

Of course, in this world only I knew the story.

They were all there. The Walrus, the Mad Hatter, the Cheshire Cat, the March Hare, even the Caterpillar.

I read the explanations on the various information placards and could only think, *Everything you think you know is wrong, you overeducated assholes.*

But where was the real thing? The informational cards showed a pictorial of the dig, and there was a map there . . . On a low mountain overlooking the Valley of the Tennessee. A national historic monument, the best preserved Fourth Dynasty coronation temple in the Southeast, it said.

Chattanooga.

Most cities and most towns are in specific places for good geographical reasons. That was one reason why so much of what I already knew still held true from world to world. Capitals were usually put where they were for political reasons at the time they were established and then they stayed where they were because it was too damned expensive to move them. Cities, though, tended to be at the limits of navigation on major rivers, at one or the other side of major mountain passes, or where there was something of great value to mine or grow.

Chattanooga—on a major navigable river, at a major bend in that river, in the fertile valley between mountain passes— was where it was here for the same reason it was where it had been in past worlds. And why the temple, or whatever it really was, was where it was, too.

Now what I needed to do was to find a way to get there, a reason for doing so, and enough time and resources to uncover what the original excavators did not. I doubted that the Command Center was inside the pyramid; it would have been found by the insatiably curious team who'd dug up the temple in 1874.

But it was there. I was *sure* of it. And waiting for me, if I could reach it and if I could get into it.

I was sure that the answers had to be inside it, one way or the other. Only the Command Center was common to all the lives we could remember and even the ones we could not. Only the Command Center had the records, the backups, all the information. Al, and possibly the others who worked with him, knew some of what was there, maybe most of it, but their memories were now just recordings and not accessible inside their heads.

The problem was, this wasn't the kind of society that did things entirely as individuals, or even in pairs. It was a communal, clannish social structure that didn't really allow for individual activities. Nor was my salary good enough to support that kind of trip; because people moved as groups, one didn't buy a ticket on a long-distance train like I had on the commuter run that had brought me here. Groups rented a train car. Everybody else walked, and that would take a lot more time than vacation would allow.

So near and yet so far.

It took more time and something of an accident to give me a possible solution to the problem. Just as the culture was communal, so, too, was it a vast, specialized bureaucracy, and in the interior department it was even more so, since nobody was supposed to know anything without cause. I discovered the flaws in this system when I was romanced by a file clerk in personnel. The clerk, a thirtyish person named Sandy Boyd who had real charm and was kind of cute, was one of those people who loved living dangerously, and I discovered this when I was lured to an office in the western wing, top floor, up where some of the senior bureaucrats had their palatial offices.

The room was large, with a whole wall of glass looking out on the city and the river, and it was well furnished with a large, executive desk and very thick plush carpeting. There was a dining nook and a dumbwaiter that could be used to accept food deliveries. I felt nervous just to be there.

"Whose place *is* this?" I asked, gaping.

Sandy laughed. "Mine."

"Don't give me that! I know what you make!"

Boyd shrugged. "Nevertheless, it's mine. Through my office come all the room allocations, expense requests, and furnishing orders. Each is on an appropriate form, and each has to be filled out in quintuplicate with absolutely zero deviations, no carbons—you know the drill. Well, I happened to notice that when Proconsul Larue was promoted six months ago, nobody else was assigned to his old office. It's a real desirable place, but its availability just fell through the cracks, and now nobody's sure if it is or isn't anybody's. Well, it's assigned to personnel, to a Senior McGregor, assistant to the Committee on Internal Security. I ought to know, 'cause I made McGregor up. I filed all the proper forms in all the proper places, and then I ordered the furniture, even allocated a stipend for food and drink as needed and a supply account as well. I've had it for all this time."

"But—that's fraud! And nobody's said a word?"

"This is an agency that deals in secrets. The fact that McGregor doesn't exist only means that there's a good reason why somebody powerful wants this office maintained. The only way you can get into trouble here is asking too many questions. Come—let's enjoy some good food, good wine, the soft carpet, and the pretty view!"

Until that moment, with all my lives of experience, I hadn't realized what a square nerd I really was at heart. How *simple*. The power of the bureaucrat's forms combined with a penchant for secrecy could give me access to almost *anything*. Okay, the penalties might be stiff, and if one got really greedy somebody would certainly catch on to most of it, but, within reason, if one were careful, modest, and plotted things right, one could have a little of the good life.

And that's how I began doing research on just what forms and what functions would be necessary to send me south. It was absurdly easy. Some loaner forms, government vouchers, and a cover story that was kind of a variation on my trip from Sharpsburg to Georgetown, complete with letters of introduction and credit. I got a lot of help from Sandy, who'd trusted me with the secret of the luxury office knowing I might well lower the boom. In fact, we moved into a small flat together a few weeks after that revealing tryst. Sandy had become very attracted to me, it seemed, without my even realizing it, and that move was the last test to see if there was anything there. When I didn't betray Sandy, and we continued to date, that had kind of sealed it.

New clans tended to start out with two, one tending to take the domestic and sexual male role and the other the female. I hadn't realized how badly I'd needed somebody else until that point, and I found myself falling in love. When Senior Brown raised objections and started to throw some roadblocks in our way, we did pretty much what we felt we had to do and got a quick civil marriage. It stopped some of that interference, since marriages, once done, could not be undone. When and if either of us strayed, new companions would simply be brought into the marriage until we had a clan of our own. That was the way these things worked. Henceforth I was Jayce Cord Boyd, and Sandy was Sanford Boyd Cord. It had a kind of symmetry.

Sandy was also invaluable in setting up what I wanted to do. "Okay, so I can get us on a honeymoon leave and imply we're also on some kind of official business so we'll have an expense account, but why Chattanooga? I got to tell you, I'd rather go to Florida or the Gulf or someplace like that."

"So would I, for a real honeymoon," I admitted. "But I'm looking for something that's hard to explain but will blow your mind if I can find it. I think it's near the ancient temple atop Lookout Mountain. I have to find out. If you love me and trust me, and we can find this place, you won't regret it, I promise you. If you think I'm crazy, well, there's nothing much I can say but I got to go. My biggest fear is that I'll get there and won't be able to find it, that it'll be really buried. Still, I got to go."

"If you have to, then I do, too," Sandy told me. "Still, what is it?"

"I'm not tryin' to be coy, honest! It would just be too weird to try to explain. If we find it, all will be clear. For now, let's just say, well, it's something way ahead of what we have now, something from another world."

"You're *kidding*!" Pause. "You're not kidding? Where'd you learn about it?"

"I—well, let's just say I got the clues from sleeping around . . ."

I have to admit that, considering my past, I had genuine and I think justifiable paranoia about everything and everybody, even Sandy. In all the other lives I could remember, I'd eventually converged with most of the others, whether they were aware of their pasts or not, and I saw no reason to believe that it wouldn't happen here. Sandy had a lot of Rick's charm and was just as sexy, but had not one whit of artistic talent. There was also a kind of crooked resourcefulness that was reminiscent of Al or at least Lee, but, again, it just didn't seem to fit. I really began to wonder if maybe Sandy was just Sandy. That would be okay except for what I might have to do if indeed I did get into the Command Center. I didn't want to abandon another person I felt close to just because they were what Al's crew had called "spooks." To me, no matter what, they were people. They were self-aware, they thought, they interacted as individuals. Nobody understood that better than me.

So, I had a sense of ambivalence about Sandy's status. One part of me wanted my mate to remain my partner and to not abandon or harm that person, while another part of me wanted desperately to not have to deal with another of the Elect who might turn out to be somebody I didn't like at all . . .

I put it out of my mind. Whoever or whatever Sandy might have been, it was impossible to recognize, and Sandy was fine with me just as Sandy.

We went first-class on the train; I was sure that if this didn't work out and we had to return to Alexandria we'd both wind up in jail sooner or later, but we were young, crooked, and in love. I won't describe the trip much, but I can say that, aside from very good meals on the government till, we didn't look at a lot of scenery. Sandy took it for granted that I was operating on secret information surreptitiously learned and not some harebrained vision, but, of course, there was no guarantee we'd find what the archaeologists hadn't. For my part, I felt sure that the center would be reasonably concealed until somebody showed up who could use it, and that some ignorant lout or government agent wouldn't be permitted to find and enter it and maybe muck things up.

Other than not finding the place, my other worry was that it would be in bad shape. That lower level had been mostly destroyed the last time I was there, and it was a dead certainty that not everything would be repaired or regenerated. Somehow, even though it, too, was merely a virtual-reality construct, it had a greater connection to reality—whatever and wherever that was—than any of us had. It was a core program, a separate "reality" running concurrently and within the greater whole.

The train went first to Atlanta, a far different city than I thought of when hearing that name. It was old, even antique looking; an Atlanta in which the Civil War had never happened and which had never been visited by a general named Sherman.

We took a day there rather than making an immediate connection. This was as much my doing as Sandy's; somehow I didn't want this to end, even though I desperately wanted that center, powered up and totally under my command, as much as I ever wanted anything. So we stayed in a really fancy old hotel, saw some of the tourist attractions, and both got our hair done. I liked the long, billowing reddish blond hair and kept it, only restyling and trimming where needed; Sandy preferred a shorter kind of pixie cut, easy to wash and manage, and it was the right look for that boyish face anyway.

I admit that I was in that immature "cozy and safe" frame of mind, at least for the time being, when I liked the way things were going and had a hard time thinking about heavier matters. Still, the Mock Turtle's threats were always lurking in a dark corner of my mind, and an ugly ape face haunted my dreams. This time I couldn't let somebody else carry the burden and try and ignore the whole business. This time, it was me or nobody.

I didn't really have a lot of time alone to think, which is when I did my best objective evaluations, but there were occasions when Sandy would be asleep that I was able to try to put things together. Having almost forced myself to board the train to Chattanooga, and now checked into a midlevel hotel there, I began to wonder if my personality really was the right one for this job. True, I'd had the guts and strength to do what I had to do when faced with an emergency, but, every time, I'd retreated behind somebody else's will and tried to pretend that these hard decisions didn't exist.

It really wasn't a lack of courage, although it might have been a lack of personal ambition. It was more like a rebellion, a refusal to play the game unless forced to do so, to try to make the best of what was dished out instead of always being somebody's football.

As I lay there in the darkness, though, a totally different thought came to me, one that was far more unsettling. Every single time I'd been a player or pushed into acting, somebody had been there, or had come along, to give me an easy exit. Whatever I wanted most, but which would also take me out of play, tended to show up at just the right time. Riki and I had run away from Al in Yakima, and Wilma and I had been panicked into that rabbit-hole vortex that provided an easy exit, away from Al's rage. Then I'd literally split into parts, but all the parts had the common personality trait of wanting to run away and have a regular life and to hell with Al and the institute. I had some of the Command Center's power in my hands, so to speak, when one of those parts actually managed to move its consciousness along the electrical and telephone networks inside the complex. Right then and there I had, at least potentially, all the answers, yet all I really wanted was to escape.

And I'd been a scared little bunny, running from Al as usual, in that world where I was the boy-wife, full of fear and confusion and a desire to get away.

The Dodo was digging a hole to China to escape rather than ask for a hand up out of the hole . . .

The Red Queen, the Mock Turtle had called me. It was all that I could do to run hard enough to stay in the same place . . .

Metaphors represented real things, after all. The Mock Turtle had threatened to abandon me as an ape, a nonplayer, if I faltered again. Was that a literal threat, or did it mean that if I ran away again for some mindless and temporary happiness and safety, I might as well be an ape in the jungle with no thoughts beyond the pleasures of the moment?

They couldn't pull me out of this because I wasn't giving them any damned help. I was digging down to China . . .

The next day, fairly early but after a substantial breakfast, we took the tourist tram to the base of Lookout Mountain and then the steam-powered cable car to the top.

The temple lived up to its billing. While the folks in the National Museum had done a superb job of duplicating it to scale, there was something to be said about standing there looking up at the thing full-sized, reeking of history and dead civilizations, against a backdrop panorama including some drifting clouds below the summit.

They barred people from walking up it, since hooves and steel shoes would have ground the temple down pretty fast, and I didn't want to even think of racing upward on that steep ramp. Still, there they were, flanking that ramp from base to top, ancient renditions that had all sorts of explanations as to godlike figures and mystic symbolism, all of which might have been correct for this place and this culture. Only I knew that, in truth, they were something else entirely. The original artist—Tenniel, I seemed to recall his name was—would have either been appalled or, more likely considering the two books, vastly amused.

Sandy looked it all over and muttered, "Creepy critters. So—where's the mystery stuff? Inside?"

I shook my head from side to side. "Not likely. That place has been pretty well picked over by the archaeologists. I think the contents, what there was left or what was discovered, are back in Alexandria." I sighed, trying to think. "No, this isn't a vault, not really. It's a billboard. Now the puzzle is to figure out what it's advertising."

Walking completely around the structure didn't help. In fact, it was a kind of pentagon, with all five sides the same—steplike with the smooth, steep ramp. What could it be pointing to? I doubted if there was any mysterious hole in space-time or anything like that to hide the Command Center. No, it would be real and physical. But where? Where could it be that a century and a half of archaeology and tourism hadn't blundered into it?

Sandy read one of the monument signs. "That's interesting. One of the sides is a foot smaller than the other four. Wonder why? It looks so, well, *precise*."

It was precise. Okay, so now we knew which direction, and I assumed that the next position didn't include up. Down, then, from that short side—but how far down? We went over and soon found ourselves on a rocky outcrop beyond which was a sheer drop. There were no trails down there; no stops on a cable car, either. If it was down there, then I'd have to wait for the invention of the helicopter to find it. These bodies weren't designed for cliff climbing.

There were definitely no secret entrances between the base of the temple and the edge of the cliff; it was solid rock without question. So—where was it? And could I get to it if I found it?

"Any idea what it looks like?" Sandy asked me.

"Hard to say on the outside, but, basically, it's a building," I replied. "And not a little one, either. Maybe a city block long, two or three floors. Nothing that would be as obvious as that temple. That's the problem. It's got to be totally hidden, yet big."

Sandy sighed. "I hate to tell you this, but I think it was a bum tip. You couldn't hide anything from anybody up here, not that size."

We took the cable car down, finally, with me in particular feeling very discouraged. I *knew* I was right, knew it was right here, waiting for me. This was what I was in this world to do— to get in there with minimum resistance.

So where the hell was it?

I tried to find it from the ground level, extrapolating as much as possible, but the angle was so steep and the clouds so low that I couldn't even see the top of the mountain, let alone the temple.

Disheartened, we went back down and found a good local restaurant for dinner, then walked along the river in no hurry to get back to the hotel. Sandy wasn't nearly as depressed as me, of course, but, then, Sandy didn't know what I knew and was half humoring me anyway.

At night, I could look up and see the mountain, kind of a blackness with small lights illuminating the various attractions and, of course, the illuminated cable car. The top had no lights that I could see; the temple closed at dusk, and in this world there wasn't much purpose to aircraft or radio or TV beacons, all three not having been invented yet.

"Let's go up to the room," Sandy urged, trying to sound sympathetic. "It's been a long, tiring day anyway. We can continue tomorrow."

"You go on ahead if you want," I responded dejectedly. "I'm just gonna stand here for a little bit and try to think." I turned and gave a little kiss. "We can have a night off, I think."

Sandy shrugged, but seemed to sense what this meant to me. "Okay. I'll be waiting."

Within minutes, I was alone on the walkway by the riverside, leaning on the iron fence that ran along the top of the levee separating me from the river itself, and just staring at that big, black mass.

Okay, Mock Turtle, so what the devil do I do now? Learn to fly?

It was frustrating, just staring into the blackness, oblivious to barges, riverboats, other walkers along the banks, my concentration totally on that damned mass.

Damn it! I ought to be able to sense *it!* I told myself. I was almost a part of it, and it a part of me, the closest thing to something truly *real* that I had to hang on to.

And I *could* feel it, feel something, anyway. Something that told me that it was there, that I was right.

Come on! Come on! Where are you? Show me! Show me! Show me now!

A pencil of greenish light shot from the top of the mountains, apparently coming through a cloud and continuing on down into the valley, striking a point not on Lookout Mountain but on the valley floor. It was quite some distance from where I stood, but it appeared to be on this side of the river, somewhere in the hills just beyond town. An arrow, a beacon, from that short side, following that steep angle down much farther than Sandy and I had considered.

It was a nice night and there were a number of others about, many looking where I was looking, yet none of them seemed to be able to see the green line. It was for me alone. I'd turned it on, I'd brought it forward by force of will. Now it was time to follow it up, while my adrenaline still flowed. I trotted over toward the hotel, and was startled when, about a block away, I heard Sandy call me from a dark alley.

"Jayce! In here! *Fast!*"

I was puzzled, but I turned and soon was in the shadows. "Sandy! I found it! At least, I think I know how to find it!"

"Huh? Yeah, yeah, that's nice, Jayce, but we're in trouble. I barely got out of there, and then only because the concierge inadvertently tipped me off. They got the place staked out! They're after me, probably you, too!"

"They? Who are 'they'?" *C'mon! Not Al or that crew! Not here!*

"IPs. I think maybe I overdid this one. Somebody caught on!"

IPs . . . Interior Police. The feds were after us.

I sighed. "I don't care how tired you are, then, we have to walk. We have to reach this point before somebody reaches us," I told my suddenly panicked mate. "Otherwise, it's all over."

XI

ANSWERS ARE NOT SOLUTIONS

I hadn't counted on having to do this secretly, or on the run, but it made things all the more imperative that it be done as quickly as possible.

As I expected, Sandy couldn't see the beacon, but it remained rock solid to me, and there wasn't much choice on the part of my crooked mate but to trust that I had at least some idea of what I was doing.

"Are you out of your *mind*?" Sandy called as I trotted along, focused on the end of the beam. "We got to get out of here! And quick!"

"To where?" I called back. "We've got some money on us, but that's about all, and it sure as hell won't take us to some island country with no extradition. It wouldn't even take us far on the train, and they can monitor that. You need an ID to get anything, so we walk and we live off the land. Do you have any idea how long it would take us to get to even Mexico on foot? A thousand, maybe fifteen hundred miles? Those are *feds*, Sandy. Our own ever-lovin' crew. We can't just change our names and dye our hair and live in the wild across a district boundary. Uh-uh."

"Then we got to think a little. We could do heavy stuff. Who would care about heavy-lifting workers? Or maybe we should just give ourselves up!"

That idea wasn't in my constitution, not in this life. Funny—the first crisis, and here I was taking over and Sandy was the one wimping out. I didn't feel at all bad. Nervous, maybe scared, considering the circumstances, but, if things had to fall apart fast, well, this was at least a good fit.

"You got any rich relatives or high Electors in the family? I mean *really* rich, like the kind that buys federal judges? I sure don't. That means paying back what we stole plus a fine. Fifteen, twenty years at hard labor with your balls cut off so you can't screw your way out with a baby—uh-uh. And if we managed to hide the fact that we were two smartasses and got prole jobs, what then? Just as much hard labor, not much better living conditions, worse food, and you wind up doin' it all preggers 'cause you have a kid a year on top of it. Nope. Not when there's one other chance."

"*What* chance? Your ancient space creatures and their base? Baby, I hate to tell you, but I never really bought that shit. I was just humoring you. I'm not sure I'm not trottin' off in the dark toward some wild hallucination of yours."

I pulled up short, reared a bit, then turned and faced Sandy. "You humored me this far; what's the cost of humoring me a little more? Just come on and stop whining and let's see who's nuts." I paused a moment, then said, more softly, "Honey, they're gonna catch us, you know. We can't hide out and we can't run, not us. But never give up until you have to. I did that more than once and it never helped a bit. I'm asking you to trust me, to believe me, no questions asked."

There was a moment of silence, with just the distant sounds of the city and the splash of waves from a passing barge hitting the side of the levee. Finally, Sandy said, "Okay. Lead on."

I can't tell you what those few words meant to me, since I more than anybody knew just how totally insane I sounded.

This time Sandy was where Mr. Cory Maddox had once been, and I was playing Cynthia Matalon's White Rabbit with total confidence.

> *Don't know how I sing this song,*
> *'Cause everything we think we know is wrong...*

It was a lot farther than it looked, and the distant clocks were chiming three in the morning before we approached the position, sleepy, hungry, and exhausted. The river wasn't the most reliable source of drinking water in these parts, particularly downstream as this was, but we never even gave it a second thought. In fact, we waded in to the waist, the water surprisingly comfortable, and not only bent over and drank but let it cool us down as well.

Finally, Sandy hauled out of the river and flopped on the bank. Even after all this time, the limberness of this body was something of an amazement to me, somebody who'd always thought of the centaur form as fairly rigid. I followed and lay down beside Sandy. It was pretty quiet this far downstream and growing increasingly foggy as well.

"How much farther?" Sandy managed, sounding pretty well all in.

I looked up across the river and found myself almost blinded by the direct beam. I got up, turned, and followed it, relieved that it really *was* striking on this side. If it hadn't, I wasn't at all sure where the next bridge would be.

"Just up there," I whispered, suddenly feeling more nervous than tired. "Another three or four hundred yards."

I helped Sandy up and we walked slowly on, my eyes focused totally on the point where the beam sliced through the fog and illuminated an area just ahead. When I reached it, it was almost a disappointment. It looked like a drainage tunnel, maybe four and a half feet wide, old and no longer in use but clearly of the modern era. Well, it would be. Anything less would have attracted attention.

"In *there*?" Sandy said, nervous and doubting once more. "It's awfully dark in there!"

The beam was dead center on the big old concrete pipe. "You can wait here if you want," I replied. "I have to go in. I have to follow this to the end."

To get inside I had to bend my torso almost straight forward. Even at that, it would be next to impossible to turn around once committed. I earnestly hoped I wasn't being the insane idiot Sandy thought I was.

Sandy sighed. "Go ahead. I'll not only be behind, I'll probably be in your behind, but let's get this over with."

I have to admit, we didn't have to proceed more than twenty or thirty feet in before I began to doubt myself. The darkness was as absolute as anything I had ever known, and it was damp, dank, and smelled of incredibly well-aged sewage. My hair brushed against cobwebs and spiderwebs and moss and lichen, and, as was almost inevitable, you could hear the sounds of things scurrying about. Rats most likely. Maybe even worse. I didn't want to think about them and prayed that none got into my hair or bit into a tendon.

Ultimately, we reached a point where it was clear that there had been some kind of shifting. The old pipe was cracked and disconnected from our end, and there was a lot of debris. I would have loved to have been able to see what was going on, and I whispered, "You got a match? There's something here."

Sandy had a habit of smoking little cheroots; I liked big, fat cigars myself, but I didn't have any of them with me.

I felt Sandy press forward, our hands met, and I got the box of safety matches. It was a little painful to be stretched out forward so unnaturally like this. I fumbled, got a match, closed the box, and, with some difficulty, got it finally to light.

It took a few moments for my eyes to adjust to the sudden blinding flare of the match, but the sight I saw gave me hope. Something—shifting mud, a rock slide, earth tremor—had moved and broken the old pipe. The reason why the thing had only had a trickle in it was because water couldn't really get much beyond this point. When the pipe had fallen, it hadn't caused the dirt and rock to fill in, though. It was curiously smooth between the edge of the old pipe and the new side of the tunnel, big enough for somebody my size to squeeze through, with effort. Two more matches and I'd made it to that point.

"Stay here," I told Sandy. "If I get stuck, I'll need you to pull me out. If I find what I think is behind there, I'll call for you to come forward."

In the dark because I needed both hands to squeeze in, I managed to twist and turn and get myself in between the old concrete piping and the curiously smooth wall. It went back maybe two body lengths, then made a sharp turn. I turned with it, wondering if I hadn't just killed the both of us, when suddenly there was a wall in front of me. A metallic wall. I groped around, found a handle, pushed it down, and opened the door inward.

The emergency lights came on automatically.

"Sandy! Come on!" I practically shouted at the top of my lungs. *"It's here!"*

I squeezed into the entryway, noting that only the top two-thirds of the door was accessible, but, with some scrapes, scratches, and bruises, I was inside.

It looked eerily familiar. All too familiar. Most of my memories of this place hadn't been very favorable, either. For the first time in any memories I could call up, I was here without Al, Dan, Les, Rita, or even Alice. If anybody'd come through to this incarnation via the Command Center, they were still wired up. It was pretty clear nobody had been in here in quite some time.

I heard Sandy behind me, cursing and stretching, even as I luxuriated in being able to stand in a normal upright position once again. I shook and felt my hair with some alarm. It felt grungy as all hell.

"This damned piece of insanity better—" Sandy was muttering, then, breaking into the room and looking up at the entryway and lights, suddenly stopped and took in a deep breath. "Oh, my god! What *is* this place, Jayce?"

I sighed. "It has a lot of names, hon. The Control Center, the Command Center, the institute—and probably ten thousand more long forgotten." I walked slowly forward, locating myself. This was the side entrance, near the clinic. I felt for the main lights, found the panel, and flipped them on, not really expecting them to work.

Slowly, almost theatrically, the neon lighting blinked and flashed on all around, bathing us in bright light. I walked slowly forward, my hooves making little sound on the industrial carpeting.

I was so taken with making it inside this quickly that for a moment I forgot Sandy. Suddenly, after looking into the empty and darkened clinic, almost to reassure myself that Les or Al wouldn't pop out, I turned and saw that Sandy was still just standing there, barely inside the door, looking awestruck and totally terrified.

"Come on," I invited soothingly. "It's just a building. I don't think anybody's been here in a very long time."

Sandy didn't move, but that cute boyish face looked over at me still filled with terror. "You—you *knew* about this, didn't you? You didn't learn this from the interior department. You've *been* here! You *know* about all this!"

I took a deep breath. "Yes, I knew it was here once I saw the clues. No, I haven't been here, not in this world. I'm sorry, Sandy, but it sure as hell beats a chain gang. Being here, now, is my sole purpose in this life. Don't be scared of it, even though it can be the scariest nightmare in all creation. It's like everything else of great power—it can be used or misused depending on who's got their finger on the controls."

Sandy still didn't make a move. "Who—what are you?"

"I'm the same Jayce as always. Nobody switched us in our beds or invaded your old mate's body. I've been honest and up front with you on most of this, I just couldn't tell you everything 'cause you wouldn't have believed it. You still wouldn't believe a lot of it. The truth is, honey, I don't know the answers. This is the first time I've been here without the baddies in charge so maybe I can learn a little. The only thing I can tell you right now is to forget what you thought you knew. This will blow your mind. As somebody once said to me, everything you think you know is wrong. All but one thing. I still love you and I won't hurt you. Come on. I'll show you around the joint."

Sandy still looked horrified, but I saw the expression on the face change as the mind said, *Snap out of it! This is Jayce, not somebody from Mars! Besides, this may be the biggest payoff yet!*

The upper control room was there, as always, and there was power to the console and the monitors.

Sandy was allowing curiosity, even fascination, to overcome some of the fear. "What are *those* things?"

"Huh? Chairs." That's right! Sandy would never have seen a chair anywhere in the world. Huge reclining half beds and divans, yes, but not chairs. Who in this world could sit in one? "The people who created this place used to sit in them. They weren't quite like us."

Sandy examined a high-backed wheeled office chair as if it were a flying saucer. "What sort of creatures could use these?"

"Apes," I replied. "Naked apes. Kind of like us if you cut off the hindquarters and back legs. Just imagine your back went straight to an ass and then the front legs only. And no hooves. Broad, flat, soft, monkey feet."

There were apes in this world; I'd seen them at the Federal Zoo. I knew the mental picture that my description must have shaped in Sandy's mind, but it was close enough. Even apes had only one sex in this world, but they tended to kind of become either male or female for a specific mating period rather than always being capable of both.

"*Monkeys* built and ran this?"

"Not monkeys. Monkeys have long tails. A kind of ape. No tail. An ape with a brain like ours." I decided to leave the part about two distinct sexes out for now. This was mind-blowing enough.

I also was a little worried about Sandy all of a sudden. Not only was this a scary wonder, it also represented, of course, a way of ingratiation to the powers that be. To deliver this technology would certainly mean dropped charges, and probably more. While I hoped Sandy's love for me was as strong as I felt, who knew what would happen when I depended on that? A lot of people have been betrayed by lovers for all the right reasons—give us a million bucks, a warm-weather villa, and forget we exist, and we'll give you the keys to the universe. I'd felt that way myself more than once in past lives. I went over to a live console and tried to remember some of the basics. It had been a long time ago, but, in here, it seemed to come back when it was needed.

There were other physiological limits than just the chairs, though. Our fingers were very long, longer than the palms were wide, and not just ending in thin nails but capped by thick ones that covered the entire end of each finger, pointed on top, tapered a bit underneath, but hard as a rock and without any nerve endings. The typewriters we'd had at the interior department were designed for these kinds of fingers; these terminal keyboards were not. I realized that I would be reduced to hunt-and-peck with two fingers, but it worked, tough as it was for a touch typist to do things that way. I typed in the automated security codes and changed the passwords, and had the computer seal the perimeter. It was true that there was probably a master code that would allow another of the Elect in if he made it this far, but he wouldn't remember it, would he? I'd had my doubts even when I knew all this had to be here. Would I have gone ten feet into that pipe if I had no idea what I was looking for or why I was there?

The seal had the effect of locking any usable exit unless a valid password was typed in first. Sandy needed never to know about this little insurance, but it made me feel a whole lot better. It was also true that the language we had was called

English but really wasn't quite the same language as that of the builders of this station, nor did it use the same Roman alphabet. The difference in the hands alone had shaped the written language into something that functioned the same but looked a lot more like cuneiform. That meant that Sandy was unlikely to be able to make out much on the screens, or type in things that would result in anything other than gibberish. A quite literate scribe had been turned into just one of the illiterate masses the moment this place was entered.

Next I managed to bring up the maintenance report. The air was stuffy; I turned on the air filters, set the temperature, and checked out the power systems. Power, as always, came from below, from that place where none of us could look.

The air-conditioning coming on startled my companion. "What's that?"

"Air-conditioning, air freshening, temperature control. It's gonna be absolutely perfect for us, and we'll get that staleness out of the air as well. I've checked all the systems and we're secure and in good shape. Just don't push any buttons without asking!"

"How'd you know how to do it?" Sandy asked me. "I mean, how do you know all this if you're not somebody different?"

I thought a moment. "Hard to explain. Maybe the best explanation is that there really is something to reincarnation. Those of us who know about this are born with that knowledge, and when we wind up here, it comes out. I won't insult you by saying it's really that simple, but that's the short version." I looked down and cursed softly under my breath. "On the other hand, I've got to be very careful about typing with these fingers on those keyboards."

"But—this looks fairly new, and everything's turned on! This *couldn't* have been buried for centuries here!"

"It wasn't, because those centuries were backfilled after it arrived. Time and space, a lot of things we take for granted, just aren't true, at least in this context. I can only tell you that this place is real. It's almost a god machine. I don't know who built it or why, but maybe here I have a chance to find out. That's what it's all about. In any event, I'll be able to use this to get us a much better future than we faced going back into the hands of the feds."

Sandy diplomatically decided to ignore the strangeness of the situation and focus on the pragmatic, a very wise choice under the circumstances. I saw the fear going, too, replaced, at least a little, with a bit of avarice.

"You got any magic combination for food and water? I'm starving!"

I laughed, relaxing. "I think I can work something out. Usually this is out in the open, hooked up to the world, and you order out for food, but there are definitely backups here." Once you'd had long discussions with walruses and mock turtles you didn't tend to think that conjuring up some wine and sandwiches would be a big deal, and it wouldn't—except that life was too short for me to do it all by two-fingered typing. That meant using one of the VR helmets, where I could interface more directly with the computers and give them an unambiguous picture of just what I wanted.

That meant heading to the lower level, a place I wasn't at all sure I was ready for, at least not yet. Still, Sandy was right— we needed food and drink, and then a long, solid sleep.

I could fully understand Sandy's thinking because not just my immediate surroundings were backfilled; although it happened slower and somewhat differently, by this point I remembered everything about my life here from childhood through the present. As had happened with less dramatic changes, I felt native and comfortable in this form, and found it very hard to relate to ape-humans on more than an academic level. Still, I remembered, even if in a distant way, and I knew this place.

The virtual-reality interfaces were also designed for a different physiology. There was no way either of us would fit in any of the life-support modules, at least indicating which form was closer to "real." The head-mounted helmet, visor, and form padding fit, anyway, although the ears were a bit off and the helmet less comfortable than I remembered. Still, I felt pretty confident when I put one on, saw the console come up, and tried to enter.

I could see the display, but there was no direct contact. It was like the early head mounts, where you could see and hear, but not feel and certainly not interface with the machine at the speed of thought. I looked at the status readout and it indicated that I was showing signs of illness, but that didn't bother me. Our bodies ran at a higher temperature and the machine was sensing what it thought was a high fever but which to me was normal. I removed the helmet, checked the console, and tapped in a request for diagnostics starting in ten seconds. I put the helmet back on and waited. It didn't take any time at all to come up with a message.

"Head Mount Device not worn," it stated. "Awaiting interface."

What did it mean by "not worn"? Damn it, I was wearing it! I took it off again, and checked the screen. There were dozens of parameters it checked, all of which had to be right or nothing would work. All seemed fine except . . .

LIMBIC SYNC: N/A.

Limbic Sync? The brain uses forty cycles per second as the frequency for passing the bulk of information inside itself. The Brand Boxes were also set at this frequency so the interface wouldn't cause seizures and would remain in the range the brain could use. I'd designed the helmet under the same principles several lifetimes ago.

Instantly, I understood that there were more differences than hands and hooves here. We obviously used a different brain frequency. *Shit!* So close and yet so far . . . !

How long would it be before we'd have to leave, probably walking right into the feds and long, hard time? It seemed that the water fountains, for some inexplicable reason, actually worked—but food was definitely lacking. Neither of us had a whole lot of body fat to live off of while I worked on an answer.

"Well," I sighed, "we both got a few ornies left. May as well eat them and sleep on it. I don't know about you, but I'm too damned tired to think of a way around this tonight."

Sandy nodded, yawning. "If worse comes to worst, we'll figure out some way for one of us to sneak out and pick up something," came the comment. "Right now—sleep is it."

I turned the lights off in the lab area and we settled in for sleep. I couldn't shake the idea that I was missing something here, but Sandy was right. I was too exhausted to think straight.

In all the lifetimes, there was some connection between all the Elect and this place, either directly or through one of the backup centers. Proximity alone was part of it—even at this very low standby level I'd felt that the Command Center was here, and I'd seen the energy that only the Elect could see pointing to this spot. We were still not at any kind of activation level, but, just being here, particularly on the lower floor, there was a sense of connection, of being one with the power of this location. Maybe I couldn't talk to it in the manner I needed to. Somehow, though, I had the sense that the great machine knew I was here and knew just who I was.

VR . . . Virtual Reality . . . Everything you think you know is wrong . . . She runs as hard as she can just to stay in the same place . . . The Walrus and the Cybernaut will speak of many things . . .

My watch said that it was six-thirty, but whether that was A.M. or P.M. I had no idea. Most likely morning, of course, for how could I sleep over fifteen, sixteen hours? Still, I felt far too rested, almost overly rested, for it to have been a mere three or four hours.

I had dreamed, but no creatures from Wonderland were there, or so I felt. I couldn't really remember the dreams, except to sense that they were pretty conventional.

I looked over and was startled to discover that I was alone. That brought me awake fast. Where the hell could Sandy have gone? Not out. A quick spring to a nearby terminal and a request for security status showed everything still sealed and intact. But if not out, then where?

Splashing some cold water in my eyes from the nearby water fountain, I turned and called, "Sandy? Where you at, honey?"

There was silence, which really unnerved me now, so I went looking, first checking the more open first floor, then coming back down to the lab area. About the only places left to look were down that dreaded corridor, in the storerooms and small offices, and back to where, the last time I'd been there, reality had been melting. I'd avoided that area up to now, fearful of what I might find, but now I headed down, opening the doors as I went, following the colored stripes. I was now down to the lunchroom, where Rini had been kept prisoner for so long. I went to it, opened the door, and found Sandy eating a sandwich.

"Hi, baby! I didn't want to wake you! You were out like a light!"

I stared not at Sandy but at the sandwich and the large plastic bottle of Coca-Cola on the table. "Where did you get that?"

"There's a room back there. I woke up and couldn't get back to sleep. I had to take a piss something awful and couldn't figure out where to do it, so I started looking. I never did figure it out, so there's a wastebasket full of pee in one of the offices here. Anyway, as I was searching, I saw this room, and I heard the humming of some kind of machinery or something back there, so I opened it and found it was real cold there. Not freezing, but cold. And there, stacked up in big boxes, were these. Sandwiches of all kinds, a bunch of containers with stuff I wasn't too sure about, and case after case of these drinks."

I didn't remember any such room, and I could draw the floor plan of the Command Center in my sleep. Still, there it was—a door where one hadn't been before, made of metal, and inside was a full-blown refrigerator, maybe ten feet by ten feet.

Sandy had taken down and torn open a number of boxes,

and they included a lot of basic prepackaged subs, tuna salad, all the usual stuff. On the other side were industrial-sized cartons with sixteen-ounce plastic bottles of Coke, Diet Coke, root beer, Sprite, and orange soda. I took a couple of cold-cut subs and a bottle of Coke and came back out, thoroughly confused. Even so, looking at them, I could read the labels. The Coke had the usual logos and trademarks—totally unknown in this world—and the line "Bottled under authority of Coca Cola, Inc., Atlanta, Georgia U.S.A." The subs listed a "Betterton Foods, St. Louis," as the manufacturer, and asserted that they were in fact registered at somebody's Pennsylvania Department of Agriculture.

"You took a chance eating some of this without checking with me first," I noted.

Sandy shrugged. "Like we had a choice? Besides, it looked like real food to me, and the stuff in the bottle looked like dark ale. It's not, it's some kind of flavored sugar drink, but it's not bad."

I smiled and nodded. "About the only thing that we need now is some good coffee," I commented a bit wistfully. Even in this world I kind of lived on the stuff.

At that moment we both caught the scent of fresh-brewed coffee and stiffened as one. "Uh-oh . . ." Sandy said, and both of us turned our heads to the back of the room.

There was a large percolator there, and the red light was just going off indicating that it had finished brewing. There were cups on the table, and even piles of sugar, nondairy creamer, and teaspoons.

"I don't want to make you nervous," Sandy commented nervously, "but that wasn't there when I came in. That wasn't even there when you came in. It wasn't there . . ."

"Until I asked for it," I completed, nodding. "Just like that refrigerator was never in this room when I was in here in the past."

"Ghosts?" Sandy suggested nervously, looking around.

"I don't think so. I've never been in here when I've been the one in charge. I think the machine, or machines, that run this place, that maintain and preserve it, somehow know I'm here and that I'm one of the ones they're supposed to recognize."

Sandy walked back to the table with the percolator on it, sniffed once more, then touched the side, first with a nail and then slightly with a palm. "*Ow!* It's really there, all right! And it's really hot!"

"It's as real as anything else here, anyway." I think I was beginning to understand now. When Rini had flowed into here to exact revenge and rescue some people, she'd seen this place not only as it is but also as blueprints and schematics. This was a design, a program, just like all the created worlds and the people in them were programs. Where had it gotten this? It knew my needs, probably read out my thoughts as I slept. I remember thinking in despair that I was going to be forced out when just a few weeks' worth of cold-cut subs would do.

Where had this come from? Maybe from a convenience store sometime in a past life. That would be ironic. With the powers of God, or at least god potential, I struck the ground and commanded that the earth spring forth a 7-Eleven. No wonder they'd never put me in charge of anything around here!

I tried some of the coffee. It tasted like my old favorite Colombian special from Starbucks in the distant past, and it brought back very pleasant and calming memories. Perhaps not just memories, which never seemed real, but feelings, a sense of a simpler life, fewer questions, better times, security.

So maybe if I could conjure up my favorite coffee, freshly brewed, and all the cold-cut and tuna-salad subs I could eat, perhaps I could figure out a way to interface more directly with the system.

Sandy was scared again, and I went back and gave him a therapeutic, reassuring hug.

"But—who's doing that? It's *creepy*!"

"Don't worry," I responded soothingly. "Even though I didn't realize it, the one doing it is me. It's getting all this from my mind and creating it. I know it looks like magic, but you don't know the half of it." *Not magic at all. Illusion. All of it nothing but damned illusion. Even, to some extent, us ourselves.* The rules of this universe said we needed food and drink, so the player was provided compatible food and drink. Where did it come from? Not exactly from thin air; no, it came from the same place as all the rest of this world had. It came from my own mind, from my own memories, down to the smallest detail that had been recorded but not consciously retained. That was how it did most of its tricks, really. It picked our own minds, experiences, and memories. That was the Brand Box system. Even if you didn't write the program, that detail I'd remarked on from the beginning, the tiny cells and root structures of the leaves, the tastes and textures—they were there because they were created from and compared to what I knew, what I had experienced, what I *expected* to find. I was a participant in the illusion, willing or not, consciously or not. For those details that couldn't be culled, the program went to other memories, other data, and, finally, to various databases probably linked together in a worldwide network.

Not the worlds, though. Not entirely. There it took a template from the subconscious, compared it against the "real" world, made the necessary changes, then extrapolated as necessary to create a new society. We weren't centaurs, a combination human and horse. We started off with that concept, but then the computers had created real creatures capable of evolving logically, and the kind of world and society that would be the most likely result of that physiology.

This world *had* been created out of some fantasy of mine. It was too comfortable, too familiar, as alien as it seemed. That was why, in spite of the physical limitations and differences, the maintenance program responded to me. I was the one who could set the passwords; I had the keys to the front door. For the moment, I was in charge of the house.

The problem was, how could I get beyond it?

At least, with food and drink, we were not going to be cast

out from Paradise. Now the trick was finding the keys to unlock the wonders of the Garden.

At least we had the food-service and janitorial programs going. I had to take a leak myself, and when I went to the room where Sandy had fouled the wastebasket to do likewise I discovered that the basket was empty. It was an out-of-the-way room of no other use to us; we designated it the latrine and used it without much regard for the carpeting or decor. It was always cleaned up after we left. I had the impression that it just vanished, was just canceled out, but never in our presence, never in our sight, where we could catch any of the routines working.

Yes, there were rest rooms there, and they worked, but getting our forms over those toilets was hardly worth it. Maybe at some point I could figure out a simple design for the computer that would create a state-of-the-art bathroom for this form, but I had much to do before allowing myself that luxury, including figuring out how to talk to the machine directly. It was still communication on an unconscious level, and that wasn't good enough.

I was very nervous about going down to the core control center at the bottom of the building. The memories I'd had of the last visit weren't very nice at all, and I was afraid of what I might find considering it was the site of the crash.

It was with some relief that I discovered that it looked none the worse for wear. Whatever repair had been done to the system had also repaired this place. Those nice leather chairs were of little interest and, in fact, were a bit of a pain since some were bolted to the floor, but the consoles were very interesting indeed. These were the masters, where the main program could all be set up and accessed. Upstairs was basically local Brand Boxes and maintenance of the larger setups; here was where you actually could shape the programs.

Of course, that wasn't quite accurate. I could no more write a program for my world as it now stood than I could wave my hand and create a livable Mars. It was a matter of structured queries, of creating templates and specifying limitations, so that the computers themselves would write the programs that would do what you wanted. Trouble was, the more ambitious you wanted to be, the more of the power source you had to tap. The results hadn't been all that promising so far. At best, all Al and his crew had seemed to manage was getting enough power to punch through and create a new random universe. Then he could do the same damned thing over again and again. Big deal. But the last time somebody other than Al had tried it, they'd crashed the whole system.

And I alone survived to tell thee . . .

But was that true? Could these terminals at least tell me the current status of all those I'd known?

It took a lot of careful poking and probing, always staying away from the newly intact red button and other dangerous controls, to find even the simple database for the first of the queries. The interface seemed deliberately designed to befuddle novices and even people who could handle routine computer work, but it wasn't something I couldn't figure out. I knew the basic UNIX variant used in the upstairs units, and it really was extrapolating from that point that finally got me where I wanted to go. Even with only minimal power to the consoles, I felt the enormous potential centered in this large room, power that could create worlds—and crash everything. I was attuned to it in some way, but not in the ways that would allow me to use the Maddox or Brand method of conscious access. That would come later. For now, I needed to know the basics.

It took me several tries to structure the first question in a way that elicited a proper response. It turned out to be LIST PERMANENT PARTY.

On the screen scrolled a list of names. Familiar names. Old names. But not any of my names. I needed a correlation.

LIST PERMANENT PARTY NAMES CURRENT.

There I was, with even my marriage accounted for. Jayce Cord Boyd. And how many others? I needed to be quick with my wrong-fingered reflexes to pause the display at each screen and count. Fifty-two names.

CORRELATE LIST PERMANENT PARTY NAMES CURRENT > ORIGINAL NAMES.

The query worked, but it wasn't the result I'd hoped for. The names listed on the left as original party were as unfamiliar as the names on the right. The only difference was that there was a definite sexual breakdown, and it wasn't quite the sort that I expected. One or two were ambiguous, but I pretty well felt certain that I had thirteen male names and thirty-nine female ones. Three girls for every boy. In a bisexual society, that was a really interesting division.

Why?

That would take a lot more work to answer than simply getting this far.

Al at least had been right, whether it was memory or gut instinct. The name across from Jayce Boyd was Mary Ann Howarth. So I *had* started off female. That really didn't disturb me, although I thought I made a pretty good male, too. What was more interesting was that one of the twelve men's names on the list was Mark Stephen Howarth. Brother? Father? Husband? Maybe I could find out, but not quite yet.

I had to fiddle with parameters and try to remember my basic programming skills to get the next query right, and, even then, I wasn't sure if the answer would be there. Still, a backup is a backup. At least, it *should* be.

CORRELATE LIST PERMANENT PARTY NAMES > ORIGINAL NAMES << NAME IN PAST THREE UPDATES.

The records weren't all complete. A few listings just weren't there, and some others were partials, but there was more than enough to get what I needed to know.

There I was, of course, easy to find. Cory Maddox, Drew Cordell Maddox, and Jayce were all there, as well as Mary

Ann from the original list. And Al was there, too. Almira
Starkweather, Albert Starkey, Al Stark, and here Al was
Sonjay Parath, of all things. But on the first list, the correlation
list . . .

"No!" I screamed at the terminal. "I don't believe it!"

Sandy, who'd been dozing, suddenly awoke with concern.
"What's the matter? You all right?"

"I—I don't know. Not anymore."

I tried several more attempts at structuring a new query
based on the new list, which this time I remembered to
save and use as a single comparative. I had to know if there
were more detailed initial personnel records. I had to know
why, in the original permanent party list, Al and I had the same
last name.

The card finally came up, complete with an almost three-
dimensional photo of the subject. A bit nerdy-looking for
somebody like Al, with a full and beautifully trimmed brown
mustache and short beard. Brown hair that was already in the
early stages of disappearing. Not a knockout but not repulsive,
either. Kind of average. Five foot ten, 180 pounds, blue eyes.
Hard to tell the age from the nonreferential date on the
card, but he looked to be no more than thirty or so when the
photo was taken. The box listed him as married and gave his
position in both numerical code and a word code, and then
simply as "Chief of Security." That figured. L.L.B., William
and Mary. A lawyer. That figured, too.

Mary Ann was even more of a letdown, I'm afraid. The
face staring out from the terminal screen was not one that
gave me a sense of total familiarity, but how many lifetimes
ago had I worn it? It was plain, somewhat mousy, a little
buck-toothed, and wearing no makeup at all. Big, round,
tinted glasses that looked absolutely necessary covered
squinty brown eyes, and the thin, unstyled, straight, light
brown hair was cut about even with the jawline. The appended
information said I'd been five-two and only ninety-six
pounds! Looked maybe mid-twenties. Maiden name Epstein.

And, yes, married, with a reference to Mark Howarth's record number.

I was—or, at least, I had been—married to Al! And he'd *known* it. Known it all along. That was why he had taken such a personal interest in me, and why he had visited me in that Brand Box. Did he think I was going to suddenly fall in love with him again, if I ever had been in love with him?

I had a B.A. from Goucher in accounting and business administration, and an M.B.A. from Penn. Not very thrilling areas, but I had one more degree than Al—er, Mark—had. The card listed me as comptroller. Interesting. I basically oversaw and controlled all funding, and my hubby was the law. In effect, we'd run whatever it was.

And what about Rick? It was odd—I'd held the torch for Rick, male or female, in almost all my previous lives, yet I felt almost nothing for him now. Still, what had been the attraction?

His records were among those not faring as well, but I got one match that at least let me know that Rick correlated with an original staff member named—Yolanda Stuart! Holy shit! Rick had been female at the start, too! Was there some story here?

I punched up Yolanda's card. She was young, looked good spirited, but chubby, maybe even fat. Five foot five, 190—heavier than Mark! She was also chocolate brown and clearly of African ancestry. B.S. in computer science from some small school in the West, and then, surprisingly, a master of fine arts from U.C. Berkeley. Listed as "programmer 1—landscape and backgrounds."

Was that it? Had Al taken me for granted during the project only to discover me one day in bed with a black woman? If basic personality traveled from life to life, and there was good evidence that it did, I couldn't think of anything that would have infuriated him more.

In a way, it was a shock to find out all this, but, in another way it wasn't really important. It was like reading a romantic novel or watching a soap opera. These weren't people I remembered, let alone knew. All it explained was why Al had a knee-jerk reaction to me and why I had a more positive reaction to Rick/Riki and was comfortable in almost any sexual combination. It even had its humorous side—white-bread Rick had started out black. But it didn't mean anything, not now. Surely it was mere amusement at this stage.

Or was it? If these were pictures and profiles of the "real" us, then those people, somewhere, were probably in some kind of permanent deep storage, maybe even cryonic storage, awaiting our efforts to get our minds out of this stew and back to reality. That faced me with another ugly problem: I didn't want to be that plain little proto-anorexic, and I sure didn't want to be Mrs. Mark Howarth, even in just his mind.

This had simply never occurred to me before. I bet it hadn't occurred to most of those who knew about this list at one time or another.

Did I really want out of this, if that were the price?

I was glad I didn't have to face that problem yet. It was perhaps a million decisions in the future yet.

Still, something I'd been thinking while mulling over the point had gone right by and it shouldn't have. What? *Think, Jayce! Think!*

Cryonic storage. Freezing. Suspended animation chambers. Wasn't that kind of like the life-support pods? No, it was the LSP in spades, hearts, diamonds, clubs, and no trumps. Fifty-two people . . . thirty-nine women, thirteen men . . . all volunteers, all part of some project. Why the hell would they put the comptroller in there, though? Because she was the chief of security's cheating wife and he wanted her there? Probably. Kind of a disappointment, really, although in later lives I somehow learned pretty sophisticated programming.

Wait a minute! Fifty-two . . . Scroll through the original list. Where in hell was Matthew Brand? In the last incarnations listing, there was no Brand, either. He wasn't there—or, at least, he wasn't part of the fifty-two.

Time to find Matthew Brand's record, if it existed.

LIST MATTHEW BRAND ALL KNOWN INCARNATIONS.

Quite a list came up. It found him at least forty times before I stopped counting, but not on the permanent party list. And every single incarnation listed him as Matthew Tyler Brand. But how was that possible? Surely there'd be some female incarnations somewhere, sometime. Hell, he'd only been lost, or escaped, or maybe murdered within the past fifteen lives or so. Within the old Al's memories before I shot the bastard in the head.

Matthew Brand, Matthew Brand, Matthew Brand. Nothing but. Not even variations in the name as we all experienced. No changes at all. As much as this Command Center, Matthew Brand was a fixed point through all the incarnations he'd lived through.

Who and what are you, really, Matthew Tyler Brand?

"They the ones who started all this?" Sandy asked. "Pardon if I'm out of line, but they don't exactly impress me much. Hell, the head shots don't look much different from us, 'cept maybe that one with the hairy face. Now *that's* an ape face!"

We didn't grow facial hair, of course, and the faces of our people tended to look pretty much like ordinary women's faces, so the reaction wasn't surprising.

I was tired, and I was also beginning to think pretty much the same sort of thoughts as Sandy on that score. It was hard to really imagine myself having that ape-human form. It was so limiting, so plain and ugly. This form, on the other hand, was sleek, beautiful, and sensual. Hell, the more I looked at that mousy little plain Mary Ann and compared her to who I was now, with a gorgeous face, beautiful hair, sleek hindquarters, and big tits, the less I wanted to consider that face as my ultimate destiny. And comparing any of those faces to my darling Sandy . . . No, the hell with that.

Proximity to the power below always was something of a turn-on, particularly when fed by emotion rather than reason, and my emotions were racing at this moment. I wanted answers, but I didn't want out. I loved being Jayce a bit too much, and I proved it until we were too damned tired to keep it up anymore.

The next day, I went looking for Matthew Brand.

It was still very limiting to have to do it manually by keyboard input; the whole system was designed to be driven directly, but the best I could get was the primitive one-way system of a head mount readout. Input was the problem. It was slow and needed to be very precise, where putting the queries in via direct mental input would have easily reconciled my desires with machine requirements.

There were fifty-two of the Elect, as it were, and I had everything from their origin names and shorthand codes to their names in this world and life. What I didn't have on all of them was just who was who among the group I'd encountered. No Cynthia Matalon, no Walt Slidecker, but the number added up so they were there somewhere. About a third of the names had missing or damaged records; I suspected that these were mostly ones who'd not been processed through the main computer for several lifetimes but rather had used a secondary site.

Still no indicator of little creatures in a flying saucer, though. That remained another mystery to solve.

Still, while a few names weren't that familiar to me from the lives I did remember, the ones I'd encountered closely were all covered with one notable exception. Here were Rob and Lee, Les Cohn—who was, it seemed, always the doctor and was the group physician on the original list under the name Herbert Weinberg, M.D.—and Alice McKee, a cultural anthropologist named Martha O'Donahue, and Dan Tanaka, the deputy chief of programming named Tice Koroku. All present and accounted for. As I said, the March Hare people were not necessarily identifiable, but those who'd passed through here during that period were recorded and cross-matched. There was Wilma, identified as a wilderness survival expert named Monica Twin Elks. Rob was identified as a female history professor from Stanford. Lee was a chemist. In fact, most of the scientific and social science disciplines were represented; few were directly connected to computers other than Tanaka. Interesting. Why not?

There was no correlation for Rita Alvarez, and considering the last time I'd seen her and her mental state, that bothered me no end. Why wouldn't she be in the records? She was working with them, after all. Walt, Cynthia, Father Pete, that crew was one thing, but Rita had been on Al's side or her own right here.

For every answer I turned up, I turned up several more mysteries.

What were the things that the people, the "real" Elect, had in common?

They were all professional people, highly educated, with some experience, yet the oldest was the doctor at thirty-four and the average age was under thirty. All appeared to be in good health; the only one wearing glasses in the ID picture was me, and that I suspected was because I was being carried along into this project by my dear husband rather than being one of the volunteers. I couldn't see where an accountant would fit into to the group otherwise.

They were multiracial, but that wasn't the major factor. All of them had IQs well above average, most had graduate degrees or unique specializations, and, more interestingly, they had been scanned for genetic disorders. It wasn't the kind of group you'd employ on a VR project or a supercomputer project, either. It was more like the kind of group you'd put together if you were sending a sample off to another planet without necessarily expecting them to return. Healthy genetic stock, wide variety, three women for every man, cryonic freezing . . .

My god! Were we in some sort of spaceship, roaming around the computer while our bodies remained in deep freeze, perhaps trying out computer models of societies we might build someplace else? It sure made sense, but only to a degree.

Fifty-two people was a pretty tiny colony for that kind of job or those kinds of models. I felt sure it wasn't the answer but that it might contain elements of the answer.

I kept going back and punching up Matthew Tyler Brand. He stared back at me, or at least his holographic face did, a handsome, boyish hippie type born decades too late for the period. He'd have been really handsome if he'd trimmed the facial hair, at least, or maybe shaved and got a decent haircut.

Where the hell are you, Matthew Brand? Why did you put together this group and then abandon it? Did Al and his crew kill you off, or did you run because they somehow discovered the truth and weren't all that happy about it? Did they decide that they were tired of being your playthings? Was it that they didn't want to play your game anymore? Was that it?

But the image wouldn't tell me.

Sandy had gotten a kick out of virtual reality even on the basic level we could access it, and I'd found a bunch of classic games that could be played without having to directly link to the computer. Kind of shoot-'em-ups and the like, but for Sandy it was miraculous.

Even though it would be very dangerous, I half wished I had Les Cohn here. He'd make short work of doing the kind of physiological measurements and adjustments that would allow a direct interface. It shouldn't be that hard to make the adjustments, but only if I knew how to do it. On the ones I'd designed so long ago it was fairly simple, but the ones here were a lot more advanced than anything I'd done, and appeared to be sealed units.

I have no idea how long we'd been there. Time kind of lost its meaning sealed inside a mountain. My watch had long since proven irrelevant, particularly since it lacked the precision I needed to use it with any computer procedures, but since Sandy never wore watches it wasn't much good for scheduling, either.

I was in the old VR interface room trying to find anything

that would give me access to the tuning and controls in the helmets when Sandy rushed in, almost breathless.

"Jayce! You gotta come quick!"

"Huh? What? What's the matter, honey?"

"I—I was just down near the eating room! Just standing there, trying to figure out what I wanted to eat, and suddenly the phone—you know that black phone that just doesn't seem to connect, like all the others don't?—well, *the phone rang*!"

My heart skipped a beat. "The phone . . . *rang*?"

"Yeah. And when I picked it up, somebody asked for somebody named Cory Maddox!"

XII

THE PLAYERS ON
THE OTHER SIDE

I don't know if I was more angry than scared or the other way around, but even as I stormed toward that phone I knew right off one thing that had turned everything on its head regardless of who or what was on the other end.

The Mock Turtle had lied.

If in fact there was anybody of the Elect on the other end of that line, then I wasn't the only one who'd lived through the system crash with my past memories intact. And since I didn't know how to call them, let alone who to call, it meant I wasn't exactly in charge of this place, either.

I grabbed the phone. "Who is this?" I demanded.

A voice came back that, while not familiar in and of itself, had a very familiar ring to it. I might have known.

"Cory! Dahlin', is that you? Why that's jes' the *sweetest* li'l ole girly voice Ah evah did heah!"

"Where are you, Cynthia?" Now I knew I was mostly angry.

"Why—Ah'm in the li'l ole flyin' sausah, o'course. In the transit bay at the usual hideout. Wheah'd you think Ah'd be, dahlin'?"

That figured. We knew from the start and from my own

experiments there that there was a link from that place, and possibly others around the world, to the Command Center. Cynthia at her best was nuttier than a fruitcake, but she had been around a very long time, and she knew how to work things. You didn't really need a degree in electrical engineering before you could flip on a light switch or make a phone call, and she knew how to at least operate most of this equipment.

"Who's with you?"

"Well, see, that's the problem, dahlin'. The li'l boys ah heah but they'ah in some soaht of a trance or somethin', and Ah can't get a rise outta any of 'em. The LSUs were used, but theah's no sign a'tall of anybody havin' been in 'em lately. Ah been out and checked around. Everything's on, but nobody's heah. Ah been lonely as all hell, dahlin', with not even an easy way outta heah. But Ah remembuhed from way back how to use these li'l ole computah thingies with the football helmets and Ah put one on and tried to dial 'round and see who was wheah. And on all the bands, all Ah could find on any of 'em was yoah ID right theah in the headquatahs, so Ah found out Ah could patch in a phone to theah through that energy muck and heah we ah."

I frowned. "You say you put on one of the network helmets and accessed the computers through it?"

"Suah thing, sugah. Ah mean, it ain't like brain suhgury or nothin' like that."

A rather bizarre thought came to me all of a sudden. One that made no sense at all. "Cynthia—what do you look like in this incarnation?"

"Huh? Dahkah than usual, sugah. Kinda Mexican beauty, all big brown eyes and coal black haiah and that soaht of thing. Ah guess Ah'm some kinda señorita, only the details didn't come in like usual. Sorry, sugah. Don't sound like Ah'm yoah type, huh?"

I felt a little chill go through me. "Cynthia, this may sound crazy, but just humor me. How many legs do you have?"

"*What?* What kinda crazy question is that?"

"Just answer me. How many legs."

"Why, two, damn it! Same as usual. Why? You think Ah lost one of 'em or somethin'?"

I thought so. "Baby, you're not gonna believe this world you're stuck in. In fact, I don't think I can even explain it to you over the phone. You're not gonna get out of there by any usual means, though, believe me." Even if somebody were around, in this world she'd wind up more a candidate for a freak show or a zoo or, more likely, she'd be burned as a deformed monster by local peasants.

"Ain't nothin' but desut out heah," she agreed, not knowing the full implications of this. "Ah don't think nobody evah comes heah. Theah ain't even the rut road outside, and it's *cold* out theah."

I thought a moment. "Cynthia, you've used rabbit holes before. I've seen you. I know you were with Walt, but right now you're in a powered station. Do you think you could get into an LSU, connect up, and come through the energy field to here? I'm outside Chattanooga, Tennessee. This world's pretty primitive, so that may be your only way out."

"What? You want me t' will myself theah? Like somethin' outta *Stah Trek* or somethin'?"

I sighed. "You know as well as I do that nothing we're perceiving as real is actually real. Only the energy is present and it can be manipulated. I've done this mentally; I see no reason, if I've got a prepared LSU here, you can't do it physically. We'll use the energy thread from this phone line as the connection. I'll tell you how to set the console so the phone will be transferred to the LSU. Then you get off this one, go to the LSU, put that helmet on, reestablish connection. I'll set up a sympathetic unit here and do the same transfer. After a while, you should be able to see here from there. When you can, *will* yourself to be here, to come here and step out of the booth. I know it sounds crazy, but if you believe you can do it, and follow my directions, it will happen. I feel sure of it. Are you game?"

It was the first time I'd ever heard doubt or uncertainty in her. "Uh, yeah, maybe. Ah—Ah'll try."

"Well, you'll either do it or you'll have to fly that saucer here."

"Ah can't do it. Tried already. If them li'l guys ah out, so's the sausah. Couldn't git 'em to budge, and Ah been heah fo' weeks, Cory!"

This was what I was most comfortable doing. Experimental, yes, but basic computer programming and math. I'd never be able to invent, or even fully understand, all this stuff, but I sure as hell was a competent technician. I was tearing up, rewiring, reworking one of the LSU units, splicing things in, going back and forth to the keyboards at which I'd become very adept, and still keeping up a running conversation with my very bewildered mate.

Sandy, after all, had just been getting used to some of the wonders in this place and now things were getting even weirder. "This person's actually a hairless ape with our brainpower?"

"Well, sort of. Cynthia's got as much hair as we do on the head, but not that much on the rest of the body." Preparing Sandy for the concept of a biped wasn't easy, particularly one that would still have to be considered human.

"And this creature is—where? Almost three thousand miles from here, out in the Northwest Territories someplace? And in spite of that, it's going to appear here by force of will? That's—"

"Teleportation, if it were in the conventional sense, but I don't think we're really talking about a physical move at all. Consider this more a changing point of view."

"But why bring it here? I mean, what good will it do?"

"Maybe a lot. Cynthia can directly interface with the computers here. Maybe a little work will allow me, through the medium of Cynthia, to get it so that I can do it as well. If I can, things will go a lot faster and we can start doing things. I don't know about you, but I want to see the sun, breathe fresh air, and go for long morning trots."

"Yeah. Me, too. Just not with a prison brand."

"Well, okay, this is the first step."

"You talk like this ape is someone you'd rather not have around. Why bring this creature in here, then?"

"Because I know Cynthia well enough to believe that it might help more than hurt. More than a little hard to take, though. Don't worry—I can hardly wait until dear Cynthia discovers that the outsider role is maximized in spades now."

Sandy still was dubious. "You said everyone of your kind would be natives of our world just as you are. Why is this Cynthia not of our kind, then?"

It was a good question. "I'll let you know that after I have Cynthia here and can run a lot of tests." It was a mystery, and one that didn't just start and end with the flamboyant and uninhibited woman. I wanted to know what they'd been doing since I last saw them.

The most important thing was that, somehow, the saucer and its enigmatic crew, in many ways far more alien than we'd be to Cynthia, had survived as well. Maybe that Roswell cover yarn had something to it.

Damn it! That's why we were here. It was time for answers! This place had them, if only I could get to them.

Sandy frowned and stared at my frantic activity. "How do you know how to do this?"

I paused a moment and grinned. "I don't. I know what these are and where they plug in, that's all. It's the computer that's going to figure out the rest. Cynthia is going to tell it what she wants it to do." *I hope.*

Finally I was finished, and only then did I reflect that I really hadn't thought much about what I was doing and that I was in a little over my head. I thought it would work, but I had no idea why such confidence was warranted.

I plugged a comm unit into the side of the LSU, activated the attached Brand Box, and said into the mike, "Cynthia? Are you there?"

"Mah goodness how Ah hate these things!" came a response apparently from inside the empty life-support unit. "And this one's cramped as all get-out! Ah think Ah musta picked the smallest one of the batch!"

I always had the impression that they were all the same size. Still . . .

"Don't worry about it. You'll be out of there very quickly. You're in direct contact through the head mount?"

"Goodness, yes! Let's get on with this! Ah bahrely got the damn helmet on my head but Ah ain't gonna shave it 'less Ah have to!"

"Okay, stand by. I'm going to button this up here. I want you to just mentally reach out for a connection. Instruct the computer just like you instructed that saucer a while back. Tell it to transmit you here, transmit you physically."

"You shoah this is possible?"

"I'm pretty sure, yes. It's been done. Now, start counting backward from thirty. When you hit zero, clear your mind of everything except what you want the computer to do. Ready?"

"Moah than ready!"

"Okay. Start counting . . . *now!*"

I disconnected the comm unit, went to the console, and fed all the energy I could into the empty LSU. The trick was to do it through the comm link, not through the core where the energy might well destroy her. I had decided not to suggest this as a possibility to Cynthia because it might have hurt her concentration.

Now I was helpless. Either she could do it or she couldn't.

For a while, nothing happened. "Doesn't seem like she's gonna do it," Sandy commented, not sounding a bit surprised.

Suddenly, as if on cue, there was a series of high-pitched electrical whines that went through every speaker, phone, and outlet in the place. The lighting, which was of course being powered from the massive energy source below, actually dimmed, and then, with the lights going up and down and the cacophony of whines reaching a nearly unbearable pitch, the entire station began to vibrate. Not a lot, but like somebody kicked on an electric massage unit.

"Is it an earthquake?" Sandy tried to shout over the din, but I just shook my head and tried to stop up my ears.

The station went completely dark but the shaking didn't stop. Now I could see waves and waves of energy, blue-white ripples almost like water through a filter of gauze, illuminating every one of the millions of miles of wiring and cabling in the place, all now converging on just one spot.

Both of us fell to the floor, unable to keep our balance and our heads close to exploding in agony from the noise. Then there was a sharp, very loud explosion, and I managed to get my head up just in time to see the wired-up LSU, which was now getting the whole series of waves, blow its coffinlike lid right off.

And, suddenly, it was over. The sound abruptly stopped, as did the vibration. I was still half deaf, but convinced that my eardrums had somehow held. Now, one by one, each bank of lights came back on, and all that was left was a shattered LSU lid and the smell of ozone in the air.

As my hearing returned and I got back on my feet, I could only think that, somehow, I'd just murdered Cynthia Matalon. A look over at the LSU, though, indicated that this wasn't necessarily true. Out of the end of the thing stuck two bare and very human feet. Big feet.

The feet twitched, and even my still recovering ears heard a deep, throaty female voice say, "Mah goodness gracious! What a *rush*!"

Two hands came up, and then the feet were withdrawn so that she could get up out of the unit. As she did so, she proved that we weren't the only surprises in the room.

Cynthia didn't look much like her former self, but she was big. It was less of a wonder now, seeing her, that she got here than that she'd fit in the LSU at all, let alone gotten the head mount on in a working position.

As she climbed down—looking a little bit in shock but otherwise no worse for wear considering that she'd just done the nearly impossible—she looked to be at least a head taller than Sandy, who was five foot ten, hoof to head. Cynthia was at least six foot four or five. There didn't seem to be an ounce of fat on her, but she definitely had muscles to match her size. Her skin was a sort of weathered yellow-tan, and her features, from the sharp nose and big brown eyes to the almost waist-length thick black hair, marked her not so much as a Hispanic, which is what she'd thought, as it did a full-blooded Central or South American "Indian." Whatever the ethnicity, I wasn't at all sure that Cynthia realized her size.

Sandy gaped, openmouthed, at the newcomer. Finally there came almost a whisper: "How does it stand up like that, on only two feet?"

"They manage," I assured my companion. "It comes naturally. But it's not an 'it' so much as a 'she.' Note that the frontal view isn't that far from what we look like, at least down to the legs. She's a lot different internally, though." For Sandy, it wasn't just the first ape-human ever seen, but also the fact that, in our world, "male" and "female" were used to describe parts of the anatomy, and the ends of plugs and cables.

Cynthia seemed to be coming out of her shock, and the voices discussing her so analytically seemed to focus her mind more. She shook her head, took a number of deep breaths, and seemed to try to focus her eyes on us. When she did, her expression was so indescribable and so unbelieving that she looked away, muttering unintelligibly to herself. To Cynthia, unprepared for a non-ape-human world, and having just undergone an unbelievable experience, we must have looked like hallucinations.

"Oh, my *god*! What in hell ah y'all?"

"We're the people here, Cynthia. You're the creature."

That took her aback. "How's that?"

"The whole world is based on creatures like us, not like you. In fact, I really want to know why you aren't one of us, too."

"Mah Lord! Cory? Is that you, dahlin'?"

"Jayce in this world, but Cory in my memories. Sandy's not one of us, but we're mated and we're both in this together for the long haul. You know the routine. I've been born and raised here like this. For some reason, you weren't."

It took some time for her to come to grips with the concept, and even more to be able to keep from looking at us like we were out of some sort of freak show. Of course, the fact that Sandy was gaping at her in the exact same way gave some balance to the whole thing, and, at least, we were the normal ones here.

They had had some warning of the crash. The little creatures on the saucer had noted the indications, and the power at the backup site had built to dangerous levels. The computers told them that they couldn't hold, that this was a critical emergency, and, of course, none of them were in any position to stop the experiment here in the Command Center that was causing it. In desperation, knowing that the usual escape route wouldn't work, Walt had come up with the idea of opening a rabbit hole and bundling everyone as far inside as possible with the hope that it would insulate them. In that world, and under those rules, Cynthia was the boss and she'd acted admirably, at least to hear her tell it. With the energy levels so high, somebody had to be there until the last moment to make sure that the rabbit hole wasn't brought down with everything else. It was only after everybody had gotten in except her that she realized it was too late. The equipment was shorting out; there was no way that she or anyone could trust any of the automated systems to cut the rabbit hole loose. She did it manually, leaving her stranded.

"Well, then, there was only one thing left that gave me half a chance, and that was the sausah," she told us. "The little men let me in, then put up some kinda foahce field or somethin' and put themselves in that suspended animation or whatevah you call it. There wasn't no place on the thing for me, and Ah wouldn't't've fit in theah cubbyholes anyways, so Ah just buckeled mahself into the captain's chaih and braced myself. Things shook like crazy, then theah was this feelin' like goin' down the biggest hill on a rollah coastah, and Ah passed out. Didn't come to till maybe two, three weeks ago, Ah suppose. Ah been eatin' off the stoahs theah as best Ah can and tryin' t'figgah a way out. All of a sudden Ah see that the computah screens ah back on and all soahts of shit is playin' ovah them. Ah figgahed that this place must be active, so Ah rigged up that call. The rest you know."

Although I had no measure of time, it almost sounded as if our coming in here and turning on the station had revived her as well. Maybe it had. "And you don't know anything about this world, about people like us, or about any of the others? You just woke up and that's that?"

"That's about it," she agreed. "I don't even look no different than I did when I climbed into that chaih. Don't make no sense, does it? Ah got no memory of a whole incahnation. Ah don't remembah that evah happenin' befoah without wipin' out the rest."

I nodded. "You can interface with the station here. So far, I haven't been able to do that. I think my brain's running at a slightly altered frequency and I can't retune the thing to access it unless I can already access it, if that makes any sense. Now, with you, maybe we can get this place up and running and make plans for the future."

"What kinda futuah have Ah got if everybody now looks like you?" she asked, sounding really worried. "Ah mean, Ah can't show mah face nowhere on this planet if what you say is true. Ah wouldn't even mind bein' one of y'all—that looks like a body built for toughness but still foah sin, too."

After some settling down, resting a little, and a real checkout of the equipment, it was easy to proceed. The only time I'd ever seen Cynthia off her balance before was when we'd haunted her that first time back in Yakima. She still had the real power here if she wanted to use it, but her confidence was shaken. I had counted on that.

As I'd suspected, it wasn't that difficult to make the adjustments once somebody could directly interface with the computers and outline the problem. I noticed that Sandy was tense when we started out; my guardian angel, as it were, ready to smite the alien Philistine should she try something. It didn't matter. Cynthia was the real god here if she wanted it, but right now she was too off stride to do more than follow my leads.

Even more interesting was the fact that, once I'd ran all the checks from the direct mental interface head mounts, I was able to show Sandy how to do it as well. In fact, although it could be undone by any one of us, I set things up so that the computers wouldn't accept direct commands outright from anyone but the three of us. It was probably a needlessly paranoid safety measure, but after Cynthia showed up I wasn't taking anything for granted.

The next thing we did, Cynthia and I working together, was to slightly rotate the entire complex so that it was aligned with the old drainage pipe. This proved to be less of a problem than I'd thought, and allowed a proper entrance and exit without having to become a contortionist extraordinaire. We didn't have much for disguises, so this would have to be a cautious and careful use of our limited freedom, but the odds were that the feds were searching for us over a far wider swath than Chattanooga by now. It allowed for some airing, particularly at night, and a real stretching of limbs and feeling a bit of freedom again, and, with one of us shadowing the other, it also allowed one or the other of us to sneak into town and pick up needed supplies.

Cynthia, too, emerged, but only at night. She was very large and not easy to conceal, but she could climb straight up things, something our form just couldn't do. She was also able, for short periods, to observe a little of our society and finally accept the fact that, here, she was the freak.

Mostly, though, we kept the guard up, and Cynthia was able to set up a force field via the computers that kept interlopers from coming too far in should anyone discover the entrance.

We also went fishing. Not in the Tennessee River, although that would have been more than welcome, but inside the memory banks and backups of the Command Center.

A correlation of the original permanent party to the current incarnations that might have taken me hours to set up via the keyboard was a matter of just thinking the question. The answers weren't always instantaneous, but they were fast and unambiguous in most cases.

How many of the permanent party could be matched to existing people in this world? Twenty-seven, it turned out, although one of those was Cynthia. She showed up on the permanent party list as a green-eyed mulatto girl who looked not much out of her teens and was identified as Maureen Laffite— one far removed descendant of pirate Jean Laffite, perhaps?— who was in turn the daughter of Jeanne Cartier, who was identified as a psychologist. Cartier had a real Cajun look to her, but clearly had little if any African blood. Maureen's father was not identified.

Cynthia was fascinated. It was kind of like knowing you were adopted and then discovering your real parents, but the detail was sketchy. We had no correlation with anybody we knew by another name and this Jeanne Cartier. It was one of those missing records.

We located the twenty-seven and asked for what detail was available. The results were equally sketchy. Only six of those who'd started off male were in this little party—irrelevant, of course, in a society like ours—leaving twenty-one females including me and Cynthia. Less than half of the twenty-seven were in the North American region, although it was probably more notable that fully six of them were with others of the Elect. Even though that was only three pairs, it was way beyond chance. Something drew us to one another.

The rest were scattered all over. Two in widely different

areas of South America; four in Africa—including another pairing in East Africa—with another six in Europe with yet one more pair in either France or Germany, and others in what in other worlds would have been Poland, Russia, India, China, and Japan. Also noted on the map, to our complete surprise, were two other backup centers, one in southern Africa, the other in southern Russia near the Chinese and Indian borders.

There were, however, a lot of the Elect that we simply didn't know or didn't have any memory of, and others that couldn't be correlated with any name we knew. It didn't matter. The odds were that none of them knew about us except in their dreams.

"You could always go haunt them and sing songs," I suggested to Cynthia, who snorted at the idea.

"Didn't go all that well the last time Ah did that," she noted.

If I'd started out as an accountant, though, I must have been a lousy one or it must have been very long ago. I hadn't even noticed, or paid attention to, the string of numbers along the top right of each ID record. I'd simply assumed that they were database record numbers for internal use. It was Sandy, in fact, who noticed them because, of course, Sandy didn't have any firsthand knowledge of the rest of this business.

"There's something funny about those numbers," Sandy commented.

"Huh? What? They're just database tags."

"Are you sure? Look at the different colors of the letters and numbers. Most of it is just in blue, but look at the last two or three digits. They can be numbers or letters, but they're either black or red. Forget the rest of the number—it may be what you say, or it might have another meaning, but these digits are designed to stand out. I've seen enough coded government forms to know that much."

Cynthia and I both looked, neither of us doing more than humoring our native companion, but it didn't take much flipping through the records and isolating the numeric strings to see that there really was something going on there. With the rest of the string of a dozen or more alphanumeric characters looking pretty standard, the ends were decidedly not. H1 in red, C12 in black, D11 in red . . . But what did it mean?

"Son of a bitch!" Cynthia swore. "Plain as day! How'd we evah miss it?"

"Plain as day? What is? That it's a code of some kind, yeah, but—"

"Do y'all play cahds in this life? You know, reg'lah cahds, like pokah or gin rummy or that kind of stuff?"

"Yeah, sure, but—" Suddenly it hit me the same way it had hit her, and it *was* plain as day. I'd only needed a little perspective because the suits here were different—cups, balls, pentacles, and triangles. Even so, it should have been clear even when I was punching them up by hand weeks earlier.

1H—ace of hearts. 11C—queen of clubs.

"Oh, my god, that rotten son of a bitch Matt Brand!" I exclaimed. "Him and his *Alice in Wonderland* motif! We're only a pack of cards, you see, at least to the computer! Fifty-two cards, thirteen in each of four suits."

"Sexist, too," Cynthia sniffed. "The thuhteen men ah the top seven spades and the top six clubs 'cept foah queens and tens. So we got two aces, all the kings, all the jacks, and three of the foah aces."

Okay, so we were only a pack of cards and each of us had our suit and our number. But what in hell did the suit and number mean? More humor, or something more important than that?

"Let's line up the ones we know with their card and suit and see if there's any pattern," I suggested.

It was quickly done. Howarth, king of spades. Mrs. Howarth—*three of spades*? I felt insulted.

Cynthia, Wilma, and Alice were all queens; Les and Dan Tanaka were both aces, but the other two didn't correlate yet with identities we knew. Riki was a ten of spades. Higher than me, but, then, almost everybody was. In fact, everybody I knew was at least an eight or higher. I was not only a low card, I was down with the unknowns and insignificants.

"Don't feel bad," Cynthia giggled. "You done all right for a meah tray. Sometimes a tray can trump three aces. It happens, if you play the right game."

I sighed. "I dunno. Somehow I always had it in the back of my mind that maybe I was secretly Matt Brand or something, hiding out, running things from my subconscious, something like that. Now it turns out I'm barely a player. No wonder I kept running from responsibility when I had the chance! You, now, you're a queen."

And so was Wilma. High-ranking cards. "Who's the one woman ace?"

"Jeanne Cartier. Mommy deah."

Now that meant something. It had to. Seven of the top eight cards were male. One female at the top, four more near it. Everybody below a jack was female. Cynthia was right. If this was a hierarchical code, then the men were definitely in charge.

And hadn't they been, more or less? Al and Les and Walt as well; and Lee and Rob and Father Pete, Ben, Dan . . . The movers and controllers had been men, pretty much, and the women had mostly shaken things up. Even in the world with the women on top, who'd been the women there? Lee and Al . . . and Rita and Alice?

Hmmmm . . .

I was reasonably certain that Alice was a queen like Cynthia, but, when push had come to shove, who'd managed the really nasty stuff? Al and Lee were flunkies, even if powerful ones, but they'd reincarnated and didn't remember much. If you don't know you've got power, you don't really have it. Alice was high up, all right, but who had the power and position outside of the Command Center people?

Rita.

And who had held her own in a world dissolving and changing and going mad?

Rita.

But if Rita was the fourth ace, as logic said she almost had to be, then . . .

"You'ah sayin' that Rita Alvarez is my mothah?" Cynthia Matalon was appalled. *"Sistah Rita Nutzoid?"*

Well, there was something of a mental family resemblance there, I had to admit—entirely to myself this time.

"The four aces—Walt, Les, Rita, and Dan. The four kings—Father Pete, Al, Lee, and one we don't know yet. Maybe Ben Sloan. He had the right kind of position there."

Sandy didn't know much of virtual realities or even *Alice in Wonderland*, but there wasn't much of a problem dealing with the bureaucratic mind or with cards even with the suits altered. Adjusting to the ape-human suits and titles, it was Sandy who started trying to put things together.

"You've got to figure that those four—aces, you called them?—are in charge. Hardest thing for me is adjusting so that two is low and one is high. Don't make sense, but never mind. Okay—a physician, a psychologist, a chief administrator, and a computer wizard you say was second to this Brand person. Makes sense for this kind of setup. You need somebody to run things, somebody to run the machines, somebody to make sure everybody's healthy, and somebody to make sure that the job isn't too much for anybody. Of course, the psych would be the one to flip out. Never saw a psychologist who wasn't crazy."

We let that pass. You don't derail somebody when they're on a roll.

"Okay, now if we assume that you are right in identifying the kings," Sandy went on, "then you have a chief of security, inevitable in a project like this, as well as a deputy chief or strongarm type, a top technician to do the rewiring and such, and this other one, the one you think of as a religious leader, really might be one, even if it's a personnel expert. The queens are even easier. A sociologist, an anthropologist, a survival expert with a different cultural background, and, pardon, the—daughter I think the term is?—of the only all female leader. Even allowing for guesses there, and hoping I think that the jobs given are pretty much the same as the jobs would be thought of here except, of course, for the computer types, you get a strong pattern. Honey, you said straight off that it sounded like a colony. It sure sounds like that to me, too. Or, rather, it sounds like a team for building a colony."

I felt like I'd really underestimated Sandy, and I loved my mate all the more for proving me a fool. It was a team created to build a colony. Or, perhaps, to test colonies? Test all these scenarios by living them out where even killing off the colony isn't fatal to the project? I said as much.

"Makes sense." Cynthia agreed. "But sugah, it shoah wasn't supposed to wuhk like this, was it? Or was it? And, if it was, who's lookin' and learnin'? Not us."

I pulled back, unable to hide from the suspicion I'd harbored not just for a few moments but perhaps from the start of this, at least as far back as I could remember, and certainly since my experiences essentially started splitting into sections. Rini wasn't just a shadow or a spinoff creation; Rini was a real person, and more and more distinct from me.

Sandy wasn't just window dressing here, either. Much of this logic chain involved this person from another unique world whose perspective was due to thinking and acting as a crooked bureaucrat. Even Cynthia had accepted Sandy as a full and equal partner.

I couldn't run from the thought anymore.

"Suppose *we* are looking at and evaluating this," I suggested. "Suppose none of us are anything more than virtual creations inside the computer. Suppose we're just undergoing scenario after scenario, world after world, in an endless series of social and economic experiments?"

They both looked at me like I'd just dropped in from Mars.

"Speak foah yo'self. Ah know Ah'm moah than just some computah routine."

"Like Sandy and Rini?"

She opened her mouth again but nothing came out. Sandy was also silent on this, but I could tell that the same feeling that was so disturbing to the two of us was giving my lover a little sense of satisfaction.

It was more than just a feeling on my part, or even living with "spooks" who had as much or more depth to them than some of us did. It was also being able to look at us, many of us, over a number of lifetimes, worlds, cultures. To some degree, those I knew best tended to be the same sort of archetypes in life after life. Overall, my personality, which I'd always considered lacking in guts and ambition, was sure as hell as much an archetype as anything. Cynthia—she was even more the same nutty Cynthia than ever. Al was the fanatical security man and jilted lover.

"And if that's somehow so, who's been pushin' you in all those silly costumes?"

I was ready for that one. "That's almost too obvious. It's Brand, and maybe others. Brand, who's on the other side of the looking glass and injecting himself inside in a number of guises based on poor little Alice. He's a card, too, only not one in the standard deck. Matt Brand's the joker. When he needs to jump-start something, get something off the dime, or kick something into termination and reincarnation, in walks another character. If he wants us to jump one way, he can threaten and demonstrate the power of a wild card as the Mock Turtle or nudge as the Walrus or change directions as the Caterpillar. It might be more than Brand. Something put us at war, one group fighting another. Mostly the high cards, but with a few of us lowly pawns dragged in now and then, particularly when Matt needs a jump start. You, Walt, Father Pete, sometimes Riki and some others, against the rest. Rebels, maybe, of some kind. Maybe you're just to keep the pot stirred and prevent the Als and Dans and Les Cohns from taking over completely."

"That's a *horrid* idea, if I do say so!" Cynthia maintained.

I shrugged. "Maybe. Maybe not. Think about religions. Father Pete's Catholic Church for one. We're all the creations of God and a heavenly hierarchy. Heaven is defined as good, but the same angels who can slay a whole army single-handed and bring plagues and other horrors to the wicked don't raise a hand to stop world wars. What's the difference, really, between us being creations of other beings and subject to their whims like the ancient Greek and Roman gods and what almost any religion also teaches?"

"But they throw in free will," Cynthia pointed out, really growing upset by this line of argument.

"So? If we didn't have free will in each of the setups then how would they know whether or not the system would work and, if it does, where the flaws and trouble spots are?"

There was silence for a little while, and then it was Sandy who broke it.

"I hate to interrupt, since I actually like the idea you have, but now that I've seen Cynthia, here, I can't buy it."

I stared at my mate. "Huh? What do you mean?"

"If your idea is right, why us? What good is it to learn about a society of people who evolved into the kind of creatures we are now? What does it teach? If it turns out that we have the best way of the batch, what are they going to do? Grow hindquarters and two more legs? What about that, Cynthia? Can your people transform to order? And, if they can, why haven't you seen more variants? No, honey, it just doesn't wash. I'm afraid you really are here."

I considered the logic, but still wasn't totally convinced. "Maybe *none* of us are real. We're nothing but a pack of cards. A video game for the technologically advanced. If these machines can create whole worlds, worlds that feel and smell right, detailed down to the last cell and bacterium, and peopled with complex creatures that can truly think, then how do we know if any of us are real? That we're not just the playing cards on the vast mosaic of the world that other players are pushing around for fun. Whole lives lived in an instant, perhaps. We may just be the diversion between dinner and bedtime." I was getting very depressed.

"Oh, shush up, both of you!" Cynthia snapped. "Y'all sound like the Catholic Chuhch. Gods and devils, tests and martahs, wheah in the rules of the game even God's gotta get crucified! Theah's only one way to settle it and find out the real truth, if anybody can find it, damn it all!"

We both turned and looked up at her. "And that is . . . ?"

"Why, you win the goddamned game, that's what!" she snapped. "Then find out what happens next!"

I shook my head. It was, in its own, sweet, simplistic way, the only real solution after all. If we win, somebody claims victory. Either we cease to exist when the game's done, or we get rewarded, promoted, or we get the answers. There was only one slight problem.

"Um, Cynthia? Just what card game have we been playing?"

"Don't mattah. Oh, it'd be a bit easiah if we knew, but that's maybe a paht of the game. Sho' 'nuf deah old Al nevah figgud it all out, and he had most of the cahds most of the time. Now, maybe the fuhst thing to do is find out wheah he kept goin' wrong."

The computer was brought into the deductive loop, although I wasn't sure if that was a good idea or not. Bringing the computer in too far hadn't done Al any good, either. What had he been trying to do with that power-up business? Bring up so much power he could dictate virtual reality? Maybe, but if that was so, why hadn't he managed it without things going wrong? Even the women last time hadn't managed it. They'd almost destroyed us all.

It wasn't the computer, but some ancient memories that helped me out a bit on this.

"Al wasn't playing a true game, as such," I noted. "Every time, what he was playing was fifty-two-card pickup."

But was he? Did Al bother in most cases with any of the lower card rankings except me? And he had a personal reason for keeping tabs on me.

He had three aces handy—including Les, who was content to play his game most of the time, knowing he could trump Al if need be—and a not so loyal but pragmatically allied Rita. Kings, including himself, were also three in number. Lee and Ben were allies; only Father Pete had been opposed. Two queens, but Wilma and Cynthia were always opposed.

Hell, what we had was one ace, one king, two queens, a jack sometimes, a ten sometimes, otherwise single digits. No wonder Walt couldn't win. The only thing that kept him from total defeat was the little creatures in the saucer, who together probably represented a fifth ace, a wild card as it were. Not enough to win, just enough to keep from losing.

By hook or by crook, willingly or dragged in and stuck in their own miniature Brand Box worlds, Les and Al had collected the top ranks. He'd powered up with most of the high cards present and awash in the energy he unleashed, and it hadn't worked. It had been okay to a point, but then, at some stage, they'd lost it and crashed into a dead end. And yet, every single time, they kept going in the same direction, did the same sort of things, and crashed. Even without Al, and maybe without Les, although I wasn't really sure of that, they'd gone that route and wound up bringing the whole system down.

Al and Les kept having all the cards, literally, and they still couldn't win.

We spent a lot of time on the problem to no avail. "We're missing something," Sandy sighed.

I nodded, then stopped. "Yes, we are missing something! Twenty-five people! Twenty-five of the Elect. Twenty-five cards."

Suit analysis. We hadn't really done that. Sure, we'd recorded the suits, but had we ever really *looked* at them? If everything meant something, we couldn't afford not to.

Ultimately, we could only deduce the identities of thirty-

seven of the people, so we hadn't really tried much in that
direction, but now it suddenly seemed like the thing to do, and
it was pretty simple to correlate the suits as well as ranks to
those we recognized. I made the list based on the names I'd
had from my earlier memories, when all this started, and which
Cynthia would know as well. It just made it simpler to stick to
one more familiar set. By this time, at least, we had filled in
more blanks:

Clubs

A: Dan Tanaka
K: Ben Sloan
Q: Dorothy Sloan
J: Michael Standish
10: Bernadette Standish

Hearts

A: Rita Alvarez
K: Lee Henreid
Q: Cynthia Matalon
J: Rob Garnett
10: Jamie Cholder

Diamonds

A: Walt Slidecker
K: Father Pete
Q: Alice McKee
J: Herbert Koeder
10: Sally Prine

Spades

A: Les Cohn
K: Al Stark
Q: Wilma Starblanket
J: Larry Santee
10: Riki Fresca

Some relationships came instantly clear. The clubs, for
example, had both couples that tended to stay married from
incarnation to incarnation. Rob and Lee, whose personalities
and attractions couldn't be more dissimilar and, frankly,
incomprehensible to most, were both face-card hearts. As a
low diamond, if Riki found me attractive, I'd be helpless. If in
fact Cynthia was Rita's daughter in the original incarnation or
reality as indicated on those ID cards, then the ace and queen
of hearts also made sense. The programmers were clubs. The
expert professionals in various fields were mostly diamonds
and hearts. The spades had one-of-a-kind skills of some sort, I

felt sure. The physician, the security chief, the sociologist, the head of the motor pool or whatever. In a sense, all were in some way administration, even Larry. They kept the operation running so the others could do their jobs. A couple seemed a bit of a stretch, but they were educated guesses for slots where we had only partial or little information.

But what about a correlation to this world? How many of the names above would match to the people we knew, and in what suits?

The answer was, quite a lot. It wasn't in who we could compare as much as who was missing when we made the list. Of all the names, only Cynthia was a heart and she was in the wrong form for this world and thus out of place. There was no trace of any of the others in the hearts list, either identified or postulated. The spades were here, as I well knew, from the bottom—me—through the top. Somewhere Al was doing the usual in a body like mine, as were Les, Wilma, even Riki. But no hearts save Cynthia, and no diamonds at all, or so it seemed.

We in this world weren't playing with a full deck.

Did the others not make it through the crash and transition? If so, how to explain Cynthia and the Command Center's general status check that said all monitored personnel were active?

If the hearts and diamonds weren't here, where were they? I wasn't at all upset with the idea that Rita wasn't here; Father Pete and Walt were people more closely missed. I'd swap some of our spades for those diamonds. Still, it seemed clear that we had the black suits and not but one of the reds. Where the hell were they?

"I've been going over all this," Sandy commented, "and the accounts you and the ape gave, and there's one thing for sure. Three of a kind, even aces, doesn't do it, nor three of much else. If we're playing poker here, then no matter how many high cards this Al had, it was never higher than four jacks and maybe not that. Four tens, maybe. That's not enough to win, that's pretty clear. You may absolutely need four aces to do it right, in which case you're sunk. The odds of that happening

again are pretty slim from what you say. But a straight flush beats four of a kind. Your turtle thing could brush you off because you were just a three, but if you were part of a two through six combo, you'd beat four aces in poker. Ever think of that?"

"No, but it does make me feel a little better."

"The trouble is, we don't know or can't identify a string of lower spades to be sure we'd have a sequence of the same suit," Sandy continued. "And we don't have any of the top rung whose identities we are fairly sure of. In fact, bring them in here and educate them, open their eyes, make them believe, and they'll be running things and we'll be mopping the floors."

I nodded. In my own wake-up call, my earliest complete lifetime memories, anyway, I hadn't been able to do much against the project or Al, and Cynthia had been able to toy with me at will. When I had Riki with me I had a little more power, but only enough to be able to run like hell. Even supercharged, with some power from the Caterpillar and more drawn from the slow but steady power-ups, we'd done little more than hold our own. Only when Wilma came aboard did we have enough power to use in anything like an effective manner. Taking the cards all as numbers, the best Riki and I together had been was twelve, a king, without the experience or knowledge to use the power. Add Wilma and we became a twenty-three count, enough power when combined together to take on any individual, but hardly a threat to an experienced team headed by kings and aces. Since a solid twelve, a real king, Al, had managed in the end to isolate us, take out Riki, reduce Wilma and I to a combined fourteen, and still beat us down, it wasn't just numbers. That helped, but it wasn't the answer.

It was an odd kind of card-game math where experience also counted.

Things weren't going any better on this when, one day, just by accident, I saw Cynthia leave by a route I'd never realized existed before. I was down near the main control center, checking something, and didn't even know she was there. I turned the corner and suddenly saw, for one brief moment, a rabbit hole open up right in the center of the control room! Cynthia then got up and walked into it, then vanished.

A few minutes later it opened again and she reemerged carrying a small soft-sided suitcase.

I stood there, openmouthed, as she casually walked in and didn't even pay attention as the hole closed once more behind her.

I cleared my throat, and she saw me.

"Mah goodness! You *stahtled* me!"

"I startled *you*? Cynthia, you just left and came back via a route I never dreamed existed."

"Huh? Oh, that. Why, I figguhed you knew 'bout that. Once Ah found the location of this place the hahd way, Ah didn't have no problems findin' the link."

"Where, exactly, did that lead? Where have you been?"

"Why, back at the backup centah, of coahse. Wheah else? Ah wanted to pick up a few things I'd left theah some time ago—couldn't bring much the fuhst time, remembah—and check on the li'l old dahlin's in theah cute li'l spaceship."

I was thunderstruck. All this time and she hadn't even mentioned that she could do this? Still, this was Cynthia, after all. Insanity might run in the family but at least this family member was on our side, more or less.

"And how are things?"

"Still quiet. The li'l deahs are still frozen. Ah know they ain't dead, 'cause Ah can see that they got some kind of monitahs wuhkin', but they ah out of this round. Oh—brought some flash-frozen steaks from the nucleah warfahre bunkahs, by the way. Ah know you two eat meat, and this is great stuff. Only the best for the generals, Ah guess. Bettah than those damn sandwiches, anyway. Got to get some ingredients for a good gumbo sometime, or maybe some good Cajun spices and a hot plate. Ah do a wondrous blackened redfish."

I couldn't have cared less about the steaks, even though

they were appealing. "You can open one of these any time, anywhere?"

"Well, mostly, yeah. Local routes, anyway. Walt, now, he could open one all the way into the next life or to any points he needed. He had *powah*. Me, Ah jes' use it to pop in and out of places and foah quick getaways. Ah got to have been at both places befoah Ah can open a path through. Why? You knew we could do that, didn't you? Ah mean, how else did Ah haunt you that one time back in Seattle, and how else did we get supplies and personnel in and out of the place theah 'cept usin' these tunnels?"

So much for security codes and the keys to the front door.

"Can you take me up there?" I asked her.

"Shoah, dahlin'. Ah can take anybody a'tall. It ain't much but a walk. You been through 'em yo'self. Not much left 'cept the sausah, the food lockahs, and a good kitchen. Ah told you it was in the middle of nowheah. Was a little funny this time, though."

"Funny? How?"

"Well, see, Ah sweah Ah locked it up and shut it down to standby befoah Ah left last time. But when Ah come in this time, it was all messed up, wide open, and everything was back on full."

The neck hairs began to tingle. "We're gonna find or create some weapons," I muttered, as much to myself as to Cynthia. "Then we're going back up there."

If somebody had been there in between her visits and changed things, then somebody else had memories and knowledge and knew how to use them. Somebody who just might also be able to figure out things and open up a rabbit hole, perhaps following Cynthia through.

We needed allies with power and knowledge, but we also didn't need high-ranking enemies in hiding. Either way, we had to find out who the hell was also playing the game and fast.

XIII

HALF TRUTHS AND
NAME BRANDS

I was uneasy about leaving the Command Center unoccupied, since what Cynthia could do, at least six others also might be able to do, and I could no longer trust the Mock Turtle's assurances, let alone ignore the idea that whoever or whatever was behind that creature was also "advising" others as well. I'd taken as many precautions as I could, including resetting the head-mount inputs to give an ugly surprise to those of either race that might try using them without the proper security codes. If you were a three and hadn't the intrinsic power, that didn't also mean you were stupid. People like Al and Walt and Cynthia and Rita and the others had so much power they often relied upon it too much. That could be as much a weakness as a strength.

The obvious solution was to leave Sandy back at the Command Center with a weapon of some kind, but Sandy had never been any farther west than we were now and wouldn't be talked out of coming.

In my current world, the region from northern California all the way up the West Coast was Russian.

"What kind of weapons y'all want?" Cynthia asked us. "That is, that might be wuhth much of anything?"

"If I could get them, I'd say a shotgun for the close-in stuff would be best," I told her. "And a rifle with a good telescopic sight, long-barreled and clip-fed, maybe thirty-caliber with steel-jacketed ammo would be a better second gun."

She grinned. "Look ovah theah," she told us.

We did, and "theah" was a big box, like a shipping trunk. I knew it hadn't been there before, not even when we entered the room, but it was there now.

I wasn't even surprised to discover inside a good twenty-gauge shotgun, double-barreled, with four boxes of sealed commercial cartridges, and a superb Remington 30-30 rifle with a top-of-the-line scope and several boxes of steel-jacketed cartridges.

"Any more surprise powers you want to spring on us, Cynthia?" I asked, feeling really helpless and out of it. If she could do this, then what could an ace or king do?

I'd already seen some minor demonstrations of that power by Al and Les way back in the warehouse lifetimes ago, and by Rita as well. But Cynthia wasn't even one of the top two power cards!

"Ah wish Ah could do that, too," Cynthia sighed. "Truth is, though, Ah can only do it when Ah'm in this buildin' and on this level and theah's power on, or in the backup centah. Outside of those places, Ah'm as helpless as you ah to conjure most things. Ah got some good ol' Louisiana mojo, but it's got its limits, too, and ain't wuhth diddly foah conjurin'. Walt, now—theah is a conjurah!"

I could guess.

I wasn't at all thrown for a loop by the fact that she and others could do this sort of thing, given their power and position, since everything around us was a fake, totally fooling our brains into thinking it was real. I was after the "That Which Is Behind All That," as the Buddhists might say, with no power of my own. Of course, they wanted to merge with that being; right now, I just wanted to shoot it.

I had never been through a rabbit hole that wasn't taking me to a new world and new incarnation. Even though they were among the most bizarre constructs of the system, they seemed more real in the context of games and immortals and the rest than the familiar world outside.

This one was smoother and more rounded than the big ones I knew. It was no problem for Cynthia's bare feet, but shod hooves slipped, and it was very slow going for Sandy and me.

Interestingly, there was a junction point, just like on the big ones, where you emerged into this vast electronic nightmare going forever in all directions. At least at that point the trail was flat, if too smooth, and had handrails.

Sandy gaped at the size and scale. I, on the other hand, for the first time really looked at what we were seeing. I'd always accepted it as a metaphor for the great computers, but now I wasn't so sure. Part of me wished even now that I had climbed straight up there when I'd been an orangutan; not even Cynthia could do it now. Another chance blown, I guessed.

Suppose this was the computer, or at least our little corner of it? Suppose this was where things were very slightly exposed to our mind's eyes?

I couldn't help but wonder what the hell would happen if a bomb went off in here. Would it just make virtual damage, or would it kill us all, or liberate us? Was there ever a point when any of us dare take that chance?

Back into the tunnel again, and now we went not to some new video game or great wall of static but rather to an end inside the control room of the desert facility.

A fifteen-minute walk, I thought, depressed. *Three thousand miles . . . as easy as that.*

Sandy and I had to jump a few feet down to the floor, and we made something of a clatter, while Cynthia just sat on the edge and then let herself down quietly. She was nervous about the noise we'd made; the place was definitely turned on full again, and I could even feel that energy surge that came with a power-up, no matter how limited that was here. There was also evidence of previous habitation—some candy wrappers with half-eaten bars, clearly not even weeks old, and the discards of military-style prepackaged meals from the larder. The sauce from spaghetti in one of them hadn't even dried completely.

I looked up at Cynthia and she nodded grimly. "Ah left everything clean and neat as a pin," she assured us in a loud whisper. "And with nothin' left on but the low-level lights and air system. Ah sweah!"

I believed her. The expression on her face and the tenseness in her body was more than enough to convince me.

Somebody else either was here, or had been here very recently. I doubted if they'd gone far, through a rabbit hole or anywhere else. You didn't eat those prepackaged military meals unless you had to.

Sandy had the rifle over one shoulder, I had the shotgun over one of mine, with ammo in a waist belt with pouches. We both took our weapons down and checked and loaded them.

"You got the advantage on me," Sandy whispered to me. "I haven't even sighted this beauty, but you just have brute force. Your lead."

Actually, considering where we were and the relative powers of all of us, Cynthia led and with my blessings.

We systematically checked everywhere we could on the base, even around and inside the flying saucer that still sat in its cradle. Cynthia was right about one thing: the little creatures were sealed in chambers with some sort of gas, and they were out for the long count. I wondered if that wasn't what was also true of the real Elect. Were these creatures "real," or were they just metaphors for the real "us"?

As before, we turned up signs that someone had been there, and recently, but didn't find the somebody who had made the signs. They were either powerful enough to mask themselves or expert at hiding.

"What about doing a perimeter search outside?" Sandy

suggested. "That would be the logical place to go. Besides, I could use something other than concrete beneath me—my ankles are hurting—and I could sure use the outside to sight in this rifle. Or is it just too exposed?"

I laughed. "It's exposed, all right, but if this is still where it had been before, then it won't matter."

Of course, it wasn't clear that this is where it had been. Cynthia had said that there were no roads at all, not even dirt ruts.

Going up the long stairs meant for ape-human feet wasn't easy, but we managed to get to the top while Cynthia insisted on staying on watch below. Opening the hatches and double doors above wasn't nearly as tough, and we finally managed to squeeze out.

It was the desert, all right. The same desert, but in the province of Sudalaska, not Washington. They didn't like the name Washington much around these parts.

There was no sign of a base or control tower on the eastern horizon, but that was to be expected in a world that hadn't yet figured out how to fly. Rocket power was well understood, if not yet fully developed, but the very concept of an airplane was considered impossible.

There were no evident tracks of much of anything around us, which meant that whoever was coming into or living in the station below either was still there or had left by unconventional means. I wasn't sure if the road going north-south was there, either, but it was unlikely that Cynthia had looked that far. Still, a run the two or so miles up to the craggy pass where, lifetimes ago, Riki and I had spied on the activities of the station was very much what our forms were designed for, and the fairly hard desert earth was no problem, either.

Still, we were both breathing very hard by the time we made it, illustrating just how out of shape we'd become trapped in the Command Center for so long.

Off in the distance there was still no sign of habitation, but far off in the distance you could see the incredibly high Cascades. We were where I'd assumed we'd be.

Sandy used the telescopic sight to survey the terrain. "Nothing. Pretty creepy place, too. No food, no water, no roads or human habitation. No, thanks. Let the Russians have it. I'll take the cool, green East."

Using some rocky points to sight in the rifle, we then headed back toward the nearly invisible station. At least this was pretty much all downhill.

We reached the hatch and Sandy groaned. "It's gonna be a pain getting back *down* those infernal steps!"

"You'd rather sit out here and bake?" I suggested sarcastically.

"Who goes first?"

I did, and it wasn't any picnic. It took me twenty minutes to descend, and several times I feared breaking an ankle, but, in the end, I made it, and, after me, about ten minutes back, came Sandy.

"Cynthia?" I called, my voice echoing through the large underground room. "Where are you?"

Sensing something might be wrong, I gestured to Sandy to split up from me and come in to the entrance of the saucer "hangar" from two directions. We couldn't hope to surprise anybody—horseshoes made an awful clatter—but if we both moved at once the resulting cacophony of hoof claps would mask position to somebody lying in wait.

I wasn't as concerned about where we were as I was over Cynthia, and who else might be there. She didn't tend to be all that careful under the best of circumstances.

I took a look inside the hangar but it was impossible to see every nook and cranny. The only way to draw someone out was for one of us to go in and be exposed while the other covered. Since I only had the shotgun, with its limited range, I went in and Sandy covered.

I kept the shotgun loosely in front of me and went slowly out into the open, straight down the center of the room. The silence, save for my hoofbeats on the floor and the sound of the air-conditioning units' steady humming, was unnerving.

"Cynthia!" I called out, my voice echoing in the hollow emptiness but too high and too thin to last for long in such a space.

I reached the saucer, still in its berth, and heard nothing from within. Now I could see the whole rest of the hangar, and it was as deserted as it seemed. Nervously, I found some partial cover and motioned for Sandy to come ahead.

We took up the same positions as before, with Sandy covering me, and I entered the smaller but still spacious control room with its consoles and LSUs. This room you could see fairly completely once inside the door, and there was nobody there.

Nobody. Not even Cynthia.

I sighed and turned to Sandy. "Great! There's no way out of here, and she's gone. That means she took a powder through a rabbit hole and deliberately stranded us!"

"Looks like it," Sandy agreed. "I hope she wasn't lying about the food, though. It's gonna be a long walk to get anywhere at all."

I looked around and found one of the consoles that I remembered from a couple of lives ago as having monitored the Command Center. I went over, kicked the chair away, and started typing. It kept asking for passwords, and I took a chance that nobody had bothered to change them. Walt never did have the world's greatest memory, so they were pretty easy to remember.

If I'd been able to use any of the head mounts I might even have been able to monitor what was going on back in the Command Center. As it was, while I now knew the procedure, I didn't want to do anything that might activate other things I wanted left as surprises back in Tennessee.

Instead, I typed in a serious of queries on life-forms, locations, and power levels within the Command Center. Walt and his March Hare Network had used these to keep a wary eye on Al and friends; now maybe I could do the same.

Several life-forms showed up, identified on the screen by record number.

1D477-334-895-446-952R. 1D, huh? Walt. It figured. And 12H, which was Cynthia. Voluntarily? I wondered. Probably, I answered myself. She and Walt were always partners of one sort.

Also 12C and 11C. Ben and Dorothy Sloan? But they'd be our kind! What the hell were they doing in there? And 12D as well. Father Pete. Damn! I really liked him!

"What's going on?" Sandy asked, knowing I could read the displays.

"Trouble. We've been suckered, that's what. Cynthia was a plant. She contacted us to find out who was there, what we knew, what we were doing, and how defended the Command Center was. Then we brought her in so she could map it to a rabbit hole. Finally, when they decided that they were ready, she returned from one of her conferences with them and allowed me to see her getting out of the hole. So now we come over here, eventually we go outside, she brings in her crew from someplace and off they go in her rabbit hole to the Command Center, leaving us here high and dry."

"You can't do anything with this stuff?"

"I could do some things, yeah, but only on a limited basis. This wasn't designed as a primary center of power, particularly as long as the original was running. I sure can't do much of anything against them, and I figure they probably got things locked down here so I can't do much but watch. It doesn't matter, though. At least I hope it doesn't. They have to come back here. They won't be prepared to stay there. Then we may be in a better position."

"Huh? What do you mean?"

"When they try and run the Command Center through the head mounts in the main control room they are going to get a nasty series of shocks. And while there are some real powerful folks there, not a one is a decent programmer. I ought to know.

I worked for Walt once upon a time, and, as good an actor as he was, I knew for a fact that he didn't really understand the principles I was working with. He's a boss, not a mechanic. The only programmer there is Ben, and I suspect he's had his head a bit scrambled even if he does remember his programming. In fact, I'm counting on it if he tries it. Dorothy's no programmer, either, and Father Pete even less so. If they had Dan Tanaka with them my goose would be cooked; even Bernadette or Sally might be dangerous. Ben, though—I'm not so sure anymore. No, they're going to come back here. Let's go see if that food's available. We might as well get comfortable."

"You sound pretty confident," Sandy replied, worried. "What makes you think that anything you can do would make a difference? As I remember, you weren't a programmer originally, either."

I nodded. "Right you are. But, particularly thanks to Walt and Al and a lot of experimentation, I've done something people are supposed to do but somehow forget others do it, too."

"Yeah?"

"I learned, honey. I learned . . ."

Dinner was quite good and cooked in a real kitchen for a change, and there was even an extensive wine cellar that contained top vintages from worlds that perhaps no longer existed. Walt was a real connoisseur. We even had some time for a little after-dinner romantic exercise before we heard the splatter of big ape feet.

If that was Walt, he definitely had improved himself this incarnation. He was maybe six foot four, with muscles on top of muscles, looking almost like a poster child for gymnasiums everywhere. With a stony but ruggedly handsome face and coal-black hair that fell to his shoulders, he seemed of the same Amerind racial group as Cynthia. He was better endowed as a male than Sandy and I were to boot. Being stark naked was no big thing when you had that kind of body, and Cynthia, standing next to him, made the perfect mate and companion. They were so stunning a couple I almost didn't notice until last the submachine gun in his hands, nor the twin pearl-handled revolvers in holsters on an ornate leather belt hanging from Cynthia's hips. It was her only clothing.

I got lazily to my four feet and smiled sweetly. "Hello, Walt," I said in my sweetest, sexiest voice. "I assume that is who you are. And Cynthia. Miss me?"

"Can it, Cory," Walt snapped, sounding anything but amused or patient. He had a commandingly deep baritone, though. "I want the codes."

I shrugged. "Oh, c'mon, Walt. You know me. You know me better than I know myself, I bet. I mean, you had me going with that Mock Turtle bit, and probably others as well. I should have instantly remembered your March Hare impersonation, but I was in a bit of shock at the time. Hell, you've had me jumpin' through your hoops for the *longest* time, ever since you made that one slipup and gunned down that kid. All for our benefit—Rick's and mine? Why, Walt? Why would a ten and a three mean anything to somebody with your rank?"

Walt frowned, but I could see there was some growing respect for me in his eyes that made me feel much better. "So you figured all that out, huh? Part of it was that interface you came up with. You'd actually invented most of it in the previous life, but then you'd gone and gotten yourself killed, and your notes were destroyed. Not even Tanaka could get it to work, and the one working prototype we found functioned just long enough to show that you had solved the problem. We had to have it. All those lifetimes with the shaved heads, the probes in the skull or in the spinal column. All out of the way, all gone, thanks to what you somehow had chanced on. Then the other side forced the company into sale before we had the thing into production. Everything you see here is refined from those early company prototypes, you know. They knew we couldn't make more, particularly not without you. We tried to scare you into our arms, but you jumped the wrong way. After that, you became, well, irrelevant except for one thing."

I nodded. "I was originally Al's wife and I was cheating on him. He never forgave that, and it was in the Brand Box informational files so it never really died as a piece of information. His ego's fixated on me. So, wherever I was, Al was going to be nearby, or vice versa. You couldn't keep a close eye on Al without tipping everybody off, but you could keep a real close watch on me most of the time."

He cracked a wry smile. "As long as I had you or your position, I had the location of the Command Center and all of my enemies who were worth worrying about. This kept me in play. That last one drove us a little nuts, though. Applied Physics in San Antonio! It was the biggest irony of all, too. Thanks to you, Al had been reincarnated as a woman but without his memories. My organization recruited her! When she and the others came for you, and stayed for romance, they were actually reporting to and working for us!" He chuckled. "Cory, you are so fucking *naïve* it's unbelievable! You think that if one side is the bad guys, the other side has to be the good guys! My god! You believe in soap operas and romance novels!"

I sighed. "I don't get it, Walt. Who the hell is 'us'? And what exactly do you want?"

"I want to win, old buddy," Walt replied. "You never did get it, because you never figured out that you were way too far down to be a player. You tried to either be one or attach yourself to one, but you were just a pawn, as you were intended to be. As for 'we,' well, my team, of course. Oh—I think you know my daughter, here, don't you?"

"Hi, y'all," Cynthia cooed sweetly.

"Your *daughter*! And Rita . . ."

"Her mother. I admit keeping that fact from her for a long while, but she forgave me. At least she did after punching me out. We were never married. In fact, Rita really was a nun at the time. Worked for Father Pete. The two had a kind of illicit tryst. They burned, and that meant to hell with the pope. Of course, that caused them a lot of problems. Pete finally broke it off and pretty much is convinced that he's dead and undergoing punishment in Hell. He might be right for all I know. Rita, well, she walked away from it, disavowed every-thing. When I met her she'd fuck anything that walked, male, female, sheep, goats, I dunno. You coulda knocked me over with a feather when she wound up on Brand's team. I don't remember any of it, of course, but I have the Brand Box recordings to rely on."

"All this family hist'ry's well and good, Daddy, but Ah'm gettin' mighty boahd heah," Cynthia said, pouting.

He nodded. "I need the codes, Cory. Give them to me."

"What's the matter, Walt?" I asked. "None of your experts able to figure them out? What happened?"

"You know damned well what happened. Cynthia assured me that she'd interfaced without problems, so Pete put on the master head mount, brought up the power to just ten percent, and attempted an interface. The next thing we saw, his entire body seemed to turn to energy and vanish."

"He's okay," I assured them. "He's just inside one of the smaller Brand Boxes. I can't be sure which one, but it might be kind of amusing if he's trapped on that luxury resort with nothing but naked women around tempting him. If he wasn't in Hell before he would be in that one."

"Very funny. How the hell did you even do that?"

"Didn't Ben tell you? It happened to him two lives ago."

"I recruited the two of them this go-round based on the searches you did with Cynthia. Yeah, we got all the data here that you pulled up there. You got no idea how long I wanted to be able to do that directly. They weren't that far from another of the backup centers, so we managed to lock on to it and create a rabbit hole to there. Between that and the backups here, we had them back in your unique but fascinating form. Trouble is, the backups don't replace seven years of advanced training and seven more years of practice, mostly under Brand

himself. Ben also seems to have developed a deep phobia
against putting on a head mount and interfacing. Wonder how
that developed?"

"Something Al and the others taught me. But you made him
do it anyway."

"Well, there wasn't much choice, and Dotty is even more
scared of that place than Ben is. We figured you'd reset things
so only those with your form and wavelength could use it,
which would have been real clever. Ben finally was, well, per-
suaded to try. Imagine my surprise and disappointment when
the same thing that happened to Pete happened to him! That's
when our thoughts turned to you." The gun came up and
pointed straight at me. "Time's up, Cory. The codes, please."

It was my turn to crack a smile. "You know that won't do
anything, Walt. Kill me and the codes are gone. I'm not on any
recorder here. Not yet, anyway. My life record stops before I
laid down the codes. The trap isn't mine; I suspect it was Dan
Tanaka's, or maybe even Matt Brand's. It seems most like
Tanaka. I think that's what happened to Brand, Walt. I think he
triggered this trap and got sucked in and was scared enough he
decided not to be found. I triggered it accidentally on Ben
once, and I had it done to me as well. I knew it was there, so I
looked for it. Then it was simply a matter of activating it.
Shoot me, and I won't remember the codes, either. You'll be
stuck in the Command Center with no way to access anything
at all. A Dan Tanaka with that genius could certainly get by
them even without direct memory, so long as you fed in the
backup near-life data so the tools would be there. But you
don't dare try it even if you can convince Danny to change
sides. Danny polished off Brand because Brand was the only
one smarter and more powerful than him. That made Dan
essential. You don't dare trust him to put on the head mount
and figure out the puzzle. If he gets in, he takes over again.
That means you need me. Kill me and it's all over for you
anyway."

I could hear power going on and rising inside the chambers

and equipment even as I spoke. Walt was activating his own center of power, inferior though it was, almost in spite of himself. He was mad as hell and it was all directed toward me.

"Death isn't even in my mind," he said, low and threatening, becoming pretty damned scary even to me. Now was the time when I saw whether or not I really had the nerve that this would take. "Everybody can be broken. You, me, *anybody*. Cynthia knows a ton of stuff beyond anything I can dream up. All sorts of stuff. You forget that I made a monkey out of you with just a threatening gesture. Imagine what I could turn you into now!"

I thought I might be able to solve this one, but I wasn't sure. Before I could reply, though, I felt cold steel against my head. I froze and looked out of the corner of my eye and saw Sandy holding the rifle on me.

"Sandy? What the hell are you doing?"

Sandy looked over at the couple. "Look, you creatures, we're lovers, but there's no way I'm gonna let you or anybody put us in the torture chamber. I'll blow my darling's head off and then do it to myself before I'll allow that."

"Sandy! *No!*" I said, nervous still at that finger on the trigger. "That's not the way!"

"Cory's right, you know," Walt said evenly, but I could feel his fury. It was physical. "Put it down. It will solve nothing. All it will mean is that, sooner or later, Cory and I will have to go through this all over again."

"No! I don't know what kind of—*things*—you are, but I'll tell you this: You're not only freaks on the outside, you're monsters on the inside. Both of you are out of the worst horrors of the human soul. I may not be much, but I know that there's no dealing with your level of evil."

"You have no idea, you goddamned little *spook*, just how much evil you're dealing with!" Walt snarled.

I felt the gun jerked away from my neck, but the momentary relief that brought was replaced with horror as I turned and saw Sandy pushed back against the wall as if by an invisible hand. I moved to help my mate, but Cynthia suddenly turned and stared intently at me with a level of concentration I never thought she had. I felt myself powerless to move, able only to watch in deepening horror as Sandy, the terrible strain showing in that wonderful boyish face, found that determination and faith often weren't enough. The arms moved, the rifle turned up, and, in spite of a tremendous effort to resist, the barrel went into Sandy's mouth . . .

There was a tremendous roar that echoed around the walls of this terrible building as the trigger was pulled, and Sandy's skull and brains and blood went flying, coating everything and spreading against the wall even as the rest of that still untouched and wonderful body slid liquidlike to the floor, twitched, and then was still.

I no longer thought, I no longer cared. I screamed a primal scream that must have echoed back through every horror and tragedy in the histories of the worlds, and I felt Cynthia's hold weaken. I brought up my shotgun and fired both barrels of grapeshot. The explosions sounded even more horrible than the single sharp boom of the rifle, and the shot spread out so that it not only cut Cynthia nearly in half, it produced hundreds of rivetlike bloody spots across Walt's magnificent body. The shock, and the fact that I could even do something like that in spite of his awesome powers, caused him more than a moment's disorientation and confusion, and that was more than enough. I kicked off and launched myself right into him, knocking him over. I didn't give him a chance to recover, either, taking the shotgun by the barrel and bringing it down hard against his skull over and over and over again until I heard it give and felt his body jerk and then die. I kept pounding and pounding and pounding until there was no more left of his head, of his brains and skull, than he'd left of Sandy's.

I don't know how long I kept it up, and when I realized, dimly, that it was far longer than enough, I turned to Cynthia.

She was already dead, of course, and there was very little else I could do to either of them.

I went into the hangar for a few moments and grabbed a bulkhead to steady myself while I cried and I cried and I cried until no more tears came, leaving only the deep hurt and anger. Father and daughter weren't enough. I wanted all of them. I wanted the kind of situation the Mock Turtle had promised me. I wanted all of them dead, all of them ignorant, all of them but me.

After a few minutes, I steeled myself, went back in, and dragged Sandy's headless body out of there along with what remained of the skull. There was no way I could get that body up those stairs and outside for a decent burial, but Sandy should have some respect. The body should not be left in the same room with that scum. As best I could, I put the body into one of the LSUs and managed, by folding and bending it, to close the lid. If not a burial or a funeral pyre, at least it would be a coffin and a crypt.

Next I walked over to the saucer, sitting there, silently, on its docking mechanism.

"Brand!" I called, cursing my voice at this point for being so weak-sounding but still adding an edge to it that I could never have achieved before. "Haven't I paid the price and more, Matthew Brand? Haven't I just proven I'm a player no matter what rank you arbitrarily assigned me so long ago? Come on out, Matthew! I think I've been a plaything long enough!"

For a moment there was silence, only the air-conditioning continuing to hum, and I almost thought I hadn't gotten it right, or, if I had, I'd done my bit now and would be cast off. I wasn't about to be cast off, not if I had to climb those stairs and walk back all the way to Chattanooga.

I was beginning to fear that I'd have to do just that when, very suddenly and without fanfare, power came on in the saucer.

Slowly, all emotion, even fear, drained from me. I walked

up the ramp and into the open door, then up the fairly easy
stairs to the central-command structure of the saucer itself. The
little men were still in their frozen cases, but in the command
chair at the center of the room there was another figure,
a figure I'd seen mostly in pictures and videos very, very
long ago.

He was a young man, like the rest, probably thirtysomething
though looking much younger. He had a scraggly beard and
long, flowing hair, and he wore ancient, hole-filled jeans that
looked more like camouflage pants from all their washing and
hard wearing and a T-shirt that read "Beware Nuclear Ducks!
Quark! Quark!" Under any other circumstances I'd have found
the shirt funny and the man fascinating. Now I just wanted him
to end it.

"You know, Cynthia really thought she was flying this thing
now and again," Matthew Brand commented. "I have to say,
Mary Ann, that you've impressed me more than anybody in
the whole group. When did you realize that the saucer was
actually a Brand Box?"

"I guessed, pretty much," I admitted. "You had to be somewhere. You weren't in the Command Center and you weren't
directly in the records or the databases. At the same time, you
were certainly around. Not all those *Alice in Wonderland* creatures were Walt or metaphors for me and the others. I actually
think it was in the back of my mind after Cynthia picked us up
in the storm and I saw this interior. I'd seen the light and floor
patterns and the general layout before, only not as the interior
of a flying saucer. I'm not sure when it hit me, maybe not fully
until I took the walk around it one more time this trip, but I
gradually realized what it reminded me of. The Caterpillar's
lair. The command chair and operator in the center on the
raised dais, and the rings of pulsing light going around on the
floor. That first time, you flew down to Texas. You picked us
off that beach when we were high on drugs and you had an
easy time disguising this place." I looked around at the creatures. "Are they real?"

"Sadly, no. Well, not in the sense I think you mean it. They're all me, of course, but based on aliens that apparently really did crash long ago. That's why they're so convincing. As long as everybody thought they were the genuine article and that they were running the ship, well, nobody looked for me in here. The aliens were friendly but sometimes inscrutable, you see. They'd go off on their own for reasons never explained and nobody really blinked twice. Then they'd help out here. It was nearly perfect. Power, mobility, and nobody knew I was here. I had it rigged up as a kind of escape mechanism long ago."

"Are you really—there?"

He chuckled. "No, not in that sense. I'm actually inside the ship. In a sense, I *am* the ship. The ultimate Brand Box, as you might expect. One that can interact with those outside of it, but is still totally self-contained. It had to be here, of course. It wouldn't fit in the labs. Besides, Alex and Maureen needed any allies they could get. They couldn't afford to look a gift horse like this in the mouth. Doc, Tice, and Mark—they might."

I realized he was using the original names for all of us. To Brand, only the initial level was real.

"You saw what happened in there, I presume? You're almost certainly hooked into every system here. I wouldn't expect any less of you. Why did you let them do it?"

"I'm not sure I could have stopped them," Brand replied matter-of-factly. "I'm very sorry for your friend. In a sense, the natives of each world are no different than we are to our native world. Even though they exist entirely inside a computer system, they nonetheless are self-motivated and acquire knowledge, form emotional ties, and make independent decisions. I sure can't tell the difference between these independent self-actuated self-programming objects inside the bigger program and real people in a real world, whatever that is.

"Consider you, a mere three, beat to death an ace after shooting and killing a twelve. The best I could have done, as a wild card, was to bump you up to Walt's power level. Instead,

I tried suppressing them a bit without him noticing. It seems to have been enough for you to do him in, but I can't think of anything either of us could have done to save Sandy. Your mate died laying down its life for your sake. That's a pretty heavy thing for an independent self-actuating program object to do, isn't it? We've got whole religions idealizing that behavior and few that could actually live up to it. It was a horrible way to prove it, but no one can say that Sandy was not one special human being. Considering that most of humanity, both programs and players, suck eggs if they are relevant at all, that's not a bad thing to have engraved on a life, is it?"

I sighed. "I guess not. But what do I do now?"

"Make sure Sandy didn't die for nothing. I have to say that this is a pretty damned sad group that wound up here. I suppose I recruited them, or at least approved them. Maybe nobody could stay sane through all this, but by god I feel like it's my fault."

"You mean you don't know?" I was doubly crushed. What did any of this mean except tragedy if even Matt Brand didn't have all the answers?

"I don't know the origin of those cards," Brand admitted. "I *do* think I know where they are."

"The entities under the Command Center," I said flatly.

"Bright girl! It's got to be. But we can't reach them from here. There's a dimensional, or programmed, barrier that doesn't permit us to go down there. It's like looking into the sun. You go blind at best and moving toward it burns you up. Yet, somehow, you know it's the source. I'm pretty sure the card ranks are basically my own Lewis Carroll fetish, without any deep meaning. That doesn't mean that the high cards aren't more powerful than the low, but I don't think that it was truly designed that way. I think it sort of evolved because it was easier for the machines to handle. These are no mere computers. Just this backup system here moves signals at the speed of light and has a memory capacity so vast I can't even conceive of it myself. Imagine what the machines are like that run us and this world, the other world, and Command Center!"

"What do you mean 'the other world'?" I asked him.

"The one that the reds are in. The Amazonian world. It's actually quite advanced, if they'd just can those wonderful little practices like tearing the living hearts out of kids and self-mutilation. Think of the Aztecs or Mayas with guns and motors."

"But—how'd it happen? I mean, there haven't been two different universes before, have there?"

"Search me. Could be. I think, though, it was the product of the meltdown. When they jump-started the system, instead of initiating on just one unit they initiated on two. I have no idea how many linked computers there are, but that's enough. The old familiars got started on one machine, your type on the other. The reds got atomic Indians, the blacks got two more legs and one less sex. Actually, that looks like a fun form to have. Odds are that really was a possibility for us millions of years ago. Too bad."

"I find it hard to think of being anything else," I told him. "But I'm not at all sure if I want to remain this way now. It's not a great form for one person alone."

"Well, the labs and these centers exist in both universes. Walt and Cynthia used rabbit holes to get here, then managed to link to yours via that comm link you so cleverly set up. From that point, Walt could move from here to the labs as easily as Cynthia, and intersect here via other holes with his own world. We can do it, too."

"You mean you can. I sure can't open a rabbit hole," I said flatly.

"You're right—you can't. But I can. Trouble is, I can't go through one. As I told you, I'm not inside this ship, I am this ship. Kind of limiting. But I can track you, reinforce you, go with you *through* you. We've had one crash. I don't think we dare risk another. I say we gather some friends and keep the enemies out. Forget the old teams and suits and loyalties. Most of these people died the last time; they really don't consciously remember anything. Maybe it's time for some discards, huh? Maybe we go over the list as much as we can from both worlds and we pick the people who we might want at our backs and not expect at our throats. A lot of the personality and loyalty runs through life after life. When we get a group, we forget the rest, ignore 'em. Then we try, as a group, to get the hell out of this mess."

"Sounds interesting," I agreed. "I have nothing left to keep me in this world, only an arrest warrant to look forward to if I went back into society. But what makes you think we can do it without another crash, without simply wiping things out?"

"I think I can avoid the crash, but I'm not saying we won't have a lot of punches and incarnations. What I'm saying is that this time we're going to be going in the right direction. Not farther in, but *out*. Out until we reach the point where we can face those entities down there. Hook me into the system from here. I helped design this system—the computers did it, but I gave 'em the blueprints. I think it can be done."

"They'll fight, some of them. If you really thought you could do this before with them against you, you'd have done it, rather than remaining in hiding. Walt and Cynthia aren't really dead like Sandy, they're in memory storage. What makes you think you can do it now?"

"You."

"Me?"

"You demonstrated that the lot of 'em can be beaten. A three killed a queen and an ace. That was impressive. But, more important, it's been you all along. You, and Rini, and Sandy, and Riki and the others you've been close to, both world-specific and permanent party. I've had a few previous opportunities, but it wasn't until now that I thought you and the others were worth saving."

It was the kind of statement that was guaranteed to get me to go along. Frankly, I wanted revenge more than I wanted out, and I had no more reason to trust Brand and what he was saying than I did trusting Walt. Still, what the hell else was I going to do?

"Where do we start?"

"I've already attuned the head mount on this captain's chair to you. I'll vanish from here and I want you to come forward and put it on. I think the first thing I need to do is to teach you everything you need to know about Brand Boxes. But you'll have to trust me implicitly. You've seen this procedure before, but not to this degree of connection. Once the head unit integrates with your form, we will be linked more closely than lovers. It's going to be an open channel from me to you and you to me, but there will be no question who is who. Understand?"

I thought of Rini's unit and nodded. "Go ahead. If this is the endgame, then it makes no difference to me now."

XIV

TINY ALICE, THOUGH
SHE'S TEN FEET TALL

The long-barreled pistol still seemed too light, but I'd already found that the computerized gun sight made it so easy to use it was almost criminal. Brand had made several inside the saucer; I admired the mind who could inject a Brand Box into the current virtual reality and add to it!

I'd checked the subject out for a couple of evenings; had I not been playing with a wild card I could never have even considered doing this, and, even so, I accepted the fact that I was a tool of Matthew Brand. I had no idea if Brand was as crazy as the rest of us or not, or if there'd been good reason to try and polish him off, but my gut instinct, the same gut instinct that had failed me before, nonetheless said that Brand was the kind of person who didn't quite relate to things in the way normal humans did, and that he was almost bored by jockeying for power and position—he saw those as just tools for finding out what he wanted to know. He certainly knew more about the computers, the grand project, and the whole system than anybody else. If I was going to reconquer his kingdom for him, well, he did build it in the first place . . .

Arnay Oraku was so achingly beautiful that it seemed a

shame to do this, but Arnay Oraku has also been known as Dan or Danielle Tanaka, and that made Oraku public target number one.

The discovery that Walt hadn't just lied, but had lied big, was still weighing heavily on me. Instead of only me coming through with my memory intact, it turned out that everybody had incarnated rather than reincarnated because the information had been fed in from backups. It had been sheer luck that had me being the first one to spot the Wonderland figures on the temple model. Even so, while Sandy and I had been searching for the entrance and then opening up the Command Center, others hadn't been far behind. It was, it appeared, a near thing, and we were saved by the fact that everybody had different names and scrambled situations and no good way to contact one another save by happy accident.

That meant we would all eventually converge on the Chattanooga temple as soon as we discovered it. Sandy and I weren't merely being tracked down for embezzling from the government; we were being tracked down by federal agent Sonjay Parath, a.k.a Al Stark. Now, here was Tanaka dead in my sights. I couldn't hesitate; I just wanted it to be clean and unobserved. I had no love for Dan Tanaka, but I'd have loved to have his body.

Tanaka had been going to the temple regularly, and was already canvassing the riverside with a thoroughness I knew would bring the solution sooner or later. Not that Dannie could get in from the culvert side, but I didn't want to underestimate anybody who could come close to killing off Matt Brand.

Tanaka wasn't the first one I'd knocked off, but it was certainly the highest-ranking one. The first had been Dorothy Sloan. She was a tough one, since she wasn't evil and, of course, I'd been married to her in one previous life. But she'd been totally hysterical when I got to the Command Center, demanding I restore her Ben and throwing chairs and endangering equipment. Unable to pacify her and not having a stun gun, I'd had no choice.

That, of course, had launched us into the Plan. Those whose minds couldn't be changed or whose instincts couldn't be trusted were to be simply polished off. They'd be reborn next time with no conscious memories of the past, and we could ignore them, if need be, until and unless they could be brought in the same way that Riki and I had been brought back that first time. Cory the programmer and Riki the artist seemed like ancient history now.

Tanaka trotted up a dark, narrow alleyway toward the room hired for this expedition, and at that point the master programmer was most vulnerable and least exposed to others. With a sigh at having to fry that beauty, I let the pistol lock on and pulled the trigger.

A beam of white, crackling light went out, struck Tanaka, enveloped and outlined the entire form, and then winked out. That was the beauty of this weapon: aside from some light ash that would blow away in the next breeze, it left no traces. Now, anybody Dannie had been working with would simply have his or her paranoia fed.

I felt no regret, no remorse. The worst thing I was thinking immediately afterward was that my scalp itched and that the wig still felt wrong.

"Very good," said a voice in my head. *"But at this rate it'll take forever and put some of them on their guard. We need to do a little recruiting. Who would you trust with your life?"*

My life was an open book to Brand, as was most of the rest of me. Using the computer at the backup site and whatever he had built into that saucer, Brand had essentially read out my entire structure at least to the cellular level—or my program object as he called it—dissolved me, and reconstituted me with a high-powered wireless head mount integrated into my skull and interfacing constantly with my brain. In effect, I had become an extension of his Brand Box; everything I saw, did, or felt was registered and recorded there, and communication was nearly instantaneous. The code was such that it gave me a bald head just like Rini'd had before, and Brand indicated that, while he could probably induce hair to grow, it might cause some interference. So, I wore a shorter black wig, which hurt my sense of pride in my blond good looks, but it really changed the way I looked. He'd also given me very dark brown skin and coal-black hindquarters; I virtually disappeared into shadows. I was also bigger and stronger, and at night my eyesight verged into the infrared. I was redesigned less as a person than as an appliance, Matt Brand's appliance, for doing Matt Brand's work.

But Matt Brand couldn't get into the Command Center. He'd hid himself so well that he now lacked a body; what I had seen on the command chair was merely a hologram. I, on the other hand, could easily get in, and I was now an extension of Brand. I sincerely hoped that I had chosen correctly, because I had no escape from his control.

Before I could start figuring out the locations of the few trustworthy people, I ran into them in a bar in Chattanooga that had proven irresistible to others who'd seen it in ads. The Temple Chaser, it was called, and it was seedier and smellier than you thought upon first impression.

I saw them enter as a triad, a three-way marriage that was not unusual in this world. We were still somewhat herd types; we felt more comfortable when we weren't alone. I might have been the one exception, but, of course, I was never alone.

I could tell that they were of the Elect, but not who they were. We tended to radiate a kind of magnetism that tipped the others off, something too subtle to be aware of unless you knew it was there but that made us all eventually come together in any incarnation, consciously or not.

Al had been in and out of the bar often, having the same feelings that I had, but lacking the ability to figure out who was who with so much radically changed. The fed, in fact, came in shortly after the trio, accompanied by an unfamiliar petite golden blond stunner with ivory skin, ruby lips, big green eyes, a golden palomino hindquarters, and a blond tail that was tied off and curled up in an incredibly sexy way.

Al was a pretty big person, maybe six-one or -two, with chiseled features that were pretty much all business and the most common brown hindquarters. It was an imposing body, but Al looked like a fed.

The companion was so small I almost thought it was a child or teen; no more than five foot one or two, perfectly proportioned in every sense, but looking so delicate that the beauty stood an even chance of getting crushed in a dive like this.

The little one, though, definitely was also one of us.

They had clearly noticed that the trio was also of the Elect and were now about to make their move. Fidelity to group marriage was encouraged, but if the three were really married they might be trolling for more.

Most likely they were trolling for others like us.

I stayed in the shadows near the far wall, watching them, nursing a drink, and wishing I could hear what was being said.

"Tune in on any of them," Brand instructed. *"Just look and concentrate. I don't think they'll be aware of it, unless you call attention to yourself."*

I wasn't sure what he meant, but I looked over at them, tried to tune out the noise and smoke in the bar, everything but them.

"You're new in town," I heard Al's voice saying. The background noise was still there, but it was as if their conversation rose above the din.

"Yes," the senior one responded. This one seemed a bit chubby, with high cheekbones and unusually large breasts that needed support from a bra but didn't get it; Amerind, perhaps? Amerind of the centaur people? "I am Unqua—it means Speaks Too Loud. These two are siblings—Mandy and Kris Cornado, who I bumped into when we toured the temple today. And you are?"

"Sonjay Parath. And my lovely companion here is a medical doctor at the general hospital in Atlanta, here visiting."

"Mela Stong, at your service," said the small one in a surprisingly firm and professional voice. I still bet that the doc could turn on the charm on command. If that was Les Cohn, the change in manner was dramatic, although the profession and bad taste in friends continued.

Okay, I had Wilma, Al, and Les pegged, but who were the near twins?

I accessed the records mentally, hoping for matches on both contemporary and older levels. Larry Santee! And—Riki!

The question was, did Wilma and the other two recognize who was in front of them?

I always liked Les; I never could figure out why he kept siding with Al, except, maybe, that he knew more about Walt than I had and had chosen the lesser of two evils. I hoped so. Having zapped Tanaka into the next life, and ready to zap Al if I had the chance, I really didn't want to dissolve that little blond bombshell.

Interesting . . . All my life in this form, I'd tended toward the "female" urges, but since taking on Brand's connection I barely had such fantasies anymore. I felt more and more like the guy who never saw a breast he didn't like and wanted to bed every woman he saw.

The conversation that followed was basically small talk; eventually they accepted an offer by Al and the doc to walk them back to their hotel, but there was nothing untoward going on. I followed in the shadows, keeping a discreet distance, but my zap gun was at the ready. I wasn't about to take Al here; the idea was to leave the impression that people vanished, not that they were being killed. Still, I was more than prepared to do it if it became necessary.

Brand wasn't sure he wanted to do away with Al, either. With these others here, we had the chance to put together a complete hierarchy of spades, ace down to ten anyway. In the ape-human world that paralleled this one, Brand noted, Rita was busy collecting hearts, not knowing, possibly, that she was missing her queen. With Walt and Cynthia out, among others, there was no way to complete a full set of one "suit" and test the theory. With Dannie, Dorothy, and Ben also counted out, you couldn't do it with clubs, either. Spades, though, were still intact.

And now, here they all were, ace down to ten, all in one place, all of one suit. It was almost too good to be true.

"Probably a trap," Brand agreed. *"Still, how else are we going to find out?"*

"Can you take on both Les and Al?" I asked him, concerned. *"Seems to me that we don't add up to all that."*

"It depends on your friends. If they're dependable, we have the edge. If not, then we'll have to do some quick shooting and try again in the next life."

That was not a cheery thought. Still, I was impatient. It had been so long now, and so many people had been hurt. There had to be, if not an end, then at least a reconciliation. Hatred, bitterness, fighting through worlds without end—it had to stop.

As might be expected, it was the doc who sensed me first. So small and delicate, the golden-haired beauty stopped, looked back, a quizzical look on its face. "Hold it," Les, or Mela, said to the others. They all stopped and turned to look at the small one, as puzzled by the comment as the doc was by sensing me.

"There is somebody following us," the doctor told them. Al whirled and stared out into the darkness, and I could feel a little bit of magnetic-like pull when those cold eyes swept over my hiding place.

I realized that in one sense I had the advantage even without the gun. I was hidden and I didn't look like anybody they knew. I stepped out into the dim light, looking steady and hard, and walked slowly up to them. None of them seemed particularly tense except for Al, of course, who was just being Al. I, however, was not being Cory.

"Good evening, citizens," I said pleasantly. I took out a cigar, stuck it in my mouth, and lit it with a safety match. The effect was to illuminate my face and reinforce the fact that none of them had the vaguest idea who I was. I looked down at the tiny golden-haired physician.

"That's one hell of a look for a nice Jewish boy," I commented casually, puffing on the oversized stogie.

I'll give Les this: he didn't panic. "Yes, I admit this was a startling departure for me in more ways than one. And you are . . . ?"

"In good time, Doc. Agent Parath—you're becoming more like Al Stark again. I liked you better as Almira. Efficient without being so . . . dour. And here is Unqua, a shaman I'll wager. And what do Mandy and Kris do for a living when they're not looking at temples to Wonderland?"

Everybody got the idea now. I was enjoying it, frankly. For the first time, it was me singing the song, and all of them doing the guessing.

"We work for *Collier's* magazine, if you must know," Mandy responded, showing a little Riki in the tone and attitude. "I'm a photographer and illustrator, and my sib is a nonfiction writer. And, like the doc asked, you are . . . ?"

"Interesting," I responded. I never thought of Larry Santee as a writer. As the world's greatest tractor-pull driver, maybe, but not as a writer. Oh, well. "As for me," I continued, reaching up, loosening the gum, and then peeling off the wig, "I represent Matthew Brand. He would like your word that you will behave and act honorably. If so, he would like to bring you to where you want to go."

"Let me just pick up a couple of things at my room—" Al began, but I cut him off.

"Now or never. No signals, no calls, no nothing. We all walk together. No guns, no knives, no silly stuff. What do you have to fear? Even Brand is only one person, and the two of you alone have a ton of power. All five of you can take most anything."

"Except somebody who's directly linked to the computer," Al responded. "I seen your type before."

I know you have. "Well, it's a pleasant night for a stroll. Shall we take a walk, or call it a night? If we call it a night, Mr. Brand has instructed me to say that we call it a world, too. There won't be a second chance in this one, and neither Mr. Brand nor I will lose control in a punch. What do you say?"

I was happy to see Wilma as something other than a vegetable, but, of course, she, too, was running off a backup. "So, you're Al the security man and you're the doctor?" the shaman asked, incredulous.

Al smiled. It risked cracking the face, but it was better than nothing.

"I'm going to walk down to the river. Who's going to follow me?" I asked them.

"You win," the doc responded. "We'll all go. We've come too far to crash and burn now."

I reattached the wig so as to not startle others we might pass along the way, almost regretting doing so. It was nearing the end of the summer, and the heat and humidity and little flying insects were at their peak. I'd much rather have left everything off, especially the wig.

As we walked along, I found myself pretty well surrounded. It didn't bother me.

"Are you really in contact with the elusive and mysterious Matthew Brand?" Al asked me. "I've been hunting for him since forever."

"Well, I found him. Pardon if I don't say where and how right now, but let's be clear. He's on my network. I can speak to him as easily as to you, and he to me."

"Huh! So why us? And why now?"

I briefly explained the personnel encoding of the cards and suits and the possibility that it actually meant something. I then told them their ranks. Both of the twins were amazed that they were that high up in the pecking order; Wilma seemed surprised that she wasn't higher.

"Have you seen or been contacted by any of the others?" Riki asked, sounding just curious.

"I've seen a number. There are a lot of them already dead."

"What about Cory?" Riki asked. "I—we had a thing, you know."

How much I know that! Still, of all the ones I expected to have no memory, Riki was one at the top. "How do you even remember Cory? You stuck with her and the kids until old age, didn't you? And that was two worlds ago. You shouldn't remember much of anything about Cory. For that matter, Unqua, you shouldn't have any past memories, either. You were in a near vegetative state."

"I was in an entirely vegetative state," Wilma agreed. "But my being is not just dependent upon some master machines. The trees and rocks and spirits of the Other Side know, too. I recovered with them in their world, nursed at their teat, and was restored while another world went past up here. I emerged stronger than I have ever been. With that power I have been able to raise that which is not to be thought to the foreground. When I met the sibs, here, I knew that Kristy and I both had the Knowledge. With that, we were able to bring what was inaccessible in Mandy's mental dark corners to the forefront. I knew Riki. We had been as one in the green fire once."

"Then you should know who I was as well," I told the shaman.

Wilma gave a short gasp, but said nothing more. What had not been known before and still wasn't known to the two high cards was now known to those who should.

When we reached the culvert, lying back of the river and off behind the bushes, I gestured. "After you."

"In *there*?" The doc wasn't too thrilled, and the others seemed uncertain as well.

"I could have killed any or all of you at any time," I told them truthfully. "I have no reason to betray you now."

"Oh, hell, I'll go in," Al grumbled. "If I fit."

"It's tight, but you'll get in. I've just deactivated the security system at this entrance for a period of time, but I don't want to leave it down long." Not that it mattered now. The ones I feared most were ape-humans, and they didn't have the road map—yet.

It was a lot easier to get in now that we'd slightly reoriented the door. Of course, with the security in place, anybody who entered would follow the tunnel all the way back to God knew where and never see the branch-off at all.

"It looks just the same!" Al gasped, sounding like a kid who just now found its favorite toy, thought lost forever.

"The chairs are piled up in storerooms," I told them. "Got tired of tripping over the useless things."

Al was chuckling and checking over things, mumbling to himself, and not paying a lot of attention.

Les looked over the small medical office and single examining room that he'd used for so long. "Amazing. It's both primitive to what I know and more advanced than anything we have now here. Not that I could be sure that most of this stuff was useful for our anatomies."

I looked around. "Excuse me. I think I ought to rein in laughing boy," I commented, and went after Al.

The security chief had a little trouble getting down the stairs, but I knew Al was going back to check on the sets of localized Brand Boxes. I caught up with him quickly.

"They're all there," I assured him. "All the small stuff. Of course, it's mostly ape-human stuff, but it plays. None of your old prisoners are in there, though. When things got restarted they began from zero."

"Doesn't matter! We'll go for a slow power-up, then—"

"With what?" I asked him.

"Huh? What d'ya mean, 'with what'? With this!"

"You're no programmer. You're a security chief, a cop, an administrator. Your whole being is in protection, even if it means keeping everybody in creation under lock and key and even if you don't know who you're protecting them from. You got a doctor. A real good, interesting doctor whose job it is to oversee everybody's health and well-being and administer the experiments with the boxes. Doesn't know beans about how they work, just preps 'em. You got a native priestess who thinks she got her memory back from the trees and the rocks. Finally, you got an artist and photographer who never could handle computers right and a motor-pool chief turned travel writer. You never did anything right even when you had top programmers, and here you've got none."

It just hadn't occurred to Stark. "Tanaka! I know Tanaka's here. I already tracked old Dannie down."

"Gone. Dead. While you were so damned paranoid that the janitor was gonna steal state secrets and playing power trips on these machines with your mousy little wife, all hell broke loose. What kind of a security chief are you, Sonjay 'Al' Parath? You let old Dannie effectively murder Matt Brand, your boss and project leader, right under your damned nose and you didn't even know it! In fact, I can see by your expression that this is the first time that thought ever entered your fucking little peanut cop mind!"

Al turned deathly pale. "My god! You mean—Tanaka? Impossible. I had every square inch of this place bugged, monitored, and videotaped."

"Yeah, you depended on your machines. But who programs this place? Who was chief programmer, Al? Who set up the master program that let you monitor and examine all and sundry? Little old Dan Tanaka, that's who. The one who then ran everything. The real boss. Who was gonna stop him? You? You were buffaloed completely, totally under his control. The doc? He was happy doing what he was doing here and sneaking off into his favorite sin Boxes. It was easy. He ran that department. He just didn't give a damn."

The others were coming down now, and I didn't care who heard us.

"But you said you were in touch with him! That you were Brand's agent!"

"I am," I assured him. "But Brand's got no body, Al. He can't incarnate or reincarnate. He's stuck inside a specially made, specially modified Brand Box that only somebody with his genius could have come up with. It put him out of or on the edge of the action, until now."

Al was genuinely horrified. Not so much, I think, at the news about Brand or the truth about Tanaka; rather, he was horrified because I'd just told him to his face how he'd been a fool all along. Suddenly I could almost read his mind.

"You can't go kill Tanaka, Al. I already did that. And I killed Walt and Cynthia and the Sloans just for starters. They'll be back, of course, next time, but not as any threat, not for a while." *But not Sandy, damn them all! Sandy will never be coming back!*

"So what do we do?" he asked me, sounding totally deflated. And that, to me, was worth living to see. Not worth what it had cost, but it was still satisfying. And what I was about to do was pure icing.

"To answer your question," I said, looking straight into those steely if now stricken eyes, "I'm Cory Maddox. And Jayce Boyd. And Mary Ann Howarth. And the only chance you have is to park that damned ego and play along."

As an old Southern saying of the centauroids went, the bottom rail had somehow flipped to the top.

"You were a lousy cop and a lousy husband," I told him. "Now let's see if you can do something right for a change."

"Just what do you propose to do?" Les asked. "I mean, Cory, no offense, but you aren't in Tanaka's league as a programmer. You had one bright idea, and, who knows, that probably came from some other life somewhere and maybe some other mind."

I wasn't insulted. "I agree, Doc, I'm not super on my own, but I have access to the best. I'm basically just a mechanic, but I'm a good mechanic. Give me the expert's plans and blueprints and access to their systems and I can remake the world. And I've got all that. Matthew Brand has handed me that."

"Just what are you proposing to do?" Kris/Larry asked. "Every time any of *them* tried anything, it blew up on them. Either they wound up having to move to the next life 'cause the built-up energy would fry 'em, or they *did* fry."

I nodded. "But this time we're not following the March Hare, the Mad Hatter, or the White Rabbit, and we're through listening to Tweedledum and Tweedledee and the Cheshire Cat. Now we do it the way of the Walrus."

They all looked at me as if I were stark staring mad. "Come again?"

"The Walrus. It's an image that's followed me from life to life to life. A cybernetic walrus, more or less. It's been pretty silly, but it still kept insisting on saying things to me in riddles and metaphors. Every one of us has gone down at the end of those rabbit holes. Down, always down. Even the punch is down. But every time we ever tried to look down, at what was under here, we were prevented by fear and energy and a sense of horrible danger. We've been going the wrong way. I don't know for how long, but we've been moving the wrong way all the time. We finally crashed the system going down, and split into two worlds. What's next? Four? One for each suit? Then what? Do we get so fragmented that we lose ourselves forever, or do we fight a four-way war of the worlds? Uh-uh. It's time we stopped going down."

Les in particular seemed to see where I was going. "Those pathways, the rabbit hole openings at the halfway points—I always thought of them as exposed areas of the great computer we were trapped inside of. But they couldn't be that, could they? Not really. In a real sense they're no more 'true' than we are. They're only a series of static programs, strings leading from one to another."

I nodded. "Don't think of them anymore as circuit boards. Think of them as, well, elevator shafts. I want to bring us all together downstairs, but this time not try to remake the world in our image. I want us all to get together and push."

"This is what Brand thinks is correct?"

"He thinks it's worth a damned good try."

One by one, they sighed and nodded. Finally it remained not for Les or Wilma or Riki or Larry to say it, but rather Al. "Let's do it."

All of the others had head mounts and were hard connected into the main boards. The linkage of mind to computer was "soft," but we could never do this in these bodies with the LSUs. That was the wrong route to go.

I tied them all in to the main console, with me acting as net administrator and the primary server. Brand, through me, was connected in as well, and brought with him the power of the backup unit and the enormous Brand Box that was the saucer.

"I'm going to bring up the power slowly, but steadily, unless something goes wrong," I told them, all contact now being mental. *"When you feel the power surging into you, share it, don't fight it or try to keep it exclusive. Let it gather as one huge pool. At a concensus, we push away. Understood?"*

They knew what I meant, and I felt a rush of power. Whether we managed to pull this off or not, for the first time we were working together, not as employees, not under pragmatic alliances, not under coercion or as a result of behavior programmed through the Brand Box. Alice had fallen down the rabbit hole; now it was time for the cards to lift her back up.

"Up to five percent. All nominal. Going to ten. Ten percent. All nominal. Going to fifteen . . ."

The surge was something I had felt before many times—we all had—but this time it wasn't controlling us. This time, we were inviting it in and not pushing it away. I felt Al instinctively resist little and try to grab a chunk for himself; I doubted if it was even a conscious act, but I gave him a mental

rap on the knuckles and he stopped it. I had a lot of grudges
against Al, and he knew it, but compared to Walt and Rita he
was merely a pimple.

According to the station records, any attempt to go over
fifty-percent power had resulted in disaster. They'd either had
to let go or they burned out and punched through to relieve
the pressure. Wilma and I had been rescued, more or less, from
Al at about forty percent, and that had given us enormous
power just by being in close proximity to it. We were passing
forty now.

I cannot describe the sense of godhood the energy buildup
gave all of us. I felt as if I could create any world I wanted,
change shape and form, rend continents and oceans just for
starters. And that was at below fifty percent.

Just at fifty I felt it beginning to slip, and it took a moment
for Brand to come in with reassurance. *"You're doubting!
You're scared shitless because this is where it all came apart
before! Ignore it! Relax! Let the pool continue to build! Don't
grab at it, don't fear or withdraw. Keep going! Let it wash over
you, go through you!"*

At sixty-five percent I felt myself go free of my body. I rose
on an ocean of green pulsing energy, looked down, and saw
my own body standing there, legs rigidly locked, eyes closed.
One by one, I sensed the others come up as well, and I felt
what they felt and saw what they were seeing in the pureness
of thought.

To Les, it was an unexpectedly childlike sense of total joy
and fun; for Al, it was harder, fighting off every attempt to gain
control of the situation. Al was the type who would always
hate roller coasters because he couldn't drive them, yet think
nothing of piloting a rocket ship if need be. He was the weak
link, we all sensed it, and we all were moving constantly with a
tiny part of our minds to shore him up.

At eighty percent, the station itself dissolved into its blue-
print mode, with everything three-dimensional but mono-
chrome, drawn with lines of force as if by strokes of an

architect's pen, every wall, room, device, and wiring harness labeled and charted.

And then we were no longer in the Command Center at all, or in the cave, the tunnel, or on the surface. We rose up, the entire river valley spreading out before us, a great full moon overhead unobscured by clouds, while, below, the snakelike river was bathed in ground fog.

We continued to rise, until the whole city was below us. I no longer had any conscious control of the power regulator, the server, or anything else; I was one with the others and looking in wonder, seeing, perhaps for the first time, not just down or up, right or left, but all directions simultaneously.

There were other small green lights down there. It was most unexpected, but we reached out to them and they began to rise toward us. With a start I realized that they were others of the Elect, also drawn here by the clues or the temple or by impulses they could not understand. The lesser spades, of course, and whatever was left of the clubs as well. Here were Mike and Bernadette Standish, and Betty as well, and several more, welcomed into the pool if they chose to rise. Some did not; some were too fearful of what they saw or sensed, or did not understand. It was too bad, but it wasn't necessary to have them.

The bubble continued to expand; we began to draw from Africa and South America, from Europe and Asia. *Come one, come all, if you dare!*

And now the world itself began to dissolve, taking on the builder's view. Numbers. Numbers and shapes and labels. What about the details? We had provided the details. That was the genius of the whole Brand setup. We imposed order on the plasma by what we knew and what we expected to be there. Each of us knew a little something that would add to the detail, which would then be incorporated as needed into the program. When things were clearly defined, the logic engine would kick in and create the structure of the cells, the bacteria and spores, the veins in a leaf, and those, too, were imposed on the new master program the way the tiny details had shown up as required in the most limited Brand Box.

In our universes, effects created their own inevitable causes, not the other way around.

The world vanished. The universe vanished. They had no further reason to exist. We were at maximum power and we knew it, but we had no idea where we were.

Or did we? Below now was the vast chamber going up and down into the infinite, and over there another rabbit hole leading to an entirely different universe. The red universe. We could see the redness, feel it, feel its hatred like some vile blood that would dissolve any of us at a touch. It was gathering, congealing even as we had done, but it was not so far along.

We watched it boil and solidify and writhe upon the face of the Earth like some despicable, tortuous mud. We hated to see it, because it contained not just the remaining evil but also some of our friends, trapped in its bloody, foul grip. Out of pity, out of hope, perhaps out of love, we reached out to it, inviting it within our community of minds. It saw us, and we felt its hatred. It suddenly and maliciously leaped out for us, its head a monstrous, hideous contortion of tooth and fang, serpent and wolf that nonetheless formed Rita's face.

We withdrew more in sadness than in fear as it fell short of reaching us. How many innocents were victims of that insanity, lust, and greed for power? Those weren't elements foreign to any of our natures, either; some of us were just better at resisting temptation and keeping those urges in check.

"Rita and the others are cohabiting the Command Center!" Brand warned us. *"Damn! It exists now only in their plane!"*

"What do we do?" the others asked. *"Is it all in vain? Do we give this up and sink back to do battle?"*

"No!" Al said. *"It's just Rita. The others are being pulled along by her. It's my job to deal with her!"*

"You can't do it alone," I told him. *"You don't have the power, and she's insane. The last time, she crashed the system. She'll do it again, and we may not be up to a third time."*

"Then we'll all go," Al responded. *"But I know the way in this case. In this kind of matter, I'm in the lead."*

And here was the crux of the problem. How much could we trust the little weasel? How many of all the horrors that Al perpetrated were done for what he perceived as noble motives, and how much for self-aggrandizement? The others, even Wilma and Riki, seemed willing to go along, and Brand was being obstinately neutral.

It was really my call. At this juncture, the way it went was up to the three of spades.

There must have been something I found to love in the jerk once. Maybe it was still there.

Brand's security system had prevented Rita from breaching the Command Center core, but she was preventing anybody else from getting there, either. It caused an eerie sight: Rita and several others—I sensed rather than knew that they were Alice McKee, Rob and Lee, Sally Prine, Herb Koeder—making up a tribe of fierce ape-human warriors in painted and tattooed muscular bodies, wearing pieces of human bone as jewelry, but holding machine guns and worse. They stood there in the control room like ghosts; we could see right through them. They almost certainly saw our centauroid forms the same way; standing there frozen but taunting, hooked into the controls so that they could not.

Rita saw us and opened fire. The bullets went right through our comatose bodies and started ricocheting off the walls. One CRT imploded with a bang.

Just as Riki and Wilma and I had drawn enormous power from simply being near a power-up once, so, too, did Rita and her crew draw from our own power supply, keeping us in check and allowing them to breach the security with some of the bullets. Al, with all that power and the authority of both Les and Matt Brand, was ready.

"The day I can't take an anthropologist nun is the day I hang it up!" Al swore, and concentrating on Rita and Rita alone, using our combined power and united will, Al's frozen body came alive and glowed, becoming slightly transparent itself. Rita was so busy trying to wreck the place that she barely noticed, and when she did, Al launched himself directly into her midsection forehooves first, the way I had come at Walt.

She came back up and struck Al a vicious and painful blow to the neck with her elbow. She was insane but she wasn't incompetent. Not knowing the physiology of this kind of creature, she'd gone for the one place sure to create problems regardless.

Although Al weighed almost three times what Rita did, the savage woman threw off the centauroid's body as if it were a sack of feathers, bounded to her feet, and started doing a series of quick kicks to the security chief.

Whatever Al had tried, it hadn't worked. Everybody, including me, had paid in the past for underestimating Rita, and there seemed no solution from the mind pool other than a gut instinct to pull Al back in and at least out of the physical pain.

Suddenly it was an unexpected member of our group that moved, impulsively, without warning and without resistance. As Rita came in and prepared to blow Al to the next life with the machine gun, a look of enormous satisfaction on her face, Riki moved out and joined into Al's body. Drawing without direct thought on the power and data of the system, Al's body changed, morphing almost instantly into a great and glorious figure that seemed to rise up out of the centauroid body and tower over the crazy woman: an awesome, Old Testament avenging angel, and it was madder than hell.

"HARLOT!" the winged apparition thundered in a voice like that of God Himself. *"Now see the price for defiling the vow you made to the Lord!"*

Rita had the machine gun; Al was as much a target as ever,

but Rita held her fire. In fact, the look on her face was possibly the most awful, horrible expression of abject terror I could ever imagine.

Hands jutted out, Al's hands, tipped with solid claws filed to fine points, and penetrated Rita's chest below her breasts, ripping away flesh and bone, and bringing out a still beating, bloody heart. The angel vanished, leaving a bloody and broken Al standing there with the heart in his hands and a very satisfied look on his face.

"Poof!" he said, and crushed the heart between his hands with all his might.

The others were still there. Until now, they had been watching, expecting to see Al die, expecting to see everything blown to pieces. Now, Rita lay dead, her chest a bloody mess, her eyes wide open, her face still locked in that monstrous, horrible expression of total fear.

Riki was back with us, leaving Al, bleeding and hurting.

"Where did you get that idea?" we all wanted to know.

"That was your problem. All of you," Rick responded. *"You weren't raised Catholic. She was, and so was I. When you go over to the other side, regardless of your reasons, you still accept the entire canon. You have to, or there's no other side to go to. I just gave her a reminder of what she almost had to share with me. In my case, it was Sister Veronica's third-grade class in cosmology, taught with an evangelical fervor that gave us all nightmares."*

Al was not doing at all well and could only go on adrenaline for so long before collapsing and maybe dying from loss of blood or other internal injuries. But Al was in charge.

"All of you! Don't gape at the people, you ape-creatures! You want to come along with me and Matt Brand and all the rest or do you want to sit here and wait for Rita to rise from the dead? Your choice. I can't stay much longer myself!"

One by one they came to us, letting themselves go, allowing the green power to envelop them and welcome them in like long-lost friends.

I guess there *was* something inside Al to love; it hadn't completely vanished after all. I still didn't love the son of a bitch any, but this was the first time that I could remember that I felt like kissing him.

"Relax, enjoy, experience and feel the power and the universe," Matthew Brand told the newcomers. *"Questions later. Now is the time to heal old wounds, to join together once more as a team. When we are ready, we are going to go, together, in search of ourselves!"*

There were injuries to my soul that would never truly heal, not so long as my memories remained, but overall I had not felt such hope and such excitement in a very long time.

"Are you sure we can do this?" I asked him, still wondering how far we could go.

"Are you kiddin'? Watch my dust! I got this baby supercharged and I've hot-wired and hijacked all us dodos! Let's see where we can go!"

XV

TO THE TOP

There was nothing now, nothing but ourselves, disembodied and empowered, centered in a great shaft that seemed to vanish into infinity above and below. All the crossroads were gone; it was just us and the shaft.

And then, from below, out of the infinite, came—*structures*. Triangular affairs, they seemed to be coming in from various points and integrating into a floorlike structure around a single rising rectangle.

And now, rising through the solid mass that the conjoining of these shapes created, came a ring of light, brilliant, whirling, beautiful to behold. It rose up through the rectangle and rested on top.

"All of the labs," Matt Brand explained, *"and all of the backup units are all plugged in and networked together. I am with you now as I haven't been since I had to flee. I told you I could hot-wire anything!"*

"It's a spaceship!" somebody exclaimed.

"No," I responded. *"It's the Brand Box. The one that actually is Matthew Brand."*

"I knew he had to be from outer space to come up with all this!" Al commented.

"Actually, I'm from Cleveland," Brand responded. *"Everybody rested and set? There's no going back once we start this, I don't think. At least not the way it was. These are all the backups, all the power units, all the control rooms, everything. If they go, I don't know where any of us will find the data to reincarnate again. Understood?"*

We understood. It was too late to turn back now. Besides, to do that would mean we'd move to yet another reality, one in which Walt and Cynthia and Rita and all their evil cronies would be once more alive and well.

Now, as one, we looked beyond and *below* the platform, below all that was real to us at this point, down, down to the energy that burned and blinded, hiding the terrible shapes moving within.

We pushed off in a unified reaction, and, slowly at first, then picking up speed as we went, we started to rise.

"There's a floor up top!" somebody shouted. *"We'll be crushed!"*

"Calm down. Look elsewhere. Don't think about it. Nothing here is real," we tried to reassure them.

We struck the barrier and went through it, but, as we did, something very odd happened.

I was Cory Kassemi, back at the house, the experiment hadn't happened yet, and I was moving backward, through the city, to the ranch, to the shore . . .

We were back in the shaft and rising ever faster, but now every single part of that earlier life, every detail, from my "birth" to meltdown, was fresh in my mind, as real as my life as Jayce.

We went through the next barrier, and there were Rini and my Brand Box prison and the saucer. There, too, was the March Hare, the strange gathering of creatures, and the accident, the retreat and Father Pete . . .

Now it was clear to all of us that we were moving backward through our own past worlds and lives. We weren't actually reliving those lives; rather we were simply regaining our experiences.

Going back through my life in Seattle with Riki, I was flooded not only with all those memories of better times but also with the love I felt for her back then.

That, however, was as far back as my direct memories went. From this point, the lives piled on less as memories than as discoveries.

At least I knew now that Al hadn't been the one to kill either Rick or me as my nightmares had suggested. Not that Al hadn't been somewhat complicitous, but, like a corrupt cop, he'd justified his involvement and made some peace with his conscience by simply not thinking much about it. We knew who were the killers among us now; we'd all had a quick refresher course.

I think we all had expected the lives and worlds from this point to be more conventional, more ordinary, but just the opposite was true. A world of Amazonian warrior women where men were seduced by night and ritually murdered in the morning; Matt Brand as almost a Wizard of Oz in a futuristic vision that seemed part Buck Rogers, part Emerald City; worlds in which we understood now that the centauroid shape wasn't the only departure from our humanoid forms. There were birdlike creatures, and whole civilizations under the sea. A world that had certainly come from the mind of paleontologist Herb Koeder, in which the dinosaur had never been wiped out and in which one branch eventually evolved into a technological species; and yet another where plants walked and invented and dreamed.

So many lifetimes, so many worlds. Too many to keep track of; rather, the mind found them merging, so that only the best and worst of them and fragments of the rest remained. Love and hate were constants, but survival and growth were important as well.

And then, after who knew how many worlds and civilizations, how many forms and functions, lives and loves, struggles, defeats, and triumphs, there was a sudden, jarring, blinding light and a sense of total confusion. The experiences faded to memories, and we stood there, all of us who survived, ape-human and stark naked, in the glare of a very hot sun.

I had studied those permanent party files and the faces too long to not realize that we now were the very people whose images had stared back at me from those screens. There were in fact quite a lot of us; more than I thought were in the group when we started our journey up through the layers.

I didn't need any mirror to know that I was that mousy little Mary Ann Howarth with the stringy hair. I just wished I had the glasses that Mary Ann had worn; I could see okay, but anything outside the middle ranges of my focus was blurry and smeared. Still, I could see that, naked or not, we each had a fairly prominent, full-color tattoo on our left buttocks: playing cards, deuce to ace, in all four suits. I wasn't sure if all of us were here, but there were a lot of women and not nearly the same number of men.

I looked around, embarrassed to be revealed as a mere three of spades so publicly, and embarrassed as well that I was the most plain-looking of the group.

On the other hand, my first thought upon looking around was confusion. The area had been something once, long ago. It had the feel of a Grecian or Babylonian ruin, consisting mostly of the remains of once great stone steps, partial statues smashed to rubble, and some Doric columns and remnants of stone walls, all long abandoned, all discolored and overgrown with weeds, moss, and lichen.

Had this been a jungle, we'd probably not have known any of it was there, but it wasn't a jungle, it was somewhere in a temperate climate and the growth wasn't extreme. Still, this whole area, its ruins reaching out in all directions for what seemed like miles, had been abandoned or destroyed many centuries before.

"Is this it?" somebody asked, echoing all our feelings. "We look right, but where the hell is everything?"

Doc Weinberg, a bit older than most of us and with a slight paunch, walked up the ancient stairs and looked out from the top on the desolation.

"No, I don't think this is it," he told us. "It's close, but we're not quite there. I think we're very close to the top level but we couldn't get all the way for some reason."

"Well, we better get *somewhere*," one of the women commented. "There's no food, no water—there's nothing here."

I looked around. "Where's Matt? Where's Matt Brand?"

Somebody turned and frowned. "Who?"

The question demanded an answer, and I saw a vision of a long-haired, bearded young man, but it started to slip away the moment I thought of it.

It was strange how everything seemed to be fading. Not completely, not directly, but growing more and more distant all the time. I tried to hold on to some of the memories, if only because of what I'd learned about the others and, most of all, what I'd learned about myself, but they seemed so distant and strange, like a series of dreams.

It was odd. I had a strong sense of myself, but it wasn't any of the people I'd once been, or maybe *dreamed* I'd been. I knew that that was my husband over there making time with a blond bimbo, and I was scared and seemed out of place here. I felt ugly, stupid, and vulnerable.

"Hey! Look at this!" one of the women called out, and several people gathered around. "On this pillar. You can make out some writing. Is that a P? P-R-A-R-Y? What ends in '-prary'?"

"Humm . . ." another put in. "Maybe it's not a P. How about a B? Brary?"

"Library!" somebody shouted. "This was a library. Sure! You can see where lion statues or something else stood here. A couple of the paws remain!"

"But what happened here?" another asked. "I mean, that's English, isn't it?"

"I don't think it matters what happened," one man commented, a sandy-haired fellow with a ten of hearts on his cute little ass. "Somethin' hit this place. Bombs, plague, you name it. This was a big city once. It's nothin' but a ruin now."

My good old hubby was always best at taking charge when nobody, including him, knew what to do. He stood up there, so damned turned on it hurt to look at him, and shouted, "Look, people, we can hunt for clues later! What we need to do now is fan out while there's still light and see if we can find some source of water first, then maybe food. I doubt if we'll find anything like that in this much ruin, but fan out and see if you can spot anything farther out. If you find anything, head back here. Everybody make sure you're back here by sundown. Bring anything useful back with you."

All of what we had gone through not long ago had faded even more, as if just a dream. *Was it just another dream after all?* How could I, could *any* of us, be certain? Centauroids, flying saucers, cybernetic walruses inside a computer . . . What *was* real, except the relatively consistent personalities we maintained? Oh, I think we remembered, all right, but we remembered all of it, and that was far too much to sort, recall, or make proper sense of. The extraneous stuff was already being pushed away; something told me that, after each and every sleep, and long sleeps they would be, more and more would disappear because we simply couldn't absorb it all. Would we remain the same as we were, or would that sort produce some new synthesis? It was impossible to say.

The others were spreading out, looking to see if there was some way we could at least survive here. There would be such a discovery; I felt sure of that. These people, all of us, had almost always found a way to survive.

My mind churned with too many half-remembered variations of me for me to properly function. I marveled that most of the others could. I was male, female, centaur, mermaid, angel, and demon, and many other variations over too many worlds to count. They were already running together in my head, snippets of this and that, a vast collection of moments, like a massive motion picture in which each frame was from a totally different story. I couldn't make sense of such things, and my brain rebelled and began shutting it all out. How many lives had Al said he'd kept straight in his head? Ten? How many had I? Not even those memories were absolute. This mob of past lives was the same as all other mobs: an incomprehensible babble.

There *was* a Cory Maddox synthesizing out of all of them, though: a sense of identity, of self, that I knew was pretty much the real me. The trouble was, while it wasn't much, it was all I had.

I was too scared to go out there on my own, and too miserable and alone to just sit and pray for a miracle. With nobody much interested in me, I began to look around the ruin. Someone, somewhere had put us here, right in this spot, for some purpose. Not gods, not demons—some intelligence that was real. I was sure of that. The massive computer had never run wild; there had always been *somebody* there, disguised in the campfires of the shaman's world or attempting to break through into the Command Center. Some human intelligence had been there when the computer crashed, someone had saved me and the others and tried to get us out.

It wasn't paranoia, it was hope that fueled my conviction that, even if we couldn't know who they were or even be aware of them, we were always being watched by someone. We should have extracted, of that I was certain. We should not have stopped here, short of that goal. If we'd stopped here, somebody had stopped us. Who? Why? And where were they?

Why were we abandoned in the middle of a ruined but once modern city, at the remnants of the library?

I began to survey the area immediately around the site. Eventually, on the far side, I discovered what I thought was an

entrance leading underneath. I didn't want to go in there, not
without a light, but something was drawing me, inviting me in,
almost compelling me to enter.

It's not real, it's not real, something kept whispering.

I slid inside in spite of myself, and was suddenly engulfed in
cool but totally frightening darkness.

Lights came on.

It was such a startling thing, so unexpected, that it almost
scared me more than the darkness. What business did lights
have going on down here, in the basement of a centuries-old
ruin? Where was the power source for the lights, and who had
turned them on?

I looked ahead and saw a descending passage, a great hall of
stone heading off into the depths of the earth. It was lit and
clearly drawing me; I felt I had to go.

The lighted walls had murals on them, precise and intricate
mosaics, depicting a great civilization that seemed almost
familiar. There were people like us, and images of big cities,
airplanes, cars, and farms. There was even, near the end, pictures of a couple of kinds of spacecraft for launching people
and objects into outer space.

The passage curved around and then opened up onto a platform. I knew what this place was, or had been, although I
didn't know how I knew.

There was a rush of air and a roar. I felt something coming
toward me, but I didn't flee. Instead I stood there and watched
as a subway train emerged from the tunnel and stopped at the
station platform. There was nobody driving the train, I noticed
that much.

The doors opened, and, emboldened by my newly found
courage and curiosity, I got on. The doors closed and the train
roared off into the tunnel.

The train went past many deserted stations but stopped at
none of them. Finally, it reached the end of the line. The car
stopped, the doors opened, and I got off, not knowing if or how
I'd get back.

There was a man at the end of the platform. He was dressed in a ratty T-shirt and even grungier jeans, and I doubted if he'd cut his hair or beard in years. Still, he was better dressed than I was.

"Hello, Mary Ann," he said in a familiar, pleasant voice. "I'm very happy you found the courage to come."

"Mary Ann . . . Yes, that's my name. And you—you're . . . You're Matthew?"

He grinned and nodded. "Yes. Matthew Brand. Sorry to have had to stop the progression before reaching the very top, but, you see, that would have destroyed me and possibly most of you as well. Come on. There are some real advantages to having some control over virtual worlds. It can do wonders as a teaching tool."

I walked with him but didn't touch him; he had almost a divine aura about him.

"You said that going all the way would destroy you and most of us?"

"Yes. You see, you're real. Not real *here*, this is just another computer-generated illusion as most of those people will eventually decide if they can keep their wits about them. But you're real *someplace*. You pretty much knew that, of course. All fifty-two of you actually exist on one plane of reality. The real one, as far as I know."

"I figured we were all real, or had been once. I wasn't sure if we still were."

"You—all of you—are still very much physically alive. The thing is, I'm not. Oh, I'm the guy who invented a lot of the computers and programs that designed and constructed the more complex computers that built and programmed the system. I don't know how it was done myself, but I was the one that started the ball rolling, the guy who discovered the basic principles. I admit I stole the best ones just like the official line says. Stole 'em from a flying saucer. It crashed, we—meaning the government types—got hold of it, but nobody could figure the damned thing out. Not its propulsion, not how you drove it. Finally, when I went to work for the National Security Agency designing better snoop computers to decode the universe, I happened on the folks who, decades later, were still part of a team trying to figure it out. I managed to help write the program and design the computer that could do it. The integrated head mount was one result. The marriage of human and machine. It was the greatest game machine ever designed. You've seen some of the simple early games. They're at the end of what came to be known as rabbit holes. Leftovers, really. Child's play, but they wowed 'em at the time."

"So all the stuff at the start, in the lectures in the first world I can clearly remember, was pretty much true."

He nodded. "And, of course, I had my Wonderland Wax Works, a perfectly legit company that masked what we were really doing, which was creating the most breathtaking simulators and scenarios you could imagine. We tried for all the themes and variations. I started with the Brand Boxes and little worlds, then graduated to more complex themes. Tice Koroku—you remember him as Dan Tanaka—came in to help build the bigger stuff, but by then it didn't matter. Before we went much further, we discovered that our computers were building their own replacements, repairing their own systems, and expanding down right into the bedrock. They seem to have grown impatient with us and decided to continue their own development of our principles at a faster speed."

"They took over?"

"Well, sort of. So long as we kept them happy, it didn't matter. We brought in anthropologists, sociologists, psychologists, historians, geographers, astronomers, paleontologists, you name it. Everybody with a world they thought would be interesting to build, study, maybe even live in for a while. That was fine, but then, one day, some of them wanted to leave. That wasn't acceptable. They had so many possibilities for different worlds in their minds, the computers didn't want to let them go. They weren't just building what the experts designed

anymore. Oh, no. They were building worlds based on our
dreams, our fantasies, even our nightmares. Eventually, you
see, the computers picked their own group and sealed them in.
Whoever was inside the lab at the time got nabbed, too. They'd
long ago found that even ordinary people often had extraordinary fantasies. The old nightmare was that computers were
going to take over the world. Maybe it was my own failure, but
my dear machines became true voyeurs."

"Us, you mean. You're talking about us."

He nodded. "There'd been a project at one point that dove-
tailed with ours that was part of disaster planning. Some scenario about killer viruses, or maybe it was nuclear terrorists. I
don't recall. At any rate, because we had the computer
capacity, the government set up a parallel project using some
of our excess computing power for maintenance. The idea was
to create a knowledge base of healthy, young, active people
who might well be able to rebuild a civilization. The ratio of
women to men was part of this, based on computer simulations. Somehow, this crossed over with our VR routines. One
day, see, there happened to be thirteen men and thirty-nine
women in the labs. Strictly accidental. Something in one of the
computers determined at that instant that this meant the colony
had to be preserved and this was the start of disaster. Everybody was trapped. Ah! Here we are! Just around the corner
here . . ."

We turned around a sharp bend and suddenly were hit by a
very cold blast of air. It was decidedly uncomfortable for
somebody with no clothes on, but the sight was so stunning
that at first I didn't care.

There they were, suspended, each in a great life-support
unit, with all sorts of wires and tubes attached to their heads
and bodies.

"This is an exact simulation of the real thing," Brand told
me. "Fifty-two of you. See? The disaster scenario meets the
computer voyeur. You're all frozen, maintained in a kind of
stasis that, excepting a catastrophic equipment failure, will

keep you preserved like this for a thousand years. Alive, asleep, dreaming the dreams of the machines."

"And you?"

"I was a threat to them. I was the only one the machines feared. I knew they were out to kill me, so I created that Brand Box existence for myself as a contingency. When I returned, after they'd sealed the building and put up the defenses, they let me in. Let me in long enough to vaporize me. They didn't want me here, even if they had a fifty-third place. They were scared of me, I think. I might have been the one person who could screw up their dirty little business. I got even with them, though. I've been haunting *their* dreams and fantasies ever since. The only thing I can't do is return to the final level. I don't have a body to go back to, you see. Here, and particularly below, in the more complex and vast nether regions, even they can't find me, any more than you could find the bogeyman hiding under the bed late at night. I'm their bogeyman, stalking their circuits, looking for ways to do them harm."

"Did you know this yourself—down there?"

"Not like I do now, but, yeah, I generally knew who and what I am and what my job is, even when so much is fragmented, so much forgotten. Still, not like the others on this level, with confused and fading memory due to overload, the technical and literary parts fading. They'll wind up starting from scratch, most of them, because that's what this level is designed for. They are the last people on Earth. Don't worry, though—there's a lot left inside even in the worst of them, and some of it is always there. If not right up front, at least in your dreams."

I had been there before.

"You don't give me much hope," I told him. "We'll never get out of here!"

"Oh, there's an end. A thousand years, or earlier if there is a danger to more than five percent of the colony. The computers will still be there, of course, probably at a level of complexity we can't imagine since they continue to evolve at a fantastic rate, but there is one thing for certain: When you wake up, and live out that last life, you will really die. That's where you have it over me. I'm stuck here, forever, causing them no end of conniptions but still trapped. A truly permanent party. You see, since I'm already dead, I am, like Mephistopheles, forever in Hell. And now you know."

"Yes, now I know. And I'm disgusted, discouraged, and depressed."

"Want out?"

My head came up. "You just said—"

He grinned. "I can't do miracles, but I could get you out. Is that really what you want? You can always rejoin the soon-to-be-savages up above. Have babies, die quick, go on to the next level."

"No thanks. If I could get out, I—I don't know, though. All the others. There are some good people there."

"I can't do it for them. The computers would catch on. Some of the folks, like the doc, should be with the group anyway. The rest—well, some of them should have their LSUs shattered. You know who I mean. And I can't mete out justice all by myself. I have some power, but not enough control, and I'm hardly omnipresent or omnipotent. Besides, if I use too much power in jiggling events, the computer will find me. I've carved out a few areas where they can't see—you've been in one or two, interestingly enough—but they are outside any of the main programs. I can't influence anything from there."

"The shaman world! That's one! And the garden . . ."

He smiled and nodded. "See? You're a lot smarter and more capable than you think you are. Still, this isn't your fight. You're an innocent victim whose main crime was trying to bring her rat of a husband lunch at just the wrong time. You've been an amazing treasure for somebody who wasn't even supposed to be here. You want out, you know the score, and, for the moment, you're outside the matrix but where I can find you. That's why I can get you out. I can get you out by putting just enough delay one level up so that I can allow another person in. That's all the machines care about."

I hesitated. "So if I get out, then somebody else is trapped?"

"That's about it. There are folks up there willing to do it, some of whom might even be useful. Besides, I kind of think that the computers would love to have a little different mix and they're pretty well stuck with this lot. The problem is contained, more or less, in that department."

"But anybody new won't have that wealth of experience that, at least on the subconscious level, the rest of us have. No matter how smart and prepared they think they are, they're gonna be fresh meat for a very long time, aren't they?"

He just shrugged.

"How long do I have to think about this?"

"Not long, I'm afraid. We better get you back to the station or you're going to freeze all over again anyway."

As we walked back, I tried not to think of the decision. "That bank of LSUs—the real one, I mean. That's what we couldn't look at, wasn't it? Our real bodies, in suspension, below the labs?"

"Sure. I told you you were smarter than you thought you were. To allow any of you there kind of gives away the game and would open them up to attack. Destroy the LSUs and you destroy the computers' vicarious lifeline. If anything actually happens to all of you, or even most of you, the computers would come crashing down once again."

The train was coming. I knew I had to make a decision. "I don't want this, world without end, virtual realities up the kazoo," I told him. "On the other hand, I also don't want to be responsible for anybody else trapped in this endless Purgatory. For now, that consideration has to outweigh the first option. If things are starting again, we'll wind up back here sooner or later I'm sure."

"Maybe. You don't know how much time has already passed, or what the world is really like up in the real plane now. You might not have as long as you think. You sure you don't want to reconsider?"

"I'm sure. I survived so far. I think I can keep doing it."

"You won't be able to hold on to or make sense of all your lives, but I'll leave the current string in your mind, starting with the programmer in Seattle. That'll give you a leg up on them, since you now know who's who and what's what. I can't make you into Wonder Woman, but you'll at least have a little knowledge, the most dangerous thing. Don't try coming back here, though. The power won't be on again."

"I know. But sooner or later we all will get out of here. At least, all of us who deserve to. Somehow there's a way, no matter what you say."

I would have kissed him good-bye, but he wasn't really there, of course.

Now, at least, I knew the enemy. Now, at least, I had something to fight, something to fight for, and I knew who my friends were.

I had no intention of going through the same hellish experiences again. At some point we'd get through to that one final level. At one point we'd wake up in our cocoons, or we'd reach down below the Command Center to our real minds and bodies in spite of the machines and, in that moment, we'd beat them.

I could wait until then. I knew the lives had their own rewards, and what was truly important to one who had to live them.

As I climbed back out into the ruined world, though, I had a strange vision, one not consistent with anything else I knew, but one that might well have been another of those memory frames.

The fifty-two of us, there, as I'd seen them with Brand, but not deep in stone, not in and of the Earth, but in the center of a great ship, a ship traveling through space to a place impossibly distant, a new life, a new colony, its trained nucleus frozen but still dreaming, dreaming of worlds that were and worlds that might be. Volunteers, eager pioneers, the hope and guarantors of humanity's survival out among the stars.

Was that a true vision, or was it something Brand had handed me? How could any of us really know?

Someday, though, we *would* know. Someday a way would be found.

Until then, or until we reached some far destiny, we would survive.

XVI

EXEGESIS

Matthew Brand walked down the corridor and turned not left, to where the stiffs were, but to the right, down yet another corridor, and out into the office. A colleague looked up at him and nodded. "Think she bought it?"

"Oh, she bought it," Brand assured the other man. "Look, we can't get 'em out without killing most of them, at least with what we know now, and the colony was getting ugly the farther in it got, so we had to do something. The crash proved that."

He continued on, past cubicles and computer screens and out into the lobby area, where the Coke machine was. The sun was streaming in, and he could even see Mount Rainier hovering ghostlike over the Seattle skyline.

It was going to be a nearly perfect day, weatherwise.

The board had asked him how long he thought he could keep secret from the press and public the fact that an experiment had gone so wrong, that the NASA universe-ship simulations had caused the minds, the personalities of the test subjects to cross the boundary from biological to computer and interact, creating their own worlds, time and again, beyond their abilities to reintegrate. The crash had given one hope, since everybody had been wiped out at once and it was possible to reload the personalities from the backups one by one. It hadn't worked, though. There was a basic flaw in the system: You couldn't turn off the simulator runs without wiping out their minds, a fate worse than murder to him and many others. You couldn't wake them up without the same thing happening. So, it just went on, a great discovery becoming a dull and boring maintenance operation.

Nobody felt sorrier for them than he did. Hell, what kind of an existence must it be to never know what's real and what's not, to discover, not once but over and over, that the reality everybody else took for granted was a fake?

He didn't have any change, so he fed a dollar into the bill slot and pressed the button for Diet Coke. The machine whirred, and then the can popped out at the bottom while the changer give him back fifteen cents. He reached in, pulled out the coins, and checked them as he always did. He never did trust machines.

Two good old Washington nickels, but what was the third one? Canadian? He looked at it a moment.

It was a Cory Maddox coin.

He dropped it in the charity box on the way back and tried very hard not to think about it again.

ABOUT THE AUTHOR

Jack L. Chalker was born in Baltimore, Maryland, on December 17, 1944. He began reading at an early age and naturally gravitated to what are still his twin loves: science fiction and history. While still in high school, Chalker began writing for the amateur science-fiction press and in 1960 launched the Hugo-nominated amateur magazine *Mirage*. A year later he founded The Mirage Press, which grew into a major specialty publishing company for nonfiction and reference books about science fiction and fantasy. During this time, he developed correspondence and friendships with many leading SF and fantasy authors and editors, many of whom wrote for his magazine and his press. He is an internationally recognized expert on H. P. Lovecraft and on the specialty press in SF and fantasy.

After graduating with twin majors in history and English from Towson State College in 1966, Chalker taught high school history and geography in the Baltimore city public schools with time out to serve with the 135th Air Commando Group, Maryland Air National Guard, during the Vietnam era and, as a sideline, sound engineered some of the period's outdoor rock concerts. He received a graduate degree in the eso-teric field of the History of Ideas from Johns Hopkins University in 1969.

His first novel, *A Jungle of Stars,* was published in 1976, and two years later, with the major popular success of his novel *Midnight at the Well of Souls,* he quit teaching to become a full-time professional novelist. That same year, he married Eva C. Whitley on a ferryboat in the middle of the Susquehanna River and moved to rural western Maryland. Their first son, David, was born in 1981.

Chalker is an active conversationalist, a traveler who has been through all fifty states and in dozens of foreign countries, and a member of numerous local and national organizations ranging from the Sierra Club to The American Film Institute, the Maryland Academy of Sciences, and the Washington Science Fiction Association, to name a few. He retains his interest in consumer electronics, has his own satellite dish, and frequently reviews computer hardware and software for national magazines. For five years, until the magazine's demise, he had a regular column on science fantasy publishing in *Fantasy Review* and continues to write a column on computers for *S-100 Journal.* He is a three-term past treasurer of the Science Fiction and Fantasy Writers of America, a noted speaker on science fiction at numerous colleges and universities as well as a past lecturer at the Smithsonian and the National Institutes of Health, and a well-known auctioneer of science fiction and fantasy art, having sold over five million dollars' worth to date.

Chalker has received many writing awards, including the Hamilton-Brackett Memorial Award for his "Well World" books, the Gold Medal of the prestigious *West Coast Review of Books* for *Spirits of Flux and Anchor*, the Dedalus Award, and the E. E. Smith Skylark Award for his career writings. He is also a passionate lover of steamboats and particularly ferryboats and has ridden over three hundred ferries in the United States and elsewhere.

He lives with his wife, Eva, sons David and Steven, a

Pekingese named Marva Chang, and Stonewall J. Pussycat, the world's dumbest cat, in the Catoctin Mountain region of western Maryland, near Camp David. A short story collection with autobiographical commentary, *Dance Band on the Titanic*, was published by Del Rey Books in 1988.